Genesis Days | Part II

Producer & International Distributor
eBookPro Publishing
www.ebook-pro.com

Days of Genesis Days Part II
Eyal Cohen

Translation: Yossie Bloch

Contact: eyalcohen51@gmail.com
ISBN 9798831508543

Contents

CHAPTER THIRTY-FIVE

The Mission

The crickets chirping around the tent conveyed a feeling of tranquility, even as the whistling wind caught the fallen leaves and made them dance. Abraham was sitting alone in his tent, reclining against a big pillow filled with wool sheared from his own sheep. A smile rose to his lips as he recalled a meeting from a few hours earlier.

He had encountered a young man in the study hall. The newcomer seemed to be struggling to comprehend a philosophical point. He approached Abraham determinedly and said: "I'm sorry, but I can't stop thinking about what you said earlier, that it is inconceivable for God to be limited in any way."

Abraham chuckled and replied: "But I did not tell you that."

The student looked at him puzzled: "So now you're telling me that God has limits?"

"Certainly not!" Abraham retorted, prepared for the young man's confusion.

"But you just said that you didn't tell me God is limitless, so doesn't that mean the opposite is true?!" The student looked upset and unmoored.

"Heaven forbid! That God is limitless is quite true. However, it is not I who told you that, young man. I surmise that it was my son Isaac, whom you discussed the issue with."

"Your son, Isaac?!"

Abraham laughed agreeably: "Ah, my young friend, you are still new to our camp, correct?"

The young man nodded, befuddled.

"Let me resolve your confusion. My son Isaac arrived at the camp only a few days ago. My son and I look like twin brothers, there are almost no noticeable differences between us. That is why you have mistaken me for him."

A look of astonishment came over the tyro.

"You know what? I will show you! Wait right here," Abraham requested and left the tent. A few minutes later, he returned with his son Isaac.

The novice did a double take, unsure whom he had spoken to and when. "It really does not make sense!" he protested in frustration, "it is impossible to tell who is the father and who is the son!"

After the new student had taken his leave, Abraham relaxed again, running his hand over his black beard, and looking at Isaac. While he was grateful for the youthful vigor God had allowed him to maintain in his old age, he could not help but think that it would perhaps be better if a supercentenarian and his young son did not look exactly the same. He calmly closed his eyes, sinking into a pleasant sleep.

"Father!" Isaac's alarmed voice awoke him abruptly.

Abraham opened his eyes to find Isaac bent over him, his body shaking, and his face terrified. "Father, what happened to you?" he asked apprehensively, relieved that the patriarch had not breathed his last.

"What's the matter? I just fell asleep for a bit..." Abraham smiled, marveling at his son's sense of urgency.

Isaac looked mesmerized. "That's not what I meant," he said anxiously, "Father, look at your beard."

Abraham did so, and he was stunned to see that over the course of his brief nap, his facial hair had turned white as snow. "Apparently, the Lord decided that people should be able to distinguish between us," he said gracefully.

"But how? Why?" Isaac was concerned about his father's strange appearance. However, Abraham gave him a look that seemed to rebuke the child. "Of course, Father, it's probably for the best," his son conceded, suddenly realizing the importance of the matter.

Still, while his new visage was not a matter of concern for Abraham, his soul was indeed troubled. His face abruptly became very pensive, as if he were diving into the depths of his mind. There was a look of sadness on his face that was not typical of him. His mind seemed to be wandering into distant lands, into the mists of the past.

"Father, is something else bothering you?" Isaac asked anxiously.

"You know, my son, that your mother and I, may her memory be a blessing, got married when she was fifteen years old, and I was twenty-five years old, but we did not live together until quite a few years later." Abraham seemed to warmly embrace the memories of his wife. "We lived a full and beautiful life; it was not always easy, but your mother was always by my side when I needed support. Even though you were born many years into our marriage, we always had each other.

"Now, the life of a married person differs vastly from that of a single person. The bonds of matrimony totally change the people who enter that covenant. The commitment to caring for another fills each person with a completely different purpose. Moreover, when children are born, a person changes even more. One's life does not truly begin before one has taken on the twin responsibilities of marriage and family."

Isaac looked at his father, realizing where he was going with this talk. "I think the time has come, my son, for you to marry and start your real life," Abraham declared wholeheartedly. "Indeed, that is the reason I summoned you from the academy of Shem and Eber. You studied with them for three years, but now the time has come for you to start building your own family."

Isaac looked at his father trying to find the right words: "But who am I to marry? There are a lot of families in our camp, but…"

"No, absolutely not!" Abraham cut off his son. "Marrying one of the girls from our camp is not an option. You know they are all Canaanites; their conduct is decent right now, but consider where they come from. You have no way of knowing if they may return to their corrupt habits a few years down the road. They cannot be trusted at all!"

Abraham sighed. "I know these people well. For years I have walked this land, its length and its breadth, and I have attempted to spread the faith. I can testify that apart from Eliezer — who is not from here but came with me from Harran — none of my followers have stayed for more than a few years. As long as it's easy and nice for them, they follow me. To my great dismay, they are not following the Lord, but only me. They waver constantly, as nothing is truly rooted in their hearts."

Abraham kneaded his face with his hands, rubbing his eyes as if he were seeking a solution.

"So maybe Eliezer's daughter? …" Isaac asked nervously.

"God forbid!" Abraham was shocked, "Eliezer is a righteous and abstemious man, but he is still a descendant of Ham, whom Noah cursed. Can we cleave to a family line which is accursed?"

"So, who? The daughters of Aner, Eshcol, and Mamre?"

Abraham shook his head. "You probably do not realize, but I have been thinking about this ever since the Binding. I shiver as I think what would have happened had the Lord not stayed my hand from sacrificing you. Just the thought of your passing before you could produce offspring makes my hair stand! If you had been married and had started a family, at least your sons would remain after you to continue your line.

"One day, as I mused about this, God's word came to me in a revelation in which He told me what had happened with my brother. His wife Milcah bore him eight sons, while his concubine Reumah bore him four more. The youngest of Nahor and Milcah's children is named Bethuel. Bethuel has become a father too, and his little daughter was born three years ago — on the very day of your Binding.

"This child, named Rebecca, must be destined to be your wife. The wonderful thing is that she was born on the same day as you were bound to the altar. If Rebecca were not destined to be your mate, why would the Lord deliver such a prophecy to me? I think we should try and take this daughter of Bethuel, for you, as a wife."

Isaac lowered his eyes, but hiding deep within his heart was the hope that perhaps he might finally find a mate. For a while, he had been plagued by the idea of having to marry one of the girls in their camp; now, this horror dissipated. He realized that it was not for nothing that his father had received a prophecy that came to inform him of the growth of his brother's family, that there was a reason behind it.

"As you wish, Father," he finally said, beaming to match the smile blooming on Abraham's face; of course, the secrets of Isaac's heart were an open book to the father who loved him so.

"Eliezer," Abraham turned to his servant, who had come running to his tent, "There is a very important task I need you to do for me."

Eliezer nodded, ready to give his life for his master.

With a serious expression, Abraham said to his servant: *"And I will make you swear by the Lord, the God of heaven and the God of the earth, that you shall not take a wife for my son of the daughters of the Canaanites, among whom I dwell. But you shall go to my country, and to my kindred, and take a wife for my son, even for Isaac."*

The pain of disappointment washed over Eliezer: "But my lord... I thought that perhaps... if you would agree, then..." Eliezer stammered, desperately trying to speak the thing he wished for most of all. "You know I have my little daughter... she's a very good girl... and I thought..."

Abraham looked at his servant out of the corner of his eye, distressed that he had to disappoint him. "Eliezer ...", he said gently, trying to appease him.

"Yes, I know..." A tear ran down his cheek: "I just thought that maybe if Isaac took her for a wife, she would make him very happy..."

Abraham put his hand on his friend's shoulder to comfort him: "You understand that she cannot marry Isaac."

Eliezer wiped the tear from his eye: "Yes, my lord, I fully understand. You know, these are just the thoughts of a doting father."

"Do not worry, I will find her a suitable groom soon," he promised his servant. "However, I need you to travel back to the land of my family. That is where you may find a suitable wife for my son Isaac," Abraham insisted.

Eliezer thought for a moment, "But, sir, if the woman does not want to follow me here, should I take Isaac there?"

"Absolutely not!" Abraham said emphatically. "One of the reasons I want you to go and bring a woman to my son from afar is to cut her off from her father's house! Do you know what effect a corrupt society has on human beings? Moreover, when the family itself is corrupt, then the influence upon the individual is all the more pernicious. That is why I command you to go far away and take a woman for Isaac from the other end of the earth. That way, she will be severed from the dangerous and malevolent stimuli of her family home."

Hesitantly, Eliezer raised a concern: "It may be that the woman will not be willing to leave her home and her family."

Abraham's reply was confident and categorical: "*The Lord, the God of heaven, who took me from my father's house, and from the land of my nativity, and who spoke to me, and who swore to me, saying: To your seed will I give this land; He will send His angel before you, and you shall take a wife for my son from there. And if the woman be not willing to follow you, then you shall be clear from this my oath; only you shall not bring my son back there.*"

Eliezer agreed, taking an oath upon a sacred object that he would faithfully carry out his mission.

It was noon, and Eliezer and nine of Abraham's servants finished loading up their mounts, each man bearing fruits, vegetables, and delicacies. Silver vessels, gold vessels, and jewelry were also placed upon the camels.

Abraham and Isaac looked at the convoy that was preparing to set out. Before them was a long-expected journey of seventeen days, a journey through deserts and mountains towards Harran, northeast of the land of Canaan. The ten servants were dressed in their best robes, as befitting the importance and respectability of their master.

Abraham approached Eliezer, handing him a rolled-up scroll: "Here is my will, in which I bequeath all that I have to my son, Isaac. It may be of help to you."

Eliezer bowed to his master and mounted the camel, ready for the long and arduous journey.

Chapter Thirty-Six

Rebecca

"**R**ebecca!"

The scream that erupted from the dining room did not surprise the young girl. The beautiful hazel eyes no longer opened wide in fear when her name was mentioned in shouts. Even the shadow of a smile rose on her lips, realizing the source of her older brother Laban's anger.

"Where are you? Curse you, girl!" The shout could be heard again, now by the door. Rebecca opened the door slowly, looking at her brother's face, enflamed with rage.

She thought with a smile: He looks like he's about to explode any moment.

"Were you looking for me, my dear brother?" she asked innocently, confronting her angry brother.

"Where's the chicken leg?" Laban screamed in obvious anger.

"The chicken leg..." Rebecca seemed to be pondering her brother's important question. "I know Mother roasted a chicken for lunch. Is it missing a leg? The leg I was supposed to eat?" she mused calmly.

"Yes! Where is it?!" Laban kept shouting, as if Rebecca were far away from him.

"Why do you ask?" she replied as she lowered her eyes to cover for the smile that gleamed on her face.

"Why am I asking?! You want to know? I will tell you why I am asking! Because if you tell me again that you have given your dish to some stinking pauper, I do not know what I will do!" Laban shrieked angrily, knowing of his sister's deeds.

"I'll tell you what to do..." Rebecca replied coolly, "you will eat your lunch anyway; even if some stinking pauper — as you say — dies, you'll still stuff your face without thinking twice."

Laban's hands trembled with anger at his little sister's boldness. "I tell you, this will not pass in silence! I guarantee I'll teach you a lesson!" he shrieked.

"You know I hear quite well; stop screaming and leave me alone. Just back off and give me a break. I have more important things to do than listen to your whiny voice," she said contemptuously, turning her back on her brother, who was rooted to his place in anger.

"Father, you must do something about Rebecca!" Laban said to his father Bethuel, as the two of them sat down to lunch. "Even today, she gave her food to some stinking pauper instead of eating it herself. Every day she eats only bread and drinks water, instead of eating the food Mother prepares. She gives her meals to the poor, and it gets them used to coming to our house and asking for charity and food. Our house is starting to resemble your uncle's house, if the tales about him are true. The riffraff are constantly banging on our front door, demanding food!"

Bethuel looked at his son in disbelief. "I do not understand where she got this madness for distributing food to the poor. If they want something to eat, let them go somewhere else and find work! She does not understand that we work hard to bring a piece of bread home!"

Laban bit into another large piece of the chunk of meat he held in his hand: "You have to explain to her that our financial situation is not the best either. We have many expenses!" he objected, as he gulped from the large glass of wine in his other hand.

Bethuel looked troubled: "Deborah!" he boomingly shouted to his wife, knowing she was always nearby when he dined.

"Yes, my lord," Deborah replied, chastened.

"Call your daughter, Rebecca. Tell her to come to me right away," he ordered without looking in the direction of his wife.

Bethuel referred to Deborah in this way even though she was not Rebecca's biological mother, who had died in childbirth. Deborah had married Bethuel soon after, and they all thought of her as Mother — not that it helped the attitude of the master's house.

"Now bring us something else to eat!" Bethuel berated her. "Your daughter causes me so much anxiety, I need more to eat in order to calm down.

A few minutes later, Rebecca arrived. "Did you call me, Father?" she asked quietly, placing the tray — heavily laden with meat — on the table.

"When will you stop this behavior of yours?" he demanded angrily, snatching a juicy piece of meat from the tray.

"What behavior, Father?" she asked innocently.

"You know what!" screamed Laban, knocking over the bottle of wine on the tablecloth, trying to raise his fleshy body from the chair and stand on his feet.

A grin stretched across Rebecca's mouth, seeing her brother try to stand up quickly: "There's no need for you to get up, brother. You can keep lying on the puffy cushions; you actually look just like them."

"Shut your mouth!" Bethuel screamed bitterly at his daughter. "Stop this behavior right away and start acting like a human being! If you are bored and have nothing to do, I can promise I'll make your life interesting!" The veins stood out on Bethuel's red face, as he watched his clumsy son spill more wine onto his clothes as he tried to straighten in his seat.

"So, it's boredom that's your problem? You have nothing to do, so you are looking for thrills!" he continued without waiting for an answer, "I'll make sure you're never bored! I will make sure you have no time to mess with nonsense. Deborah!"

The door opened immediately, Deborah standing in the doorway, trembling before the rage of her husband. "Yes, my lord," she whispered anxiously.

"Listen to me carefully! From now on, only Rebecca goes to the wellspring to fetch water! Tell all the maidservants and manservants that anyone else who dares to do so, aside from this girl of yours, will feel my wrath! She will also bring water to the manservants and maidservants! Maybe putting her to work will put a stop to all her nonsense!" he declared, offering a brilliant solution to his thorny problem.

"Very good, my lord," Deborah whispered, a tear running down her cheek. The mother and her daughter left the room silently, although they still managed to hear Bethuel's sigh as they left: "Who will marry her...?"

"Why do you have to antagonize him?" The mother whispered to her daughter wistfully, "Look what you've done to yourself now."

Rebecca looked at her mother in pity, knowing how difficult Bethuel made Deborah's life. "Mother, I'm not doing this to upset him. I just cannot live this way! I cannot see the poor people coming to ask for a piece of bread and close my eyes as if they are not there. I prefer to die then to live like a beast that thinks only of itself." Tears flowed from Rebecca's eyes: "What is my life worth, if I have to marry such a man! I would rather die now than have to live that way!"

Rebecca wiped the tears from her eyes: "I have to go get water.

Mother, do not be sorry for that! I'm happy to do it. Perhaps I cannot show kindness to the paupers, but at least I can show kindness to the manservants and maidservants…" Rebecca paused for a moment, considering whether or not to say the following words: "And to the beasts as well, I can show kindness!" she blurted out with a sigh.

The path to the wellspring delighted her young heart. The outing meant release from the stress and the unending shouting in the house that constantly cast a pall over a soul which was joyous and carefree by nature. Lightly jumping from rock to rock, Rebecca descended to the wellspring, her heart singing even as her father's offhanded question echoed in her ears. As she walked, she could not help but think about it.

She mused: But really, who will marry me? I'm so different form everyone here. People whisper behind my back, like I'm crazy and abnormal. It is so beastly the way people want me to accept whatever abuse the riffraff want to indulge in with me, just to slake their animalistic desires. People think that because the girls my age act in this feral way, I ought to ape their behavior. They even justify this inhumane conduct with all sorts of excuses and justifications. So, am I the one with the problem? How do I know that they are wrong, and I am right? I am still a young girl, barely three years old; yet I think I am smarter than all of them. But maybe I'm the one who's mistaken?

These questions threatened to overwhelm her, even as she tried to figure things out for herself. Could she justify her way of life, which was considered so bizarre by everyone she knew?

"Maybe… maybe… maybe… Wow." Rebecca stopped in her place, forcing herself to stop wandering down that path of speculation. "No! They are not right! There is no way, no angle from which their views make sense. They are utterly wrong."

Then the doubts rolled back in: "Yeah, genius… what makes you so sure?"

Then she cried, her voice echoing into the distance: "Because I am, and that's that!"

Still, she could hear the laughter in her head, trying to push her off course. The mocking voice within challenged her: A little girl who knows better than all the people in the world? You alone understand, awesome genius? In all the world, the great secret was revealed to you only, and everyone else is mistaken?!

Rebecca felt the warm tears welling in her eyes, her soul ripping to shreds by feelings of self-doubt and recrimination, which threatened to push her off the path of righteousness which she had chosen for herself.

"No! I'm not alone! There are others like me, who think like me!" she said aloud, struggling with the ridicule erupting from within her to stymie her.

But the voice continued: Yes? Who, for example? Neither your father nor your mother, neither your brother nor your kinsmen. Not even one person in the city agrees with such a fool!

Rebecca tried to find counter-arguments to silence her persecutor: "I have some friends who understand that I am right! And more than that, there is one person in our family... so Father once told me. He is Abraham, father's uncle, brother of Grandfather Nahor. Abraham and his wife Sarah did not think like the whole city, not like all other people around! They were even willing to give up their lives for their faith! I am not alone in the world, there are other people who think like me..." Rebecca felt that she had dealt a triumphant blow to the voice trying to confuse her.

Her feet led her to crest the hill, and now she could see the wellspring below, from which she was supposed to draw water. Her hand gripped the massive jug, twice as big as her head; clearly, the way back would be much harder, with a full load; but she girded her loins with the decision not to give her brother the satisfaction of seeing her fail at such a punitive task. Her young legs pumped as she rushed down the hill, realizing how little time she had before the sun would set. The bright light of the sun dazzled Rebecca's eyes, even as she noticed the brilliant figures standing by the wellspring. Who were they?

"Something very strange is happening here," Eliezer had thought upon his arrival a few minutes earlier. He rubbed his head, which was adorned with a glorious turban with gold and silver threads woven into it. "The landscape is not the same as it was a few years ago when I was here. And how it changed utterly in an instant!" In the distance, Eliezer saw a figure grazing his sheep. He turned his camel toward the man, and the convoy followed in a line behind him.

The sun began to tilt west slowly, advancing toward the far horizon. It painted the bright end of the day in shades of orange. "Excuse me," Eliezer addressed the shepherd in the language of Canaan, looking in amazement at his clothing, uncharacteristic for the area.

The man looked at Eliezer in surprise; the servant's elegant mien aroused fear in the face of the man, who did not seem to understand Eliezer's language.

"Where are we?" he asked the petrified shepherd.

"I do not understand you!" said the shepherd in the language of the land of Harran.

Eliezer tried to recover and regain the language he had not spoken for decades. "Where do we be?" he asked, stumbling in the shepherd's tongue.

The shepherd smiled calmly, realizing that the people did not want to attack him but only to ask him a question. "In the land of Harran, not far from Ur Kasdim," he replied happily.

"Are you sure?!"

The man laughed: "Certainly, I live not far from here; Ur Kasdim is a little beyond this hill. Five minute ride on a camel."

"Thank you," said Eliezer, feeling a tremor run through his body as he realized the miracle he had experienced.

He thought to himself: A seventeen-day ride has passed in three hours. It is, of course, by the merit of my master Abraham...

From the top of the hill, Eliezer looked down, and a wellspring appeared before him. Eliezer and his men went down to it. "We will stop here by the wellspring," he told his men, who seemed preoccupied by the miraculously swift passage between the land of Canaan and Harran. They made the camels kneel down by the wellspring, but they did not bring their mounts any water. There was no need to bring water to the camels, as the ships of the desert had had their tanks filled just a few hours earlier. Abraham's men leaned against the kneeling camels, enjoying the end of the sunny day.

Eliezer approached the wellspring, hearing with pleasure the rippling of the stream flowing deep below, seeing the crystal waters rise slowly upward like a fountain. The wonder of the water coming up to meet him was a true sign of Divine Providence, by the merits of his righteous masters, Abraham and Isaac. He offered a prayer of gratitude for the miracle, then turned to the matter at hand.

He thought to himself: Everyone needs water; evening is usually when the women come out to fetch water for their homes. We should wait here until the women come to draw water.

Eliezer felt the hesitation that arose in him: But how do I know who to choose for Isaac, my master's son? How do I know that the girl is decent and worthy to be Isaac's wife? I have no idea whom to approach if some girls come to the wellspring...

Eliezer felt pressure, the magnitude of the mission threatening to suffocate him now that he had the time to reflect on it.

Then, he came to a realization: It is not up to me, but God Almighty! Just as He has so far miraculously led me, so He will continue to lead me!

Eliezer closed his eyes, composing a prayer: "*Lord, God of my master Abraham, send me, please, good speed this day, and show kindness to my master Abraham. Behold, I stand by the wellspring of water; and the daughters of the men of the city come out to draw water. So let it come to pass, that the damsel to whom I shall say: Let down your jug, I please, that I may drink; and she shall say: Drink, and I will give your camels drink also; let the same be she that You have appointed for Your servant, even for Isaac; and thereby shall I know that You have shown kindness to my master.*"

Eliezer mused to himself: If the girl lets me drink from the jug, and then she takes the water to her house, she is a stupid girl, for she does not know if I am a healthy or sick person, and she might harm her family. If she spills the contents of the water left in the jug on the ground and fills it anew with water, then she does not have virtues, as she might embarrass me. If she gives the water left in the jug to the camels, this will prove that she is both wise and virtuous, and that she deserves to marry Isaac.

Eliezer opened his eyes to see a quite young girl approaching the wellspring from the other side, leaping nimbly from rock to rock, her jug on her shoulder. Eliezer, feeling unable to stop himself, ran towards the girl. She quickly filled the jug of water from the wellspring, which suddenly seemed to overflow toward the girl. The girl deftly put the full jug of water on her shoulder.

Rebecca looked out the corner of her eye at the elegant man running toward her. A shiver of fear gripped her body, as she stared at the old man rapidly advancing.

Eliezer stopped in his place, realizing that his action must have frightened the young girl. "Please, young lady, could you give me some water from your jug?" he asked in a soft voice, praying that God would continue to grant him success.

"Gladly, my lord," the girl said, lowering her jug from her shoulder, handing it to Eliezer. Eliezer sipped some water from the jug and returned it to the girl.

Rebecca looked at the jug, which still held plenty of water, almost to the brim, even after the strange man had drunk a little of it.

She thought quickly: What will I do now? I cannot take the left-over water to the house, lest he be ill. I cannot even pour the water out on the ground before him, as that might embarrass him.

The seconds passed, as Rebecca glanced at the camels kneeling a short distance away: "My lord, I will give your camels to drink as well, until they are full," she said. She ran over to the camels, pouring the water from her jug into the troughs nearby.

Eliezer looked happily at the girl approaching him, feeling that God was granting him success. The girl filled water again and again from the wellspring, giving water to all the camels.

Eliezer rejoiced, thinking: This is a girl suitable for my lord's house. She is so clever and so kind! Instead of simply pouring out the leftover water before the camels to avoid the dilemma, she fills the troughs to the brim, going back to the well again and again. Moreover, she acts as if it were the most natural thing to do, as if I were alone and infirm, even though I have a squad of strong men with me. Her character is impeccable — but what about her lineage? If only she were to be from the family of my master Abraham!

The young girl finished her work, watching with pleasure the camels drinking their fill from the brimming water troughs. Her gaze was full of joy at the kindness she has done, her quick breathing showing the great effort she had exerted. Eliezer went to the camel he had been riding, took gold jewelry from one of the packs and brought it to the girl, who was astonished at the beauty of the items.

"No, my lord. I require no reward for what I did," the girl whispered, embarrassed, as Eliezer approached her, with a gold nose-ring adorned with a precious stone and two precious bracelets in his hands.

"Who are you? Is there a place in your house for my people to sleep for the night?" Eliezer asked, sure that, thanks to his master, it would turn out that the girl hailed from his master's family.

"*I am the daughter of Bethuel the son of Milcah, whom she bore to Nahor,*" the girl answered gravely, unsure whether it would be for good or ill. "*We have both straw and provender enough, and room to lodge in,*" she assured him, "for as long as you need." She knew that her father would not refuse to let rich guests into his house, as they would pay a lot of money for the hospitality.

Insisting that she take the jewelry, Eliezer jubilantly reflected: She is none other than the granddaughter of Nahor, my master's brother!

He joyously bowed to God in thanksgiving. "Blessed be the Lord, God of my master Abraham, who has not forsaken His mercy and His truth toward my master; as for me, the Lord has led me in the way to the house of my master's brethren!" he declared aloud.

As Rebecca heard the words of Eliezer, revealing that he was from the estate of Abraham, trembling took hold of her body; she could not believe that she was hearing the very name of the man whose household she so longed to join. Could she dare let hope into her shattered heart? Would this man rescue her from her misery and take her to the domain of his master? "My lord, wait here, please..." she said to Eliezer and ran toward her house, leaving the jug of water behind.

The way back seemed long, refusing to end. The short minutes seemed like an eternity as she was consumed by the fear that the stranger whom she had met would disappear like a mirage.

Deborah's door opened impatiently, as she looked at her daughter, who was breathing fast.

"Where's the jug? Why didn't you bring water?! Do you want to drive your father mad?!" Deborah cried in alarm, seeing her daughter without the water she was sent to fetch. "What's in your nose? What's on your wrists?! Where did you find that?!" she said in amazement, noticing her daughter's jewelry.

"Mother! Abraham! He sent his servant! He's by the water! He's there! We need to get him!" The torrent of exclamations pouring out of the girl was bewildering.

"What Abraham?! What servant are you talking about? Who should you bring? Where's this jewelry from?!" Deborah responded to her animated daughter.

Rebecca tried to calm down. She took a deep breath and made a conscious effort to present the situation comprehensively and comprehensibly. "I went to the wellspring, to draw water like father said. On the edge of the wellspring, was a splendidly dressed man, who asked me to give him water to drink. I gave him a drink, and he gave me this jewelry. He asked whose daughter I was, and I told him. Then he bowed and thanked the Lord. It must be his god, who sent him to the house of his master's kin. Do you understand? He is a servant of Abraham, the brother of Grandpa Nahor! "

"Show me that!" Laban's voice snapped Rebecca back to reality. Her brother was standing in the doorway behind her. He reached out his clumsy hand to grab the precious gold bracelets. "He gave it to you for some water you drew for him?!" he asked, a triumphant spark in his eye.

"Yes..." said Rebecca, turning her gaze from her brother's greed in disgust. Laban turned on his heel, then ran stumbling from the house, towards the wellspring.

"Hey... hey there! Wait, my lord!" came a call from the top of the hill towards Eliezer. Eliezer looked up and saw a clumsy guy running towards him heavily, falling and stumbling in his attempt to accelerate his gait. Eliezer looked with a smile at the young man as he arrived, huffing and puffing, and painfully holding his sides.

With a manufactured smile, Laban declared: "*Enter, you blessed of the Lord; why stand outside? For I have cleared the house, and made room for the camels,*" said Laban, holding out his hand to grab Eliezer's. "Come, my lord, please, I have cleaned the house; it is clean and tidy, my lord." Laban pulled Eliezer's hand, urging him to go to the house. "It was not easy to clean the place. I took out all the statues and idols so that you and your people could enter there. I understand that my lord is of the house of Abraham, brother of my grandfather, Nahor.

"I've heard a lot of good things about your master... I'm really gratified and excited to welcome you to our home. All my efforts are worth it just to enjoy your presence; it's not something for which one should get paid at all. It's not that I worked too much — just a few hours of very hard work. I understand you gave my dear sister jewelry because she gave you some water to drink...

"That's a bit excessive, I do not require so much..." Laban pulled Eliezer towards the house, and he motioned for his men to follow.

The camels were brought into the pen, and Laban unloaded their baggage, trying to see what the big packs contained. His eyes lit up as he saw the fancy vessels. Laban ran to bring fodder for the camels, while Eliezer's men opened their packs so that they could eat. Laban hurried to fetch tubs of water, and humbly washed the feet of Eliezer and his men.

"My dear father is waiting for you, my lord," said Laban to Eliezer, "I have made sure that we prepare a meal for my lord that will surely please your palate, my honored lord," he said with a fake smile. "Please, my lord, come with me to my father, who is breathlessly looking forward to meeting my lord," he flattered Eliezer.

"Happily," said Eliezer, though his fondest wish was to bring the nauseating fawning encounter to a conclusion as soon as possible.

"Father, this is Eliezer, a member of the house of Abraham your uncle, who has arrived in our fair town," Laban told his father as he entered the room. He introduces the important guest to the master of the house.

"Sit down, my honored lord," said Bethuel, gesturing with his hand at the large cushion beside him. "Will you see to some refreshment for our esteemed guest?" he asked his son.

"Yes, Father, I'll be right back with the food."

"And how is my dear uncle..." Laban heard his father start a conversation with the guest as he left the room.

"I'll take the guest his plate!" said Laban to his mother, who was filling the plates with various delicacies at her son's command. Laban took the loaded plate, placed a particularly large piece of meat on top, and stepped from the kitchen into the pantry for a moment. He took a small vial out of his pocket and poured its contents onto the piece of meat, then shook the plate so that the meat settled in place among the other items.

He thought, with a sly smile: When the guest dies, it will not be a problem to get rid of the men who are with him and to seize all the baggage that is on the camels. Not only that, but Abraham's son will then be unable to marry any of the Abrahamic family, out of fear that his servant had already betrothed one of the women, making all of her kin forbidden relations!

He entered the dining room. "Please, my honored lord, please eat! My lord must be famished," said Laban with a wide smile to the guest, placed his plate humbly in front of him.

Eliezer looked at Laban's face, beaming with glee. "I will not eat until I have spoken," he said emphatically, spurning the plate in front of him.

"Speak, please, my honored lord," said Bethuel.

"I am no lord," he corrected them. "I am the son of King Nimrod, but I have served Abraham for decades. It is the greatest honor to serve such a great master."

Bethuel and Laban looked at Eliezer in amazement. The knowledge that Nimrod's son went and made himself a slave to Abraham had long been forgotten. The recognition that this important and wise man had decided to dedicate his life to serving Abraham raised their uncle's stock even more in their eyes.

"*I am Abraham's servant. And the Lord has blessed my master greatly; and he is become great; and He has given him flocks and herds, and silver and gold, and menservants and maidservants, and camels and asses.*" Eliezer noticed the beady, greedy eyes watching him as he described the extent of Abraham's wealth.

"*And Sarah my master's wife bore a son to my master when she was old.*"

They looked at him with puzzlement, and he elaborated: "Yes, she was ninety years old when she bore her only child!"

He then dramatically produced the parchment from his robe: "*And my lord gave to his son that was born to him all that he had.*" Laban and Bethuel eagerly perused the document and marveled at the great wealth that Abraham had.

The door creaked slightly, Rebecca entered the room carrying two plates laden with food, using the trays to shield her body from view, because her father was not willing to buy her clothing that was less revealing.

Laban looked at his sister in disgust: "Put down the plates and get out!" He commanded angrily, "and you better not eavesdrop behind the door!"

Rebecca put the plates on the table and left the room quickly.

"Yes, and what good is it to us?" Laban asked boldly after the door closed.

Eliezer smiled at the two men: "*And my master made me swear, saying: You shall not take a wife for my son of the daughters of the Canaanites, in whose land I dwell. But you shall go to my father's house, and to my kindred, and take a wife for my son.*"

Laban laughed lightly, rubbing his hands together with glee: "And who said anyone would agree to give his daughter to the son of your master Abraham?"

Eliezer's laughter surprised the two: "I thought so too, let me tell you! *And I said to my master: Perhaps the woman will not follow me.* But you know my lord, you have probably heard of the years he lived here, and of the miracles done for him..." Eliezer looked at the father and son with a threatening look. "Well, my lord reassured me, told me not to worry about it, for an angel from heaven would accompany me on the way I go, and that indeed turned out to be the case, as this very afternoon I left the land of Canaan and within three hours I covered a distance that should have taken seventeen days. And I know that the angel who took care of bringing me here quickly also made sure that Rebecca was the first woman I met, even if my prayer was not the most precise and focused!

"And I came this day to the wellspring, and said: Lord, God of my master Abraham, if now You do prosper my way which I go. Behold, I stand by the wellspring of water; and let it come to pass, that the maiden who comes forth to draw, to whom I shall say: Give me, I please, a little water from your pitcher to drink; And she shall say to me: Both drink you, and I will also draw for your camels; let the same be for the woman whom the Lord has appointed for my master's son. And before I had done speaking to my heart, behold, Rebecca came forth with her pitcher on her shoulder; and she went down to the wellspring, and drew. And I said to her: 'Let me drink, I please.' And she made haste, and let down her pitcher from her shoulder, and said: 'Drink, and I will give your camels drink also.' So, I drank, and she made the camels drink also. And I asked her, and said: 'Whose daughter are you?' And she said:

'The daughter of Bethuel, Nahor's son, whom Milcah bore to him.' And I put the ring upon her nose, and the bracelets upon her hands. And I bowed my head, and prostrated myself before the Lord, and blessed the Lord, God of my master Abraham, who had led me in the right way to take my master's brother's daughter for his son."

Eliezer smiled at Bethuel and Laban: "You know? Many years have passed since the four kings abducted Lot, my master's nephew. You must remember what happened in the end, right?" Eliezer's voice sounded menacing. "Many years have passed since we went out to war, my master and I. The memories of days gone by always evokes nostalgia…" Eliezer sighed sadly at times past. "You see, the Lord is quite exacting with anyone who attempts to injure or distress my master."

Eliezer looked into Bethuel's eyes subduing him with his sharp gaze. *"And now, if you deal kindly and truly with my master, tell me;"* Eliezer paused to stare meaningfully at Bethuel. *"And if not, tell me,"* his brow furrowed in fury; *"that I may turn to the right hand or to the left.* My lord Abraham has kin beyond the House of Nahor. Should I turn elsewhere, to seek a match from the another branch of the family tree of Terah? That would be most unfortunate — for you!"

Bethuel looked away from Eliezer's piercing gaze, and turned to look at his son, seeing the sweat dripping down his round, pampered face. His eyes pleaded for his son's advice.

"The thing proceeded from the Lord!" blurted Laban in terror, fearing that the man sitting in front of him would be angry with them. *"We cannot speak to you bad or good. Behold, Rebecca is before you."* In his heart, he reflected: Fortunate are we to be relieved of this burden!

Then Laban grinned, *like one who discovers a great treasure.*

Aloud he said: "They sound like a match made in heaven. *Take her, and go, and let her be your master's son's wife, as the Lord has spoken.*" In his heart, he sneered: If you can make it out of here alive.

Eliezer bowed to give glory to God: "I am very glad you made the right decision. Can you call Rebecca and her mother, please?" he said to Bethuel.

"Deborah! Rebecca! Come in here!" Bethuel thundered towards the door.

The door opened quickly, revealing that the two women were standing right behind it.

"Come in and close the door!" Laban ordered, outraged that his sister had defied his orders.

Eliezer sorted through the large pack he had brought with him to the dining room, rifling through its contents until he found garments, splendid in material but modest in cut, in the appropriate size for Rebecca. "My lady, please take these. They suit you far better!"

Rebecca rejoiced at the sight of the new clothing, which accommodated the modest style which had always appealed to her. The servant also took out gold and silver vessels, telling her: "My lady, please accept these gifts, which my master sent for you."

Laban stared at the vessels inlaid with gems, gleaming in the candlelight. Eliezer took some precious items and delicacies from his pack and gave them to Bethuel, Deborah, and Laban.

"And now, my dear friend," Eliezer turned to Laban, "if you will kindly show me to my men, I want to see that they get along, that all is well with them." He patted his shoulder, like an old friend, "Come with me, and I will give you some more presents, my friend," he whispered in Laban's ear.

"But you did not eat?!" Laban hissed, feeling he was missing his chance.

Eliezer grinned: "My master Abraham taught me that whatever

one eats must be prepared in accordance with God's law and healthy living. I must decline."

Eliezer and Laban left the room, leaving Bethuel and the two women. "What did he want...?" Deborah asked with trepidation.

"That is none of your business!" Bethuel looked at his wife angrily, knowing she had heard everything. "Get out of here now and leave me alone." Bethuel felt that he had missed a golden opportunity — literally! How much could he have demanded for Rebecca's bride-price; had not he not been intimidated by Eliezer and his tales of angels and battles?

"And get these plates out of here — but leave me one!" he roared.

Rebecca picked up two plates and left the room.

"Bring me the slave's plate! Aren't you ashamed to bring the big portion to the slave instead of me?!" He screamed in frustration, pulling towards him the plate presented to Eliezer.

"I get no respect in this house!" he said resentfully, as he ravenously bit into the big piece of meat.

"Father, I was able to get him to give me—" Laban said happily as he entered the room, seeing his father slumped on the large cushions. A strange feeling gripped Laban, seeing Bethuel in repose. "Father..." he whispered and walked over. The half-eaten large piece of meat lying at his father's feet made it clear to Laban what had happened.

The sound of roosters crowing woke Eliezer and his men. Eliezer hastened his men to prepare the camels for their departure. He was aware of the sudden death that had occurred the previous night, but he was ferociously determined to avoid any delay.

"I heard what happened last night," he told Laban and Deborah, sitting stone-faced around the table. "I am very sorry, and I share your grief... Apparently, the joy of his daughter's betrothal was too much for his heart to bear, and his soul went back to its Maker."

Deborah nodded her head, looking for some hint of loss and grief in her heart, but finding nothing but relief.

Laban's eyes darted side to side, avoiding the gaze of anyone who tried to make eye contact with him.

"But I'm sure he would not want the mourning for him to delay the joy of Rebecca's nuptials," Eliezer continued, violating the silence of mother and son.

"I'm not sure," Laban replied. "Indeed, this is a bad omen!" Carelessly, he mumbled: "He wasn't the one who was supposed to die." Then, realizing what he had said, he jumped out of his seat: "I mean, he didn't deserve to die... He was such a decent man!" he half-yelled.

"I understand..." Eliezer replied, glaring at Laban murderously. He realized that there had been yet another miracle on his wondrous journey.

The silence dragged on, Deborah stared at her son, knowing what he had done, loathing the thought of staying in the house with him.

"I ask that you call Rebecca, and I will take her, and I will go to my lord," Eliezer said, without hiding how much he wanted to escape the viper's den.

"I do not know... Perhaps this is not the right time for Rebecca to leave... Perhaps she should stay here for a year or so, and then you can come back to take her," Laban said, hoping to extort more gifts from Eliezer.

"I also do not think it is worthwhile for her to go now...", said the mother, afraid to be left alone with her son and the miscreants around him.

Eliezer glared ominously at Laban: *Delay me not, seeing the Lord has prospered my way; send me away that I may go to my master.* Dispatch me immediately, unless you want to end up like your father!"

"You know what? *We will call the damsel, and inquire at her mouth*, if she even wants to go with you," said Laban, seeking escape from the bind that he'd almost put himself in.

Eliezer nodded with a smile, "By all means..."

Rebecca entered the room at the sound of her mother's calling. A smile hid on her face, like a prisoner whose sentence is done and awaits release. She wore the clothes that Eliezer had brought here the previous night, her bags already packed for the journey.

"Rebecca, do you seek our consent to send you with this man, to marry his master's son?" Laban asked his sister.

Rebecca giggled: "Of course, I seek your consent," she said, looking at him in horror, "but if you refuse, I will leave regardless!"

Laban cleared his throat self-importantly, as if he were a lord acting beneficently towards his vassals. "Then, I hereby consent to send you along with Abraham's servant and his men!"

Deborah raised her tearful eyes to Eliezer, pleading, "Can I come with you too?"

"Happily," Eliezer said to the woman who was the only mother Rebecca had ever known.

"And so," said Laban, standing tall with pride, knowing that all his father's property now belonged only to him, "it is time to bless the bride!" In the name of the household he now headed, he declared: "*Our sister, be you the mother of thousands of ten thousands, and let your seed possess the gate of those that hate them.*"

Laban smiled jubilantly, thinking: They say that children take after their mother's brother, so may all your offspring be like me!

Rebecca felt a pain in her stomach, knowing her brother's blessing would not benefit her at all.

Rebecca and Deborah got on the camels, but they were not alone. Some of her friends, who had decided to embrace her approach to life, also accompanied her, eager to join Abraham's camp.

Finally, they were all ready for the long journey ahead of them, a two-and-a-half-week cross-desert trek.

CHAPTER THIRTY-SEVEN

Keturah

"I must do something," Isaac thought to himself. "Now that Eliezer has been sent to fetch me a wife to marry, my father will be lonely. Although I know that he does not feel lonely, since he is constantly engaged in his studies, still it is appropriate for him to have a wife. When the Lord created the world, He said, 'It is not good that the man should be alone; I will make him a suitable helpmate.' It makes no difference whether a given person is young or old, one needs a partner. I must bring it about, come what may…"

"Father, may I come in?" Isaac asked as his heart trembled. Doubts as to how his father would receive the act shook his body.

"Of course, son. Come on in, please."

"Father, Eliezer will probably be back in a few weeks, right?"

Abraham saw the apprehension on his son's face. With a calm smile, he tried to relive the tension his son must be in approaching his marriage.

"Father, God commanded man to take a wife, right?"

The tension in Isaac's words conveyed to Abraham a fear that he had not clarified to his son the importance of married life.

Abraham nodded calmly to his son.

Isaac continued: "God did not limit the duty by age; whether a man is young or old, he ought to have a wife, right?"

"True," Abraham told his son.

"If so, Father... I hope you do not get mad at me..." Isaac did not know how to say it. "I mean I have a surprise for you..." Abraham looked at his son in amazement.

Isaac turned to the tent door: "Keturah, can you come in, please?"

A woman entered the tent, covered from head to toe, her eyes tearing with excitement, her mouth murmuring.

"Hagar?" Abraham said in amazement and got to his feet.

The woman fell to her knees, bowing to her son's father: "Yes, my lord. Hagar was my name; but Isaac, your son, told me that from now on my name will be Keturah."

Isaac approached his stunned father: "Father, I inquired about her a lot before I dared to bring her to you," he whispered in his ear. "This woman has bound herself (*keshura*) for more than thirty years, that no man should approach her. I have asked everyone, far and wide, about her deeds; everyone says her deeds are as pleasant as incense (*ketoret*) to heaven. Her reputation is impeccable! So, I told her that her name ought to be Keturah and not Hagar. Ishmael, your son, has returned with her, he and his wife and sons. They have really changed, Father; everyone who knows them praises them."

Isaac hesitated, trying to figure out how to sum up his appeal: "'*It is not good for man to be alone; I will make him a suitable helpmate,*' said the Lord; and as you said, Father, whether a young man or an old man, he should have a wife."

Abraham put his hand on his son's shoulder affectionately: "You are right, my dear son."

Isaac came out of his father's tent, borne on the wings of his joy. The sun, inclining towards the west, caressed his radiant face in its warm light. Isaac hurried toward the open field, seeking to carry a prayer of thanksgiving from his heart to God for granting him success in this endeavor. Flowers in a variety of colors greeted him, a spectacular carpet of the beauty of creation, sending intoxicating fragrances into the air. It was a seemingly infinite space, not far away from human habitation: a vast meadow, over which songbirds and butterflies hovered. Hands spread out to the sides, as if gathering into them the wind blowing around his body, Isaac sought to embrace the whole world happily. The hairs of his sidelocks were tossed in the breeze, beneath the turban that sat on his head.

His heart dissolved, then filled up, expanded, flew into virgin regions, rocketing to the skies. Eyes closed in prayer, he felt himself merge with the beloved Creator of All Existence. His lips opened in thanksgiving, a song of praise and exultation for the Author of Reality.

Nullifying self...

Merging...

Connecting...

Incorporating...

For a long time, Isaac poured out his discourse before his Creator, acknowledging, glorifying, and praising with utmost grace from the bottom of his heart, in gratitude for the past and hope for the future.

Finally, Isaac opened his eyes, finding it difficult to part with the feeling of union, feeling as if he were suspended between the two worlds.

His eyes beheld from a distance a caravan of camels approaching him. Isaac went towards them, seeking to bring the guests into his father's tent.

Eliezer smiled to himself, realizing that the miracle he had initially encountered was now repeating itself. The land he knew so well came into view at eventide, the field which his master had bought in Hebron. His eyes saw, from a distance, his master Isaac standing in the heart of the field in prayer, within sight of the burial place of his righteous mother. Joy filled his heart, knowing that he would soon announce to his master and son his success in his important mission. Eliezer saw Isaac finish his prayer and begin to advance toward the caravan. "He is, of course, looking for guests; he cannot imagine that it is we, who have returned in two days from Harran," he thought cheerfully.

A glorious figure, beaming with majesty and splendor, approached the caravan of camels.

Rebecca stared at the approaching figure; her eyes dazzled by the light enveloping the man who looked as if he had descended from the highest heavens to earth. Hypnotized by the sight before her eyes, she did not pay attention to the fact that she was riding a camel. She leaned over to catch the wonderful sight and almost fell off.

Awestruck, Rebecca reverently asked the servant: *"Who is the man walking in the field toward us?"*

And the servant said: "It is my master," affectionately adding, "your husband-to-be."

Rebecca took her veil and covered her face, lest the holy man see the face of a woman. Eliezer jumped off the camel, jubilantly running to Isaac, who was shocked by the delegation's swift return. The two friends embraced in affection, and Eliezer told his master everything that happened to him from his departure until his return. Eliezer and Isaac, embracing each other's shoulders, led the way as the caravan followed them. The sun was now sinking below the horizon.

As Rebecca entered Sarah's tent, the light which had gone out three years earlier reignited, spreading a glow through the camp as in the days when Sarah was still alive. The appearance of a cloud of holiness enveloped the tent as before Sarah's passing, returning to its place. The aroma of the baked pastries and stews fills the air, intoxicating the members of the camp who had so missed the lady who had taken care of all of them. The tents were opened, inviting guests to satisfy their hunger as in days of yore.

"I feel like Mother is back," Isaac told his father, who came out of his tent, smelling the scents spreading through the camp.

"I, too, feel that there is again a worthy lady in the camp," said Abraham, lovingly embracing his son.

CHAPTER THIRTY-EIGHT

The Twins

Atop Mount Moriah, the Place of Binding, a cool wind whistled through the brush, rattling their bones. Isaac and Rebecca had arrived at the site where he had been bound decades earlier, in order to pour out their prayers before the Gates of Heaven, hoping to arouse the Attribute of Mercy for both of them. Each picked a spot to petition God that their years of childlessness, now numbering nineteen, might finally come to an end.

The restless sound of each one's crying tore at the other's heart, the suffocating unarticulated pain cutting deeper than a deafening scream. Tears streamed down their faces, landing in silence on the saturated land. Murmuring groans inadvertently emanated past lips trying to stifle anguish; but each could hear the other's agony, stabbing like a sword. Feelings of futility and desolation overwhelmed them as they begged for salvation, to become complete as they deserved, to enjoy the fulfillment shared by so many other couples.

Isaac and Rebecca were broken, shattered by the idea that each was accountable for the other's pain, responsible, guilty. The fear was mutual, though neither dared voice it: I am the source of my beloved's distress, I am the sinful one, I am the reason God withholds children from us!

"Lord, I know that I am not entitled to ask, that my actions are sullied," her lips murmured. "I do not ask based on my rights or my deeds. I beg for the sake of my righteous husband, the man who twenty-two years ago stretched out his neck for the slaughter before You happily. The man who gave his all to You without batting an eye, son of the man who has spent his entire life telling the world of Your presence and what You seek from Your creations. Even though I am not worthy, act for Your great name's sake, and give Your saintly son the seed to succeed him in following Your path." The prayers erupted spontaneously, the eyes swollen from daily crying. The pain seemed unbearable. The heart, sealed in an endless effort not to upset her righteous husband, burst amid the waves of tears breaking through the fortified dam.

"Not for me and not by my merit do I beseech You, Father in Heaven," his lips murmured, "but on behalf of this righteous woman. A girl who grew up in battle with an evil and despicable people and kept herself on guard. The rose that blossomed among the thorns, the girl who grew up and became a righteous woman who made sure to follow Your way to the limit of her ability and beyond. I cannot ask in my own right because I dare not; I grew up between two righteous people who led me all my days on Your path. I ask only on behalf of Rebecca, who grew up between Laban and Bethuel and still remained innocent and perfect in her deeds. On her behalf, I beseech You..." The prayers were carried, joining each other, knocking on the Gates of Heaven: "Nineteen years have passed since my wife came to my house. Ten years I waited for her to be old enough to have children. Nine years have passed since then, and we still have not had the privilege of experiencing Your mercy on us, to grant us fruit of the womb."

Rebecca pleaded: "My husband's father waited for Sarah for ten years from the time they came to the land of Canaan, for her to become pregnant. Then, once a decade had passed, he took Hagar as a wife, at Sarah's request. I do not know if I can withstand that trial, and to ask my husband that he should take a maidservant as a wife... Please, have compassion upon me..."

Isaac pleaded: "Please, act for Your great name, and let me have all my descendants be solely from this righteous woman You have chosen as a wife for me. I cannot even think of taking another wife or a concubine, please..."

The couple returned from their pilgrimage to Mount Moriah, having poured their hearts out to God. Isaac returned to his studies, wondering when the Lord would answer his prayers. More than anything, he was weary.

Then, one night, a whisper roused him in the dead of night. "Isaac..." He was slumped in the study hall, his eyes having surrendered to the increasing fatigue, slumber falling upon him. His head rested on the scroll lying on the old table, his arms hanging limp from the sides of his exhausted body. Isaac slowly opened his eyes, trying to clear away the cobwebs of sleep clinging to him, strand by strand.

Rebecca, his wife, stood over him, with a subdued smile on her face, trying to hide something.

"Yes, darling, I probably fell asleep. Are you alright? Do you need anything?" he whispered to his wife apprehensively, surprised by his wife's visit.

"It seems to me that everything is more than just fine," she whispered, giving up trying to contain the resplendent smile that transformed her delicate face, while tears of joy flooded her cheeks. Isaac's eyes still inquired, not understanding his wife's hint.

Rebecca put her hands on her stomach with a sublimely happy

smile: "I think this is it…"

"What?" Isaac rubbed his eyes, as if trying to find out if he were dreaming.

"It's over!" Rebecca laughed with pleasure, "The Lord has heard your prayer, my dear husband, and with God's help we will soon have fruit of the womb."

"Are you sure?" Isaac felt his heart fill to the brim with joy, stopping himself from bursting into tears of happiness. "Are you sure?" he asked again with a smile.

Rebecca nodded affirmatively to her rapturous husband. "Yes… I've been feeling this way for about two months now, but I did not want to tell you, so you wouldn't be disappointed if it turned out to be nothing. For about a month, I have been waking up at night with strange sensations, sometimes nausea. Now, it has become more frequent, so I asked a number of the women in the camp casually about what early pregnancy is like… That's exactly what I'm going through," she said with a radiant face.

Isaac jumped to his feet as he saw his wife's expression change, as a queasy feeling gripped her. "Oh my, I'm nauseous again. I must go!" she said, hand on her mouth, and ran out of the study hall.

Six months had passed since Rebecca began to feel the changes taking place in her body. Her belly swelled at a very fast pace, far beyond what she had seen among her friends and the women of the camp. Day by day, the pains knocked her down, sending her to bed, as she lacked the strength and capability to do anything but lie down. She knew when her husband would come to visit, gathering strength all through the day to look her best at that time, as she tried to hide from her husband the anguish she was feeling.

Strange emotions washed over her, feelings that all the women she asked found unfamiliar. There was a feeling as if the child in her womb was trying to tear her body apart and escape through her abdominal wall, as if it wanted to kill her. When she infrequently mustered up the courage to leave the tent for a short walk, she felt very strange sensations. When she passed the entrance of a study hall, she felt as if the child in her womb was squeezing out, a feeling that put a smile on her face; but on the other hand, when she passed an idolatrous temple, she felt a similar sensation, a feeling that clouded her heart.

Rebecca's agony seemed inexplicable and unbearable; she fruitlessly looked for a diagnosis and a cure for her condition.

One night at the end of the summer, she found herself outside. The coolness soothed the heat radiating from within her. The tingling in her swollen feet dissipated a little from the comforting cold, as she walked in the camp, wondering whom to turn to. As if inadvertently, her legs led her to the opening of her father-in-law's tent, her eyes half-closed in pain, not seeing where her body was being led.

"Good evening, Rebecca. Did you go for a short walk?" Abraham asked, leaving his study hall.

"Yes… more or less…" Rebecca whispered, clenching her jaw to keep a moan of pain from issuing forth, feeling that the fetus was about to tear through her and charge into the study hall her father-in-law had just stepped out of.

"Everything all right? Do you feel well?" Abraham looked with concern at his tormented daughter-in-law. "Wait a minute, I'll get you a chair," he said and ran quickly into the tent. "Sit down, darling, I'll get you a glass of water to drink."

Rebecca accepted the water, ashamed of herself for bothering her righteous old father-in-law: "Sorry, my lord, I did not want to bother you."

Abraham smiled lovingly at his virtuous daughter-in-law: "Happily! It's no bother… are you alright?" he asked with trepidation as he saw his daughter-in-law's mortified face.

"Yes... I'll be fine... I hope..."

"Do you want to tell me what's going on? Maybe I can help! I may be old, but I still remember something from days gone by," he chuckled, trying to calm down and comfort her with his smile.

"What shall I tell you, my lord!? I do not understand what I have!" she lamented and burst into tears. "Something is wrong with the pregnancy. The pain and agony I am experiencing is unnatural, not rational. My lord knows that I am not a pampered princess, but the pain I am suffering drives me mad..." The crying turned into a pitiful sob: "Sometimes I think I'd rather die than endure this sorrow... When I pass a study hall, I feel like the fetus wants tear my body apart and escape, but when I pass by idolatrous temples, I feel too, that he is tearing me apart and trying to leave... I do not know what is happening to me. I can no longer bear it... What do I have? A kind of hybrid creature that studies Torah and worships idols at the same time?!"

Abraham looked at his daughter-in-law helplessly sobbing from her torment, trying to think how he could help his righteous son's wife. "I have an idea... wait here a few minutes..." Abraham said and started running toward the corral. A few minutes passed, and Abraham arrived with a cart drawn by two horses: "Let us get you into the cart..."

"Where are we going?" Rebecca asked her decisive father-in-law in bewilderment.

"We are going to Shem son of Noah," he declared with a tone that brooked no objection or hesitation. "As I said, I am old, almost one hundred and sixty years old; I have seen many things in my life. However, he is older than me, already five hundred and fifty years old! His study hall has been established for centuries! Certainly, he can tell us what the grief and pain you are suffering from means. Do not worry, he is not that far from here."

With Abraham's help, Rebecca got in the cart, knowing she had nothing to lose. As they traveled, she grew excited, thinking of an encounter with the great sage who had survived the Deluge on the Ark.

Abraham jumped out of the cart like a young boy, eager to meet the man who had been his guide through such critical times in his life. More than twenty years had passed since Shem had come to comfort him on the day of Sarah's burial.

Abraham entered the old building, the place remained just as it was in his youth, as if the decades had rolled over the landmark without leaving any impression upon it.

Shem sat bent over a scroll, just as he had done many years earlier. Abraham cleared his throat, drawing the attention of Shem immersed in his study. Shem looked up from the scroll: who had come to disturb him in the dead of night? Light filled his eyes, seeing Abraham, his diligent disciple from decades ago. They embraced warmly, like old friends after a long separation.

"My master, my dear teacher, I am overjoyed to see your face," Abraham proclaimed rapturously. "You have not changed, not one iota!"

His teacher touched Abraham's face, marveling at the snowiness of the hair: "I too am glad to see you, my friend. Your white beard flatters you wonderfully," Shem replied with a loving smile. "What brings you to me? And who is the lady who is with you?" he asked, seeing Rebecca behind Abraham's shoulder, trying to shrink into herself, though her belly made it impossible.

"This is Rebecca, the wife of my son Isaac. Rebecca is the daughter of Bethuel, son of my brother Nahor," he replied. "The truth of why I have come to you is as follows…" Abraham began to tell him what was happening to his young daughter-in-law. Shem sat down, put his face in the palms of his hands thoughtfully.

The silence in the room sent a shiver through Rebecca's body.

The feeling that the child inside her was quiet and calm, infused her with a sensation of comfort and relaxation which she had not experienced for many months.

Shem rubbed his face with his hands, drawing himself inward, deep and calm breaths breaking the abysmal silence. A few minutes passed, as Abraham and Rebecca stared at the elder.

With his eyes still closed, he declaimed: "*Two nations are in your womb, and two peoples shall be separated from your innards; and the one people shall be stronger than the other people; and the older shall serve the younger.*"

Rebecca understood that what she heard was a divine prophecy, the Lord speaking through the righteous Shem son of Noah.

Abraham and Rebecca said goodbye, trying not to waste the scholar's study time. The two boarded the cart to return to Hebron.

"I did not quite understand what he was saying ..." said Rebecca to her father-in-law, turning over the terse oracle in her mind.

Abraham hesitated briefly, then explained: "You are pregnant with two sons, one of whom will be righteous and one of whom will not," he said, trying to soften the blow. "They will not get along; they will constantly fight each other. When one is triumphant, the other will be humbled. The older child will eventually be subjugated to the younger."

Rebecca felt calm in her heart despite the harsh prophecy that one of her sons would be wicked and fight his righteous brother. "At least he is not to be a monstrous hybrid creature who studies Torah and worships idols simultaneously!"

"One more moment and he's out, my brave fighter... Just one more push and..."

The midwife looked at the woman in the throes of childbirth, empathizing with her distress. The long hours of labor had left their mark on Rebecca. The dripping sweat wet the sheets around her head. Another midwife lovingly stroked the head of the pious lady, who dedicated herself to helping anyone in need. A scream of pain erupted from the mother-to-be, as if the flesh of her womb had been torn inside her, unbearable pain that left her weak and bleeding...

A loud crying sound was heard. The midwife looked at the newborn in disgust, feeling the thick hair covering the little head in her hands. Lingering glances were exchanged by the two midwives in silence, trying to stay calm and not startle the woman still in labor.

The child's body followed the head. The disgusted expression of the midwife worsened when she saw the body covered in red hair, like animal fur. Her initial thought, that the baby's red color was due to his mother's blood, was rejected as she saw his red furry body. The baby came out completely, the midwife's face expressing panic, seeing that a tiny, delicate hand was grasping the red-furred heel. The first midwife took the crimson infant while her colleague helped the mother through the birth of the second child.

Rebecca closed her eyes, surviving the pain by clinging to the hope that everything would soon be over, that she would get to the other side of her agony. Soon, the other child came out, a small, skinny baby who was weakly bleating.

The new mother remained on her bed powerless and breathless, feeling that the pain she had experienced was not in the slightest similar to what her friends had told her.

The two midwives look at each other miserably, gesturing at the mother's bleeding body. They could not bring themselves to articulate the unmistakable prognosis: the trauma to Rebecca's body, caused by this birth, was irreversible. She would bear no more children.

The two midwives tended the mother with devotion, trying to staunch the bleeding and assuage the agony. "What of my boys?"

Rebecca asked, her voice faint amid the miasma of pain and exhaustion.

"Everything is fine, my dear, the children are just fine, do not worry... you need to rest, sleep and gain strength," the midwife by her head whispered as she massaged her with love and pity.

Rebecca gave into her fatigue, so her battered body could begin to mend itself.

The midwives whispered among themselves now that their patient was out of imminent danger. "Poor thing! She will need to regain all her strength of mind and body to deal with this... baby? Can you even call him that? This red demon, he already has hair, teeth... as if he were already fully made (*asui*). For the life of me, I do not understand how this boy came out of these two parents, so meek and mild..."

"I have never seen anything like it in my life; I think he should be called Esau, because he is indeed fully made, straight from the womb... A full-grown child!"

Eight days passed, and the initial shock had almost passed. Due to the firstborn's unnatural appearance and his blood-red color, Abraham and Isaac decided that it would not be right to circumcise the child at the traditional time. "His blood needs to circulate fully, and then we will decide when to circumcise him," Isaac told Rebecca, as they looked with slight askance at their ruddy firstborn.

Rebecca went to the other crib, picking up her sweet younger son in her arms. She embraced the tiny body in boundless, unlimited love.

"Bring him, Father is waiting for us," Isaac whispered warmly, lovingly to his wife. "The sun is rising soon, and we must hurry to keep the commandment of circumcision as the day begins."

Isaac and Rebecca approach Abraham's tent with reverence. The men of the encampment stood in anticipation of the couple coming to circumcise their son. Abraham sat on a high chair, serving as the godfather of his grandson, the second son of his second son, continuing on his beloved path. In holiness and purity, Isaac circumcised the baby as Abraham held the baby in his lap.

"And his name shall be..." Isaac said with his eyes closed in devotion.

"Jacob," claimed an unseen Voice, shaking everyone in the tent.

And the boys grew; and Esau was a cunning hunter, a man of the field; and Jacob was a quiet man, dwelling in tents. Now Isaac loved Esau, because he did eat of his venison; and Rebecca loved Jacob.

Right on time, the gentle, familiar knock sounded on Isaac's door. The clear knowledge that Esau was there brought a smile to Isaac's face. The realization that his son was a strong and powerful man stood in stark contrast to the faint sound of the knock.

Esau entered the room, head bowed, his hands carrying a tray laden with delicacies that he had toiled to prepare himself for his father. His dress was elegant and neat, clean and unwrinkled. In submission, he places the tray on the table and hurried to kiss his father's hand, smiling at him. "Father, I made it exactly as you requested, venison shoulder in mustard sauce, with rice and a fresh vegetable salad," he sighed with a big smile, revealing his large, prominent teeth.

"Thank you, my dear son. Please sit by my side a little, and tell me what you learned today," Isaac asked as he took a small piece of meat from the tray to eat.

He thought to himself: I must bring him closer to me. His ruddiness is not only physical; it affects his temperament and tempts him to violence. I must guide him down the path of decency.

"Father, is the food tasty?" Esau inquired, eagerly anticipating his father's compliment.

"A taste straight from the Garden of Eden..." Isaac replied and conspicuously savored another tiny bite. "Well, my dear child, what did you learn today in the study hall? "

"Ah... we learned... ah yes ... The lesson today was about tithing!"

Esau stuttered, trying to recreate in his head what Jacob had been listening to in the study hall, as he passed by the window.

"Father, may I ask a question?" Isaac nodded affirmatively, encouraging his son.

"If you must tithe all the produce from the earth, then what about salt and hay?"

Isaac smiled with pleasure at his son's clever question. "No, my dear boy, neither this nor that. The salt, you see, does not grow from the ground; it is mined, and thus exempt from tithes. As for straw, it is animal fodder, not human food, so it too need not be tithed."

Esau seemed to be pondering his father's answer, internalizing the important lesson.

Isaac put the piece of meat down on the tray and looked at his son seriously. "Look, Esau, there is a very important issue that we need to talk about. Please, I beseech you to do what I ask."

Esau nodded. "Whatever you ask, Father! You know that whatever you want, I will bring you."

Isaac looked at his son with hope.

He thought: The truth is that Esau is exemplary in keeping the commandment of filial obedience. He never refuses my requests; he does not even hesitate to do them! He even changes his clothes when he comes into my study. I hope that the merit of this good deed will help him and direct him along the path of truth.

"What should I bring you, Father?" Esau asked, happy to do his father's will.

"I do not need you to bring me anything, my dear son," he said with a smile, caressing his son's hairy hand. "I want to ask you something completely different. You are already thirteen years old," he began to explain. "When you and your brother were born, your skin color was a little red, and I was afraid that the blood was not yet circulating well in your body, so there would be great danger for you to be circumcised then. I circumcised your brother Jacob when he was eight days old, when the Creator commanded us, but I could not circumcise you then. Grandfather and I decided that the best thing would be to wait until you turned thirteen, and then we would circumcise you."

Isaac looked at his son, who looked like an animal caught in a trap. "I know that at this age the thought of it is very frightening, but you know my older brother Ishmael? He too, was circumcised at the age of thirteen, and nothing happened to him..."

Esau suddenly craned his head towards the window: "What's that? Sorry, Father, I think I hear someone calling me... I'll be back soon..." Esau fled the room, leaving his father alone.

"Poor boy ... he must be very scared to do what I asked him to do ... In a few days, he will overcome the fear, and seek me out again to do what I said."

Isaac pushed away the almost-full tray, turning inward, wondering what he could do about his son.

CHAPTER THIRTY-NINE

Birthright

The tent was packed with Ishmael's dozen sons, Abraham and Keturah's half a dozen sons, and their numerous offspring. They were tensely anticipating the words of their patriarch.

Abraham leaned over the table in front of him, as if unaware of the people gathered in his tent. The sound of Ishmael's coughing drew Abraham's attention to the crowd assembled before him. Abraham smiled at the faces that looked at him with anticipation, waiting for him to speak his piece.

"My dear children and grandchildren," he began at last, "I know that my days on this earth are drawing to a close. I will soon leave this world, ascending on high to be judged and accounted by our Heavenly Father."

Those gathered glanced from one to the other, as if asking: What does the old man want from us?

Abraham laughed to himself, continuing to smile: "You ask yourself, 'What does the old man want from us?' Well, as I said, I have but a few days left, and because you are all my offspring, I wanted to allot you your share of my inheritance." He beamed with barely concealed joy.

"You are all the offspring of my concubine Hagar, now known as Keturah. As you well know, your mother is the daughter of Pharaoh, king of Egypt. Now, when I was in Egypt together with my wife Sarah, Pharaoh gave us many gifts. Years later, King Abimelech of Gerar gave us even more, a thousand pieces of silver."

Abraham looked at his descendants as they marveled at the immense fortune. "I will divide all this wealth among you," their faces turned joyful. "But ..." Abraham paused, looking at the tense faces, "that is all under one condition ... provided none of you stay here with your family. You must take your households and depart from the land of Canaan. Go to the land of the children of the east — or anywhere else — as long as you do not remain in this region."

The assembled, longing for the legendary wealth of their forebear, looked at each other apprehensively. Zimran, oldest of Abraham's sons after his remarriage to Keturah, asked apprehensively, "How will we survive in the land of the children of the east? They are all sorcerers there!"

"There is a solution to this too," Abraham said with a grin. "I will teach you sorcerous incantations, how to bind spirits and demons to serve you; the spells they know are nothing compared to what I can teach you. With the money I will give you and the incantations I will teach you; you will quickly become honored and respected members of those communities. I do not command you to do this for your detriment, but solely for your benefit. If you stay in this area, you will soon wage war upon the descendants of Isaac; and if you do so, you will be destroyed and inherit eternal hell. Although you are all meant to be his slaves, you will not be enslaved right now; but only in the future when the Blessed One's kingship will be revealed to the world. Then, you will be the first to come and subjugate yourselves to Isaac."

His tone changed ominously. "Whoever refuses to go, rest assured that you will not only lose your inheritance, but you will not live out the year." Abraham's offspring looked at him in fear, knowing that if he decided to target them, they would not live long.

"And so..." Abraham summed up, "who ready to get his share and leave this place?"

Everyone raised his hand, as Abraham smiled with satisfaction.

"Now go rouse your families, load them on your carts, and gather the livestock. Leave one cart empty, bring it here, and I will load it with your parting gifts," Abraham ordered.

His descendants dispersed quickly, to fulfill the commandment of Abraham.

"Ishmael!" Abraham said to his eldest son, whose face was gloomy.

Ishmael stopped in his place, feeling a twinge in his heart. How could he be forced to leave his father after he had worked so hard to improve his character, correct his deeds, and follow the Godly path of his father? "Yes, Father," he replied, humbled.

"I know it will be very difficult for you to leave this place; I very much understand your heart's distress. That's why you and your family will stay here until the day I die. However, once I depart this mortal plane, you will have to leave this place with your family. You are my firstborn, and nothing will ever change that; but your mother Hagar was enslaved to my wife Sarah when she became pregnant with you. Thus, you are not entitled to be my heir; you are the son of my wife's slave. Sarah was your mother's mistress, Sarah was your mistress, and now Sarah's son Isaac is your master. You must always remember that you are enslaved to the sons of Isaac, and all your descendants will be slaves to his descendants."

Abraham looked at Ishmael's offended face: "You know that your grandfather Pharaoh gave your mother to Sarah as a gift, because he understood that to be a slave in a God-fearing house was better than being a princess in an idolatrous household. I know that you have quit idolatry, that you follow the path of the Lord; but this is how things must be forever. Know that even though you are enslaved to Isaac legally, he will not subjugate you practically. Still, you will have to leave this place immediately after my passing. Until then, stay with us."

Upon hearing that he would be able to stay at the patriarch's side until his dying day, Ishmael fell to his knees, kissing the feet of his father.

The bustling camp near Hebron had become relatively quiet. The sons of Keturah and their families had left the great encampment a few weeks earlier.

The rain dripped lazily, drumming on the tent sheets. The blowing wind that accompanied the staccato sound made a soft and melancholy melody.

Isaac sat hunched over at the foot of his father's bed, the tears flowing from his eyes, refusing to stop.

Abraham looked at his son, with a thin smile on his face, "Do not be sad, my dear son. *I go the way of all the earth* because my time has come. I have had the privilege of living a full life, a life of worshipping God, and now it is my time to give an account and a reckoning for all my deeds."

Isaac stroked his father's hand, which was half-lying on the bed. He knew that he would soon have to say goodbye to his father, mentor, friend, guide, and protector. The father who had encompassed, for him, the totality of human society; the mentor, directing him to the truth but deliberately letting him find it on his own; the friend who had always lent him an ear, helping him right the wrongs; the guide who had always sought to uncover the path best suited for him; the protector who watched over him, his righteousness shielding all who took shelter under his wing. The captivating smile never vanished from the lips always expressing love.

"I am one hundred and seventy-five years old; at the age of three

I began to serve the Creator. I went through various and strange experiences in my life, and precisely because of them I clung to the Creator. Death is not the end, as you know; it is the gateway to new life — an alteration of image and reality, one I eagerly await. I will soon rejoin my spouse, the love of my life; and you will be left to tend to our flock."

Abraham grasped his son's hand firmly, encouraging him before they were forced to part: "Keep the destination in sight as you blaze new trails! Teach your followers how to pave paths for themselves — roads that suit them, the ways they ought to tread."

Abraham raised his hand weakly, wiping the tears from his son's eyes. "In just a moment, I will leave you. You must bury me next to your mother in the cave I bought for us."

Abraham closed his eyes calmly, joy spreading over his beaming face. Isaac felt his father's grip loosen, as his fingers opened, and his breathing stopped.

Isaac grasped the top of his robe and tore it deeply, exposing his chest heaving with grief. From lips wet with tears, he proclaimed: "Blessed be the True Judge."

The funeral procession set out, Isaac and Ishmael carrying their father's body. Shem and Eber and all the nobles of the land came to attend the funeral of the greatest of men, a role model, and symbol for all humanity.

Isaac and Ishmael entered the cool cave, a soft light emanating from it. Sarah, lying in her grave as on the day of her death thirty-eight years earlier, as if patiently awaiting her husband to join her. Abraham's body was silently set by his late wife. Tears of longing and loss filled Isaac's eyes when he saw his mother.

Then Isaac and Ishmael emerged from the cave, facing the large crowd which had accompanied Abraham on his final journey.

"Woe to the ship that has lost its captain, woe to the world that has lost its leader..." Isaac eulogized Abraham right there and then. The encomia lasted for hours, as Isaac and Ishmael sat mourning the death of their father.

"Who allowed you to hunt here without my explicit permission?!" The aggressive rebuke jolted Esau, who was standing at the edge of the clearing, his taut bow pointing at a small doe. He flinched slightly and missed his target. Esau turned around to see who dared to interfere as he worked his venatic magic. There stood an old man — swarthy, wrinkled, hairless. He was glaring at the red-haired youth.

Esau responded with defiance: "And who are you, geezer, to hold me accountable for my actions? I don't answer to you or anyone else! You'd better make yourself scarce; you don't want to get into it with me!"

The old man responded with derision, which made Esau tense; the self-confidence infused in the dismissive laughter made it clear to him that the elder was a dangerous man, sure of himself in a way the young hunter had never seen before.

"Oh, I don't want to get into it with you, ginger boy? Or are you really a girl? No, you're so furry, you must be an ape! But you can talk like a man, so that's not quite right." The old man smiled, motioned for Esau to approach. "Come, orangutan orator, let us get into it!"

Esau plastered a smile on his face: "Before I end you, perhaps you might tell me your name, so I can add it to my list. I always prefer to know whom I kill; it's good for my resume," he said with a wide grin that displayed his prominent teeth.

"My name?" the old man smirked. "You think you will add it to your roster of kills?"

Esau nodded, returning a laugh to the confident man: "Yes, your name, old man, I do not know how useful it will be for the resume, but if it does not help, it at least will not hurt ..."

"I actually think it will prove useful, orangutan; you must have heard of me. I am Nimrod son of Cush! Do not trouble yourself to tell me your name, because I would never bother to put it on my resume!" He announced this confidently, expecting the crimson devil to fall to his knees and apologize.

Esau looked shocked for a second, but soon regained his composure. "Ah... I've heard about you ... the weakling Nimrod, the man who cannot even beat a baby, if not for the special clothing he wears," Esau said in a dismissive voice, as a storm raged within him.

He thought quickly: Father told me once that as long as he wears his clothes, no one is able to beat him; I have to get him to take off his clothes.

"Yes, my beautiful clothes are can be very helpful sometimes ..." Nimrod smirked arrogantly.

"Weakness is all one may expect from dotards!" Esau taunted him. "A nothing like you always finds something to hide behind. Every dam needs a sire to protect her, while a bitch like you has enchanted clothing for protection. You know... not long ago, I saw a woman who looked like you, a weakling, not far from here. The truth is, she was nothing special, but I thought for her sake she ought to know what a real man looks like. Do you know her? Same complexion, same build. She bears a striking resemblance to you!"

"What are you..."

"So, you do know her..." Esau laughed aloud. "Do not worry, I did nothing to her that you would not have done yourself!"

"That was my granddaughter, newly betrothed this week..." Nimrod hissed angrily.

"At least she will know how to appreciate a real man. A man who is not trying to hide behind his mother's skirt. Old and helpless cowards always try to hide, like rabbits," Esau looked at Nimrod contemptuously, seeing the rage rising in his face. "The sad thing is, even if you manage to kill me, you pathetic excuse for a man, you wouldn't be responsible. It's your enchanted robe! There's nothing in your resume… maybe your clothes have a resume, but not you, coward!"

Nimrod spat an angry chortle. "Is that what you have to say, orangutan?! Then let us fight, hunter versus hunter. No special garb, just blades!" Nimrod began to take off his clothes, looking at the hairy youth, knowing from his vast experience that he could defeat him even without the clothes.

As he disrobed, he thought: This is a foolish act. This boy is causing me to do something I've never done before. But this orangutan had his way with my granddaughter…. In a few minutes, I will slay this crimson ape, and then I can dress again in my regalia!

Naked, the old man and the young man faced off, approaching each other, blade in hand. The polished steel gleamed in the sunlight.

"Orangutan, you cannot take your fur off you, right?" Nimrod leered at Esau. "No matter! In a few minutes, I'll skin you and present your hide as a gift to my granddaughter; at least she will use your red fur as a rug. Is your name like that of humans, ape?"

Esau smiled at Nimrod, knowing the history between his grandfather Abraham and this man who would be killed in just a few moments. "It seems to me that my grandfather will be very happy to see the gift I bring him, the man who threw him into the fiery furnace over a century ago. You probably remember him; they called him Abram then."

Esau continued to advance, slightly hunched over, tossing the hunting knife from one hand to the other to confuse his opponent "Grandfather had a son named Isaac, who bore me: Esau. Now I will avenge Grandfather, striking down his longtime nemesis." Esau grinned at Nimrod's astonishment.

Nimrod smiled back happily: "If not the grandfather, I will at least get to kill the grandson; you can really see that you are his grandson, you have the same degree of hutzpah."

A distance of two paces separated the fighters. Nimrod glanced up, looking past Esau's shoulder. Esau turned his gaze to see if anyone had come to the aid of his enemy. At that moment, Nimrod rolled across the ground, slicing Esau's leg with his dagger. A shriek of pain erupted from Esau, who felt the blood dripping from his leg as he leapt to dodge his wily foe.

"Nice trick, old brigand. You continue to hide behind invisible people..." Esau grunted as he put a smile on his face, rising above the sharp pain.

"I just wanted to see if your blood is as red as your fur," Nimrod smirked.

Esau advanced rapidly toward Nimrod in a furious manner, his right hand holding the knife. Nimrod stood, waiting for his raging enemy to commit a lethal error. Esau waved his hand holding the knife as he prepared to stab his enemy from above; but Nimrod raised his dagger to stop the blow of the knife. Esau's right arm took the blade of Nimrod's dagger, while his left hand caught the knife tossed to it from the right. His knife tore into the flesh of Nimrod's belly. The combatants moved away from each other, nursing their injuries for a split second.

"You are a decent fighter... for an orangutan," prodded Nimrod, trying to cover the expression of pain on his own face.

Esau looked at his enemy with restrained rage. All his life, he had suffered humiliation based on the way he looked, a bizarre and homely creature; now, his loathing found a focal point in this old man, whose verbal jabs were more cutting than the swipes of his dagger. The red-hot fury spread through Esau, "You'll never call me orangutan again!" he screamed, charging at his enemy as best he could on a lame leg.

Nimrod looked at Esau, who was rushing towards him: "The orangutan is enraged; now he will make a fatal mistake!" As Esau came within one pace of Nimrod, his trailing foot hit a stone. Esau lost his balance and fell on his face, his forehead hitting a large rock.

Nimrod thought, throwing himself at his foe: Here the orangutan's anger has tripped him up. A moment more, and he will be no more!

Nimrod smiled to himself, already feeling the rush of victory; soon the body beneath him will be a corpse. However, Esau turned, flipping over on his back, smirking at Nimrod, who was sure he had lost consciousness. An expression of bewilderment came over the old man's face, as he tried to find a way to change the trajectory of his jump in midair.

But it was too late, and Esau's knife was raised towards Nimrod's face. Aided by gravity, he thrust the knife deep into Nimrod's chin, splitting the skull. The tip of the long blade protruded beyond the crown of Nimrod's head.

Shoving the royal corpse off of him, Esau got to his feet, pulling his knife from deep within Nimrod's brain. He felt the sharp pains throbbing in his arm and leg, sensations hardly felt in the heat of battle.

Esau looked with pleasure at the carcass lying at his feet: "You were a good fighter… but not good enough." He grinned to himself as he knelt on his knees, ready to remove his enemy's head as a trophy.

"Your Majesty... King Nimrod ..." Not-too-distant shouts could be heard, drawing closer. Horses' hooves pounded the ground not too far away. Esau raised his head, fear washing over his face. He realized with a start: Of course, my fallen foe was a king, and he would not hunt alone. Here comes the cavalry…

Esau felt like an animal falling into a trap. He abruptly rose to his feet, abandoning his plan of beheading his enemy. As quickly as he could limp, he grabbed his and Nimrod's discarded clothing, stumbling to a cave at the edge of the clearing, from which he could observe what happened next.

Ten armed horsemen found the slain king, lying in disgrace on the bare ground. Fury and astonishment intertwined on their faces. One of the horsemen bent down, feeling the warm blood dripping from his master's body: "The killer must be near," Enoki, lord commander of the army, told his comrades. "We must apprehend the regicide, so we can avenge our king. This pathetic miscreant must be somewhere around here. You!" he ordered, pointing to one of the warriors. "Go back to camp and summon all our fighters to join the hunt." The rider jumped agilely on his horse, galloping from the clearing at a blistering pace.

"He certainly didn't flee in the direction we came from, so we must look in the other directions," said Enoki, who suddenly found himself in a position to inherit the leadership of the nation. "We will go in threes; the scoundrel who dared to murder our divine lord must be a very dangerous and cruel man. Pay attention to any suspicious person; he also took our master's clothes, so he is even more dangerous." The cavalrymen jumped on their mounts, galloping away in search of the killer.

Esau looked at the horsemen as they disappeared into the distance, devising a strategy for escape as he dressed his wounds and his body.

He thought helplessly: Soon the whole area will be filled with soldiers coming to hunt me. I have no chance unless I can get back to Grandfather's camp. They will turn over every stone until they find me and execute me! My only chance to survive is to make it to Grandfather's tent. They will surely not try to enter Abraham's camp, after he managed to destroy all their warriors many years ago!

He mused: This place will be swarming with soldiers any minute; I have no hope unless I get moving and get out of here right now!

Esau crept forward towards the camp, hiding from enemies emerging from every corner. His hunting excursions meant he knew how to keep to the thickets and bushes, the thorny undergrowth, crawling on his belly so that his red head would not pop up and attract attention.

He slowly reached the outskirts of the camp, reconnoitering as he approached to make sure the late Nimrod's soldiers had not yet arrived.

A pleasant scent beckoned from his brother Jacob's domicile, pulling him reluctantly to enter the tent on the outskirts of the camp.

Holding his growling stomach, he thought: At least I'll eat something, I hadn't noticed how many hours have passed. Otherwise, hunger will kill me before any soldier can raise his sword!

"I'm hungry! Give me food! What do you have in the pot?" Esau burst in without preamble. Jacob turned his gaze from the pot to his brother who burst into his tent, his eyes full of tears and pain. His expression showed disgust at the rude man, caked with mud and blood, who entered his tent without an invitation.

"It smells good, I'm hungry! What is it?! Who are you making it for?!" Esau demanded, ignoring Jacob's look of unrestrained disgust.

"I made it for Father, it's lentil stew," he said, turning his back on his brother, continuing to fiddle with the stew.

"I told you I was hungry!" Esau grumbled at his brother's back.

"And I told you it's for Father!" Jacob answered without looking.

"I'm about to die! Father can wait!"

Jacob turned around, stared reprovingly at his brother: "Father will not wait! This is a consolatory meal for Father! Grandfather Abraham passed away this morning, and he has just returned from the funeral. Father must eat a consolatory meal! You will wait!" Jacob looked at his brother's face and saw that terror had seized him.

"Grandfather Abraham passed away?!" Esau asked, realizing that his last refuge from death had disappeared and vanished.

Jacob felt the anger rising in his heart over his despicable brother, disrespecting their grandfather. "He passed away this morning, peacefully," he whispered, trying to calm himself.

"Wow, wow, wow," Esau sighed to himself, "so even this old man died in the end! Apparently, there is no judge and no justice! If he couldn't escape from the Attribute of Justice, then this is the fate of all men. He worked like an ass his entire life, and for what?!"

The hatred that Jacob felt toward his brother increased, upon hearing how Esau despised his grandfather and dismissed the belief their father had endeavored to instill in them all their lives. "I'm asking you to get out of here!" he said, trying to keep his tone civil.

"But I told you I was starving!" screamed Esau at his brother in anger.

Jacob felt a smile rise to his lips: "Sad to say, I do not work for free..." he said with a chuckle. "If you are hungry, you will have to pay!"

"How much do you want?"

Jacob laughed: "Not how much, but what?"

"What?!" Esau could not understand what his brother meant.

Jacob looked at his brother like a foolish child: "I want something you have, in exchange for the dinner I made tonight!"

Esau looked at his brother angrily, "What do you want?"

"The birthright!"

"What birthright?"

"The birthright of the firstborn," Jacob said determinedly. "As the firstborn, you have the birthright of divine service. You have the privilege of bringing sacrifices to the Lord, and that's what I want!"

Esau looked at his brother, with his mouth wide open. Would a leper, desperate to rid himself of his condition, seek compensation for transferring his malady to another? Yet Jacob wanted to pay him for this plague of the firstborn's birthright! "The birthright..." he finally said thoughtfully.

Jacob nodded.

Esau pondered this for a few moments: Father's probably going to live a long time, another century at least, considering how long

Grandfather stuck around. In another hundred years, who knows what will happen? I'll probably be dead by then!

A paroxysm of fear gripped him, as he reflected: Indeed, I may not live until sunset! At least, if Nimrod's soldiers execute me, I can die with a full belly!

Esau smiled at his brother, baring his big teeth: "Well, if you want it so much … I'll do you a favor and give you the birthright for the lentil stew."

"Swear to me by the life of Father, whom you love, that you will never challenge the sale," Jacob said, knowing his brother's wiles and villainous characters.

"I swear by Father's life!" Esau replied. "Now I'll open my mouth, and you'll pour this red stew inside!"

Jacob thought quickly: If I give him only the stew, they will say he was crazed with hunger and agreed to the sale under duress!

Jacob turned to the side of the room and brought bread and wine: "Look, my brother, I am a generous soul," he reassured Esau, "eat some bread first and drink some wine. In the meantime, I will pour you some lentil stew."

Esau sated his hunger with bread and slaked his thirst with wine. He looked at his brother with amusement — how naïve, serving food and drink triumphantly, as if he had won a valuable prize. The wine sloshed and spilled on his beard, blending with the crimson color of his mane.

"What about the stew?!" he lustily called to his brother, who was pouring the red stew into a bowl. "The deal was that you pour my stew straight into my mouth from the pot! I want it all!"

Jacob smiled at his brother, swallowing the bile rising in his throat at the idea. "Sure, open your mouth …"

The stew was poured into the gaping orifice, and Jacob tried to turn his face away to avoid the disgust he felt when he smelled the stench emanating from Esau's open mouth. Some of it splashed onto Esau's beard, red stew mixing with red wine in the red beard, a blood-colored medley.

Esau lurched to his feet, patting his fill stomach with both hands. "That really hit the spot," he said with a tooth-baring grin. "Now, I have to get going... big brother." Esau laughed and left the tent. He still had the clothing of his victim in his hunting pack

Jacob, happy with the purchase he had made, hurried to make a new pot of lentil stew for his father's consolatory meal.

Screams of terror from women and children shocked Isaac out of his reverie. He had been sunk deep in thought, remembering longingly the father who had left him. The longtime leader, the shepherd of the flock, was no more; now the responsibility for all in the vast encampment had settled on his shoulders. This had made him feel the sorrow of loss even more, the desolation in the heart. The tree in whose shadow he had lived for seventy-five years had been cut down.

Now Isaac, who had been sitting on the ground immersed in mourning for his father, was suddenly shaken to his feet, as he internalized the pounding hoofbeats of horses and whoops of warriors, mingled with the weeping of women and children, rising from the outskirts of the encampment. The realization that they were in trouble and that he was now responsible for them made him rise and rush from the tent. The scene was awful, as cavalrymen rode through the rows of tents, screaming and striking at women and children, who tried to dodge the hooves and the clubs mercilessly unleashed upon the heads of the powerless. Without thinking twice, he burst into the commotion, scanning for the leader of the invaders. Who was giving the orders? Isaac began to run forward, repelling with his outstretched arms horses galloping towards him, knocking them down with their riders to the ground, careful not to let his own people be trampled by the beasts.

The cavalry leader reined his mount to a halt, looking in surprise at the man with the familiar appearance striding towards him. Isaac leapt towards the horseman, who was momentarily shocked; the young prophet ripped the commander off his horse and tossed him onto the ground. The officer was stunned by the mighty force displayed, the unassuming man who had thrown him into the air like a naughty child.

"Command them to stop, or I'll kill you all!" Isaac ordered the prone man as he grabbed him. The tone of the speaker brooked no dispute; but the pride of the officer refused the behest of the prophet, whose outward appearance belied his martial abilities.

"And if I do not ..." he croaked in pain under Isaac's crushing grip. He was convinced that his bones would shatter any moment.

Isaac stared sternly at the commander: "If not, I will have to kill you all, and I do not want that."

"Kill us all?" the groaning man tried to put a mocking smile on his face. "I have thousands of soldiers on the way here!" he hissed in agony.

"Fool, have you not learned your lesson? No matter how many soldiers you have, you remember Abraham who fought the kings who rose up against Sodom..." Isaac waited, letting the man bring up the memory in his head. "Just as Abraham destroyed them, so I will destroy all your soldiers now! Tell them they are to stop!" Isaac saw the fear and awe in the man's eyes and dropped him in the dirt, sprawling. "Now!" Isaac commanded, bending down to take in his hand from the dust of the earth: "Immediately! Before I..."

The man raised his hands in fear: "No! Do not throw the dirt! Wait!" The horror of death enveloped him. "Stop it! Stop it all, you stupid dogs!" he shouted at his men, "Stop right now, before I decapitate you!"

The warriors relented, watching their commander in amazement. "Who are you?! Why did you come here?!" Isaac asked, having seen that all the soldiers stopped their attack, looking at their commander and the strange man who had easily overpowered him.

"I am Enoki, Lord Commander of the Army of His Majesty, King Nimrod — who was slain today. We seek his killer!"

"Nimrod was murdered today ... Fascinating! On the day my righteous father died, his evil enemy died," Isaac mused. "But what are you doing here?!" he asked firmly.

"We tracked the regicide here. We have come seeking justice." Enoki looked at Isaac, who was smiling a little. "Don't you think killers must be brought to justice?"

A slight giggle came out of Isaac's mouth: "Certainly they should! Murderers must not be allowed to continue. In our case, it seems to me that the great murderer has already been brought to justice, as King Nimrod has received his just punishment. I will not tell you that I am sorry; I will not lie. What I can tell you is that there is no murderer here. That is not our way. I suggest you gather all your people right away and go back to where you came from. Otherwise ... " Isaac raised a handful of dirt, threatening to throw it at the soldiers.

With no choice, Enoki got on his horse, motioning for his soldiers to leave as well. The warriors left the camp in disgrace, looking at Enoki, who had hitherto been the object of admiration, with displeasure.

Esau peered out from the shelter where he was hiding and breathed a sigh of relief. Peering into his pack, he examined the clothes he had stolen from Nimrod. A smile of happiness came over his face.

A party was held that evening by Esau; the slaves who were his companions came to celebrate with him. Esau sat at the head of the table, telling everyone how he had cheated his foolish brother, who had agreed to give him food and drink in exchange for the "right" to be the eldest servant carrying out the sacrificial service.

Chapter Forty

Gerar

The heat wave was overpowering. The sheep desperately sought some shade, but the trees were denuded. The shepherds tried to draw water, but the wells had run dry. The livestock bleated in thirst and hunger, breaking the hearts of those who tended the animals. Their skin cracked in the hot and dry wind. Hungry wolves attacked the livestock, ignoring the danger posed by the people guarding them. With swollen tongues, they tried to wet dehydrated lips. The scorched fields were filled with the stench of carcasses, attracting scavenging beasts and birds.

The slaves walked in the encampment, dragging their feet, exhausted in the oppressive heat, looking up, searching for a small scrap of cloud that might herald the end of the drought.

"It does not appear that the famine is about to end any time soon," Isaac told Rebecca sadly. "In the coming months, hunger and thirst will probably increase. I am afraid we will have no choice but to migrate south, towards Egypt.

"The last thing I want to do is leave the land of Canaan. The thought that I am now compelled to depart from the land promised to my seed towards a country steeped in depravity—I shudder at it!"

His voice weakened as he accepted the inevitable. "Apparently there is no choice. Tomorrow we will set out on a journey towards Egypt. "

Rebecca lowered her eyes and a tear rolling out the corner, upset at the sorry situation in which her husband, the unblemished offering, would have to descend into the land of the unclean.

"I will inform the slaves to start packing," she said and left the tent.

Evening had fallen and the sky was mostly starry, but the stifling heat continued to make it difficult to sleep. Isaac's heart was heavy, buckling under the pressure of fulfilling his duty for those who depended upon him; his mind tried to bolster it, knowing that he had no choice but to fulfill the decree of the King.

His internal dialogue left him in extreme distress.

"I must rejoice in what the Creator intends me to do! If I sit in sadness and distress because I must do something that is not to my liking, then it is heresy to the Creator!"

"Yes, but to go down to Egypt..."

"No ifs, ands, or buts! The word of the Creator brooks no alternative."

"Egypt is full of lewdness and abomination!"

"So what? Who is forcing you to join the demonic dance taking place there?"

"It is human nature to be influenced by the culture of the place one lives in..."

"Wrong! That is the way of animals, conforming to their environment thoughtlessly. Humans are supposed to have self-control, to maintain their independence!"

"True, and yet people commit acts in certain places that they would never consider elsewhere."

"It all depends on what you think of as your base. If you know where your roots lie, you will be able to overcome the challenges and protect yourself..."

"I? I do not worry about myself! What about my son? Jacob, I have no concerns about, but Esau... the blood flowing within him is raging. He will not resist the temptations that Egypt presents!"

"You will have to hold him very close to you, bring him as near as possible; show him inexhaustible love, so that he does not move away from you and is not tempted to sin."

"True, but ..."

"No ifs, ands, or buts, remember? You must redouble your efforts! Shake off the doldrums! Revive yourself, however you can! Forget your preoccupations and start serving the Lord!"

"But how?"

"You ask how?! The one who teaches the whole world how to worship the Lord asks how he will get rid of the foreign influence in his heart?! Dance! Sing! Tell yourself a joke! Make faces! What does it matter how? The main thing is for you to reach joy!"

Isaac was won over by his head and began to hum a silent song. His mind commanded: Happier! Stronger!

Isaac got to his feet, a happy rhythmic melody beginning to emerge from his lips. He clapped his hands and danced around the tent. "*Serve the Lord with gladness; come before His presence with singing.*" Chanting loudly, his voice carried and enveloped the oppressed camp, bringing smiles to the faces of the residents, joining the tune of the prophet on this stifling night.

Isaac danced in his tent until he was out of breath, a smile smeared on his lips as he fell on the padded pillow. He could hear the slaves chanting as they loaded all the property on the carts, happily preparing to embark on the long journey, his eyes closing with a sense of acceptance of the future. Contentedly, he thought: The essence of man's duty in this world is to joyfully accept whatever he encounters. True, this is the most difficult duty of all, but it is the most worthwhile!

His eyes closed limply; his heart full of joy at receiving the divine process in its perfection. *"Go not down to Egypt; dwell in the land which I shall tell you of."* He sensed the voice of prophecy speaking to him.

Isaac felt his heart leap at the oracle. "Should I stay here? In Hebron?"

"No, you must wander from Hebron," the prophecy answered. "You will be a sojourner in this land, but you must not leave the borders of the land of Canaan. Because you are an unblemished offering, you do not belong outside of the Promised Land."

The voice of prophecy continued: *"Sojourn in this land, and I will be with you, and will bless you; for to you, and to your seed, I will give all these lands, and I will establish the oath which I swore to Abraham your father; and I will multiply your seed as the stars of heaven, and will give to your seed all these lands; and by your seed shall all the nations of the earth bless themselves; because that Abraham hearkened to My voice, and kept My charge, My commandments, My statutes, and My laws."*

Isaac opened his eyes blissfully, knowing that the way of joy was the only thing that saved him from descending into the impurity of Egypt, realizing that he must follow in the footsteps of his father to the land of Gerar.

"Wow, wow, wow, look at her..."

"Shhh, tell me where you got this precious piece of jewelry?"

"Does she belong to you?"

The border guards walked around Rebecca, staring at her, admiring the superhuman beauty.

Isaac gritted his teeth angrily, knowing that if he said she was his wife, he might be summarily killed in order for Rebecca to be taken as the king's wife. "She does not belong to me!" he said angrily, trying to stand between the drooling people and his wife. "She is my sister, and she is a married woman!"

The guards laughed with each other: "If she is your sister, where is her husband?"

Isaac answered the obvious question thoroughly: "Because of the famine in the land of Canaan, her husband went to look for a place to find food; in the meantime, we came here, maybe we will find something here to satisfy the hunger of our house. Probably, in a few days, her husband will join us here."

"What is your name?" asked the commander.

"Isaac son of Abraham is my name, my lord; and what is your name, if I may ask?" Isaac asked the elderly but daring officer, who looked old-faced.

"I am Phicol, lord commander of His Majesty King Abimelech's army," he replied, looking at the man standing in front of him. "Are you the son of Abraham the Hebrew?" he asked, as the memory struck him like thunder on a clear day. The familiar face was literally the face of Abraham, who had come to Gerar more than seventy years ago.

"Indeed, yes," Isaac replied with a smile, recalling the stories his father and mother had told him about the king of Gerar and the commander of his army.

"So maybe you're lying, and she's not a married woman? Or maybe she's really your wife, like Sarah was your father's wife? Or maybe you're just skimping on this beautiful woman and don't want to give her to the king?" he asked with a grin, trying to hide the fear that had taken root in his heart.

"I tell you she is a married woman, and these are her two sons!" he said, pointing to Jacob and Esau, who stood on the sidelines watching the interaction with restrained anger.

Laughter erupted around them. "Is this her son?!" one of the guards asked, pointing to Esau. "What? She married an ape?!"

As Esau heard the words, his hand started moving towards his dagger, only his father's stern gaze stopped him from attacking the man laughing in front of him.

"Come monkey, do you want to go to a little fight?" the guard asked Esau with a smile. Esau examined the guard, realizing that he could easily subdue the clumsy, fleshy man who was trying to provoke him. However, his father's glare stayed his hand, saving the foolish soldier from his just deserts.

Esau looked down and removed his hand from the dagger's sheath.

"Good boy," the guard laughed, seeing Esau surrender to him.

"So, I understand that you want to come and settle in our country for a while," said Phicol to Isaac, who nodded in agreement.

"If so, King Abimelech will have to approve this. You know that there is a possibility that famine will come to our land as well, so His Majesty will have to decide whether to let you stay in the land or not," said the army minister, gesturing to Isaac to follow him, along with the entire camp.

"I do not know what I would have done to this man if he had been her husband. I would probably have slaughtered him and taken her as my wife," one of the guards said to the other.

"If you had done that, I would probably have slaughtered you later, and taken her from you for myself," his friend grinned, knowing that he would have done so.

Abimelech looked at the commander of his army in amazement: "Are you sure that this is the son of Abraham who was here about seventy years ago or more?" he asked in astonishment.

"It's as clear as day," Phicol answered decisively. "He looks just like his father. There's no mistaking that."

"And you say that he identifies the woman with him as his sister?"

"Just like his father said," Phicol replied with a smile.

"What is it with this family? Everyone says his wife is his sister!" Abimelech was angry.

"If your wife looked like his wife, and you came to a place like ours, I'm sure you would say anything that could save your skin and prevent someone from taking your wife," the army minister said, with a melancholy smile on his face as he recalled Rebecca's appearance.

"I do not understand where they bring their wives from, but they are out of this world! More than seventy years ago, I saw Abraham's wife, and her figure is still stuck in my mind, as if she were standing before my eyes in this very moment; now, he has come here with this woman, and I feel she too will remain in my head as a wrenching memory until the day I die! When I see this wife of his, I want to kick my wife out and throw her to hell. And you know that I only recently took her as a wife — she is very young and considered one of the most beautiful women in the country!" Phicol declared in frustration.

"Well, well, I heard you!" Abimelech grumbled, trying to distract himself from thinking too much about a woman he had not yet seen. "Make sure to put them in a place where I can watch them from my house. I want to see if she is his wife or not."

"Maybe she really is his sister, but not a married woman..." Phicol whispered hopefully. "If she is not a married woman, then..." Phicol fell silent when he saw the grim face of Abimelech, who was looking at him angrily. "Th-then you..." he stammered, "you can take her as a wife, Your Majesty!"

Abimelech displayed a rictus of fury. "Go, do as I told you!" he ordered, "and make sure they bring me something to eat. All this talk has made me hungry."

The days and weeks passed quickly in Isaac's camp. The relief they felt after the famine was palpable. The slaves grazed the flocks in the extensive pastures, thankful and happy to see the flocks recover and multiply. Isaac went around with his servants to look for the wells which his father Abraham had dug. The wells were found and re-excavated.

People from all walks of life made their way to Isaac's tent to learn what the Creator desired from His creatures; the wellsprings of wisdom overflowed and saturated all seekers of wisdom. The green fields were plowed and sown, the grain overflowed — a hundred times more than one might expect. Jacob kept himself in the study hall, explaining and instructing all prospective students his areas of scholarship.

Over time, their resistance to the culture of Gerar faded. They no longer felt like strangers in a strange land. The fear that some man would come and try in his impudence to take his wife disappeared. The concern that anyone might learn about Isaac's true relationship to Rebecca receded, as a feeling of security and calm rested on the camp.

Evening came; darkness began to spread its wings over the camp preparing for the night. Isaac walked innocently towards his wife Rebecca's tent, entered the tent, and closed the flaps behind him.

Night fell on the sleeping camp.

Dawn broke over the camp, light creeping over the horizon. The deep darkness retreated before the advancing brilliance of the day. Isaac peeked out of Rebecca's tent, looked around, and quickly snuck out, making his way back to his own tent.

Little did he know that Abimelech could see everything from the tower of his palace, overlooking Isaac's encampment. He took note of Isaac as he surreptitiously left Rebecca's tent ahead of the advancing sun. All night he stared at the tent; from the moment he had seen Isaac enter it, he had not looked away from the tent door. In the middle of the night, he had snuck into the encampment, and listened to what was happening in the tent. An hour later, he had returned to the window of his tower and waited to see when the "brother" would leave the tent of his "sister."

"Go and call Isaac immediately, let him come to me!" he commanded the guard standing in the doorway of his royal chamber.

A few minutes later, Isaac entered the king's presence with slight apprehension. The feeling that his secret had been revealed due to his own carelessness gripped his heart.

"Isaac, my friend, how are you?" Abimelech looked at Isaac, with a cruel smile smeared across his face. "I hope I did not wake you too early."

"Not at all, Your Majesty, it brings me joy to see your face."

Isaac smiled at Abimelech, trying to ignore the enmity he felt the monarch had for him. "I feel quite well, and I am so grateful to Your Majesty for hosting us in this beautiful land."

"And your dear sister, how is she?" the king smiled sarcastically.

"Oh… thank the Lord, she is quite well too."

"My friend, I want to ask you a question. I believe your father would call it a matter of ethics, of God's law."

"Of course!"

"Then let me ask you: is it permitted, in the eyes of the Lord, for a brother to marry his sister?" he asked, glancing at Isaac.

Isaac pondered for a moment, realizing that his secret had been revealed: "No, sir, this is strictly forbidden."

"If that is true, what were you doing last night in your sister's tent?!" he snapped at him, looking at Isaac as if he were a sinner caught red-handed.

Isaac ran his hand over his face, clearing his throat: "Your Majesty is correct," he said, lowering his eyes. "As Your Majesty undoubtedly knew from the beginning, she is not my sister, but my wife."

"So why did you identify her as your sister?" Abimelech rebuked him.

Isaac looked straight into the eyes of Abimelech: "I feared for my life, Your Majesty! If I had told you the truth, I might have been killed so that you could take her as a wife."

Abimelech glared: "*What is this you have done to us? One of the people might easily have lain with your wife, and you would have brought guiltiness upon us.*"

Isaac continued to stare at Abimelech, thoughts of the future possibilities running through his head: "But what now?" he needed to know.

Abimelech put his hand on his shoulder, feeling the pain, which had healed many years ago, radiating again: the pains brought on him by the mother of Isaac on the night he had attempted to touch her. "I will raise alarm among all my people, and warn them not to touch you or your wife," he conceded, with no choice.

"What do you think you're doing?" Isaac's shepherds started shouting, descending the steep slope toward the well they had dug a few days earlier.

The shouts of Isaac's shepherds brought a vengeful smile to the Philistines, who stood on the edge of the well and poured mud into the pure water that Isaac's shepherds had discovered.

Swords were drawn by the Philistines, ready to shed the blood of Isaac's shepherds. "You have no right to come to our land and do whatever you please!" The Philistines laughed at the shocked shepherds. "You can try to stop us if you want," they said, waving their blades.

The shepherds looked in horror at the swords, knowing that they could not overpower the armed men. "But why...?" they asked in pain as the people filled the water source with thick mud.

"You ask why?! What hutzpah! You came here, took all the best of what our country has to offer, got rich at our expense, and you still ask why!" Hatred was visible in the eyes of the Philistines.

"Yes, we demand to know what your claim is! What do you have to answer?" asked one of the young shepherds boldly, "Several months ago, we dug water wells in the Gerar, and you blocked them on the pretext that the water belonged to you. Then we moved away from you and again you came and blocked the wells we dug under the pretext that we were corrupting the land. Now what are you saying?"

One of the men approached the young shepherd with a hard face, the drawn sword nearing the throat of the young man planted in his place. The shepherd's face expressed fear, but he did not flinch as the blade approached.

With blazing eyes, the armed Philistine spat at him furiously: "What am I saying, parasite? Do I need to speak slowly so you'll understand? Fine, then: flee! Leave the country before we slaughter you all! What? You think you can come here on the pretext that you have a famine, and then loot our precious resources? You came here as starving refugee, but bit by bit you buy another plot of land, take over all the treasures of nature, get rich at our expense. You have brought us famine, but you dig wells and live like kings!

"And at the height of your hutzpah, you are still trying to bring people to your way of life, teaching people your pathetic philosophies, confusing the youths trying to make their way in life through your false religion. I have offered my son, who fell into your net, to come and work for His Majesty King Abimelech, and he said to me, 'I would rather work in the manure of Isaac's mules than for all the silver and gold of Abimelech.' I do not know how you enchant them and the whole land, but I tell you, if you do not leave here quickly, it will cost you all your lives!" The man pressed his sword to the young shepherd's throat. "We mean every word we say" he whispered, the blade biting into the young man's flesh. "Do you understand now?" Isaac's shepherd nodded his head slightly, fearing the Philistine might slit his throat.

"Now go and tell your master what we told you. I hope you understood us well." The man turned on his heels, gazing at the well-filled well: "Come on, we have nothing more to do here," he told his companions.

"Apparently, we have finished what we had to do in this place," Isaac told the shepherds, who came to him after the well was sealed.

"We will dig another well at the border of the land before we leave, so that these unfortunates know that there is nothing in our hearts against them. For this well, they will not contend with us. From there we ascended directly to Beersheba in the land of the Negev. "

In short order, the shepherds dug the well and Isaac and his men left the land toward Beersheba.

Joy filled the heart of Isaac when he came to Beersheba. In a prophetic vision, it was revealed to him that he had done the right thing in leaving Gerar; the providence of God would accompany him and his seed after him.

Isaac's servants rose early in the morning to dig a well, while Isaac built an altar and offered a sacrifice of thanksgiving to his God. The sound of many horses galloping shocked him. Isaac hurried out of his tent to see what was happening.

King Abimelech and Lord Commander Phicol, along with a detachment of soldiers, had arrived at the camp of Isaac. Isaac watched his frightened men, shrinking from the new threat in their midst.

Isaac's eyes flashed fire as he addressed Abimelech, who got off his horse and stood humbly in front of Isaac. *"Why have you come to see me, seeing that you hate me and have sent me away from you?"*

Phicol looked at his silent master. "Lord Isaac," he said in a flattering voice, "we do not hate you; we have seen that the Lord has been with you." Phicol gestured with his hand over Isaac's great camp. "So that there may not be any misunderstanding between us, we have come to make a covenant with you as we did in the time of your father, peace be upon him."

Isaac snorted contemptuously at the flattering Phicol.

"I know we did not behave properly sending you away from our country. But you know, people start talking, and we were afraid that someone in the nation would do something stupid. Now we have come to you to ask for your forgiveness and to make a covenant of peace with you," Phicol looked down.

Isaac laughed to himself: "The good you did for me...?! Do you mean that you did not murder us?!"

"Let's sit down and eat something," Isaac said. One of Isaac's servants came to him quickly, as he gestured towards him, running to fulfill his master's command.

Isaac, Abimelech, Phicol, and his men sat down to eat together. In the morning, Abimelech and his men rose up to return to their land.

"My lord!" one of the slaves happily turned to Isaac, "we have found water in the well which we dug."

CHAPTER FORTY-ONE

Blessings

 ou must listen to me. Do not defy me!" Rebecca glared at her son Jacob. Her peremptory tone convinced Jacob that she was determined he do what she commanded.

"You cannot deny that your brother is an unscrupulous man, whose thoughts are nothing but evil. Do you know why your father has lost his sight? I know for a fact, those two termagants your brother married have blinded your poor father with the smoke of their idolatrous incense. Esau even lied about the names of those Hittite harridans! There's Oholibamah daughter of Beeri, whom your brother claimed went by Judith, a name expressing gratitude to the Lord; and Adah, daughter of Elon, whom your brother claimed went by Basemath, because supposedly her deeds were as pleasant as spices (*besamim*). He had the hutzpah to marry them when he was forty, as if he were as righteous as your father, who married me when he was forty. Of course, he spent all his single years messing about with every woman he came across, whether she was married or not — and now that he is married, he has not changed his behavior at

81

all!" An expression of disgust appeared on Rebecca's face, mixed with sadness because this creature had come out of her womb.

"But you, Jacob — thank God, I was privileged to have you study in the academy of the righteous Shem, may his memory be a blessing, and Eber, may he live long. You have been studying the wisdom of the Lord ever since we left Gerar when you were eighteen years old. Thirty-two years you studied there, until Shem's passing a few years ago. My sole comfort during those decades was the knowledge that you were delving into the will of God and that you were far from your brother.

"The big problem is that your brother, all those years, served your father faithfully. I can't say why he worked so hard at it. I am sure he was not motivated by love. He would even change his clothing and apply cologne before he entered your father's presence — regardless of how often or for how long he did so."

Jacob pondered why his mother was repeating the whole family history. His mother held one hand in the other, as if trying to calm the tremor which had seized them. The usually smiling face now looked worried and restless.

"Mother," Jacob spoke in a loving tone, understanding his mother's pain, "if you're so upset because I'm not married yet, do not worry, I'm sure I'll soon find the right match." Jacob's captivating smile caressed his worried mother with love.

Rebecca looked at her son in consternation, realizing that she had not yet told him what she had to say, urgently. "I'm sure of that. You know who will be the happiest?" she grinned. "A few days ago, I heard the news that about a year ago my brother Laban and his wife Adina had twins, Leah and Rachel. Adina sent me a message to tell me that my older son would marry her older daughter, Leah, and my younger son her younger daughter Rachel... Poor Leah," Rebecca whispered sadly, thinking of the unfortunate fate of the woman who would have to live with Esau.

"Still, that's not why I summoned you," she said emphatically. "I learned something today, via the Holy Spirit..." Rebecca stopped, pausing to make clear to her son the import of her next words, "Your father has commanded Esau to bring him delicacies so he may bless him tonight. It is a very important night, the fifteenth of Nissan; in the future, this date will be a turning point for the great nation which is to emerge from Abraham. It is a spiritual watershed, a time of miracles; that is why your father wants to bless your brother tonight. This is not trivial matter; the whole future depends on this blessing.

"The legacy that your father's father, Abraham, received from the Creator and gave to your father, that all his blessings would come to fruition, is about to be handed over to Esau — and we cannot allow that."

Jacob felt embarrassed by his mother's pressure: "But, Mother, what can we do? It's Father's decision what to do with the blessing he received. Unfortunately, I do not think there is a way to convince him to pass the blessing on to me."

Rebecca stared into her son's eyes: "We are not going to convince him! We are going to... let's say... prevent him from making a bitter mistake."

Jacob looked thoughtful: "But how? You said he told Esau to hunt game for him and prepare a feast. I know Esau; it will not take him long until he manages to catch something. What can we do in such a short time? It won't be easy to persuade him to withhold his blessing from Esau."

Rebecca thought for a moment how to explain the plan to her son. "We won't try to persuade him not to give the blessing to Esau ... We will just have to divert the blessing from him to you! You will pre-empt Esau, and your father will give the blessing to you!"

Jacob laughed a little: "Is that all? I go into his room and tell him to give me the blessing before Esau shows up? No way he'll agree!"

Rebecca smiled at her innocent son: "Obviously, he will not agree, unless he thinks you are Esau; then he'll bless you willingly."

Jacob looks surprised by his mother's words: "How will he think I'm Esau? We look completely different; we don't even sound alike!"

"I thought about that, too," Rebecca said with a mischievous smile, "and we have Divine Providence, thanks to your brother," laughed Rebecca. "He thinks he's so smart! He's worried that you'll impersonate him, speaking gruffly and roughly; so he coordinated with your father that he will imitate your manner of speaking. So, when you go in to see your father, you have no need to change your voice; just speak normally, which will convince your father that you are Esau. The mighty hunter has outwitted himself!"

Jacob seemed shocked at the idea of tricking his father: "But, Mother, that's a lie! It's tantamount to stealing!"

Rebecca looked at her son reproachfully: "No lying, no thievery! You told me the day your grandfather passed away, peace be upon him, you bought the birthright from your brother Esau for the lentil stew you gave him, right? And more, I know that when I became pregnant, I conceived you first, and then your brother, even if I cannot prove it. So, you are actually the elder of his sons," she said firmly. "And even if it were not so, we cannot let your father commit the grave mistake of bestowing his blessings on Esau. You would not let a blind man trip over a stone, right? Well, your father's blind spot has nothing to do with his vision; it's his affection for your bother. We must not let him stumble. You know it's your duty!"

Rebecca shot a hard look at her son.

"This is the struggle that has been raging since the day the world was created, the battle over which power will rule the total universe. Eve and Adam failed in their battle, accepting the advice of the serpent, and thereby allowing death into the world, the war between the forces of light and the forces of darkness. The fight for the souls of man, towards faith or towards heresy, Abel or Cain. Noah lost his battle as well. He barely saved his skin and his family. His son Shem also tried but was unable to bring the world back to the true path. Abraham, who was the reincarnation of Adam; and Sarah his wife, the soul of Eve — they fought against Nimrod, good versus evil. Abraham, your grandfather, succeeded a little in defying Nimrod and instilling faith in the world; Your father too walks in his father's way. Since the first human sin, the whole world has been involved in this fight of good versus evil. Unfortunately, to this day, evil usually prevails.

"You know, being pregnant with you and your brother I would feel strange feelings. As I passed the study hall, I felt pain as if one of you were struggling to get out, but as I was passing an idolatrous temple, I would feel the same. At first, I was very sad because I was afraid I would have a child who would be an agglomeration of good and evil. When your grandfather Abraham took me to Shem the ancient, he made it clear to me that there were two sons in my womb, one all good and one all bad. Your brother, unfortunately, is the root of evil in the world. It hurts me a lot to say this about my son, but that's the reality. In the early years I tried to deny it, tried to suppress the idea that the root of evil had come out of my womb, but I have come to terms with it.

"Unfortunately, though, difficult as it is to say this..." Rebecca wiped a tear from her eyes. "Your father refuses to understand that the root of evil we must try and overcome has emerged from our union. Your brother is rooted in villainy, as you know; he will resort to any means to connect with vice and corruption. If he gets the blessings from Your Father, His power will increase to dimensions that no man can ever overcome. Control of the world will be given to the forces of darkness, which will bring humans down to the lowest level. The lusts of the flesh, gluttony, and greed will rule all creation until they fawn to its final destruction, as almost happened in the generation of

Noah. You have two options," Rebecca concluded, "either you listen to me; or you refuse and bring complete destruction."

"But what are we to do?" he asked apprehensively.

"You will now run to the flock and fetch me two goats. I will cook them for your father as he likes. In the meantime, you will put on your brother's clothes, what he wears while he serves your father. You know that even he does not trust those two snakes he married. He is not willing to leave anything of value with them; he entrusts everything of value to me, because he suspects that they will steal things from him. After you get dressed, you will enter your father's room with the food; he will eat and then bless you! Easy as that!" said Rebecca with a smile.

Jacob felt a tremor in his body, thinking about deceiving his father and stealing the blessings; yet if, God forbid, the blessings would be given to Esau, it would be a global catastrophe. Thus, he felt compelled to agree to his mother's plan. The preoccupation with the consequences of what might happened when his brother learned of the ruse was pushed to the margins of consciousness.

"But, Mother, if my father decides to touch me to confirm my identity, he will immediately feel that I am not Esau, for I am a smooth man, and he is a hairy man. God forbid, he might even curse me for trying to deceive him," he said apprehensively.

"I thought of that, too," Rebecca said directly. "We will skin the goats you bring me, and from that we will make hides to wear on your neck and on your arms. He will not notice the difference. Do not worry; he will not curse you! And if so, the curse will apply to me and not to you! Now, quickly run to the flock, and do as I have commanded you! We are wasting precious time!"

"Damn it, nothing's going right for me today! What's wrong with me?!" Esau walked quietly among the trees, trying to catch game to bring to his father, as he told him. The tangle of tall, familiar vegetation seemed for a moment to be trying to thwart his mission. The minutes ticked by, the night was soon down, and he would not be able hunt anything. A fawn, lazily munching on grass, appeared before Esau. Esau progressed slowly, angrily beating back the urge to shoot an arrow and be done with it.

"Today of all days he had to tell me that I couldn't just kill an animal—I have to slaughter it with a knife! Not only that, but he also demanded I catch an animal from the wilderness, not from anyone's field." The fury in his heart rose; he was frustrated by the realization of how difficult it was to ritually slaughter an ownerless animal, rather than grabbing and killing whatever he found, without thought to whose it was or how it died. He had to make progress carefully, avoid making noise lest the fawn be frightened and slip out of his hands. He was so close he could almost touch it! He jumped on the young deer, which collapsed beneath his weight. From his belt he took a rope, expertly tying the frightened fawn's legs. Esau happily got up, went to fetch the knife and bow he had left behind so that they would not obstruct his movement. Esau returned to the place of the fawn, and to his astonishment, he saw that the fawn had vanished, his rope in pieces on the ground. A shout of despair and anger shook the forest, chasing the animals away from the place; a moment later, the trees erupted with birds taking flight. The frustrated Esau resolved to return home; he would ignore his father's command and grab whatever crossed his path first.

Esau makes his way back to the camp, striking with his sword angrily at any branch or bough unfortunate enough to be in his way. As he approached, one of his dogs ran to greet his master happily. The unfortunate canine was unceremoniously decapitated, and Esau swung the carcass over his shoulder: "What does it matter what the old man eats? As long as his stomach is full, he can bless me!" he said to himself.

A faint knock rattled Isaac's door. Isaac raised his head, looking without seeing in the direction of the door to his room, which slowly opened at his invitation. Full moonlight shown through the large window, illuminating the room with no candles lit. A fresh breeze rustled the curtains drawn to the sides, heralding the impending summer.

Isaac sat on his bed, raising his face towards his guest. The breeze brought to his nostrils the aromas of a feast for one. His bright face formed a smile, welcoming the caller. His snow-white beard shone brightly in the moonlight, shifting slightly in the night breeze.

"Father..." the soft voice said, as if trying to burrow unassumingly into the noises of the night.

Isaac strained to hear and identify the voice. "Who are you, my son?" he asked, marveling at how good Esau was at imitating Jacob.

"It is I," the voice whispered and hesitated a little, giving a space between the statements, "Your firstborn... Esau," he continued. "I have done as you told to me," Jacob's voice said to his father, "Please get up, and eat my game, so that your soul may bless me."

Jacob's heart beat violently within him, like a deer trying to escape the hunter tracking it.

The thoughts ran through his head: I'm not lying at all. Father asked who I was, so I said, "It is I." Then I said that his firstborn is Esau. Moreover, I have done what he has asked of me many times. I am not even misleading him, for it is surely clear that I am altering my replies to avoid a blatant untruth.

Isaac pondered, trying to establish the identity of the person standing in front of him. "How did you find game so quickly, my son?" he asked, trying to puzzle out the identity of his interlocutor.

"For the Lord your God made it happen for me," Jacob whispered to his father. Isaac stared at his son, thinking to himself: Esau is not accustomed to invoking God, but now he speaks of "the Lord your

God"?! Perhaps it is not Esau but Jacob

"Come here, my son, that I may touch you. Are you my son Esau or not?" said Isaac to his son.

Jacob advanced toward his father, his heart galloping, as it might burst, his flesh vibrating in terror. Isaac ran his hands over his son, who was covered in goatskins. The familiar feeling of the hirsuteness of his son Esau deceived him; he felt a certain strangeness he could not comprehend. *"The voice is the voice of Jacob, but the hands are the hands of Esau,"* he said in bewilderment. "Are you my son Esau?!" he asked.

"I am," said Jacob, thinking: I am Jacob.

Isaac breathed deeply, the inability to identify his caller was confounding his spirit.

"Serve me your game, my son, so that my soul may bless you," he said, trying to push down the gnawing doubts within him.

Jacob served his father the dishes his mother had prepared, pouring him wine with a bouquet that recalled the Garden of Eden. Isaac ate the exquisite meal, appetizer, aperitif, and entrée served by his son. He felt his spirit expand joyfully as he was about to deliver his blessings to his son on this important day, a day when his son's sons would witness unprecedented miracles.

Doubt still gnawed at his heart: "My son, give me a kiss!" Jacob shuddered but leaned down and kissed his father on the cheek.

Isaac took a deep breath, inhaling the secret of his son's perfumed clothes — a heavenly experience. He was relieved and elated, finally convinced that his son Esau had begun to change his ways.

He exclaimed: *"See, the smell of my son is as the smell of a field which the Lord has blessed. So, God give you of the dew of heaven, and of the fat places of the earth, and plenty of grain and wine. Let peoples serve you, and nations bow down to you. Be lord over your brethren and let your mother's sons bow down to you. Cursed be every one that curses you and blessed be every one that blesses you.*"

With that, the blessing was irrevocable.

A shout shattered the silence. "Father!" someone called from outside the room. Jacob realized that his time was up; Esau had completed his mission.

Jacob leapt up, slipping behind the door just as Esau flung it open. Esau entered the dark room, approaching his father tensely. *"My father will rise and eat from his son's game, so your soul will bless me!"* he said in a commanding voice, standing in front of his father, who was sitting on his bed.

Jacob slipped out while his brother's back was turned, fleeing from the place before Esau would see him. The knowledge that his brother might kill him the next time they met was real and inescapable.

"Who are you?" Isaac asked his new caller in amazement.

Esau looks at his father in bewilderment: "I am your firstborn son Esau!" he declared passionately.

Isaac began to shake as the realization hit him: it was the real Esau standing before him now. His thoughts were running wild, as he tried to understand what had happened in his room over the past hour, and why Divine Providence had allowed this bizarre thing to occur. Isaac wondered: *"Who then, is he that has taken game, and brought it me, and I have eaten of all before you came and have blessed him? Even so, he shall be blessed!"* Isaac said to Esau, accepting that Divine Providence had led him to bless Jacob even though he had not meant to do so; he felt what had happened was for the good.

Isaac sniffed the pungent odor rising from the stew Esau had brought him. In disgust, he thought: That cannot be a clean animal.

Esau screamed in impotent rage and frustration, realizing that his younger brother had managed to take the blessing he had so longed for. The blessing for which he forced himself to serve his father for many years had been stolen from him, never to return. His hope that he and his offspring would always dominate his brother and his descendants vanished.

Isaac felt terrified of his son yelling in anger; he realized the raging man in front of him would let nothing stand in the way of what he wanted. Such a man was not worthy of receiving the blessing he had just given; if Esau had received it, he would have used it to destroy the world.

Esau gnashed his teeth: *"Bless me, even me also, O my father!"* he screamed at the old man lying, shaking on his bed.

And he said: *"Your brother came with guile and has taken away your blessing."* Isaac was worried about his violent son's reaction.

Esau took the tray in his hands and threw it at the wall. He lamented: *"Is not he rightly named Jacob? For he has supplanted me* (vayakeveini*) these two times: he took away my birthright; and behold, now he has taken away my blessing."* He furiously kicked over the pot Jacob had used to serve his father.

Whispering, Isaac tentatively asked his firstborn: "He took away your birthright? How did he do that?"

"You do not know?! I once asked my crooked brother to let me eat the lentil stew he had made; he agreed on the condition that I give up the birthright. I was hungry so I agreed, and the scoundrel just fed me bread and stew!" Esau ranted. "Don't you have a blessing for me?!"

A slight smile crept onto Isaac's face. He thought: So, thank the Lord, I did bless the rightful firstborn. He tried to conceal the joy flooding his heart, grateful for the Divine Providence that he had encountered, and which had misled him, as it were. He explained contentedly: *"Behold, I have made him your lord, and all his brethren have I given to him for servants; and with grain and wine have I sustained him; and what then shall I do for you, my son?"*

Esau, however, would not relent. He was desperate knowing that any consolation prize he received now would be far inferior to what his brother had taken. *"Have you but one blessing, my father? bless me, even me also, O my father."* A cry erupted from his throat, as two tears fell from his eyes for the first time in his life; a third tear welled up, then receded.

Isaac keenly felt the sorrow that filled the heart of the son who had served him faithfully for many years; he had to appease Esau or risk losing him forever.

"Behold, of the fat places of the earth shall be your dwelling, and of the dew of heaven from above; and by your sword shall you live, and you shall serve your brother."

An agitated growl sounded from Esau's mouth.

"And it shall come to pass when you shall break loose, that you shall shake his yoke from off your neck. When Jacob and his descendants veer from the rightful path, you will be able to assume control over them."

Esau looked at his father in disgust, feeling that all he wanted was to murder his rogue brother. A tremendous thud shook Isaac, sitting on his bed. The pot in which Jacob brought the food to his father was kicked viciously again against the wall.

Esau came out of his father's room grumbling and growling. He vowed in his heart: *Let the days of mourning for my father be at hand; then will I slay my brother Jacob.*

Rebecca gripped her hands tightly as she paced around her tent. The Holy Spirit had revealed to her Esau's homicidal intent; but her firstborn was so wrathful, she was not convinced he would in fact wait for Isaac's passing. Esau could attack at any moment, and what would happen then? Would her twins kill each other?

. The servant whom she had sent to call her younger son had been ordered to do so quickly but quietly, and it was not long before Jacob entered slowly. His face expressed shame and unease, confusion and consternation, joy mixed with sadness over his deeds. He'd had no choice, he acknowledged, but he had still acted in a way diametrically opposed to his honest and truthful nature.

Though the concern on Rebecca's face was apparent, it betrayed little of what had she had experienced over in the last few hours. Her stress was palpable, indicating that her call to him was not just to get information from him about the success of her plan.

"Listen to me carefully!" she said without preamble. "I have been informed that Esau is plotting to kill you."

Jacob tried to interrupt, telling his mother that Esau would not dare touch him while Isaac was alive, but Rebecca cut him off.

Desperately, she said: "There is only one thing to do: you must flee!" She stifled a groan at the thought of what might happen otherwise. "Until your brother's fury subsides, and he forgets what you have done to him, then I will send for you and retrieve you." The thought that her beloved son would no longer be by her side broke her heart. *"Why should I be bereaved of both of you on one day?"* she whispered, knowing that if Esau attacked Jacob, both might perish.

Rebecca held her son's hand, pleading, her teary eyes expressing the pain of the separation forced upon them. "Please, my dear son, do what I ask of you," she said softly. Rebecca began to cry faintly, hugging her son to her lap, as if he were a tender child.

Jacob began his journey at his mother's command. A pleasant springtime sun greeted him as he left.

At a light run, he left his parents' home. The journey to an unknown place disturbed him a bit; he was concerned about being so far from a source of spirituality. Then, a smile spread across his face, as an idea flashed in his head. "I will return to the academy of Eber for a while! I learned so much in my years there, internalizing the Word of God; but what about all the wicked people out there?

The righteous Eber learned from his forebear Shem, a survivor of the Flood, how to deal with villains and scoundrels. He will teach me how to deal with such rough characters. Then I will be able to confront even the most desperate men — the liars and the thieves and the murderers. Only when I am prepared to face those who may wish me ill can I begin to think of building a family for myself."

With a pack on his back, Jacob felt his feet happily carrying him towards Eber's academy, his heart rejoicing at the thought of reuniting with the man who had taught him so much for so many years. Only then could he confront faithless and corrupt men — those motivated by a strong desire for honor and power, willing to do anything in order to obtain control.

"So, what do you want?" Ishmael looked intently at Esau, who was sitting across from him.

Esau lowered his eyes trying to give his voice a soft, submissive tone: "I've come to ask my lord for the hand of his daughter, Mahalath."

There was silence. Ishmael looked at his nephew with suspicion; the rumors of the man's exploits had reached far and wide. Clearly, Esau had an ulterior motive. He thought: This creature wants to marry my daughter, but why? What is he planning? Is it just so he can marry a woman who is a grandchild of Abraham as he is?

"Why do you want to marry my daughter?" he demanded bluntly.

Esau maintained his humility, answering the old man humbly: "My lord surely knows that I have two wives. Unfortunately, they displease my parents. When I married them, I thought that they would reform, that I could influence them to follow the path of my fathers and accept upon themselves the yoke of heaven. Unfortunately, I was deceived, and they continue in their way and worship their idols. I thought that in order to please my father and mother, I would marry a fine, decent woman like your daughter, and my father would at least have some peace of mind at the end of his life."

Ishmael snorted contemptuously: "Why would you have expected them to accept the yoke of the kingdom of heaven?! Since when are you a God-fearing man?"

Esau sounded offended. "I know that much slander about me has reached my lord, but most of it is not true. Did my lord forget what was said about him when he was young? There were many bad reports about your behavior when you were young, but later on you repented and changed your conduct. Do I not have the right to repent? You too married a woman who was less than perfect, to say the least. Aisha was her name, if I am not mistaken. Only after you got married to Fatima did you begin to repent. Am I right? Why would you prevent me, your nephew, from taking the first step to getting closer to our Father in Heaven?"

Ishmael watched Esau. The thought that he might have never had the chance to repent sent a shiver down his spine. "I understand," he said thoughtfully, "there is truth in what you say..."

Nebaioth, the son of Ishmael, who sat still throughout the conversation, looked at his father, who seemed to approve of the match. A faint smile came over his face. He knew that Esau's velvet tongue concealed his disingenuousness; but his cousin could be a powerful ally, as together they might be able to overpower Isaac, who had taken Ishmael's birthright and all of Abraham's property.

"Very well then," he said with a smile. "I wish you nothing but health and happiness. I will tell the women to bring dinner, and tomorrow we will consummate the marriage."

Ishmael and Esau looked in amazement at Nebaioth, who was in such a hurry to get it done; but then they shrugged, smiled, and shook each other's hands, sealing the deal.

A few hours later, weeping and wailing filled the night throughout the camp of Ishmael. Their patriarch had died in his sleep. Ishmael returned his soul to its Creator at the ripe old age of one hundred and thirty-seven.

The wedding of Esau and Mahalath was postponed for a week.

Then Esau returned to his parents' house with his new wife; she joined his household, where his Hittite wives remained just as before.

CHAPTER FORTY-TWO

Pursuit

ho's there?" Rebecca was alarmed by the rustling at the back door. Now that she was a centenarian, she could not move as swiftly as she once had — and her grandchildren, Esau's rambunctious lot, were running her ragged as they entered young adulthood.

But the man she faced was no youngster; his full beard and robust frame were fully mature. He bore a striking resemblance to Esau, but no... after fourteen long years... It was...

"Jacob!" she exclaimed, weeping for joy.

Her younger son smiled broadly. "Mother, I've returned! Don't worry, no one saw me come in the back..."

Then his mother's face crumpled, the tears of delight turning into tears of despair. "Oh, my sweet boy! You have just returned to me, but I must send you away again."

"No, Mother, you don't need to do that! When I left here, I was a naïf; but now I know the ways of the world. Eber has trained me well, and I fear no man. Not even Esau."

"Edom."

"What?"

"He calls himself Edom now."

"Like *adom*? The color red?"

"It is part of his identity. He is no longer a lone hunter. He has troops now, he forges alliances in the land of Seir, he has sons who fight alongside him. I can see that you are a man, but your brother has become more than that. Can you face down an army on your own? Even your grandfather had allies, disciples, Eliezer his lieutenant!" She shook her head. "No, my son, it is not safe for you here. The fury of Edom still burns red-hot, while his power has only grown. You need to go far away and to build your own house, if you can ever hope to confront him." She struggled to her feet, sighing heavily. "Come, my dear. It is time for your father to send you towards your destiny — and the house I left almost a century ago."

"Jacob, my son," said Isaac, staring into the eternal gloom that was his lot. Jacob stood awkwardly, a little dizzy from the events of the day.

"You are about seventy-seven years old today. Your mother and I think that the time is ripe for you to take a wife and build a house for yourself. *Arise, go to Paddan-Aram, to the house of Bethuel your mother's father; and take you a wife from there of the daughters of Laban your mother's brother,*" said Isaac to his son.

Jacob looked at his father, miserable at the thought of renewed exile. Convinced he could not stay, he still felt guilty about the blessing he had seized from the intended recipient. "Father, I'm sorry..."

"There's nothing to be sorry about," Isaac said with a smile, when he understood the meaning of his son's distress. "*And God Almighty bless you, and make you fruitful, and multiply you, that you may be a congregation of peoples; and give you the blessing of Abraham, to you, and to your seed with you; that you may inherit the land of your sojournings, which God gave to Abraham.*" Isaac lovingly patted the shoulder of his son, who fell at his feet and kissed his hands. "Now, my beloved son, do what I have told you, and go to Laban the son of Bethuel, your mother's brother, and take a wife from his daughters."

The tears flowed in the furrows of his cheek, as Isaac hoped he would meet his son again in this life. Isaac handed his son a pack full of gold and precious stones so that he could pay the bride-gift to his future father-in-law.

A satanic smile sat on Edom's face. The rumor that Jacob had returned to his father's house had reached him. His heart leapt at the possibility that he might finally have the opportunity to take revenge on the brother who had stolen his blessing.

Eliphaz, his firstborn by his wife Adah, looked at his smiling father in amazement.

"Listen to me carefully, my son," Edom knew the boy's skills, even at age thirteen. Edom would have gladly killed his thieving sibling himself, but he could not take the risk that his father might learn about it.

The alternative, he thought, was a brilliant plan. Eliphaz and his friends would chase after Jacob and kill him once he left the land of Canaan. Their parents, who believed that their son had set out on his journey to a distant land, would know nothing of the assassination. He himself would be able to truthfully tell his father that he had not touched Jacob with his hands. Then, after Jacob failed to return during Isaac's lifetime, Edom would inherit everything upon their father's death.

"Go now, gather ten of your most dangerous friends, and chase after my brother Jacob. I command you to kill him and bury his body in one of the caves. Tell your friends they must keep this a secret, I do not want anyone finding out. When you return, I will pay them what they deserve. Do it all as quickly and quietly as possible."

Eliphaz looked at his father with a smile: "It will be my pleasure and honor to fulfill your will, my father. I am already on my way."

Edom patted Eliphaz affectionately on the shoulder, happy that his son was following in his bloodstained footsteps.

The sky was full of stars as Jacob left, dispersing the gloom of the dark night. Jacob slipped slowly out of his father's tent, aware of the danger he faced. The long journey ahead did not deter him. He considered it likely that Edom would chase after him, and he was afraid. After all, for almost a decade-and-a-half, it was Edom who had served their righteous father. No doubt, he had accumulated merits in the spiritual ledger, as it were, which might benefit him in his war against his younger brother. In addition, the thought of the time he would have to take off from his studies until he reached Harran disturbed him. "But I am still fulfilling a great commandment," he tried to encourage himself. The road to Harran suddenly seemed easier.

Jacob made his way to the northeast, leaving his father's encampment in Beersheba behind, breaking into a run as he approached the Jordan River. Joy spread in his heart as he realized that he was on his way to the place where he would find a wife and fulfill the great divine commandment to be fruitful and multiply. His legs were light, carrying him as if he were hovering above the ground. The landscape quickly changed: "This is the road to Hebron," he observed, "and here is the road to Mount Moriah." He could not stop moving, running towards his goal. The green banks of the Jordan River appeared before him, and he slowed his pace, looking for a convenient place to ford the river.

"Uncle Jacob!" A voice, calling out of the dark of the dissipating night, stopped him in his place. His eyes trying to find the source. Straining in the predawn dimness, raising his staff which glowed with spiritual power, he could now see a mounted force approaching him. The riders stopped a short distance from Jacob, quickly jumped off their horses, and drew their swords.

Jacob felt the swift beating of his heart, forcing himself to calm down and imbue his voice with confidence. "And who are you, my friends?" he asked with good humor.

"I am Eliphaz, son of Edom your brother, and these are my faithful friends," said the young boy with a self-assured smile.

"How can I help you, my dear nephew?" Jacob asked, understanding the purpose of Eliphaz's arrival.

Eliphaz laughed, with a rolling voice: "You can help me keep the commandment to honor one's father."

"With great joy," said Jacob, "what did your father command you to do, my dear nephew?"

"Ah... he ordered me to kill you," chortled Eliphaz.

Jacob sounded pensive: "Unfortunately, I cannot help you with this, my dear boy."

"Too bad, so I'll have to do it without your help and with the help of my friends," Eliphaz chuckled.

"Murder is man's work, Eliphaz, and you are still very much a boy. So are your playmates. This is not a game." Jacob laughed in a dismissive voice. "You know, I should be insulted that you think your uncle is so easily dealt with, but no matter, I forgive you, sweetie." Jacob raised his staff, which gleamed in the darkness.

Eliphaz felt the self-confidence that had accompanied him so far had faded. His companions no longer brandished their blades; the man standing before them would offer stiff resistance, it seemed. Yes, they outnumbered him, but attacking him seemed to be a dangerous proposition, perhaps even lethal. They were transfixed by the gleaming staff Jacob twirled adroitly.

"Listen, you scamp," Jacob said as if speaking to a young child, "I really do not like telling you this but it seems to me that you are a wise boy. Now, I abhor the thought of hurting children, but if you leave me no choice, I will not be the one to lose my life today. So, why don't you rascals scurry home to your mothers. They're probably worried that you haven't come home for supper yet." Jacob rolled up his sleeves, as if readying himself for fisticuffs. The boys backed away a little, as Jacob took a slight step toward them.

Eliphaz felt embarrassed and frightened. His bookworm uncle, who had been studying at Eber's academy for years, suddenly seemed frightening and threatening. His psychic power was palpable, and Eliphaz felt a tremor in his heart. It was clear he and his companions could not never harm Jacob. "But my father commanded me," Eliphaz sighed, his voice sounding broken.

"I see, darling," Jacob said in a conciliatory voice, "it's a little difficult for me to help you with your mission, but I have a good solution that will set everything right."

Jacob smiled lovingly: "Sheathe your playthings, sweet boys," he ordered.

The young men complied, with downcast eyes. Jacob approached Eliphaz with a smile. Eliphaz took a step back with apprehension. "Do not worry, darling, I will not hurt you. Here's what you need to do so you won't disappoint your father. You've been studying with your grandfather Isaac, so I've heard."

Eliphaz nodded in silence.

"So, my father is your teacher, and your teacher commanded me to go to Harran. By not interfering with my fulfillment of my father's command, you fulfill the commandment of your teacher. Is that clear?" Eliphaz hung his gaze on his uncle, nodding his head like a small child.

"And if you studied with my father then surely you have learned that if you have a commandment from your father and a commandment from your teacher, the latter takes precedence. That too is clear?" Eliphaz's look conceded the matter.

Jacob continued to speak with a smile to the shocked Eliphaz:

"Still, so that you won't be in full defiance of your father's command, I can do you a favor, my dear boy. I will give you all my possessions, and I have quite a few," Jacob patted his full pack.

"If you take my pack, then I will be penniless. And a pauper is likened to a corpse, so it will be as if you killed me, from a certain point of view. And you will also have gifts to give to your sweet friends, who have come with you all this way."

Eliphaz looked up, staring at his uncle, wondering: Why is this imposing man willing to sacrifice so much just so I won't break my father's command? "Really?!..." he asked in amazement.

Jacob laughed with pleasure at the sight of the excited boy: "Surely, my dear boy," he said affectionately, pinching Eliphaz's cheek, handing him his heavy pack. "Here you go, sweetie; now hurry home, so your mothers won't worry anymore."

Eliphaz looked at his uncle in awe. "Thank you, Uncle Jacob," he whispered. "But, Uncle Jacob, if you have clothes left you will not be really poor," Eliphaz stammered.

Jacob looked at his nephew thoughtfully, "You are right, darling, I will give you my clothes too," he said and began to take off his robes as he entered the river. "Now I'm truly destitute," he told Eliphaz, who was looking at him in amazement.

"And what about the staff?" Eliphaz asked, hoping to get his hands on that as well.

"That, darling, I cannot give to you; it must remain with me." Jacob smiled threateningly at the boys: "Now, sweet boys, you should get out of here before I regret the gifts I have given you."

Eliphaz and his friends got on their horses and returned to Beersheba.

Jacob stood naked, immersed up to his neck in the cool waters of the Jordan. He heard the hooves of a galloping horse. Soon a rider appeared, dismounted, disrobed, and waded into the river. A few seconds later, the rider was swallowed up in his place, disappearing before Jacob's eyes. Jacob waited a few minutes, realizing that the Supreme Providence has supplied him with clothes in exchange for the garb taken from him. Jacob returned to the riverbank and put on the clothes of the horseman who drowned; but the horse was frightened of the stranger, so it reared and galloped off into the distance.

Pleasant rays of sun began to spread over the land. Jacob looked at the Jordan River flowing slowly in front of him, sorry that he had to leave the Promised Land for a foreign land. He felt a twinge in his heart, knowing that banishment was his fate and he had to embark on his journey. Jacob approached the clear water and placed his staff in the water, which split before him. Exile lay on the other side.

He walked on and on, lost in a series of thoughts, swept away in the current within his mind: Why is it my destiny to be displaced and distanced from the Holy Land? Why am I not an unblemished offering like my father, who was never compelled to leave the country?

Even as his feet trod the ground, his thoughts floated loftily skyward: Is my service of God deficient? Am I not worthy to live in Canaan? Has the land vomited me out like an irredeemable sinner?

Jacob felt that melancholy was filling him, but he shook himself out of it: I must strengthen my faith! My father had a certain job to do, and I have another job. He had his mission, I have mine. And why should I even look at others? Providence is personal and precise, so it is fruitless to compare my work to the work of anyone else in the world! Come on, come on, grin and bear it! Rejoice in your lot, all is well with you! "Jacob felt the smile spread across his face, just as he reached the crest of a hill — and found himself looking at a foreign landscape.

He surveyed the unfamiliar area, which was filled with people dressed in strange clothes. They spoke a different tongue as well, but he recognized it from his grandfather Abraham's house, the language of the land of Harran.

"Where are we?" he asked the first man he came across.

"In Harran!" the man replied, looking at the stranger with surprise.

Jacob suddenly realized that the road had contracted beneath him; in no time at all, he had reached Harran.

In shock, he wondered: Could it be that I left the borders of the land of Canaan without stopping at Mount Moriah, where my ancestors prayed, to speak to God?!

Jacob turned on his heels to return back to Mount Moriah even though it was clear to him that the journey was supposed to take several days. Instead, in the blink of an eye, he found himself standing on the summit of Mount Moriah, at the site of the altar on which his father had once been bound.

The position of the sun made it clear that the day was still young. Jacob shed tears of thanksgiving and gratitude for the miracles and wonders that were taking place before him. He whispered his appreciation for the past and his hope for the future. Warm tears washed over his face, running down his beard. His arms were outstretched, pleading to the heavenly heights, heart pounding. For long hours, he stood in prayer, merging with his Creator.

He felt a complete release from the distress he had felt at leaving his country and being exiled to a foreign land. He was filled with the sense of purity and right that comes after true prayer from the bottom of one's heart, knowing that everything which happens emerges from perfect love. He thought to himself, looking at the sun that had begun to move westward. There's plenty of daylight left, so I'll go to Harran; at least another four hours before nightfall.

Jacob tried to walk away, but he felt like a stone wall was blocking him. Looking up, he saw the sun rapidly sinking, visibly falling to the horizon. "The sun is setting," he whispered in amazement, "as if the Lord is extinguishing it."

Jacob felt an exhaustion he had never experienced before. In all the fourteen years he studied at Eber's academy, he had not put his head down to rest, but suddenly felt that he must lie down. He took twelve stones, placing them around his head so that they would protect him from predators. Jacob's eyes closed, a pleasant, sweet sleep enveloping him.

A vision of prophecy took over his slumber.

And he dreamed, and behold a ladder set up on the earth, and the top of it reached to heaven; and behold the angels of God ascending and descending on it.

The guardian angel of Egypt rose two hundred and ten rungs and fell...

The guardian angel of the kingdom of Babylon rose seventy rungs and fell...

The guardian angel of Media rose fifty-two rungs and fell...

The guardian angel of Persia rose one hundred and eighty rungs and fell...

The guardian angel of Edom rose but did not fall!

A tremor gripped Jacob's body: "Will Edom's guardian angel never fall?"

"As it came up, so I will lower it!" the prophecy answered.

"And now it is your turn to climb."

"Master of the Universe, will I too rise and then fall?"

"Just as I never fall, so too you will never fall!"

Jacob stumbled in the dream, refusing to ascend the terrifying ladder.

"If you had ascended, you would have nullified all the rungs that these others climbed; but since you have declined, your descendants will have to endure the burden of the exile. You will not bring the world to its final correction," God declared.

Tears welled up in Jacob's eyes: "Master of the Universe, will it be like this forever?"

"Finally, I will avenge them and plant them in the land of Canaan, and I will finish off all the nations among whom I have dispersed them," a comforting Voice told him.

Jacob felt as if the whole land were being folded underneath him, as if he were covering, with his body, all the land of Canaan.

"I am the Lord, the God of Abraham your father, and the God of Isaac. To you and to your seed I will give the land whereon you lie. And your seed shall be as the dust of the earth, and you shall spread abroad to the west, and to the east, and to the north, and to the south. And in you and in your seed shall all the families of the earth be blessed. And behold, I am with you, and will keep you wherever you go, and will bring you back into this land; for I will not leave you, until I have done that which I have spoken to you of."

The vision of prophecy faded. Jacob opened his eyes, trembling at the very prophecy that served him. *"Surely the Lord is in this place; and I knew it not,"* his lips murmured in trembling, feeling the fear of God that filled his whole being: *"How full of awe is this place! this is none other than the house of God (beit E-lohim), and this is the gate of heaven."*

Jacob looked at the stones he had put in front of him; they had merged into one giant stone. A jug of oil appeared to him, as if out of nowhere. Jacob took the oil and poured it on the stone. With reverence, he named the place Bethel, the house of God.

"If God will be with me, and will keep me in this way that I go, and will give me bread to eat and garb to wear, so that I come back to my father's house in peace, then shall the Lord be my God, and this stone, which I have set up for a pillar, shall be God's house; and of all that You shall give me I will surely give the tenth to You," Jacob vowed trembling.

He felt his feet easily leading him away after being assured that he would be protected on his journey.

CHAPTER FORTY-THREE

Rachel

With Jacob's sights at last set on the city of Harran, in the region of Paddan-Aram, he could marvel at the breeziness of the journey. His feet barely needed to move as the landscape rapidly shifted beneath him, in the blink of an eye. He was filled with the pleasant afterglow of the prophetic vision which he had been granted. His heart was full of hope for a rosy future, positive about the expected developments.

His mother's words came to his mind: "Just as I was summoned to the well where Eliezer stood looking for your father's future wife, you too, will find she who is meant for you at the well; and just as I am beautiful," his mother blushed as she described herself, "you too will find a beautiful woman destined to be your wife."

The land flew beneath his feet, deserts changing into meadows, ending in mountains. The gorges were filled and replaced by fields and vineyards. The caressing sun, standing in the sky, barely moved. His heart fluttered in the pleasant rays of sunlight.

A group of shepherds came into view, sitting by a well that was covered by a large stone. Jacob was upset by the apparent laziness of the herdsmen lounging by the well instead of grazing the flocks? It was clear to him that the animals were not their own, but that the men were indolent day laborers. Their clothing was markedly different than that of Canaan, which he had left but only a short time earlier. Jacob slowed down. He turned to the young shepherds, who were looking in amazement at the strange man approaching them.

"Hello, my honored brothers," Jacob began, trying to enter into conversation with the people. Their only response was to shake their heads at him.

Jacob thought they might be Harranites, since their clothing resembled that of the man he had met the previous day, who had said he was from Harran.

"Brothers, where are you from?" he asked in Aramean.

"We are from Harran," they replied casually, trying to get rid of the annoying stranger.

Jacob stared at them, amazed at the speed with which he had reached Harran again; for the third time in two days, he had experienced a miraculous shortening of the way. He was also excited for the impending meeting with his mother's family. "Do you know Laban of the house of Nahor?" he asked hopefully.

The men looked at Jacob angrily: "We know him!" they said, their tone indicating that they would rather not know him.

"Is all well with him?" he asked, as if ignoring their peeved tone.

"Well enough!" they answered in disgust.

A small flock could be heard approaching; the shepherds raised their eyes to see who it was. "Here comes Rachel the daughter of Laban, ask her whatever you want to ask. You two are alike, chatterboxes," said one of the shepherds, to the laughter of his friends.

"Why don't you graze the sheep?" Jacob asked, ignoring the shepherd's sarcasm, forcing himself not to look up where the herdsman was pointing. "It is not yet time to gather in the flock; water the flock and go grazing."

"What's so hard to understand?! Can't you see the rock lying on the well?!" said one of the shepherds with contempt. "We are waiting for the other shepherds to come, and then together we will remove the stone. We cannot take down a rock like this alone, but only with the help of five people."

"Rach!" One of the shepherds called out to the young woman coming down the hill with her flock: "There is someone here asking about your father; come talk to him, he is driving us crazy!" The shepherds laughed with pleasure.

Rachel approached slowly, leading her father's little herd. Until recently, her father had had many animals and herdsmen, but not long ago a plague had broken out among her father's herds, leaving him only a few sheep. Her father was forced to fire the shepherds and let his daughter graze the few remaining sheep. Her twin sister, Leah, was unable to do the job, her eyes constantly aching from bouts of crying.

She thought to herself, forcing herself to keep walking the sheep to the well without raising her eyes to look at the man asking about her father: My poor sister, she is constantly told about the evil man she is supposed to marry when the time comes. She cannot stop weeping over her fate, so her eyes hurt all the time. I wish I could make her not have to marry Esau. She is such a good woman; she does not deserve an evil husband.

"Rachel, here's an old man asking all kinds of questions about your father. Answer him so he'll leave us alone," said one of the shepherds, ogling Rachel as she stood there, eyes downcast. "Maybe after you get rid of him, we can sit and chat a little? It's not nice how you avoid us. After all, your name means 'ewe,' and I'm a shepherd. I can water your flock. I know how to treat… ewe!" He leered and jeered, to his companions' amusement.

Jacob felt the urge to look up and speak up. In his heart, he knew that the newcomer was his intended wife. For a moment he raised his eyes, feeling that he must marry Rachel. His heart skipped a beat, sensing an unfamiliar emotion. "I must water the flock! She is my cousin!" he declared. Without thinking, he walked over to the stone laid across the well, as the shepherds laughed uproariously. He placed his hands on the rock, feeling its weight; then he shoved it hard, tossing it to the ground like the lid off a pot.

The shepherds looked at the old man in awe; their eyes widened in astonishment when they saw the water shooting up the walls of the well, flowing over the lip of the well. After all, they had placed the stone on the source to prevent anyone from stealing the shallow waters. Now, it was overflowing!

Jacob took Rachel's flock in hand, leading the sheep to the streaming water, quenching their thirst. With an inexplicable impulse, Jacob approached Rachel and kissed her on the head. Jacob's eyes filled with tears, weeping audibly, knowing that she would one day be his wife — but they would not be buried alongside each other when the time came.

"Look at him! Utterly shameless! Is that what he dares, to kiss a strange woman in public?!" one of the shepherds shouted at the weeping Jacob.

Jacob looked at the herdsmen, taking two steps toward his accusers. Immediately, they jumped to their feet and fled for their lives, fearing the strong man who removed the stone from the well.

"Who are you?" Rachel asked, startled by the encounter.

"I am Jacob, son of Rebecca, your father's sister," he told Rachel.

Rachel felt butterflies in her stomach; apparently the man standing in front of her was her intended husband — the innocent and honest man whom she had been told about ever since she had been a little girl.

Jacob looked at Rachel, sensing her emotion, knowing that she too recognized that he was her intended husband. "Will you marry me?" he said, feeling the words come out of his mouth as if by themselves.

Rachel was struck for a moment, joy rising in her heart contradicting thoughts about her father and sister, Leah. "It will not be that simple," she said with abysmal seriousness.

"Why?" Jacob asked, knowing that Rachel wanted to marry him.

"I do not know what your mother told you about my father, but unfortunately he is a very shrewd cheater," she said sadly.

Jacob laughed out loud, "If he's a cheater, I can be a cheater too."

"You'll be a cheater?! Are the righteous allowed to cheat?!" she asked, incredulous.

Jacob looked at Rachel: "Indeed, the righteous are allowed to deceive the deceivers. And what can he do about it?" he asked with a smile.

Rachel clarified her words, trying to crystallize the situation without having Jacob think, for a moment, that she was trying to evade his proposal. "I have a twin sister. She was born before me; therefore, she is the eldest. My father will not let me marry before her. Everything will be fine and beautiful until the wedding day; then he will put my sister in my place beneath the wedding canopy without your knowledge," replied Rachel, who knew her father all too well.

Jacob deliberated for a moment, pondering how best to manage the situation. The thought that Laban would give him his daughter Leah instead of Rachel made him feel uncomfortable.

He considered: Poor Leah is supposed to marry my brother Esau, my mother told me. If after I bought his birthright and took his blessing, I were to take the woman destined for him, surely, he would not keep quiet; he would not rest until he shed my blood like water. I'm sorry for the unfortunate woman, but I do not want to upset my brother again. I must find a solution that will prevent Laban from giving me Leah instead of Rachel.

A plan sprang to his mind, taking shape. "It seems to me that I have a solution to the problem," he said with a smile, "a code. I will tell you some codewords, and if you tell them to me at our wedding, I will know that you are my wife; if your father tries to put Leah in your place, she will not know the codewords, and I will know that she is not you!"

Rachel smiled in agreement, and Jacob began to teach her. She listened intently to what her future husband had to tell her, trying to stay focused while the shining knight of her dreams spoke to her. She was transfixed by her cousin, whose praises had been sung to her since the day she was born. Her ears tried to absorb and her mind to understand, but her heart wanted to hover towards other realms, towards the day when a son would be born to her from her future husband. She felt spiritual transcendence and freedom; she would not be forced to marry a Harranite.

"Rachel!" The words of Jacob seemed to tear her from her soaring imagination.

"Can you repeat the main points?" Rachel blushed, realizing that Jacob had noticed her drifting as he spoke.

"Yes... about... it seems to me..." She grinned in embarrassment at Jacob's captivating smile. "The name Hannah — you said it's an acronym for separating the holy portion of the dough, observing family purity and lighting candles for the Sabbath, the special commandments for a daughter of the House of Abraham."

Jacob chuckled affectionately: "There you go! I feel I should tell you what that entails..."

"By all means, it's fascinating."

For a long time, Jacob continued to describe the family customs, answering Rachel's shrewd questions, clarifying her doubts. The two sat by the well, suddenly noticing that the sun has begun to tilt to the west, heralding that in a short time darkness would come.

"I lost track of time! I have to get home!" said Rachel, jumping briskly to her feet: "Soon it will be nightfall, and I still have to bring the flock back. Father and Mother must be worried. I will run and tell my father that you have come here. I'm sure he'd be happy to see his nephew." Rachel started walking quickly, sorry she had to leave Jacob.

The door of the house was flung open, and Laban burst out of his home, running towards the well.

His daughter, Rachel, looked with a pitying smile at her father, who ran with all his might to the place where she told him Jacob was waiting.

Laban clumsily tripped over the hem of his robe, as he tried to pick up the pace. The man was about one hundred and twenty years old. Until recently he had been quite well-off, but the plague which had claimed so many of his animals had impoverished him.

He had four daughters to marry off, after all — two from his wife Adina, Leah and Rachel; and two from his concubine, Zilpah and Bilhah. The news that his daughter Rachel told him had sent a vibration through his fingers. The thought that Jacob, the son of Isaac and his sister Rebecca had reached him, made his heart rejoice.

He reflected with a smile: Many years ago, when Eliezer the servant of Abraham came here, he brought with him a huge fortune, and thanks to him I became rich. Now Abraham's grandson has come here. As far as I have heard, his son Isaac has become even richer than his father. Surely, he came here with a huge fortune!

His heart filled with joy, as he thought triumphantly: And now everything will be mine!

Laban kept running, trying not to fall on his face as he raced.

In the distance was the well, next to which stood a sturdy man, looking at the setting sun.

He wondered: Where are the camels... the slaves... the silver and gold?

Laban kept running, rejecting the notion that the man who arrived was poor. Surely, he had hidden his money somewhere!

"Jacob! My dear sister's son!" he panted as he arrived.

Jacob turned his face towards the call, smiling at the memories that came to mind from his mother's stories about her brother Laban. As Laban reached him, he thought: Just like Mother said, he probably hasn't changed at all.

Laban embraced Jacob, with ostensible love that was more paternal than avuncular; but as he did so, he patted Jacob's body, feeling for hidden riches. After a few awkward moments, his face fell, as he came up emptyhanded.

Laban moves away from Jacob a little, examining him with his narrowed eyes: "Let's go to my house, it's almost nightfall. When we get to my house, tell me how and why you have come here," he said in disappointment. As they walked toward the house, he thought: Maybe at least he'll marry Leah, so I'll have one less mouth to feed.

Weeks passed, and Laban's mood had gone from disappointment to resentment. Angrily, he watched his nephew sit down at the table, reflecting: He's been sitting at my house for a month now. He eats, he drinks, he sleeps, all at my expense — and all he does is graze the sheep for a few hours a day! I must formulate a plan on how to get something out of it! At the very least, he must properly work!

Laban hesitated, musing: Right now, he works for me for free, which means he is not liable for any animal which gets lost or dies; but if I pay him, he will be liable. And I will keep him working for the rest of his life!

"My friend," Laban said to Jacob sweetly, "you have been with me for a month, working hard all day with the sheep... I do not think it is right and proper that you work for me just for room and board. I think you deserve a salary for your hard work."

Jacob looked at his uncle, amazed at the fairness he radiated.

"That's all right, uncle, I don't need a salary. I'm happy to do it," he replied affectionately.

"No, it's wrong, my friend. You have to tell me what your salary should be."

Jacob lowered his eyes. Heart trembling, he thought: Maybe this is the moment I've been waiting for.

"If you really want to give me a salary for my work, I do not want money. All I want is a wife. I will work for you for seven years for your younger daughter Rachel," Jacob said emphatically.

Laban smiled slyly, happy at killing two birds with one stone. Not only would Rachel be married off, but he would also make Jacob his employee, liable for the lambs. "With great joy, my friend, I will give you my daughter's hand in marriage."

"Not any daughter, I mean Rachel!" insisted Jacob, remembering what his younger cousin had told him about her father's wiles.

"Certainly, I will give you Rachel as a wife!"

"Not some woman named Rachel from the marketplace, but your daughter Rachel," Jacob said grinning, trying to seal all the loopholes.

"Rachel my daughter, of course, she will be your wife!" Laban smiled with narrowed eyes.

"Your younger daughter Rachel! You will not switch their names!"

"Do not worry, dear boy! I will give you my younger daughter Rachel as a wife, once you have served as my shepherd for seven years."

Jacob nodded. "Agreed."

Laban smiled at his good fortune. "Adina!" he shouted through the door at his wife, "Bring us some wine. We shall toast to the success of this fine match."

The years passed quickly, day after day and night after night. Winter, spring, summer, and autumn alternated rapidly. Time ceased to have meaning for Jacob; now that he had an end date, nothing else mattered as he looked forward to the moment when

Rachel would become his wife. Every hour, every minute brought him closer to that blessed occasion.

In the meantime, he fulfilled the terms of his contract diligently. He cared for the lambs as if they were his infant children. Soon, they grew into rams and ewes, and they began to have their own young. The flocks of sheep were fruitful and multiplied, and soon the extra ones were traded for cattle and goats. Busy with his work, Jacob occasionally sent his fiancée Rachel gifts through her father.

The time was approaching, another year... half a year... a month... a week... a day...

"The time has come; let me have your younger daughter Rachel, as you promised me," Jacob said to Laban with a smile.

"I will gladly give her to you, my friend. You know that I love you in my very soul and that from the day you came to me I have encountered only good things. When you arrived, I only had my four daughters — Leah and Rachel, Bilhah and Zilpah — but since you have come, I have had three sons: Beor, Elib, and Moresh. In your merit, I have vast flocks and herds," Laban smiled back at Jacob. "A week from today, we will hold a bridal party in honor of the doubly joyous occasion. My daughter and my nephew are getting married!"

Chapter Forty-Four

The Switch

"La-la-la, lee-ah!! La-la-la, lee-ah!! La-la-la, lee-ah!!" The shouts of joy filled the huge tent set up in the heart of Harran. All the people of the city came to make merry, dancing and rejoicing amid the spectacular wedding feast prepared by Laban.

Jacob wandered among the many participants, amazed at the kindness they had done with him to share in his joy.

"Why have you paid me the honor of coming to my wedding?" he asked one of the guests.

"We all know that it is thanks to you that we have plenty of water. Since you came here, we have faced no drought or thirst. You have rewarded our people with kindness, so we come to repay that kindness to you," said the man, patting Jacob affectionately on the shoulder.

«La-la-la, lee-ah!! La-la-la, lee-ah!!» he shouted, joining the circle of dancers.

The large orchestra fell silent as the guests turned towards the bridal canopy, covered in white silks, and decorated with colorful flowers. Twelve men carried the canopy towards the elevated stage, on which the marriage ceremony was to be held.

Jacob watches the raised canopy, his heart trembling with joy and anticipation as his fiancée being led to the stage. He had never been to a wedding ceremony held in Harran. For seven years, he had spent most of his time far away from the town, grazing the flocks amid the ownerless meadows, so he would not inadvertently steal.

The strange customs fascinated him. Boys began to extinguish the torches which had illuminated the dimness of the huge tent, and darkness began to occupy the tent.

Jacob hurriedly approached his uncle, soon to be his father-in-law. "Why are they extinguishing all the torches?" he asked, puzzled.

Laban looked at him in shock: "Come now, Jacob, do you think we are licentious people?! With us, nuptials are performed with the greatest modesty! Do you want all the people of the city to stare at your wife during the wedding?!" Laban reproved him. "The bride must also be covered with a thick veil that will hide her whole head and body! We do not present the bride to the eyes of all! She must be modest!"

"You are right..." Jacob said apprehensively, "I understand..."

"Congratulations, Laban! What a wedding you put together for us! Really well done!" said one of the guests, sloppily but lovingly embracing Laban. The intoxicated man went on: "For such a magnificent groom, it is worth spending a lot of money on the wedding. And the bride... sweeter than a honeycomb..."

He looked at his host: "Say, how much did the wedding end up costing—" He abruptly stopped, then recovered: "No matter, the important thing is for it to be a day of good fortune for all of us!"

Laban smiled to himself, remembering the day Jacob had come and said that the time had come for him to marry Rachel.

Laban gathered all the townspeople for an emergency meeting.

"Do you know that all the blessings we have enjoyed in this city are due to Jacob, who came to live with us? He stayed here for seven years because I promised him he would marry my daughter Rachel. Now the seven years are over! If so, help me make sure he stays here for another seven years. If you help, he will remain with us and we will retain our good fortune; and if not, then both he and his blessing will vanish!"

The worried townspeople promised to help in any way they could.

"I will make sure to replace Rachel with my daughter Leah. Jacob is eager to marry Rachel. So, after he marries Leah, I will agree to give him Rachel too, provided he stays here for another seven years. All you have to do is make sure he does not know that he is marrying Leah. Make sure he thinks that he is marrying Rachel."

The locals happily agreed.

"Now, listen up! We have a problem. With all of you coming to the wedding, I'm worried that someone's lips will be loosened by the liquor, and he may accidentally reveal that the bride is Leah, and then the jig is up. To keep you quiet, each of you must give me his finest cloak as collateral. That will help you control your tongues. I will make sure everything is returned in the end."

The townspeople agreed and deposited their cloaks with Laban. He promptly took their finery and mortgaged it to pay for the wedding feast and expenses.

At the wedding, Laban remarked: "Believe me my friend, it cost us a tidy sum." He laughed at the tottering guest, thinking that once the wedding was over, the townspeople would have to pay a pretty penny to get their garb back from the pawnbroker.

He thought: What, do they think me a fool? Should they eat while I pay?! Everyone must pay his share when the bill comes due! He smiled.

Turning to his son-in-law-to-be, Laban clasped his shoulders: "Calm down, son, in a few minutes you will marry your dear wife, and everything will be behind us.

"Not only that, because I love her so much, I am giving her Zilpah as a handmaid. Bilhah and Zilpah are my daughters as well, sisters to Leah and Rachel, but their mother is a concubine, so I thought it would be appropriate for little Zilpah to be the maidservant of my dear daughter who begins her life as a wedded woman today."

Laban took Jacob's hand, leading him to the stage on which the canopy had been placed.

Rachel looked at her sister, perfumed, bejeweled, and made up.

A few days earlier, Leah had come to her and told her that she was going to marry Jacob soon. Rachel felt a twinge, her heart twisting in agony. Still, she smiled lovingly at her sister, who had cried for most of her life over her bitter destiny, the fate that befell her — to marry the notorious Esau.

Rachel hugged her happy sister, knowing that for the past seven years Jacob had been sending her presents, which had been given to her sister Leah. Tears streamed liberally down her cheeks, wetting her dress.

The groom, escorted by his father-in-law-to-be, arrived in the dark, feeling his way towards the canopy beneath which the bride was standing. The cries of the happy crowd acclaimed: "La-la-la, lee-ah!! La-la-la, lee-ah!! La-la-la, lee-ah!!"

The next morning, the sun rose over the sleeping household. Its rays penetrated the door of Jacob's tent, as the rooster's call roused him.

Jacob opened his eyes lazily, allowing himself to remain in his bed for a few moments. The memory of his wedding night comes to mind: "Rachel remembered the details of our secret code," he thought with a smile. "Lucky I gave her those signs, because I could not light the candle at night, since it was the Sabbath," he thought as he relished another brief moment of his matrimonial repose.

His eyes opened in astonishment as he realized the woman lying in his bed was not Rachel, as he had thought, but her sister Leah. Jacob jumped out of bed as if a snake had bitten him, staring in horror at the woman waking up with a smile from her sleep.

"What are you doing here?" he asked, trying to hide the deep shock.

Leah laughed happily at her upset husband: "Did you forget we got married yesterday?"

Jacob felt embarrassed and confused. Suddenly and sickeningly, the realization dawned that the strange formula the people of the city had been chanting all night — "La-la-la, lee-ah!" — was an indirect taunt, hinting to him that the woman marrying him was not Rachel but her sister. "But I called you Rachel last night, and you answered me," he said in amazement.

Leah smiled affectionately. "Father said that you have a bizarre custom. When your father would ask you if you were Esau, you would respond, 'It is I. Your firstborn... Esau.' So, if you were to ask me if I were Rachel, I was to respond: 'It is I. Your beloved... Rachel.'"

Jacob tried to smile, understanding that there was no way to undo what had been done; Divine Providence clearly wanted him to marry Leah as well.

"I have some affairs to tend to, but I will be back soon," he said to his new bride as he left the tent.

Jacob burst into his father-in-law's tent.

Laban was splayed across several cushions nursing a hangover, but he still had a self-satisfied grin on his face as he turned to his son-in-law. His plan had gone off without a hitch!

"Why did you trick me?" Jacob said angrily to his father-in-law.

Laban laughed with pleasure: "Sit down, son! You do not need to be upset!" he said, directing his son-in-law to sit on the large pillow lying in front of him.

"What did you do to me?! I worked with you for Rachel!" Jacob objected, trying not to shout out of anger.

"Sit down, my friend! I told you that you do not need to be upset! We can settle this affair with no trouble," grinned Laban, ignoring his son-in-law's anger.

Jacob sank into his cushion, knowing that he would not be able to outmaneuver the man who had expertly robbed him blind.

"Now listen to me, my dear son-in-law. I do not know if you are aware of the laws that exist in Harran, but here we do things in the proper order. The first to be born must be the first to be wed as well. I know you wanted to marry Rachel, but Leah's nuptials were a necessary prerequisite. So, I thought it would be best to take Leah first, and after Leah's bridal week, you may marry Rachel. And even if there were no such law in the country, would you want my beloved daughter, Leah, to marry a man like your brother Esau?!" said Laban in shock.

"But I..." Jacob tried to counter his argument.

"Don't tell me 'but'!" Laban looked sharply at Jacob: "I know what you did to your brother Esau: you took his birthright and his blessing. Well, if you bear the title of the firstborn, then you should marry the firstborn, Leah. Perhaps you think that the second may easily take the place of the firstborn, but we do not act that way here. You are certainly in no position to teach me about propriety and honesty, son!" Laban looked at Jacob with burning eyes. Jacob was silent as he accepted the judgment, knowing that this was the sentence for his crimes.

"Now that we understand each other, and so you do not think I'm mad at you, I'll happily let you marry Rachel too. As I said, after you finish Leah's wedding week, you can marry Rachel, provided you work for me for another seven years, my dear son-in-law. And so, you know that my heart holds nothing against you and Rachel, I will give Bilhah as a handmaid to Rachel," said Laban, settling a satisfied smile upon his face.

Jacob also tried to put a smile on his face: "So may it be," he mumbled. Inside, he was torn. He knew it was not the Creator's will for a man to take two sisters as wives at the same time. He said to himself: Nevertheless, I must marry Rachel!

After all, he knew that the prohibition had not yet been promulgated; it would only be binding in the future, for his descendants. *And you shall not take a woman to her sister, to be a rival to her, to uncover her nakedness, beside the other in her lifetime.*

Leah's bridal week passed, and Jacob married Rachel in a very small ceremony. The large crowd that had come to celebrate his first nuptials avoided the second wedding, knowing this time that attending the feast would cost them a lot of money.

CHAPTER FORTY-FIVE

Tribes

R ain poured down on the tents in sheets, the raucous raindrops muffling the choking cry.

Jacob looked tenderly but despondently at his weeping wife; he wanted nothing more than to relieve the pain of the woman he loved, who was desperate to bring children into the world. Tears came to his eyes as he saw her agony, his heart twisting in empathy.

"Bring me children!" she demanded of her husband, through a curtain of tears. *"And if not, I am dead!"*

"Please, dear, do not cry, I am sure we will soon have children," Jacob said in an attempt to lift the spirits of his aching wife.

Rachel was overcome by sobbing, even as she lobbed an accusation at her husband: "It's easy for you to talk! It does not hurt you!" Rachel observed scathingly. "You have three sons from my sister Leah already—Reuben, Simeon, and Levi — and another on the way! You do not know what it means to have no infant to cradle in your arms!" she protested, confronting her bitter fate.

Jacob feels a rising anger within him. More than a decade since they had met, didn't Rachel know that he was wholeheartedly devoted to her, his beloved ewe? All he wanted was to give her what she lacked! He acknowledged that her grief was real and justified, but he also knew that he wasn't the proper address for her claims. *"Am I in the stead of the Lord, preventing you from bearing the fruit of your womb?"* he asked, trying to counteract her pain with his anger, borne of his own distress.

Rachel's weeping swelled, at her husband's insensitive and angry rejoinder: "Is that how Isaac your father responded to your mother?"

Jacob tried to overcome the grief that gripped him in the face of his wife: "After all, I have sons, as you said; while my father, Isaac, had no sons."

"Your grandfather, Abraham, had sons, and yet he prayed that he would have a son with Sarah," she complained with bitter tears.

Jacob thought for a moment: "You are right, but he got a son from his wife Sarah only after she brought him her slave. She brought her rival into her house; that is why she bore a child."

Rachel looked at her husband, trying to calm the storm within her, realizing that although she had helped her sister replace her and marry Jacob, such an act done before the marriage was not similar to such an act performed afterwards. "Is that it? *Go in, please, to my handmaid; she may bear children on my knees, that I too shall be built up through her!"*

In the next year-and-a-half, Jacob's family doubled, as three more sons were born.

First, Leah gave birth to a fourth son: *"This time I will thank (odeh) the Lord,"* said Leah jubilantly, calling her son Judah.

Then, Bilhah bore Jacob a son. "Dan will be his name!" Rachel said happily, *"For the Lord has judged (dan) me, and He has also listened to my voice, and he has given me a son."*

Bilhah went on to have another son. *"With mighty wrestlings (naphtulei) have I wrestled (niphtalti) with my sister, and have prevailed,*" Rachel said happily, calling the second son of her handmaid Naphtali.

In the meantime, Leah became distressed that she had not become pregnant since Judah's birth. Following her sister's example, she too gave her handmaid to Jacob. Thus, even while Bilhah was pregnant with Naphtali, her full sister Zilpah became pregnant herself. Her firstborn was born just a month after Naphtali, and Leah called him Gad, lucky number seven.

Soon after, as the weather grew warm again and the wheat was being reaped in the fields, little Reuben came back to his mother's tent one day bearing a gift: mandrakes, which filled the space with a pleasing aroma.

"Mother, look what I found in the field!" he exclaimed happily, handing his mother the sweet-smelling plant.

Leah happily hugged her eldest son, stroking his head with love; but the scene was soon interrupted by Rachel, who had noticed her nephew's discovery. After all, the young boy could not know that his find was not only aromatic, but an aphrodisiac. Rachel had found some measure of fulfillment through the birth of her handmaid's sons, but she still found herself struggling with the fact that she had not merited to go through childbirth herself. Enthralled by the scent, she was determined to get the mandrakes for herself; but would Leah give up the prize so easily?

Tragically, the clandestine competition between the sisters had worn away the close sororal relationship they had once shared; now they seemed distant and disconnected, each feeling devalued and disrespected.

Rachel felt betrayed by her husband, the love of her life, who fathered one son after another with her full sister and two half-sisters; while she felt worthless and aimless, a fifth wheel while Jacob, Leah, Bilhah, and Zilpah trundled on their way. All Rachel wanted was healthy, happy offspring; but if Divine Providence would not grant her that, what sins must she have committed to be punished so?

Leah also felt wronged, in a different way. She, after all, was Jacob's first wife, but not his first love; even after Leah had borne him four sons, Rachel still came first in his heart. Leah could not overcome the realization that her husband still preferred to be with her sister, who had stolen his heart.

Leah smiled as Rachel barged in; trying to bridge the chasm between them.

"Give me, please, of your son's mandrakes," Rachel begged, her eyes full of tears as she gazed at the treasure in Reuben's hands.

Leah felt a twinge in her heart. Two years had passed since Judah's birth, and she still had not managed to become pregnant again. She felt a deep yearning to eat the fruit of the mandrakes, known for their blessing of fecundity. After all, if her sister were to bear a child to Jacob, he would only love her all the more, increasing Leah's alienation. It made her fiercely protective of the prize her firstborn had discovered. She replied, with a ferocity that surprised even her: *"Is it a small matter that you have taken away my husband? And would you take away my son's mandrakes also?"*

Rachel's retort was businesslike: *"Therefore he shall lie with you tonight for your son's mandrakes."* Even though it was her night to spend with Jacob, it would be a small price to pay for the aphrodisiac.

"Very well," said the older sister, sealing the deal with her younger sister.

The sun had set, and Jacob made his way home in the gloaming of twilight. He was exhausted from a long day with the flocks in the pasture, but he was still thinking about the day's work and planning for tomorrow; he was committed to being the best shepherd, to honor his commitment to his father-in-law and provide for his family, now a dozen members strong. "Surely everyone is already asleep," the thought came to his mind. He led his donkey past Leah's tent, toward Rachel's tent, where he was supposed to spend the night. The animal was tired as well, eager to have its evening meal of hay and get some rest.

The door to Leah's candlelit tent suddenly flew open, and she emerged, dressed, and adorned spectacularly. Tenderly, she spoke to her husband. "*You must come into me. For I have surely hired you with my son's mandrakes,*" she whispered to Jacob, with a smile.

Even though Leah had surrendered her mandrakes, she soon found herself busy with more babies than she could carry.

First, Zilpah had a child to join little Gad. Leah named him Asher, explaining: "*Happy am I (be-oshri) for the daughters will call me happy (isheruni).*" Even as she held newborn Asher, she knew that within her womb, a fifth son was growing.

Indeed, months later, she would once again have a child from her own body, Issachar. "*God has given me my hire (sechari), because I gave my handmaid to my husband.*"

Within a year, a sixth son was born to Leah. She called him Zebulun. "*God has endowed me with a good dowry; now will my husband dwell with me (yizbeleini), because I have borne him six sons.*" She was certain that Jacob would live with her from now on, as she had borne him a half-dozen sons.

However, a few months later, Leah sat in her tent with her hands on her stomach. She was pregnant again, but this time the thought of childbirth filled her with anxiety rather than anticipation.

It was known in their household that Jacob was destined to have twelve sons. Ten had already been born. She herself had six children on her own, plus two each from Bilhah and Zilpah. The thought that her little sister had not yet borne fruit of her own womb brought tears to her eyes.

She addressed God in prayer. "Master of the Universe, twelve sons are to be born to my husband; I have given birth to six and the two handmaids have given birth to two each. If I have another son, then my sister's lot will be less than that of the handmaids' — just one son. She was the one who was always destined to be the wife of Jacob: the older ought to marry the older, the younger ought to marry the younger — that's what they always told us. Please, Master of the Universe, make the fetus within me turn into a daughter rather than a son."

Tears washed down Leah's face, pity for her younger sister, as her supplication soared heavenward.

When the time came, Leah gave birth to a daughter, Dinah. She knew that the case (*din*) she had made for her sister before God had been decisive.

Shortly after the arrival of Dinah, a twelfth child was born to Jacob — this time from Rachel, after seven barren years.

The era of sadness and heartbreak was at an end, leaving Rachel embracing newborn Joseph. Rachel announced, through tears of happiness, "*God has taken away (asaf) my reproach.*" A prayer rose from the depths of her heart: "*May the Lord add (yoseif) to me another son.*"

Chapter Forty-Six

Laban's Schemes

A smile of contentment filled Laban's plump face as Jacob approached. Laban, aged and fleshy, was sprawled on quilts embroidered with silver and gold threads. Wealth and economic well-being were evident in every detail of his great sitting room, announcing his stupendous wealth to all who entered. The table was laden with plates and bowls filled with remnants of the last meal, but the next meal was already rapidly approaching.

Laban was happy to see his son-in-law, expecting more good news from him. After all, every time Jacob reported, it was to describe quantitative and qualitative increase among the Aramean's sheep, cattle, and goats.

"Congratulations, my dear son-in-law, on the baby born to you and Rachel!" Laban said with a smile, trying to make an effort, as if he intended to rise to honor the approaching Jacob.

Jacob looked at his father-in-law, repulsed by the man who spent all his days eating, drinking, and sitting in the same place. He tried to put a smile on his face for the man whose daughters he had married. "Thank you very much, my dear father-in-law, you do not have to get up. Our joy is sublime and complete now that Rachel has given birth."

"Sit down, my friend. What have you come to tell me?" His eyes sparkled with lust for lucre. Jacob laughed out loud, trying to disguise the disgust he felt at the glint in Laban's eyes, knowing that the Aramean already had more money at his disposal than he would ever be able to spend. "Nothing special; there are now about a thousand more animals among your flocks, but that does not matter, neither adding nor taking away," he said, knowing that his statement would shock his stingy father-in-law a little.

"A thousand sheep do not matter?! They are worth a fortune!" Laban sputtered.

Jacob chuckled lightly: "If you do something with them, then they are worth a fortune; if they simply stay put, it's just busywork. Still, that's not why I have come to you, my dear father-in-law," a genuine smile spread across Jacob's face. "I came to you to remind you that my term of service expires today. The second period of seven years, which you demanded that I work for your daughter Rachel, have come to a conclusion. Do not worry, I also completed the two weeks of my wedding days with Leah and Rachel."

Laban looked at Jacob anxiously, feeling that the days of wealth and serenity he had enjoyed for the past fourteen years were at an end. "So, what do you want to do?" he asked, astonished; it had totally slipped his mind that Jacob's service had always been limited in time.

"What we agreed on," Jacob replied triumphantly in the face of Laban's downcast expression.

"*Give me my wives and my children for whom I have served you and let me go; for you know my service wherewith I have served you.* You know that I have honored the terms of the contract impeccably, and that I have done my work faithfully."

Laban shuddered at the thought that his good-luck charm was about to disappear. What, was he supposed to run his own business? How could even he begin to do so?

He thought to himself: I must speak to him gently; perhaps I can convince him to stay for bit longer.

Laban cleared his throat, trying to find the words which would please his son-in-law: "*If now I have found favor in your eyes, I have observed the signs, and the Lord has blessed me for your sake.*" Surely Jacob would approve of his use of the name of Jacob's God, "*Appoint me your wages, and I will give it.*" he said flatteringly. "Had I more daughters, but I have given you four already, and I have no more to give away," he declared with a lewd smile.

Jacob, knowing his father-in-law's nature, ignored his sarcastic remark: "You know that I have served you faithfully for fourteen years. Before I arrived, you had nothing but a handful of lambs, but now they have increased and multiplied. The Lord has blessed you for my sake, as you admit. So now, I have to look out for my own house."

"What would you ask for as a gift?" said Laban in an attempt to keep Jacob in his home.

"I do not seek a gift," Jacob said.

"Please tell me how much you deserve, and I will pay you for your work," Laban tried again.

Jacob rejected the offer. "I do not want a set salary; I want a share in the blessing you receive, so my household and my family will be provided for."

"Then what do you want?!" said Laban angrily, feeling that the treasure of his household was receding from his grasp.

"*If you will do this thing for me, I will again feed your flock and keep it. I will pass through all your flock today, removing from there every speckled and spotted one, and every dark one among the sheep, and the spotted and speckled among the goats; and of such shall be my hire. So shall my righteousness witness against me hereafter, when you shall come to look over my hire that is before you: every one that is not speckled and spotted among the goats, and dark among the sheep, that if found with me shall be counted stolen."*

Looking at his father-in-law with a smile, he summed up: "Your name is Laban, meaning 'white,' so you may keep all the white sheep."

"And what of the goats? Will you leave me only the ones with white markings? Our goats are usually black!"

"Indeed, so you may keep all the fully black goats. I will take the ones with white markings."

"So, your wages will be limited to the sheep with dark markings, born of white sheep, and the goats with white markings, born of black goats?" Laban asked in amazement. He could not believe his luck; it was the way of the world for animals to have offspring resembling the parents.

"Yes, indeed!" Jacob said confidently.

Laban got up with great difficulty: "Let it be as you say, my friend," he said, happily shaking Jacob's hand. He reflected that Jacob would spend many more years working for him if his only wages were to be the sheep and goats with unusual markings.

Laban inspected all of his flocks that day, removing all the white sheep and black goats; he also selected for himself the strongest animals, leaving the weak and sickly for Jacob.

Jacob looked at the sparse flocks Laban had left him. A light smile played on his lips knowing his father-in-law's covetousness and his desire to deprive Jacob of his deserved fee. "Now is the time to act for my home," he thought with a grin.

And Jacob took him rods of fresh poplar, and of the almond and of the plane-tree; and peeled white streaks in them, making the white appear which was in the rods. And he set the rods which he had peeled over against the flocks in the gutters in the watering-troughs where the flocks came to drink; and they conceived when they came to drink. And the flocks conceived at the sight of the rods, and the flocks brought forth streaked, speckled, and spotted. And Jacob separated the lambs — he also set the faces of the flocks toward the streaked and all the dark in the flock of Laban — and put his own droves apart and put them not to Laban's flock. And it came to pass, whenever the stronger of the flock did conceive, that Jacob laid the rods before the eyes of the flock in the gutters, that they might conceive among the rods; but when the flock were feeble, he put them not in; so, the feebler were Laban's, and the stronger Jacob's.

Six years into the new arrangement, one night, Laban ordered his son Beor to take some white sheep and hide them among Jacob's flock.

"What do you want to give him presents for, Father?" asked Beor in amazement.

Laban looked at his son angrily: "Nincompoop! You think this is a gift?! Tomorrow I will visit his flocks and innocently 'find' the white sheep which are supposed to be mine. Then I can claim that he's a thief and fine him for breaking our contract. Do you understand? "

Beor smiled sheepishly at his father: "Yes, Father."

"This Jacob annoys me!" Laban said to Beor furiously, "I do not understand how he's managed it, but he already has hundreds of animals of his own. People used to come buy sheep from me, and now everyone goes to Jacob, they claim my sheep look lean and paltry compared to his sheep. He does business all the time. He sells his sheep and buys male and female slaves, camels, and donkeys! I used to be the richest man in the country, but he surpassed me long ago. I cannot begin to consider how far he may go if he continues at this pace. In less than six years he has become the richest man I have ever known, and soon he will be even richer than the king. Now go and do what I've told you. Maybe I can incriminate him in this way; then people will stop trusting him and come to do business with me again."

Beor obeyed the commandment of his father.

However, the next time Laban went to inspect Jacob's flock, he couldn't find the sheep he had sent with Beor. The flocks were moved at night by unknown hands back to Laban's pasture — a full three days' travel away.

That night, Jacob fell into a deep sleep after his long day of work. In his unconscious state, he heard the Voice of God: "Return to the land of your fathers, and to your kindred; and I will be with you."

Jacob awoke thrilled. For two decades, he had not experienced the blessing of prophecy. Between living an a foreign land and working himself to the bone, he had nearly lost the desire to be vouchsafed a vision from God. The sweat dripping down his body and the slight tremor of his hand made it clear to him that it was a true prophecy, not his imagination. He realized that being close to the evil Laban had deprived him of the closeness to God he yearned for with all his soul; clearly, it was time for him to take action, urgently.

Rachel and Leah made their way to the field, the place where Naphtali told them to come, at his father's request. The distance that had existed between the sisters has dissipated after the birth of Joseph. Leah and Rachel had returned to the relationship they had once had, accepting their reality with love. Leah was the mother of most of Jacob's children, while Rachel was the love of his life. The two women worked through their issues together, until they could accept their respective roles.

"I wonder why Jacob asked us to come to the field, I hope everything is fine," Leah told her sister with a little worry.

Rachel held her sister's arm in encouragement: "I'm sure everything is fine. Since Jacob has come here, everything has been good."

"Yes, you're right, but I still do not understand why he called us to the field. Why couldn't he talk to us at home?" Leah's voice sounded apprehensive.

"Apparently, he has something confidential to tell us, and the walls have ears. Namely, those of our dear brothers, Beor, Elib, and Moresh." Rachel laughed out loud, "When I said everything turned out well, I did not mean them." Rachel and Leah laughed, continuing to make their way towards their husband.

Jacob was waiting in the field for his wives, knowing the urgency of the matter, hoping that his wives would not procrastinate in the face of the trouble that was sure to come their way.

Rachel and Leah came to Jacob, looking down out of reverence, feeling as excited at the meeting as they were every time they met him.

"Thank you for coming," Jacob told his wives, marveling at how fortunate he was to have married these two righteous women. "I must talk to you about something very important."

Jacob thought of how to arrange his words so that they would be willingly accepted by his wives.

"I see your father's countenance, that it is not toward me as beforetime; but the God of my father has been with me. And you know that with all my power I have served your father. And your father has mocked me and changed my wages ten times; but God did not allow him to harm me. If he said thus: The speckled shall be your wages; then all the flock bore speckled; and if he said thus: The streaked shall be your wages; then bore all the flock streaked."

Jacob looked at his wives to gauge their reaction. Rachel and Leah were silent, knowing the obstacles their father had placed before their husband, constantly trying to thwart his enterprise and cheat him. They had never told him about the anger and resentment they felt towards their father, so as not to cloud his spirit.

"Thus, God has taken away the cattle of your father, and given them to me."

Jacob continued in lieu of the agreement he saw from his wives. "As I was dreaming in my sleep, God Himself spoke to me, announcing that He had seen everything I have done."

Jacob saw his wives' expressions change. They had always known about Jacob's prophetic experiences, but the thought that God had spoken to him directly the previous night and now they would hear the Divine Word inspired awe in them.

He quoted the Lord's message: "*I am the God of Bethel, where you did anoint a pillar, where you did vow a vow to Me. Now arise, get you out from this land, and return to the land of your nativity.*" How would his wives respond to this divine command?

Rachel and Leah looked at Jacob, and a smile appeared on their faces: "*Is there yet any portion or inheritance for us in our father's house? Are we not accounted by him strangers? For he has sold us and has also quite devoured our price. For all the riches which God has taken away from our father, that is ours and our children's. Now then, whatever God has said to you, do.*"

Jacob looked at his wives happily, grateful for his fate.

Rachel laughed happily, rejoicing at the idea of leaving the rotten environment they lived in for a new place: "The sooner, the better!"

The preparations were made quietly. It was to their advantage that there were constant comings and goings in Jacob's camp, with merchants and traders regularly making their way there. The four wives, with the help of their little ones, packed all their belongings, careful not to inadvertently take anything which didn't belong to them. In a few days, Laban would be leaving the main house to celebrate the shearing season with his workers, giving them a golden opportunity to slip away.

Finally, the day arrived, and the good news that Laban had gone out to his flock passed from woman to woman. In a short time, Jacob's camp was ready for the journey towards the land of Canaan, waiting only for daybreak.

"You must do it!" Rachel commanded herself as she crept silently to her father's house. "You have nothing to fear from the teraphim; they really have no actual power whatsoever!" she thought, in an attempt to overcome the fear of the act she was about to do.

Rachel entered the dark room, where her father used to bow before his god. The embalmed head of a slaughtered firstborn; under the tongue of the head Laban put a golden plate, on which he wrote impure incantations, which made it speak. The teraphim would reveal to Laban the future, and then he would actually bow to his handiwork.

"I believe wholeheartedly that there is no power in the world other than the Creator, may His name be blessed!" Rachel repeated to herself, as she entered the dim room. Candles, lit by the sides of the teraphim, dimly illuminated the horrible sight.

Rachel breathed deeply, bucking up her courage to do the deed. "I have to do it! Even though he's evil, he's still my father; I have to get him to stop messing with this nonsense! An old man who bows to a piece of preserved meat! Maybe even now the teraphim will tell him where we are going." Rachel took out the thick sack she had brought. Feeling disgusted, she pushed the teraphim into it, feeling the bile rising in her throat at the thought of the mummified head she was holding. She ran to the camel and buried the sack in the saddlebag.

The expedited journey began — next stop: the mountains of Gilead, east of the land of Canaan!

Jacob hastened his servants, who led the many flocks. Each servant grazed a small herd, so that he could drive them as fast as possible. Each maidservant led a limited number of cargo-laden donkeys or camels. The wives of Jacob were in charge of the care and welfare of the children. With military precision, each member of the camp knew their exact role in the procession.

"I have to hurry, as much as possible!" Jacob thought in his heart, "Laban's place is three days away from Harran. Surely, as soon as we leave the camp, a messenger will be sent to tell him that we have fled; he would not want to let us go with all our possessions. He would surely chase us to try to stop us from leaving Harran."

Jacob led his people as quickly as he could, over the Euphrates River and towards Canaan. Over the course of seven days, urged on and encouraged by Jacob, the camp managed to make its way from Harran to Gilead. However, by that time, Jacob's worst fears had been realized: Laban had received word of their departure, mustered his own force — composed solely of hardened men — and caught up to his fugitive family.

"They are encamped on the other side of the mountain," the tracker told Laban. "Within an hour we can reach them. It will be dark soon, and we will be able to surprise them at night and finish them off," he said, rubbing his hands together happily at the promise of loot.

"No, we will stay here until the morning, and then we will go out to their camp," Laban told his men, who watched him covetously. "Do not forget that my daughters are there, and they must not be harmed! There can be too many mistakes at night, and I don't want that. We are all very tired after this day of pursuit. In just one day, we covered the ground that took them a week! Also, this is Jacob we must confront, and he is no fool. We need to be rested and ready!" Laban turned his gaze on the great camp around him — the dozens of warriors he had gathered in Harran after returning to his city, when the messenger arrived to tell him that Jacob had fled with all his family and belongings. "We will retire now, and tomorrow morning we will face Jacob."

The first rays of the sun awoke the camp. Jacob oversaw the camp as it began to wake, facing the day when they would cross the Jordan into his ancestral home, land of Canaan. The bustle in the camp increased, as the diligent women ordered the manservants and maidservants to pack everything up and load the luggage on the camels and donkeys.

Then the sound of galloping cavalry froze the people in their place. Everyone's eyes raised to the cloud of dust rising from the horses' hooves. Jacob motioned for his servants to gather around him, the women and servants gathered the children, getting ready to protect them with their bodies.

The cavalry stopped within touching distance of Jacob. Old, clumsy Laban dismounted with uncharacteristic grace, approaching Jacob with a sober look. Jacob tried to put a smile on his face, to greet his frowning father-in-law in peace.

Laban angrily ignored his son-in-law's conciliatory smile, turning red with anger at Jacob's serene grin. *'What have you done, that you have outwitted me, and carried away my daughters as though captives of the sword? Why did you flee secretly, and outwit me; and did not tell me, that I might have sent you away with mirth and with songs, with tabret and with harp; and did not suffer me to kiss my sons and my daughters? Now have you done foolishly!"*

Jacob watches his father-in-law calmly. The situation could very easily deteriorate into bloodshed, he knew; he was a little surprised at the unnatural restraint inherent in Laban's words. Laban's blood boiled, it was plain to see, but he stayed his hand. Jacob wondered why.

"*It is in the power of my hand to do you hurt...*" he warned, pointing to the cavalry regiment with him.

Silently, Jacob thought: Then why don't you? What stops you from trying to do so?

"*...but the God of your father spoke to me last night, saying: Take heed to yourself that you speak to Jacob neither good nor bad.*" A shudder passed through Laban as he recounted this,

The smile on Jacob's face widened, knowing that Laban would not dare to try and hurt him and his family after his nighttime revelation.

He thought: Well then, what is your purpose in coming here?

He kept on smiling; Jacob knew that Laban knew his own powerlessness.

"Now you surely went because you surely missed your father's house — but why did you have to steal my gods?" Laban shrieked the accusation, realizing the absurdity of invoking the divinity of a god impotent to protect itself.

A burst of laughter rose from Jacob's servants in the face of the stupidity that Laban displayed in his anger at the theft of his god.

Jacob looked at his servants with a smiling expression, as if reproving them. "Why, did I not tell you I was going?" he turned to Laban with a rebuke. "My dear father-in-law, don't I know you well enough?! For I feared that you would steal your daughters from me! Rest assured, whoever has your gods will not live!" he declared in shock at Laban's impudence in accusing him of theft — without knowing that Rachel had indeed stolen them.

"Go through the whole camp, look to see if there is anything I have taken from your house. If you find something, take it as you wish."

Laban looked at Jacob, debating in his heart whether to do the search: "I will do it!" he finally said, deciding to find his stolen gods.

Laban turned to the tents that were still standing. He entered Rachel's tent, rummaging and searching in every sack and package; then he moved to Leah's tent, and from there to Jacob's tent. The tens of Zilpah and Bilhah were also thoroughly inspected and investigated. Laban tried to find something that belonged to him, so that he could accuse Jacob of stealing.

Jacob signaled to his servants to start taking down the tents Laban had finished searching and to load the luggage on the camels.

"Just a minute!" Laban shouted to the servants who intended to fold up Rachel's tent.

"This is my light-fingered daughter; I may not have checked well enough," Laban thought and ran again to check Rachel's tent before it was too late.

In the meanwhile, the manservants loaded up the luggage, while the maidservants help the wives of Jacob get on their mounts. Laban, flushed from the search efforts he had made, began to examine the luggage on the camels and donkeys.

Rachel sat on her camel, trying to bring a captivating smile to her face, as her father approached to inspect her mount.

"Forgive me, my dear father, that I do not rise before you, and I do not kiss you," she said apologetically, "I have my monthlies now." Rachel saw the disgust in her father's face when she told him this.

Laban forced himself to hastily check for the teraphim which might be under his estranged daughter's body. Rachel breathed a sigh of relief when her father walked away, unsuccessful.

Jacob looked at Laban from a distance, noticing that his father-in-law was trying to find something that belonged to him in order to accuse Jacob of thievery. Each teaspoon, towel, or pillow-cover was carefully examined to see if it might have been taken from his home. Exhausted by the long search, Laban returned to Jacob, who was standing in his place, and looked at him angrily.

Jacob motioned to his father-in-law to come to a more private place, so he would not need to shame him in front of the men he had brought. Laban complied with a sad and sullen look, discouraged at his inability to find even the tiniest item from his home.

When Jacob turned around, now that they were alone, he felt his burning anger become an inferno: "*What is my trespass? What is my sin, that you have hotly pursued after me? Whereas you have felt about all my stuff, what have you found of all your household stuff? Set it here before my brethren and your brethren, that they may judge between us two.*"

Jacob held an open hand out, for Laban to present his evidence. Laban's gaze was downcast; he had no response.

"*These twenty years have I been with you; your ewes and your she-goats have not cast their young, and the rams of your flocks have*

I not eaten. That which was torn of beasts I brought not to you; I bore the loss of it; of my hand did you require it, whether stolen by day or stolen by night. Thus, I was in the day the drought consumed me, and the frost by night; and my sleep fled from mine eyes. These twenty years have I been in your house: I served you fourteen years for your two daughters, and six years for your flock; and you have changed my wages ten times."

Jacob paused, calculating: "No, it was ten times ten, a hundred times, that you changed the terms of my contract to satisfy your greed. Moreover, even though I never was at fault, I paid for any damage that befell your flock. And you would have gotten away with it!"

His eyes flashed fire, remembering the bitterness of his two decades serving Laban: *"Were the God of my father, the God of Abraham, and the Fear of Isaac, not on my side, surely now had you sent me away empty. God has seen my affliction and the labor of my hands and gave judgment last night."*

Laban, however, was not chastened, and he shot back at his son-in-law: *"The daughters are my daughters, and the children are my children, and the flocks are my flocks, and all that you see is mine; and what can I do this day for these my daughters, or for their children whom they have borne."* Laban approached Jacob, putting a hand on his shoulder convivially: "Rapprochement is all I seek!" With a conciliatory smile, he proclaimed: *"And now come, let us make a covenant, I and you; and let it be for a witness between me and you."*

Jacob looked around and noticed a huge rock; he lifted the boulder to the surprise of a Laban, as if it were a pebble. Jacob turned to his sons and to those who had come with Laban: "Come, my brothers, gather stones." The sons of Jacob raised large rocks like their father, laughing at the sight of Laban's men lifting small stones to add to the pile.

144

"These were the people we were supposed to fight?" one of Laban's men asked his friend in a whisper.

"Naphtali," cried Jacob to his son, "run, my dear, and summon the people who have come her to eat with us."

They sat down to eat with Jacob and his sons, watching the young men who displayed such strength.

"Cheers, my friend," Laban said to Jacob, waving his glass of wine with a smile. "We will call this the Heap of Witness — Jegar-sahadutha, in the language of the land of Harran."

"I will call it Galeed, in the language of my fathers," Jacob said.

Laban laughed, surrendering to the words of Jacob, *"Behold this heap, and behold the pillar, which I have set up between me and you. This heap be witness, and the pillar be witness, that I will not pass over this heap to you, and that you shall not pass over this heap and this pillar to me, for harm."*

Jacob smiled at Laban, knowing that even if Laban asked his men to fight him and his sons, they would vehemently refuse after seeing their power.

Laban approached Jacob: "Can I talk to you in private?" he asked.

Jacob got up and walked with Laban far enough away that they could not be overheard.

"Look, my friend, I have a personal request from you," he pleaded. "Please do not take more wives in addition to my daughters."

Jacob smiled at his father-in-law: "Had it not been for the ruse with Leah, I would not have taken any woman except Rachel."

Laban blushed a little: "Look... you know... with us..."

Jacob laughed at his father-in-law's embarrassment.

"You are right," said Laban, recovering, admitting his actions. "I know you're abstemious and that's the issue. I am afraid you will abstain from seeing to my daughters' personal needs, if you get my drift..." Laban smiled deceitfully at Jacob.

145

"Yes, I understand what you mean. Do not worry, I will not do it. Let's go back to the people," he said, turning to his men.

A feast of reconciliation was hosted by Jacob and his sons. At daybreak, the camp woke. Laban kissed and said goodbye to his daughters and grandchildren and took his leave.

Laban's convoy turned back to Harran, while Jacob and his camp continued on their way to the land of Canaan.

As they approached the border, Jacob's young sons were struck by fear. Before them loomed prodigious figures with glorious visages — awesome but frightful.

"Who are they?" Reuben asked apprehensively.

Jacob looked at his sons calmly: "Do not worry, my sons, these are the angels of God belonging to the land of Canaan, who have come to welcome us as we return to the land of our fathers. Because this is the camp (*mahaneh*) of God, we shall call this place Mahanaim."

CHAPTER FORTY-SEVEN

The Struggle

Laban looked around with teary eyes and gazed at his ruined house. While he had spent the night at Jacob's camp, bandits had raided his home, destroyed all his property, and plundered all his money and flocks. The smoke billowing from the sheep pens testified that the looters wanted to return him to the poverty that had prevailed in his house before Jacob came to him.

"Take this letter to the land of Canaan, and bring it to Esau, brother of Jacob," he commanded his eldest son Beor, "he will know how to deal with this ingrate that has escaped from us."

My dearest nephew,

> *I hope this finds you well. I consider you not only a kinsman, but a comrade and close friend. Unfortunately, I have to tell you about your brother Jacob, who came to my house about twenty years ago.*

> *To my sorrow and displeasure, he took my daughter Leah, who was destined to be your wife. When I told him that Leah was supposed to marry you, he told me that he had managed to take advantage of you and fraudulently take*

your birthright. Thus, he claimed, he was entitled to all the privileges of the firstborn, so Leah, my eldest daughter, had to be his wife as well.

Then — this effrontery can scarcely be believed — a week later, your brother demanded my younger daughter Rachel's hand in marriage as well. When I argued that, according to him, Rachel ought to marry you, he told me that he was the second-born brother, and therefore, as the saying goes, "older to older, younger to younger."

Of course, I pointed out the illogic of his stance. I told him that you would be outraged to hear that he had taken both my daughters; but he just laughed and said he knew "how to deal with his idiot brother." (You must forgive the phrasing, but I want to quote him accurately.)

Why did I wait so long to write? Because we were under Jacob's thumb all the time he was here; the brute kept us captives in our home. Only with his departure am I able to contact you without fear of reprisal. As for the thousands of heads of sheep, goats, and cattle he took from me — well, you know the evil of his thoughts and the malice of his deeds

I send you this letter so that you may save yourself. Beware of your brother, whose sole intention is to return to the land of Canaan to kill you and your family, so he alone can inherit your father's estate.

With great love and admiration,

Your uncle,

Laban, son of Bethuel the Aramean.

A smile came over Esau reading the letter sent by his uncle.

The thought of sweet revenge was like a strong wind at his back.

"Thank you, my dear cousin," he said to Beor with a smile, "tell your father, my beloved uncle, that I thank him very much for the letter, and that I will do my best to give my dear uncle real peace of mind

The cries of the many horses gathering in the valley brought a smile to Esau's face.

Eliphaz his firstborn was there, along with Reuel and Jeush, Jalam and Korah, his other sons. They were all eager to go to war.

Esau had found many allies outside the family as well. Promising to distribute the spoils among anyone who would join him in the attack on Jacob, he had amassed a force numbering in the tens of thousands.

"Considering the vastness of Jacob's wealth, each of these men stands to walk away with twenty or thirty animals. Not bad for a day or two of work," Esau told his sons.

"Eliphaz, among these people, I want you to find four hundred who are fit to be commanders, each of whom will organize his own men. Every hundred commanders will lead one wave, in an arrow formation, to attack Jacob's camp," Esau ordered his eldest son. "And this time I expect you to be a more responsible leader than you were twenty years ago," he warned him, a withering glance fixed on his son.

Eliphaz lowered his eyes in shame: "Do not worry, I will not disappoint you again, Father."

Jacob looked at the angels who came before him:

He thought: I must find out how Esau's feels about me, whether he still resents me or whether, over these years, he has forgiven me for what I did to him. I must know how to prepare for an encounter with him.

Shaking and trembling seized Jacob as he thought of what he was about to do.

"Forgive me, divine servants, but I have a request of you," he told the angels sent to him.

They looked at Jacob, bowing their heads as if ready to serve him happily.

"I must know what my brother is planning, whether he seeks peace or war. *Thus, shall you say to my lord Esau: Thus says your servant Jacob: I have sojourned with Laban, and stayed until now. And I have oxen and donkeys and flocks, and menservants and maidservants; and I have sent to tell my lord, that I may find favor in your sight.*" Jacob cringed at giving celestial messengers such a mundane task.

"With great joy, Lord Jacob," they said and disappeared.

The wild shrieks of the people galloping towards their promised prey echoed through the air, the sound of the horses' hooves being swallowed up in the cloud of dust rising from their wild gallop.

The warriors suddenly stopped, as terrifying, unearthly figures loomed in front of them.

"Who is Esau?" asked one of the figures, in a voice that chilled the battle-hungry men. The frightened riders pointed at Esau, who stood gawping.

"Are you Esau?!" they asked in a threatening tone.

Esau felt terror grip his heart. "Yes," he said, trying to give his voice a calm, relaxed timbre.

"Strike!" one of the figures commanded its companions.

They began beating the experienced warriors, who tried to defend themselves; but the men of war were soon shrieking and moaning in pain and grief, hopeless and helpless before the other-worldly onslaught.

Esau realized the attackers were not earthly but ethereal. What could convince angels to stop? "I am the grandson of Abraham!" he screamed desperately.

The lead angel paused for a moment to consider this. "Abraham's grandson?!" it asked in bewilderment. A moment later, it repeated the command: "Strike!" The beating resumed with more force; indeed, every blow grew stronger.

"I'm the son of Isaac!" Esau yelled, hoping his father's reputation would protect him.

The lead angel stopped, telling its companions to halt as well.

"What did you say? Are you the son of Isaac?!"

The battered Esau nodded happily, glad that his words made an impression on the angel. "Yes, I am the son of Isaac!"

"Strike!" The angel commanded with a smile, and Esau's heart was gripped by terror. The angels continued to beat Esau and his men; in fact, they seemed to do it with more relish.

"I am Jacob's brother..." Esau said, feeling his weakness and helplessness at having to mention his brother to save himself.

"Jacob's brother?!" The angel said in shock: "Why didn't you say that at first? We are very sorry, Jacob's brother. We didn't know you were Jacob's brother."

The angel motioned to its companions, telling them: "This is Jacob's brother. We must not hurt Jacob's brother."

The angels disappeared as abruptly as they had arrived, leaving the warriors overwhelmed and sorrowful.

"Come, let us be on our way," Esau told his men.

"Go on alone!" some of the warriors said, turning their horses around. "We have no desire to meet your brother's friends again."

Esau looked at the warriors who stayed with him: "They are fools! That just leaves more spoils for the rest of us. Even without them, we will easily defeat Jacob and the slaves with him," he said, trying to put a smile on his face. The warriors continued on their way, with the pains of the blows preventing them from riding wildly.

An hour passed, and to the horror of the riders, the angels reappeared. They went through the entire experience again, with the angels beating them until Esau invoked his brother's name. Then again: an hour of riding, an hour of beating. And again... and again...

"Why don't you tell them from the beginning that you are Jacob's brother?!" one of the miserable warriors demanded of Esau.

"It hurts me more to need Jacob than to accept the beatings," Esau said, knowing that repeated rounds of beatings were yet to come for him before he could confront his worst enemy.

Jacob looked around. The lazily flowing river created a relaxed and calm atmosphere for the huge camp with him. The children frolicked in the light of the last rays of the sun, unwilling to end their game as their mothers called their names.

Watching the children play, Jacob thought to himself: I must try to get Esau to refrain from going to war with me. Whatever happens, I must not let war break out. I must reconcile my brother's opinion in any way! Esau my brother loves money, that is sure. I must mollify him with an extravagant present. A gift that will satisfy him, an appropriate recompense, next to which the taking of the birthright seems insignificant."

"Listen to me carefully now," he told ten of his senior shepherds. "Each of you will take a drove to Esau."

He spent the night there, and from what he had with him he selected a gift for his brother Esau: two hundred female goats and twenty male goats, two hundred ewes and twenty rams, thirty female camels with their young, forty cows and ten bulls, and twenty female donkeys and ten male donkeys. He put them in the care of his servants, each herd by itself, and said to his servants, "Go ahead of me, and keep some space between the herds."

He instructed the one in the lead: "When my brother Esau meets you and asks, 'Who do you belong to, and where are you going, and who owns all these animals in front of you?' then you are to say, 'They belong to your servant Jacob. They are a gift sent to my lord Esau, and he is coming behind us.'"

He also instructed the second, the third and all the others who followed the herds: "You are to say the same thing to Esau when you meet him. And be sure to say, 'Your servant Jacob is coming behind us.'" For he thought, "I will pacify him with these gifts I am sending on ahead; later, when I see him, perhaps he will receive me."

In addition, he supplied each of the drovers with a pack full of gold and gems. He looked at them, hoping his scheme would work.

The shepherds returned to their master with the beasts he had commanded them to bring. Jacob moved the shepherds and the flocks across the Jabbok River.

Jacob thought to himself: I cannot rely on a miracle. I must do all I can to protect my family and my servants from what my brother Esau might do.

He went through the midst of the camp. He divided his men into two cohorts, arming the men and boys with weapons to defend themselves. "I will be in the first camp," he told his men, "and the second camp will stay away from us. Thus, if Esau fights with us, the remaining camp may escape."

Jacob thought to himself about his mother's prophecy that her two sons would die on the same day. If, God forbid, he succeeds in killing me, then he will probably die too, and at least the remaining camp may escape... I must take care not to kill him, for surely my mother's prophecy will not go unfulfilled.

Jacob surveyed his men, untrained in war but arming themselves for battle. Jacob closed his eyes, raised his heart to heaven, begging his Creator that his sins do not lead to the death of any of his people... or himself.

He was worried about his spiritual state. He had spent decades away from his parents, and decades away from the Promised Land. The knowledge that Esau, in his absence, had honored their father for the past thirty-four years was galling — would that be enough to guarantee his brother victory? Meanwhile, Jacob had just forged an alliance with the wicked Laban, which certainly must degrade his spiritual status.

All he could do was seek out God in heartfelt prayer: *"O God of my father Abraham, and God of my father Isaac, O Lord, who said to me: Return to your country, and to your kindred, and I will do you good; I am not worthy of all the mercies, and of all the truth, which you have shown to your servant; for with my staff I passed over this Jordan; and now I am become two camps. Deliver me, I beg of you, from the hand of my brother, from the hand of Esau; for I fear him, lest he come and smite me, the mother with the children. And you said: I will surely do you good and make your seed as the sand of the sea, which cannot be numbered for multitude.* He may approach me as my brother, in which case I fear his behavior will negatively influence my children and household; he may approach me as Esau, in which case I fear his violent attack against my family. Either way, Lord, you are my only hope!" he pleaded with his Creator for rescue, his eyes welling with tears.

Night fell, and Jacob decided to move his camp across the Jabbok River. He thought: If I confront Esau within the borders of the Promised Land, perhaps that will be enough to tip the scales to my benefit.

Jacob began to move his family, his workers, his flocks, and herds across the ford. It took hours, but he managed to do it. He even gave special instructions to Leah to hide Dinah away in a large chest, so Esau would not see her and desire her.

"I'll go and check one last time to see if we left anything behind," he thought as he crossed the river again. Jacob looked around the place where the tents had been pitched until recently, looking for small jugs or something left behind, thinking: When the Creator showers wealth on a person, that is a phenomenon rooted in the highest planes of spirituality. Therefore, no one should neglect their property; whatever they receive, they ought to maintain and use wisely.

Jacob was suddenly slammed hard on the ground; something had jumped on his back, knocking him to the dirt. The initial thought, that some beast of prey had attacked him, was negated when he felt two hands gripping his neck. Jacob extended his elbow back, intending to hit his assailant's side, perhaps cracking his ribs; however, the elbow hit compressed air, leaving the hands holding him as before.

He thought: What is this? How is he not hurt?

Jacob bent forward tightly, tossing the one holding him over his head. Now free, Jacob got to his feet deftly, looking up at his attacker.

The figure was cloaked in gloom, but it seemed slightly transparent. Still, the face was familiar, it was the spitting image of his brother Esau, but made out of air, smirking contemptuously at him.

The phantom quickly approached Jacob, pouncing on him with its arms outstretched toward his neck. Jacob grabbed the arms, realizing that the only way to grapple with ethereal limbs was with the power of thought, knowing that everything operated solely by the might of the Will of God. Jacob pulled the figure toward him, falling on his back to toss his assailant over him and into the dirt.

"Well done!" the surprised specter said. "Where did you learn all this from?"

Jacob looked at the misty doppelganger of his brother, keeping his silence, realizing that his opponent was not a man.

The figure approached slowly, watching Jacob's movements: "You understand you have no chance at all, don't you?"

Jacob was silent, trying to figure out what to do.

"You are a wise man; you must grasp that you have no chance of dealing with me. You are just a human being, a mortal who is lost, who will soon end his life," the figure whispered with venom. Jacob was enthralled. "Your sins will be the death of you. Every struggle is actually soul against soul; there is no true substance in the physical world. I am nothing more than the manifestation of the Will of the Creator, and I will never transgress His will! But you... human... sinful.... desirous... lustful..."

As Jacob reflected on the disheartening words, the figure suddenly leapt towards him and grabbed his body in its transparent arms. "There is no point in fighting!" he spat, leering. "Your story ends tonight!"

Jacob felt the venom seep into his heart, felt his body slacken against his assailant, feeling the surrender to despair taking over his being.

"I hope you said goodbye to your family," the spectral figure mocked him. His body grew weaker, weaker still, surrendering.

Suddenly Jacob thought: "Reuben ... Simeon ... Levi ..." His muscles, which had gone limp, suddenly grew taut. He squeezed the figure — for if it grew solid enough to hold, then he could hold it well. Firmly, tightly, forcefully, Jacob gripped the wraith harder and harder, while he loosened his wrath from his tongue: "Sin? Lust? Desire? Is that what you bludgeon me with, apparition? Know that at the age of eighty-four I married — Reuben is the product of my first encounter with a woman! Laban tried to tempt me with all the pleasures of the flesh when I was in Harran, but he never succeeded. I have legendary wealth, but I have never indulged in anything material."

Jacob felt his arms crushing, crunching, crumbling his phantasmic foe. "Do you think you are superior to me?! You do not sin because you are not capable of it! I have the ability, but all my days I have fought against the temptations which taunt me. I have never violated the Will of the Creator, nor any of His laws."

Jacob felt his assailant growing weak and desperate, searching for some vulnerability to exploit. "Oh, do you think I violated His Will when I married two sisters? I did so only once I had concluded that He Himself had decreed it!" he rebutted firmly.

"But for twenty years, you have abrogated the commandment to honor your father and mother—" the attacking apparition prodded him, trying to find a chink in his armor.

"I left because they commanded it, and I stayed away because they commanded it. What greater honor could I pay my parents then to obey their orders and the Will of their God?" He tightened his grip, keeping the specter from moving.

However, the phantom had one last trick up his sleeve. "But what of your children? What of your offspring?"

Jacob suddenly felt a burning pain in his thigh, a strong blow shaking his body. He felt that his thigh had been dislocated. "You see?" said the angel. "You may be righteous; your conduct may be impeccable... but what about your descendants? They will stray from the path, and that cuts the legs out from under you!"

Jacob felt a twinge in his heart at the thought of future failings, worse than the pain in his thigh; but after a few seconds, he refuted the angel's accusation. "You cannot hold that against me. I can only do my best, raising my children and showing them the way. I cannot be criticized for what may happen years from now. The Creator judges a man only for what he has done, not what may yet occur or what he has no control over!"

They stayed locked in their struggle for hours, with the angel indicting Jacob and Jacob defending his behavior and his virtue.

Finally, the figure turned away in terror; rays of light were flashing in the east, as the day was about to begin. "Release me, dawn is breaking!" the angel said to Jacob, "I must go up to my place and sing the morning song to the glory of God."

Jacob's grip was strengthened, as he realized that the angel could not move as long as he held him. "I will not release you unless you bless me," he said firmly. "If you are an angel who wears my brother's face, then you are his spiritual representative. Concede the blessings my father gave me, and then I will let you go."

The angel looked at the beams in the east, shaking and trembling: "Very well, what is your name?" he asked urgently.

"Jacob," he replied, bewildered.

"Your name will no longer be Jacob, but Israel, because you have struggled (sarita) with God and with humans and have overcome," he said.

"Please tell me your name," Jacob asked the angel.

Now it was the angel's turn to be bewildered: "Why do you ask my name? Everything angels do is by the commandment of the Lord. Our names change according to the missions we must fulfill."

The angel felt Jacob's grip slacken. "May all of your father's blessings come true," he said, and disappeared as he had arrived.

Jacob looked at the space in front of him, naming it Peniel, *"because I saw the Lord face to face (panim el panim), and yet my life was spared."*

Jacob began to cross the river towards his camp, the sun shining, raising the gleam of its glory on the earth. He limped along, until the sun crested the horizon.

Chapter Forty-Eight

Encounter

The relief Jacob felt after rejoining his family was short-lived, as the air was soon filled with hoofbeats and war cries. A cloud of dust could be seen approaching the camp, so large it threatened to block the sun.

Jacob knew he had to act quickly. He split his family up in in ranks: Zilpah and Bilhah with their children, followed by Leah and her children, and finally Rachel and Joseph.

Jacob thought: This presentation will answer all of the accusations Esau might throw at me. No one can object to the way I married Bilhah and Zilpah, so they will be the first to be presented to Esau, with their children. Leah was designated to be Esau's wife, but we were married due to Laban's deceit, so she must come next with her children. Finally, I will present Rachel and Joseph because my marriage to her is the most controversial, since the Lord will one day outlaw this: *And you shall not take a woman to her sister, to be a rival to her, to uncover her nakedness, beside the other in her lifetime.*

Jacob glanced at Rachel, who seemed shocked by the arrangement. "Last but not least," he whispered to her reassuringly.

Jacob advanced towards the ranks of Esau's troops, carrying a large sack containing gems and pearls. His brother rode his mount defiantly at the head of his ad hoc army; Jacob hurried, knowing that it was not out of the realm of possibility that either he or his brother — or both — would perish in the next hour.

His heart was racing; all the toil of the past and the hope for the future rested on this fateful meeting. Jacob watched his brother gallop toward him, trying to dredge up positive feelings for his wild brother. Compassion and pity filled his heart as he recalled the strange hirsute boy who was ridiculed and mocked; he searched for good points in the actions of his brother, who had been held captive by the bitterness of the heart, trying to deal with his rejection from society by committing despicable acts. Jacob thought fondly of his only brother, from whom he had been estranged for so long. He tried to feel the pain of his brother, who had never in his life tasted true love, who for ninety-seven years of his life has been despised and rejected by all those around him. He sensed his heart go out to his brother, feelings of love and brotherhood he had never felt before. He reflected: He has points in his favor. After all, even if he seeks to kill me, he never disrespected our father, but showed him the utmost honor. The way I feel for him might have an effect on his inner nature. Thinking positively about him can move him from the side of evil to the side of good. If, on high, an advocate can plead his case before the heavenly court, then repentance is always an option for him. He may yet be fully vindicated!

The army advanced until Esau brought it to a halt. He dismounted and considered his brother standing before him.

Jacob looked toward Esau and perceived an invisible barrier, the Divine Presence itself protecting him. Jacob bowed to this manifestation of God seven times, moving closer and closer to his estranged brother, feelings of mercy and compassion overwhelming him.

At the same time, Esau advanced towards his hated brother the thief, preparing to kill him with his own hands; but his legs seemed to refuse to run as fast as he wanted. His heart, moments earlier, eager to shed blood, was suddenly awash in feelings of affection and pity he had never felt before.

Esau thought: For thirty-four years my only brother lived in exile, in a foreign land, because he was afraid of me. Now he has returned! The two brothers approached each other in a storm of emotions. Closing the distance, Esau wrapped his brother in an embrace, hugging him without understanding what he was going through. The renewed desire to reconcile fought the strong desire to kill, his mouth opening wide. Bite (*neshika*) or kiss *neshicha*? Esau's mouth slammed into Jacob's neck as if it were a marble column.

The pain of Esau's cracked teeth brought back the memory of the attacking angels he had met the previous night. Tears of pain filled his eyes, his feelings a jumble. Esau burst into sobs. He realized he could not change the past, that he should accept reality as it was and try to reconnect with his only brother.

Jacob sensed the hardening of his neck, the chomping teeth. He wept gratefully for the miracle given to him, ruing his brother's offense.

For a few minutes, the crying brothers stood hugging each other, childhood memories flooding their hearts. Jacob took a step back from his brother, taking him in; he felt that his brother had relented, and that there was no way he would try to harm him or his family. His hand rose toward the camp he had left far behind, instructing them to advance. Jacob and Esau began to walk toward the approaching camp.

Esau looked up at the camp; the sight of the four women walking toward them with their children left him with his mouth open: "What?! All these are yours?!" he asked his brother in amazement, knowing that when he had left the land of Canaan he had still been single.

Jacob felt his brother's indignation at the women: "The children with whom the Lord has graced your servant," he said, ignoring part of the question.

Zilpah and Bilhah approached Esau with their children, bowing before him in submission.

After them, came Leah and her sons, and they bowed as well.

Joseph, a boy of six years old, pushed in front of his mother, obstructing Esau's view of his mother as much as his small frame allowed. He thought: My mother is very pretty; this scary man may want to grab her if he sees her!

He stretched, trying to shield her, waiting for his mother to bow down. He then, bowed down in front of her body, trying to keep her safe.

Esau demanded: 'What do you mean by all this, all whom I met?'"

Jacob felt a smile tugging at the corners of his lips. "All this" indicated that he had encountered both of Jacob's delegations, the human and the angelic. Aloud, he said: "To find favor in the sight of my lord."

Esau replied: "I have enough; my brother, let that which you have be yours."

"No, I beg of you, if now I have found favor in your sight, then receive my present at my hand; as I have seen your face as one sees the face of God, and you were pleased with me." Jacob knew it would be hard for Esau to turn down a gift; moreover, his courtly manner would make it very hard for Esau to change the tenor of the convivial encounter into a menacing one.

Esau thought: Oh, so he's met angels too? Feeling the bruises on his aching body, he reflected: my meeting with them was not as endearing as his.

"My dear brother," Jacob said to Esau, feeling his brother's greed for money, "I want to give you all my riches, all the gold and precious stones I have, if you can give me one small thing in return."

"What are you asking for?" Esau asked suspiciously.

Jacob smiled at his brother: "Before that, look what I am willing to give," he said and motioned for his servants to approach. A convoy of slaves arrived, carrying large boxes in their hands, emptying the contents at Esau's feet.

The pile of gold and precious stones left Esau gaping: "What can I give you for this?" he asked in amazement.

"Not something particularly serious. All you need to do is give up something that can be said to belong to me," Jacob scratched his forehead uncomfortably, refraining from mentioning the purchase of the birthright made many years ago. "The tomb in the Cave of the Patriarchs ..." he said, looking at his brother. "I am happy to give you all this if you merely sign a contract giving me the sepulcher."

Esau's eyes widened, his face looking as if he was about to burst out laughing: "Are you willing to give all this for a grave?!" He put his hand up to his mouth, trying to keep from openly mocking his ridiculous brother.

"Take, I beg you, the gift I bring you, because God has graced me, and because I have all," he told his brother hopefully.

"You do not need all this," Esau said, staring at the wealth piled up in front of him, picking up a good stone from the ground, looking at it with the eyes of an expert: "It's too much, brother," he whispered, quivering.

Jacob produced the contract. "Just sign it for me, my dear brother, and please take it all in return," he said, knowing that Esau could not resist the temptation.

"Oh well, if you are so insistent," Esau said, signing with a triumphant smile.

Esau called to Eliphaz, ordering him to pack up the whole pile of goods.

Esau clasped his brother on the shoulders warmly. "Brother, I am so happy that you have returned; let us not part now. Come with me to my home in Seir. *Let us take our journey, and let us go, and I will go before you."*

Jacob trembled at the thought that Esau and his unsavory companions might remain near his family for an extended period of time. Instead, he tried to reassure him that there was no need for a personal escort. *"My lord knows that the children are tender, and that the flocks and herds giving suck are a care to me; and if they overdrive them one day, all the flocks will die. Let my lord, I beg of you, pass over before his servant; and I will journey on gently, according to the pace of the cattle that are before me and according to the pace of the children, until I come to my lord to Seir."*

Esau sensed that Jacob felt uncomfortable at slowing down his older brother's progress, so he volunteered some of his men to guard Jacob's camp. He said: *"Let me now leave with you some of the folk that are with me."*

"What needed it? Let me find favor in the sight of my lord." Jacob was alarmed; having Esau's rough men in his camp would endanger his family and servants.

Esau grinned at the sight of his brother, distressed by his offer: "All right. If so, you know where I am. Come meet me, my dear brother, in Seir. I look forward to your homecoming." He motioned to his son to gather their belongings and prepare to leave. With a smile, he thought: At least I have something to pay them for their trouble.

"Come on, we're going home," he told his men, galloping off.

Jacob looked happily at the army moving away from him, happily stroking the contract lying in his lap. Feeling light and relaxed after having rid himself of the great wealth he had accumulated in Harran: "There is no blessing in wealth acquired outside the Promised Land," he thought with a smile.

Jacob and his camp remained in place, on the east bank of the

Jordan, enjoying the peace and quiet away from those who pursued them. Day after day and the camp remained in place; a house was built for the family and slaves, and stalls (*succoth*) for the flocks.

Every month Jacob made sure to send his brothers gifts, smothering his lust for revenge with lucre. For a year and a half, Jacob and his household resided in the place they named Succoth.

"The time has come to enter the land of Canaan," Jacob told his family. "The days are passing, and for some reason I have entered a state of complacency. Tomorrow we cross the Jordan."

CHAPTER FORTY-NINE

Dinah

She could hear women raising their voices in celebration and song, and the sound was irresistible.

Dinah, daughter of Jacob and Leah, ran toward the window of the house, in an attempt to see what was happening outside. An only daughter in a family of eleven boys, she was cut off from girls her age.

The city of Shechem was only a stone's throw away, but she had never set foot in it. She knew that Prince Hamor, the local ruler, allowed Jacob's family to live on the outskirts of his city — but only for the princely sum of one hundred pieces of silver.

When her brothers asked her father why he had paid such an exorbitant fee — as he did not intend to settle there permanently — Jacob replied that he wanted to build an altar to his God, to offer a sacrifice of thanksgiving for his salvation from Laban and Esau. "It is not proper that I should build an altar on land that is not mine," he told his sons. "Moreover, when we leave, I want the locals to respect this place and not destroy the altar." Jacob built the altar and offered on it his burnt offerings. "I name this altar El-elohe-Israel, God is the God of Israel," he told his sons, using the name that the angel at Peniel had told him was destined to be his for posterity: Israel.

Dinah's question was different from her brothers'; she wanted to see the city just outside the fence of their home. "Dinah, my dear," Jacob explained, "I understand that you are bored with life at home, but I am not ready for you to leave the house. The Shechemites are quite wild and uncultured. It is not for nothing that their prince is named *hamor* (donkey). From his heir — whom he named Shechem too, like the town — on down, they are uncouth and unrestrained, and who knows what mischief such miscreants are capable of?

"Consider this: as rich as the land has always been, Shechem had no public institutions, no currency, no marketplaces, no bathhouses. Then, I explained to Hamor the value of such things, and he followed my advice."

Jacob looked at his despondent daughter: "Regardless, we soon will leave this place and travel to Hebron, where your grandparents live. There, you'll be able to leave the house more."

The delightful music tempted Dinah to stick her head out of the window. She could see the groups of women, young and old, singing and playing instruments just on the other side of the fence, around the garden out front. She snuck out of the house, telling herself she would only take a look, without approaching the women. Despite her desire to obey her father, she found her legs moving as if on their own.

She thought: I just want to watch them for a bit, then I'll go back inside. Surely Father did not mean to forbid me from taking a look at the women of Shechem!

She came out of the gate of the house, watching the dancing girls with pleasure; the colorful clothes, which covered the girls from head to toe, caught the young girl's eyes. The modesty with which they were dressed was inconsistent with what her father had told her about the townspeople. The dancing and melodies brought a smile to her melancholy face; her heart, yearning for freedom, leapt. A little girl slowly approached Dinah, smiling kindly at her, the stranger who had come to live near the city. A small drum was placed in Dinah's hands.

Struggling to disobey her father, she told herself, : I'll just play a bit, then I'll go inside. They seem very nice and modest.

Dinah felt her spirit flutter as she banged the drum to the cheerful melody. A soft hand gripped her little hand, gently pulling her into the circle of dancers. The jig soothed her soul, bringing jubilation to the heart of the girl imprisoned inside her home. Dinah felt the happiness and pleasure which had been so elusive for so long, bouncing mischievously along with the tune, her eyes closed.

Then the darkness deepened; a strong hand clamped over her mouth, preventing her from screaming for help as a thick cloth was thrown over her head and body. The playing stopped at once; the stunned girl was carried off in an iron grip, toward an unknown place.

Only a few stray rays of sunlight shone into the luxurious chamber, which held a large golden bed in the center. From every corner, symbols of ostentatious wealth gleamed: gold sculptures inlaid with precious stones, walls of resplendent marble, heavy embroidered curtains covering the huge windows overlooking the big city.

On the marble floor, a girl sat, disconsolate. Her torn clothes failed to conceal her battered body and her bruised soul.

In front of the girl sat a young man, moved to tears by her sorrow. "Do not cry, my dear," he whispered to Dinah as he wiped away her tears. "I'm sorry that what I did was against your will. I understand I was wrong, but please understand me, I could not resist doing it. From the day I saw you and your family come here, I could not stop thinking about you, dreaming about you, and wanting you. I cannot explain to you what I have gone through every day, from the time I first laid eyes upon you. I could not eat and drink, I could not sleep, I could not function. I only thought of you all day and all night." The young man's voice sounded shattered. "Unfortunately, I knew that if I asked your father for your hand in marriage, he would surely refuse my request. That's why I had to send the girls to sing and dance near your house so that you'd go out to them, and I could bring you to me. I want to marry you, Dinah..."

The girl's sobbing increased, as if trying to drown out the conciliatory voice attempting to rationalize the injustice done to her. As much as she hurt, her grief was magnified by the thought of what her family would experience when they learned of the heinous offense. She smacked her own face in distress. If only she had listened to her father, could she have avoided this pain? The feelings of shame and guilt overwhelmed her.

The voice of her abductor resumed: "Please, my dear, stop crying. I am not a bad person; I will be a good husband to you. You would lack nothing in the world, neither silver nor gold, neither slaves nor maids — I would give you anything. After all, you have to get married at some point. You cannot marry one of your brothers, so you will have to marry a Canaanite anyway! I could not bear to think of some other man marrying you, so I did what I did. Now I'll speak with my father, so he can talk to your father and convince him to agree to our marriage. I will make sure my father gives yours whatever he desires: silver, gold, precious stones and pearls, oxen, goats, donkeys, horses, sheep, and camels. My father will withhold nothing, until your father grants me your hand in marriage."

Shechem son of Hamor continued to speak to Dinah for hours, trying to appease her, trying to stop her heartrending sobbing.

There was a rap on the door, and Jacob lifted his tearstained face at the sharp sound. His boys were coming back from the pasture in the middle of the day, in response to his urgent summons. He tried to stop the torrent of tears, to no avail. The eleven sons of Jacob looked at their father weeping in astonishment.

Little Joseph ran towards his father and hugged him in terror: "Father, what happened?" he asked, tears springing to his eyes at the sight of his father's, without even knowing why.

His ten brothers looked in alarm at their father, aware that real trouble had occurred while grazing their father's flock. Their eyes asked the question, as they prepared for the bitter news.

Jacob looked at his sons with a broken heart. "Dinah..." he said and his voice cracked as he was wracked with sobs.

The brothers looked at their crying father in shock: "What happened to Dinah?!" Simeon asked, feeling as if his heart would leap from his chest if some calamity had befallen his beloved sister.

The father wept with sorrow: "Shechem son of Hamor abductped her..."

"What?!" Levi shouted. "He took her?! Then I will take his worthless head!" Levi, not yet a teenager, drew his sword angrily.

"He defiled her..." Israel whispered as tears rushed down his face.

The brothers' faces flushed with rage, tears of anger on their cheeks.

"Are you sure?" Reuben probed, hoping against hope that his father had misunderstood.

"Unfortunately, yes. Prince Hamor sent me a messenger to inform me of what happened," Jacob muttered sadly. "He is coming tonight with his son to discuss the nuptial arrangements. The truth is, I do not know what to do." Hesitancy and heartache were both apparent on his face.

"This reprobate took our sister against her will, and now he wants to marry her?!" Simeon hissed angrily. "It's a funeral they ought to be planning, not a wedding!"

"We have to think before we act," Israel remonstrated with his sons. "We do not want to make the situation any worse."

"Any worse? What could be worse?" Simeon said as his body

trembled with rage. "This reprobate and his shameless father need to be executed!"

Jacob looked at his sons, seeing in their faces a consensus with their brother Simeon: "This is a catastrophe, but we have to see what constructive thing may come out of it. What has been done cannot be undone. We must at least see if we can succeed in deriving something positive from this outrage, for the greater glory of God." Israel saw the face of Simeon sour: "Simeon, my dear, we must make the best of a bad situation..."

"The best of this bad situation would be his head on a pike!" Simeon roared and stormed out of the room.

Israel looked at his other sons, knowing the strength of their character and the pain they all shared. "We must think what to do," he said, as if speaking to himself. "We must not cause bloodshed and killing. Everything that happens is by the hand of God; it is all Divine Providence. Perhaps this disaster has befallen us because I prevented Esau from seeing Dinah, for fear he might marry her! Maybe if I had married off my daughter to my own brother, she would have reformed him!"

The brothers watched their father in amazement, struggling to imagine that Dinah could have changed their uncle.

Israel recovered and raised his eyes, wiping away his tears: "I want you all to be present when Hamor and Shechem come. Until then, try to think about how we should proceed. I will try to formulate a plan too."

"I promise you, when this Hamor and his son come here, I will chop off both their heads! This reprobate has had his way with our sister, as if she were one of the loose women of his city! This dog thinks we are giving our sister to an uncircumcised brute!" Simeon looked at his brother Levi, feeling that they were of the same mind on this matter.

The two brothers huddled in the small room at the back of the house, feeling an uncontrollable tremor in their bodies.

Levi looked thoughtful for a moment: "He wants to marry her, and Father wants to make the best of a bad situation, for the glory of God"

Simeon blurted out angrily, vowing: "He will never marry her!"

"Just a moment," Levi said, grinning with a dawning realization. "Listen to me, until to the end!"

Simeon paused, looking at his smirking brother, realizing that in his brother's brilliant mind a plan was beginning to form: "So what are you smiling at?!" he asked curiously.

"You'll smile soon, too," Levi replied, laying out his scheme for his brother.

In the large dining room, lit by blazing torches, Israel sat gloomily with his eleven sons across from Hamor and Shechem. As he observed Hamor's slaves present chests filled with jewels and gold — while the prince watched approvingly — his gaze hardened. The royal fools thought that the bride-price they had brought would make him excuse and forgive the misdeed done.

Hamor tried to ignore Israel's glare, knowing that he would surely have to pay a greater bride-gift to please the respectable family whose honor his son had violated. "Every man has a price," Hamor had told his son as they left the palace. "The problem is that this family is a wealthy one, so I will have to pay an exorbitant sum for your lust." Even his reproach had a lilt of lightheartedness and lewdness.

"My lord," he turned to Israel, "I am sorry that this is how things turned out, but boys will be boys..." Hamor looked at Israel, searching for an opening of agreement. "To you, what my unruly son did must seem unconscionable, I realize; but marriage by abduction is quite a common practice among our people. How do you say it? When in Shechem..." He smiled suggestively.

"Well then," he shrugged in response to the sullen expression, "to the issue at hand." He launched into his formal appeal: "*The soul of my son Shechem longs for your daughter. Please give her to him as a wife. And make you marriages with us; give your daughters to us and take our daughters for you.* The decision will be up to you whom to give and whom to take. *And you shall dwell with us; and the land shall be before you; dwell and trade therein and get possessions therein.*" Hamor looked at the opaque face observing him without reaction.

Shechem got up from his place and bowed deeply to Israel: "My father, my brothers," he said to Israel and his sons as if they had already agreed to the marriage. "*Let me find favor in your eyes, and whatever you say to me I will give. Ask me for as great a bride-price and gift as you will, and I will give whatever you say to me. Only give me the young woman to be my wife.*" His voice and face radiated sincerity, as a tear rolled down his cheek at the sorrowful thought that his petition might be rejected.

Levi got up from his seat in front of the young man, "With your permission, Father," he said to Israel. Israel nodded to his son.

"Listen to me carefully, Hamor and Shechem! We are a completely different people from you!" he said in a scolding, sharp voice. "We are a people who have made a covenant with the Creator. *We cannot do this thing, to give our sister to one that is uncircumcised; for that would be a reproach to us.*" Levi looked up at his father, seeing in his father's eyes consent and approval of his words — making the best of a bad situation, for the greater glory of God. "*Only on this condition will we consent to you: if you will be as we are, that every male of you be circumcised; then will we give our daughters to you, and we will take your daughters for us, and we will dwell with you, and we will become one people. But if you will not hearken to us, to be circumcised; then will we take our daughter, and we will be gone.*"

Hamor and Shechem beamed at this response: "Happily, young

sir, happily!" said Hamor, turning his gaze to Israel, who offered him a conciliatory look. "Do not worry: first thing tomorrow, every Shechemite will be circumcised, just like you! I guarantee it!"

Indeed, bright and early the next day, the citizens gathered in the town square, summoned urgently by their prince. The crowd nosily chattered away, the tumult rising to a deafening level. Hamor and his son looked out over the tens of thousands before them from a towering stage. Hamor's soldiers maintained order, gathering in the stragglers and quieting the townspeople so their prince could be heard.

Hamor tone was light and jovial as he addressed his subjects. "My dear, beloved brethren, have you heard about what my naughty son did yesterday?"

Hamor's smile widened at the approving responses: "The apple did not fall far from the tree!" "Do they have any more daughters?"

The prince chuckled. "Oh, they have daughters! And I want to thank you all for your help. As usual, I do not know how I could have done it all without your support and help every step of the way."

"Always happy to help you, Hamor," a call came from the audience, "especially on such happy occasions."

Laughter rolled through the crowd, as the townspeople enthusiastically applauded Hamor and Shechem smiling at them from the top of the stage. Hamor waved his hands in satisfaction, enflaming the wild crowd.

A minute passed, and the excited crowd calmed down a bit. "What now, Hamor? Are you sending her back home?" someone shouted from the crowd.

The smile on Hamor's face widened: "My dear friends, is that what you think of me? Would I do all this just for my son to have one night's romp?!" Hamor glared at them, like a father good-naturedly rebuking his son. "Do you think I would neglect my loved ones or not take care of their wellbeing? Perish the thought!" Hamor laughed at the puzzled looks: "You want to know the truth? I'm a little disappointed in you. I assumed you thought more highly of me."

The crowd's gaze was downcast before Hamor's piercing eyes. The townspeople shifted restlessly, shamed by the rebuke of their prince. "Never mind! it's not that bad, I forgive you," Hamor flashed his captivating smile again.

"I must admit, I did not let you in on all my secrets. You helped with our plan without knowing the full extent. You thought it was just to please my dear son."

Hamor fell silent, surveying the crowed, smiling like a father forgiving his rebellious sons. *"For my thoughts are not your thoughts, neither are your ways my ways,* as you know. The plan my son and I concocted is far more sophisticated than what you could imagine in your simpleness."

The people looked admiringly at Hamor, waiting breathlessly for what he might say next.

"You have all probably heard of Jacob's deeds, how he outwitted Esau and Laban the Aramean. You all have seen the intelligence and wisdom of this newcomer, how he edified us and helped us create a currency, marketplaces, and bathhouses." A murmur of agreement rose among the people.

"Do you think I'm a fool to let someone like that slip out of my hands?!" Hamor's scolding tone tore into the townspeople. "Do you have any idea how much such a person is worth?! Do you know what legendary wealth this man has?! What a brilliant mind! He managed to outsmart Laban the Aramean, famed for his cleverness and guile. Jacob left Laban's house with uncounted wealth!"

Hamor glared at the reprimanded people: "You really don't appreciate me properly, do you?" Hamor looked hurt and sad.

The crowd protested, trying to convey a message to the prince to renew his trust in them.

"My son, Shechem, risked his life for you lot!!!" Hamor screamed at the top of his lungs. "Ever since the Deluge, we have eschewed sexual immorality, but my devoted son was willing to do anything for you, to throw away his life for your good! But you..." Hamor considered his people with disgust.

His audience, stung by his rebuke, expressed remorse and dismay. Some were in tears at the thought that they had unwittingly wronged their well-regarded ruler.

Hamor stared at the humiliated crowd: "You have so greatly disappointed me, citizens of Shechem, that I have my doubts about continuing to lead you. Is there any point in executing our plan, which has begun to mature? Perhaps the best option is for me and my son to leave. We can find another town to live in, one with a more appreciative populace!" Hamor wiped crocodile tears from his face.

The people responded with desperation: "You can't leave us!" "Please forgive us!" "We didn't mean to hurt you!" "Tell us your plan, we beg of you — we will do whatever you ask!"

Hamor looked up to behold the frantic audience. "I'm sorry, I can't go on. I'll try to forgive you... but Shechem, my son, will tell you about the plan I have crafted. If you accept it, we shall stay; if not..." Hamor lowered his eyes in sorrow, wiping away feigned teardrops.

Shechem watched the downcast crowd, his heart rejoicing at his father's acting talent. "Father, I'm sorry," he announced, gazing at Hamor. "I'm so sorry the citizens did that to you, but it's probably the way of the world. Human beings never appreciate the leaders who give their lives for the sake of their people. I do not know if it makes sense to tell them your brilliant strategy..."

The crowd protested: "Tell us!" "Whatever you say will be done!" "Please, don't do this to us; let us know the plan!"

Shechem looked at the people, as if responding reluctantly to their plea: "Very well. You know that Jacob and his family are not ordinary people. After much toil and immense effort, we were able to reach an understanding with them and make peace between us. It was not easy to reach such a level of wholehearted agreement, but for your sake, my father and I were ready to debase ourselves before them, in order to reach a peace accord. The arrangement we reached states that they will settle in our land and engage in trade." Shechem chuckled, "After all, this land is big enough for the both of us. Allowing them to settle here does us no harm, but the commercial opportunities..." Shechem rubbed his hands together with pleasure.

"And not only that..." Shechem laughed. "I heard someone ask if they have more daughters, right? Well, their daughters are exceptional, I can tell you that much! Our pact with them states that we will take their daughters for us — whoever wants, any girl he wants. And our daughters, the ones we cannot marry off here, we can marry off to the family of Jacob. However, I can see that you're not interested. That being the case, my father and I will go and tell them that everything is null and void, and we will leave town." He turned to leave the stage.

"Shechem, stop, we've already apologized! We accept the agreement. Don't go!" the people begged.

Shechem, standing with his back to the audience, smiled with satisfaction. Then, he whirled around to face the people: "Are you sure you will not embarrass us? We are supposed to bring back word to Jacob forthwith."

"They did not ask for anything in return?" someone in the crowd wandered.

"Just a small matter," he remarked offhandedly, "nothing overly onerous or essential. You know these people are circumcised; and in order for the covenant made between us to be complete, we must be too. They have already circumcised themselves, which is irreversible, but we are not circumcised. All they ask is that we become one unified people. Thus, they will feel good about themselves when we take their daughters for us and give them ours. Then, they will give us all their flocks and possessions and all their beasts! All they want is for us to circumcise ourselves," he said with a smile. "Imagine: legendary wealth, everything you wish for in life; in return all you need to do is take off a small and unimportant piece of skin."

"But it hurts," shouted another person in the crowd.

Shechem laughed at the man: "It hurts a little, but doesn't your back hurt when you go to work? Here it is a small pain; after two days, three at most, it passes, and then you'll have a life of leisure and luxury for the rest of your days." Shechem looked at the people. "But if you do not want to, you do not have to!" Shechem turned on his heel again, as if he were about to walk off the stage.

"No, don't go, we want to!" the crowd cried, dreaming about the windfall coming their way.

Shechem turned back to the man who had challenged him: "Don't be afraid, my dear friend. I will show you that it is nothing to fear. I will circumcise myself before you all, so you see that it is not as awful as you think." Shechem took a knife out of his pocket, cut off his foreskin in front of the whole crowd, restraining his impulse to scream from the pain.

"You see?" he said, with beads of sweat dripping down his face. "It's not that bad."

The men began to take knives out of their pockets, circumcising themselves in front of everyone. People who tried to evade circumcision were stopped by the guards and persuaded with a threatening look to circumcise themselves as well.

Chapter Fifty

Vengeance

n the third day since the mass circumcision of the Shechemites, Simeon and Levi reached the gates, glaring at the sentries posted there, who were grimacing in pain.

"Who are you?" one of the guards asked the two boys standing in front of him, as he tried to get to his feet, falling back over his chair due to the pain of his circumcision.

Simeon laughed at the fallen man: "We are the brothers of Dinah, who was abducted by Shechem son of Hamor. We came to see if you did what we agreed you would do," he told the guard.

The guard's eyes lit up with hope: "Surely we did! Do you have another sister? I met you first! If you have another sister, I will take her for me!" he declared, remembering Shechem's promise.

Simeon looked at the man with a grin: "Yes, we have another sister. Do you want to meet her?" he asked the hopeful guard, who nodded. "Her name is Vengeance!" Simeon declared, drawing his sword. "This is your bride. Come embrace her!" he yelled as he plunged his blade into the heart of the guard.

Levi dispatched his comrade.

Simeon and Levi flung open the gates, slaughtering all the soldiers who challenged them, then moving on to the rest of the men. None of the Shechemites could oppose them, as they were all unable to stand. The brothers spent hours making their way through the town, killing all the circumcised males.

"No one will care that we killed them," Levi laughed to his brother, "for they are now a part of Israel, and no one cares if the people of Israel get killed."

"We must find where the scoundrel hid our sister, Dinah," Simeon said to Levi. "There's no time to waste — who knows what evil things he may be doing to her right now!"

The two brothers faced the palace in the heart of the city, striking down with their swords all who tried to stand in their way.

"Dinah! Dinah! Where are you?" Simeon roared through the courtyard, trying to find his sister.

The palace guards came out to challenge Simeon and Levi, trying to stop them from breaking into the chambers from which Dinah's faint answer came. The brothers made short work of them.

"What are you doing here?!" the authoritative challenge rang out behind them. Simeon and Levi both turned toward the familiar voice. Hamor and his son stood in front of the brothers with drawn swords and an aggrieved but aggressive expression on their faces.

"Where's Dinah? We are here to take her home!" Simeon demanded, approaching the unsheathed blades without blinking.

"But we agreed that she belongs to me," Shechem said, amazed.

"This belongs to you!" said Simeon, angrily cutting off the head of Shechem in front of his stunned father.

"Where is she?" Simeon pressed his sword to Hamor's throat, making it clear that his fate would be the same as his son's if he refused to answer the question. Hamor pointed to a large wooden door, knowing that this was the last action he would take in his lifetime.

"Thank you," Simeon said, executing the prince unceremoniously. Simeon and Levi entered the room. In the corner they saw their shrunken sister crying bitterly. The brothers looked at Dinah with teary eyes: "Come, dear, we're going home," Levi said, his heart aching.

Dinah's crying voice intensified at her brother's words: "I don't want to go! Leave me here, or kill me too," Dinah shouted, to her brother's astonishment, "I won't go with you!"

"But, Dinah, you must come with us," Levi whispered, feeling confused at his sister's response. "We're taking you home."

Dinah got to her feet, defiantly telling her older brothers: "It's too late for me. I'm not coming with you!"

Simeon and Levi could not understand Dinah's reaction. In shocked unison, they asked her: "But why?"

"What will people say? 'There goes Dinah, daughter of the righteous, lover of the uncircumcised?' How will they look at me? How will you look at me? Don't you understand it's too late?" she begged with teary eyes, and her resolute voice broke. "How will I look Father in the eyes?" Dinah collapsed into hopeless tears, collapsing onto the bed where she had been abused. "Leave me to die here! Who will want to marry me in my state? It's too late!" she sobbed bitterly.

Simeon approached his sister, feeling her pain and understanding her broken heart. "My dear sister, I swear by the Lord, you will always have a place in my household," he whispered. He picked her up in his arms, carrying her as her cries echoed through the palace, which was otherwise silent as a sepulcher.

"We have to keep going," Levi whispered to his brother.

Simeon nodded in agreement, and the two continued on their way to the rear gate, killing all the males in the city. The women, children, livestock, and portables they took as bounty, heading back to the camp.

A commotion disturbed Jacob's tranquil perusal of the holy scrolls.

The entire encampment was astir. Jacob stepped out of the study and left the main house, as he saw his second and third sons leading women and children, herds of cattle and flocks of sheep and goats, donkeys heavily laden with all manner of vestures, vessels, and valuables. The boys left the servants to sort out their bounty in the adjacent fields, while they advanced toward their father's house.

Levi opened the gate. Simeon was carrying the crying Dinah in his arms. Leah rushed past Jacob to welcome her victorious sons and victimized daughter. Mother and daughter wept together.

Simeon and Levi turned toward their father, who glared at them. His penetrating gaze confirmed he understood what they had done. He rebuked them: *"You have brought trouble on me, to make me odious to the inhabitants of the land, even to the Canaanites and the Perizzites; and I, being few in number, they will gather themselves together against me and smite me; and I shall be destroyed, I and my house!"*

Simeon and Levi lowered their gaze, knowing that their act could endanger their entire family: "But what was the alternative? Was our sister to be abandoned and forsaken? Is she some kind of animal, to be left in the field? Would no one defend her honor?!"

Jacob walked away from his sons, unable to respond. He needed to digest the day's events, which were completely out of his control.

Night fell on the camp, preparing for rest after the day's events. Jacob felt his eyelids grow heavy from the hardships of life, his heart pounding as he thought of his daughter and what she had gone through, as well as what they all might go through due to his sons' reckless actions. The past flashed before his eyes, the tumultuous events of his life confounding him. Esau... Laban... the angel... Dinah... and what now...?

"Arise, go up to Bethel, and dwell there; and make there an altar to God, who appeared to you when you fled from before Esau your brother."

Jacob trembled at the prophecy, the realization dawning within him: he was responsible for the calamities which had befallen his household, as he had neglected his vow for years.

As dawn broke, Jacob gathered all the camp, ordering them to inspect all of their belongings, removing any idols, icons, or images. The offensive items were then buried beneath the massive terebinth tree in their yard. In preparation for their pilgrimage to Bethel, where Jacob promised to build an alter to the Lord, Jacob ordered his household to wear their finest clothes.

As they set out, Judah patted Levi, his big brother, affectionately on the shoulder: "Next time you see action, I expect you not to leave me behind," he said with a big smile. "I ran into a trader earlier, and I asked him if any of the surrounding people heard about what you and Simeon did. He told me that everyone knows, and they're deathly afraid. They're saying that if two adolescents managed to destroy an entire city, what could the whole family do together? It seems to me, that for the time being, we do not need to fear our neighbors. They are panicking, not attacking," Judah laughed out loud. "And again I tell you, remember to let me know next time!"

Jacob and his sons came to Bethel, where they joyfully fulfilled his vow from twenty-two years prior, when he fled from Esau.

For once, a pleasant surprise awaited Jacob at Bethel. "Father, an old woman is asking to see you," Naphtali looked upset as he entered his father's tent. Jacob, who was always immersed in his studies, looked up from the scroll he was writing in. He carefully laid down his quill and covered his inkwell. He was immersed in his writing. Jacob's soft eyes met the nervous eyes of his agitated son.

"Father, she says her name is Deborah, and she has been sent by your mother Rebecca," Naphtali reported. "She looks very old. Could it be the woman who was once a kind of grandmother to you?" he asked.

Jacob quickly got up, hurrying to meet the old woman. The

unexpected encounter made his heart leap. "Probably so," he replied to his son as he left the tent.

The old woman stood in the doorway of the tent, her eyes teary with happiness, looking around at the children keen to serve and honor her. The rumor has spread through the camp; great-grandmother has arrived! All the children, from eight-year-old Joseph to fourteen-year-old Reuben, were eager to meet this link to their father's past, and they huddled at her feet.

Jacob watched the beloved old woman, whom he had not seen for decades. Tears flooded his eyes with longing. "Grandmother!" he said lovingly as he tasted the word that had not been said for many years. "How...? Why...?"

"Are these all your children?" she asked happily, seeing the dozen youngsters neatly arranged before her.

Jacob smiled happily at Deborah. "My children, your great-grandchildren," he gladly announced.

"How fortunate I am, to witness this!" she said with a joyful heart, "They seem to be such wonderful children too!" she said as she stroked the head of little Joseph, who approached her with his captivating smile.

She pointed to her wagon, harnessed to two horses, a few yards away. "That's how I travelled, and it was not too far or too hard to make the trip," she said with a smile at her grandson's lingering look. "And why have I come?" she repeated the question with a smile. "You are still relatively young," she giggled. "At my age you no longer know whether you'll get out of bed in the morning or not. Your mother received word about your arrival to Bethel, and when she wanted to ask you to come home, I jumped at the chance to come deliver the message. Like I said, at my age you cannot know what tomorrow will bring. You know that your brother has given me many great-grandchildren, but they are... not like this. I needed to see your children because I knew they'd be raised right. Now I know it was all worth it in the end." Deborah sighed with pleasure.

"Now, I can go to sleep peacefully. As for you — it's time for you to come home," she told her grandson. "As for me — I think this will be my resting place," she whispered, her hands gripping her heart. Deborah collapsed into Jacob's arms, breathing her last with a beatific smile.

Mourning descended on the camp. The children wept with their father over the death of the wonderful woman, the great-grandmother they had not known; the youngsters tried to comfort the grieving grandson.

Their grief was compounded by a rider, who showed up at the camp three days later, sadly informing Jacob of the sudden death of his mother, Rebecca. Jacob tore his clothes and sat, mourning his mother whom he had not seen at the end of her life. Even worse, was the paltry funeral held for her. It had been conducted in the dead of night, on the orders of Isaac, before Esau could attend the funeral, so that people would not rejoice over the death of Rebecca, mother of Esau. At least Rebecca was buried in the Cave of the Patriarchs, the burial place of Abraham and Sarah.

As Jacob mourned, he received a prophecy: *"Your name is Jacob: your name shall not be called any more Jacob, but Israel shall be your name; and He called his name Israel."* The vision went on: *"I am God Almighty. Be fruitful and multiply; a nation and a company of nations shall come from you, and kings shall come out of your loins; and the land which I gave to Abraham and Isaac, to you I will give it, and to your seed after you I will give the land."*

When the mourning period for his mother was over, Jacob arose to return to his father's house.

"Father," Joseph, his face full of concern, caught Jacob's attention. "Mother asked us to stop. She says the baby is coming."

Jacob stopped the caravan, anxious for his heavily pregnant wife. "I was hoping to get to Hebron before your mother gave birth, darling. It's less than a day's walk from here," he told his little son, "but it looks like you'll be a big brother by the time we get there," he said, smiling. "Run, sweetie, and tell Leah, Bilhah, and Zilpah to help your mother."

Jacob hurried to his wife's side, his heart racing. He thought: Rachel will finally be truly happy after she has two sons like Bilhah and Zilpah!

A tent was quickly pitched, and Rachel, leaning on Leah, shuffled into it. Soon the sounds of moaning emerged from the tent.

Israel paced around the tent, praying for an easy birth for his wife. The hours passed, the sun moving across the sky to set, while the moaning sounds only intensify. Night came, the moon almost full, the cold of autumn causing Jacob shiver slightly. He drew his cloak around himself against the cold.

"A little more, Rachel...." He could hear the loving words of encouragement from inside the tent, "A few more minutes and everything will be behind you, my dear..."

Jacob closed his eyes in prayer for the peace of his wife and child.

"Yes!" Leah's yell of triumph rose. "Here he comes, Rachel. Do not be afraid, it is another son for you!" The shouts of joy failed to cover up the cries of pain emanating from Rachel's mouth.

"Here, Rachel. Beautiful mother, hug your sweet son. He looks just like his father!" Leah exclaimed as she placed the baby on his mother. Rachel embraced her baby, love mingled with loss, joy mingled with pain. As the new mother tenderly cuddled her newborn, her hands fluttered over the little head: "His name shall be Ben-oni," she whispered, as if from a fog. Her caressing hands dropped to the sides of the bed, her eyes glossed over, joy mixed with grief.

"Rachel?! Rachel?!" Leah tried to wake her insensate sister.

"Rachel…" The sound of broken crying forced Israel to enter the tent. The three women wept bitterly around his wife's bed. "She said his name should be Ben-oni," Leah told Jacob in a shattered voice, knowing that her husband had now lost what was most precious to him.

Jacob wiped away his tears in pain: "Ben-oni? Son of my sorrow? Let us call him Benjamin, son of the right hand!" he declared, eyes unseeing amid torrents of tears.

Israel stumbled out of the tent in shock, grabbing a shovel in his hand and beginning to dig a grave. The earth was moistened by its running tears.

"Father," Reuben said softly to his father, "shouldn't we wait—?"

Jacob hesitated for a second, then declared: "No! Here she must be buried, although Hebron is near," he said, resuming his digging.

He thought tearfully: Indeed, we need her here, so in the future she may ask for mercy on her sons when they go into exile.

The words of prophecy were clear in his heart:

Thus says the Lord: A voice is heard in Ramah, lamentation, and bitter weeping, Rachel weeping for her children; she refuses to be comforted for her children, because they are gone.

Thus says the Lord: Refrain your voice from weeping, and your eyes from tears; for your work shall be rewarded, says the Lord; and they shall come back from the land of the enemy.

And there is hope for your future, says the Lord; and your children shall return to their own border.

The children of Israel wept with their father and their mothers. They assisted in Rachel's burial, erecting a large stone monument on her grave on the road to Ephrath, also known as Bethlehem.

Late one night, Reuben entered the tent of Bilhah, Rachel's handmaid. Some time had passed since the tragic death of Bilhah's mistress.

Anger clouded Reuben's mood as he slipped inside, a maelstrom of outrage as he thought: Aunt Rachel was a rival to my mother, but is her handmaid a rival to my mother too?

The bed of his father, Israel, which had been frequently placed in Rachel's tent, was now placed in the tent of Bilhah, Rachel's handmaid.

He thought indignantly: I cannot let this happen! I cannot allow my mother to be humiliated, that she be regarded as less than my aunt's slave-girl!

Reuben climbed into his father's empty bed, knowing that when his father arrived and saw him sleeping there, he would understand his firstborn's objection to the new sleeping arrangements.

Israel entered the tent and saw his eldest son asleep in his bed. He realized that trying to have another son with Bilhah, his wife's handmaid, had been prevented by Reuben's act of defiance.

As he left the tent, he thought: Apparently, it is not proper for me to bring more children into the world. Thirteen is not the magic number of sons for me; I must be content with those I have. Thank the Lord, my twelve sons are all righteous, pious, and whole.

CHAPTER FIFTY-ONE

The Six-Day War

"Quiet!" King Jashub of Tappuah's scream silenced the room. "You cluck like a henhouse full of chittering chickens!" he rebuked them. Those present glared at Jashub with barely restrained anger. "You cannot talk to us like that!" objected King Ihorai of Shiloh, rising to his feet, but the trepidation in his voice was clear.

"I'll talk to you any way I want!" Jashub said with a grin, "Do you think I called you here to listen to the chatter of fools?!"

"Really, why have you summoned us?" King Ajalon of Gaash demanded, astonished that the reason for the emergency meeting of Amorite kings had not been established beforehand.

However, Jashub, ignoring the question, was not done berating his companions. He went on angrily: "I really do not understand how you rule over your own kingdoms. Do you not see what is going on under your nose?! Are you so dimwitted that you do not see the danger you face?!"

"What danger are you blabbering on about?!" asked King Sussi of Sartan.

The king of Tappuah sighed, rubbing his forehead in despair: "Do you not perceive our eminent threat? Jacob and his sons!"

"What about them?"

"Did you not notice that Jacob and his sons are beginning to take over the land?! Hebron in their hands! Shechem in their hands! It won't be long before they conquer the whole land!" The fear in his voice was noticeable.

King Parathon of Hesser laughed at the idea. "Is this a joke? A father and his twelve sons, the oldest of whom is barely an adult, are going to conquer the whole land?! That's who you're afraid of?!"

Jashub fixed his penetrating gaze on Parathon. "Do you forget what two adolescents did to the city of Shechem?! You probably do not remember the fear that gripped you, when I told you it was urgent to unite and destroy Jacob and his house. At that time, you were no hero. Now, you pretend not to be afraid of them? Either you're insane or an idiot! In fact, it's more than stupidity: you are acting like an ostrich, burying its head in the ground so as not to see the approaching danger."

There was silence in the room; the kings seemed helpless in the face of the encroaching thereat.

"What do you suggest?" King Laban of Horon asked, breaking the long, awkward silence.

"I suggest that we mobilize for battle! This is war: to be or not to be! We must not be complacent and wait for them to come and attack us, unless we want our fate to be that of Hamor, ruler of Shechem," said Jashub pragmatically.

"It's not just a war for survival. Even if they do not attack, they will start instilling in people their misguided opinions, influencing our subjects to start following their distorted ways, causing our people to change their way of thinking. It is a war for our culture! For our faith! For our way of life!

"I know that most of Jacob's sons are now in Shechem; they are grazing the flocks there. If we join forces and attack them there, then we may be able to overwhelm them. Then, we can turn south and attack Jacob himself and the rest of his children in Hebron. They may not be armed, but we must take them very seriously. We cannot afford to take this operation lightly. If we unite for this, there is a chance that we will be able to defeat them, and if not, they will soon attack us, and then..." Jashub sighed from the bottom of his heart, "we have no chance."

"I'm with you!" King Sachir of Mahanaima said, "Who will join?"

The hands of the six other Amorite kings were raised one after the other, joining King Jashub of Tappuah.

Simeon leaned against a tall oak tree, the warm sun shining on his face. His thoughts raced to the past, seeing the gates of the city of Shechem, which he and Levi had conquered seven years earlier. He could not erase the sight of his humiliated sister Dinah from his mind.

The trauma had not ended with Dinah's rescue. His sister had become pregnant against her will, and she eventually bore the posthumous daughter of Shechem. The outrage constantly clouded Simeon's mood.

Dinah remained inconsolable. The sight of her daughter was a constant reminder of her awful ordeal, her bitter sobs unrelenting.

Finally, Simeon took drastic action. He took little Asenath to Egypt, placing the infant on the doorstep of one of Pharaoh's ministers. Simeon knew that the minister and his wife were childless, and he reflected: They will surely take the girl into their household and raise her as their own. This pendant, which I hang around her neck, will stay with her, and maybe the day will come when—

"Simeon, look alive!" Judah's startling shout shook his older brother from his reverie.

"What's happening?!" Simeon asked, trying to gather his thoughts.

"I'm not sure, but something doesn't smell right."

"What?"

"Look at that cloud of dust rising beyond the hill. It doesn't seem natural to me, and I also heard a sound in the distance — like horses' neighing, a lot of them."

Simeon strained his eyes and ears to see what Judah was talking about. "You're not mistaken, brother, I hear a troop of horses — and probably chariots as well."

Judah stuck his fingers in his mouth, the familiar whistling sound echoing through the pastures to all of his brothers in the area. Fleet-footed Naphtali was the first to arrive, and Judah sent him toward the towering pillar of dust at a run.

A few tense moments passed, and Naphtali ran back. "Remember those brats who sent a letter to Father, ordering him to present himself for a trial in the Shechem Valley? It looks like they've finally shown up." He gestured towards the cloud of dust: "They want revenge for their friends." Naphtali maintained his captivating smile. "They probably gathered everyone they could for the mission."

"How many are they?" Reuben asked, unsheathing his sword.

Naphtali laughed happily: "I don't see more than a few tens of thousands. They're divided into seven camps."

Judah smiled at his brother: "*A thousand may fall at your side, and ten thousand at your right hand; it shall not come close to you.* Father is with us, and we are ten brothers. We also have one hundred and twelve slaves. Isn't that enough? Perhaps that's too many!" Judah's confident tone filled the brothers with a combative spirit: "Let's go and greet the guests; but do it slowly, so we can meet them together," he said with a chuckle to his swift brother.

The brothers and their slaves began to run quickly toward the army approaching them. Their light clothing was blown about by the silent wind. They gripped their swords lightly, bows and quarrels on their backs. The brothers were divided into three groups: three of the brothers turned right, three to the left, and three in the middle, flanking the huge force approaching them.

Naphtali came to the tent of his father, who was diligently studying. "Father, I am sorry to disturb you, but the kings of Canaan have come to fight, and you asked that we inform you when they arrived."

Israel rose from his place peacefully, raised his eyes heavenward and closed them, beginning to pray: "Master of the Universe, You are our Father, You are our King. You created and formed us; we are Your handiwork. In Your great mercy, save my sons from their foes, who come to make war against them; grant them salvation, for Yours is the power and the might to save few from the hands of many. Grant Your servants, my sons, courage and heroism to fight their enemies to subdue them, and cast down all their enemies before them, so my sons and my servants will not die by the hand of the Canaanites." Israel paused for a second: "Still, if it seems good to You to take the lives of my sons and my servants, take them." Israel opened his eyes, looking with a loving smile at his son: "Now we may go to war." He easily and calmly took his sword and bow in his hands and left the tent with Naphtali to join the rest of his sons on the battlefield.

As Judah ran toward the frontlines, he looked for the king. If only he could cut off the head of the snake, the battle would end quickly. It took him a moment to find his target: Jashub, king of Tappuah.

With a platoon of ten servants, Judah moved towards Jashub. Waves of warriors faced him, but Judah and his men cut through the onslaught. Judah's nimble blade ripped through the bodies of his opponents. He thought: What a bunch of clumsy oafs!

He deftly dodged the swords raised against him, darting in, and beheading the bodyguards around Jashub. A path quickly opened up to the monarch atop his noble steed. The king of Tappuah began launching javelins with both hands. Judah dodged them, leaping from side to side, appreciating Jashub's wondrous ability to ambidextrously toss javelins. He was forced to use his sword to deflect the javelins which fell upon him with tremendous force. Judah swung around like a maelstrom, his blade slicing through all the Canaanite soldiers who dared approach him. As the corpses piled up, most of Jashub's warriors scattered, abandoning the king of Tappuah. The select few who refused to abandon their monarch fell prey to Judah and his servants.

Judah smiled to himself, seeing that the king of Tappuah's arsenal of javelins was empty. With a grin he thought: Now it's one-on-one.

Twenty yards away from Jashub, Judah lifted a boulder and hurled it at the king. The massive rock slammed into him and knocked him to the ground. Judah exulted: He is lost; now I just have to behead him.

Judah quickly approached the silent monarch. With just one pace separating the two, the king of Tappuah suddenly leapt to his feet, surprising Judah, who had been walking confidently toward his prone foe. In a flurry of movement, his blade arced towards Judah's neck; but at the last moment, Judah interposed the buckler on his arm, protecting his neck. The shield broke in two from the force of the blow, and Judah was knocked off his feet. Still, as he fell, he extended his arm in a sweeping motion, slicing through Jashub's legs above the ankle. Jashub screamed, shattered and in excruciating pain. Judah quickly chopped off the king's head.

Judah paused for a moment, regulating his breathing. Around him, the battlefield had fallen silent, as the combatants on both sides observed the dénouement of the fight between Judah and Jashub. Judah looked at his brothers, his grim grin a rebuke to them for relenting in their attack. The brothers caught the smile and attacked their enemies anew. The sounds of raging battle resumed.

"Go and help them," he told his servants, "I will join you presently." Jashub's glorious scale armor had caught Judah's eye. He set to stripping the corpse, ignoring the battle around him.

Nine horsemen, the lords of Tappuah, began to advance toward Judah as he was engaged in the removal of the armor. A small twinkle was reflected in the polished armor, as Judah raised his head slightly from the corpse. An ax blade was speeding toward his head, and Judah barely dodged it, rolling to the side. He grabbed a rock and jumped to his feet, hurrying toward the lord waving the ax. With the rock, Judah crushed the skull of his attacker, whose corpse fell from his mount.

The remaining eight lords fled. Judah whistled to his servants, who had left him to assist his brothers.

Judah and the ten slaves began to chase after the lords of Tappuah, their pursuit ending in bloody victory.

"Levi! Pay attention!" The warning from Dan alerted his older brother.

Fifteen armed fighters attacked him from behind. King Ajalon of Gaash and his lords advanced against him, with a frightened smile. Levi signalled to his twelve servants to challenge the attackers. The battle of the swords ended quickly, with fifteen bodies lying on the ground.

King Ihorai of Shiloh burst forth against Levi with his servants, his sword raised to bide his time. An arrow pierced Ihorai's head, penetrating his helmet and protruding from the back of his neck. Levi smiled at his father standing in the distance, calmly stretching his large bow, protecting his fighting sons from a distance, his lips blazing with prayer.

A feature of defeat began to grip the remaining four kings, seeing that their comrades in arms had lost the battle. There were fifteen thousand dead on the Canaanite side, while Jacob, his sons, and his slaves had emerged without casualties.

"Everybody's fine?" Jacob examined his men, "Do you have the strength to keep going?" he asked with a grin. "It is impossible to let these four kings go back to their kingdoms peacefully." Everyone smiled in agreement.

"Forward!" Jacob said and began to chase his enemies swiftly.

"Open the gates!!!" King Parathon of Hesser yelled to his men who stood upon the walls.

The guards inside the city watched the tableau before them: tens of thousands of the city's soldiers, along with their Amorite allies, stood trembling at the city gate and sought refuge. Jacob and his forces were harrying and quickly gaining on them.

"We cannot open the gates for them," one of the guards told his friends, "We cannot endanger the women and children. Only after they win, can we let them enter. "

The guards nodded to each other, descending from the wall, ignoring the king's insulting screams.

Jacob stood on a small hill overlooking the Canaanite camp on the outskirts of Hesser. "Keep going!" he said calmly to his sons, "I will join you shortly." The boys, with their slaves, continued to pursue the Amorite forces, bunched up against the city wall.

Jacob raised his bow: "One!" he counted, as he fired an arrow which brought down one of the four remaining monarchs. "Two... three... four..." The four kings fell dead from their mounts, one after the other.

The ten brothers and their slaves pounced on the frightened warriors, scattering them to every wind. The battle lasted a long time, and at the end of it four thousand more soldiers had been slain.

"Is everyone all right?" Judah asked his brothers.

The brothers bowed their heads in sorrow: "Unfortunately, three of your servants were killed in battle, my dear brother," Reuben said sadly.

Judah was mortified and angered by the news. "We will pursue them to the bitter end!" he declared. "Naphtali, check where the other warriors have fled to!" he told his fleetfooted brother.

A few minutes passed, and Naphtali returned to his brother: "They are entering the city from the opposite gate. This city is huge! It took me maybe four minutes to go around it. They must have come in while I was making my way around the wall."

The pursuing forces of Jacob began to run to the other side of town. The frightened warriors were hiding inside the city. Four armed warriors, displaying no sign of fear, came out from the gates to provide cover, smiling confidently and defiantly.

"Leave it to me," said Naphtali, "I need to expend some energy." he ran toward the warriors, who were somewhat stunned by the daring man approaching them pell-mell.

With one blow of the sword, Naphtali cut off the heads of two of the warriors. The two remaining fighters, who tried to flee for their lives, died before they could get far.

The brothers then entered the city, only to find another wall, more fortified than the outer one, before them. The huge iron gates were locked from the inside without any way to open them. Judah looked up at the high stone wall; it was as tall as a five-story building.

He quickly repositioned his scabbard on his back and began climbing the wall, sticking his steel-hard fingers into the stone grooves. Simeon and Levi quickly followed. A few minutes passed, and shouts and screams rose from inside. "Come on, let's see if they need help," Dan said to Naphtali. The two brothers clambered up the wall like their older brothers.

A while later, the iron city gates of Hesser creaked open. "Father, you can come in. There are only a few women and children left here," Judah told his father and brothers.

"Well, children," Jacob told his sons, "we will rest a little tonight. The sun is about to set, tomorrow, we will continue the mission."

The city of Sartan stood before Jacob and his sons. The high, smooth wall was out of reach, as a very deep and wide moat surrounded the city. The iron drawbridge, which was the only way to traverse it, had been raised.

"This moat must be seventy feet deep and a hundred feet wide!" Gad said in amazement at the labor invested. "We have to find a way to get through it." The brothers looked at each other, stumped.

"I have an idea!" Issachar suddenly announced. "I'll show you how we get past this." He got a running start and then leapt off the edge of the moat; his amazing jump took him all the way to the other side. The brothers, holding their breath at Issachar's vault, breathed a sigh of relief as they saw him waving at them to do the same. The nine brothers jumped over the moat following Issachar.

A rain of stones and arrows were thrown at the heads of the brothers advancing toward the wall, protecting their heads with their shields, searching for the city gate. The fortified iron gate could not be opened, and the pelting rain of stones and arrows pushed the brothers trying to break into the city to find a quick solution.

Judah looked at the wall, searching for a way to climb the slippery structure.

He hastily placed his shield on his head and pulled out two knives from his bag. He drove one knife into the wall, then stuck the other a few feet above it. Judah then began to climb the eastern wall of the city with his knives. Gad and Asher also drew their knives and began to climb the western wall. Simeon and Levi did so from the north, Dan and Reuben from the south. The people standing on the wall looked anxiously at the people climbing like spiders in front of them. Precise arrows, which pierced the necks of those trying to throw stones at the climbers, chased away the sentries on the walls. The fear which gripped them caused them to flee into the city to try to save their lives.

Issachar and Naphtali went to the city gate, building a fire under the gate. The city gate melted, and Issachar and Naphtali entered the city.

The massacre raged, with the ten brothers fighting against the enemy, which was battered by fear. Fortified towers were captured, while the brothers left behind heaps of warriors' corpses.

"Simeon..." Levi whispered to his brother with a smile. "Do you see that? It's a fortified tower."

Simeon and Levi began to run toward the tower, breaking into it, destroying the wasps' nest.

"They fled in that direction...," Simeon said to his brother. The two brothers embarked on a pursuit of the fugitives. The boulevard was empty of living people, as Simeon and Levi gave chase. The brothers grinned in anticipation as they rounded the corner — and stopped short.

Twelve armed fighters surprised the brothers, and the battle began immediately. Simeon and Levi strove to strike at the warriors of Sartan, who were fighting with extraordinary boldness and heroism; they were clearly a cut above the simple soldiers the brothers had hitherto encountered. Six warriors attacked each of the brothers, who struggled to counterattack. The brothers fought back-to-back, defending each other bodily. The combat was exhausting; the shields the brothers held finally shattered under the onslaught.

A sword swung towards Levi's head with tremendous force. "Levi!" Simeon alerted him. Levi raised his arm to deflect the blade, and it cut into his flesh deeply, almost slicing clean through. Levi pushed back on the blade, forcing it into the chest of his assailant, killing his attacker.

The battle continued. The remaining eleven warriors intensified their assault when they saw the wounded Levi fighting with one hand. A scream of rage erupted from Simeon, frustrated by his inability to defeat his enemies.

"Simeon is in trouble!" Judah called to Naphtali. The two brothers ran toward their troubled brother. Judah jumped into battle, trying to protect his wounded brother who continued to fight. Naphtali ran to fetch two shields for his defenseless brothers.

"Naphtali, run and call Father," Judah said to his fleetfooted brother.

The grueling battle continued, the sun beginning to tilt to the west. The news that Levi had been wounded in battle shocked Jacob. He ran to his sons, praying to God.

He shot an arrow from his bow, knocking down one of the warriors; a second and third fell after him. The remaining eight warriors fled for their lives, trying to escape around the corner. Asher and Dan, who had been summoned by Simeon's cry, emerged in front of the eight fugitives, killing two of them while six dodged. Judah and his brothers began the chase, catching up with the fugitives and killing them too.

"The operation is complete," Reuben told his father, smiling. "Only women and children remain in the city. We took the best of the children as slaves, then gathered all the spoils and beasts into one place."

Jacob smiled at his son: "Wonderful! Tomorrow morning, we will return to Hebron, with the help of the Lord."

"How's your arm?" Jacob asked Levi with a worried face.

Levi looked at his father with a smile: "Don't worry, Father, everything is fine. It's just a slight scratch."

"A scratch?! Your arm was almost cut off, "Jacob looked at the bandaged limb. "Tomorrow we return home, and I want you to rest."

Jacob looked at his ten sons proudly: "We will go rest now; set up guard watches until morning."

The boys nodded with a smile at their beloved father.

As day broke, they stepped around the melted city gate, getting ready to return to Hebron, their home. The voices of the captive children mourning their parents mingled with the sound of the bleating sheep, the neighing of horses, and the braying of donkeys.

"It seems to me that today we will not return to Hebron," Naphtali told Judah. "Look, there are others who have not yet learned their lesson!" Naphtali pointed toward the ranks of fresh warriors advancing toward Sartan. Judah looked at his brothers watching the next army advancing on them: "Come on, brothers, we have unfinished business!"

The ten brothers and their slaves broke out in a light run toward those coming to battle them.

The people of Tappuah, who had come to avenge their slain king, soon scattered before the sons of Jacob, trying to flee to their fortified city, while the sons of Jacob pursued them. The city of Tappuah fell, ten of the slaves of the sons of Jacob remained in the town to finish the work of plunder, while their masters launched an offensive against the people of Arbelio, who had come to the aid of the people of Tappuah.

Reuben ran quickly toward the gate of the city wall of Arbelio. He stopped in astonishment as four armed women stood before him, pulling out their polished swords.

"Lay down the swords, and you will not be harmed," Reuben told the women standing before him. "It is not our way to fight women."

The four women laughed out loud as they attacked Reuben. Repelling the remarkably precise and powerful sword blows, while trying not to hurt the women, he thought: They know how to fight better than many of the warriors I have encountered. If I continue like this, they'll kill me. I have no choice; this is war, life or death!"

"Did you finish playing?" Simeon asked Reuben, who was standing over the bodies of the four women.

"Did you see it?" Reuben was amazed.

Simeon laughed out loud: "Really, a very interesting battle," he said, "I think we should get used to it. All the women in this city fight just as well as the men." Simeon pointed to a bend in the wall:

"Come, the brothers are waiting for us there, we will breach the city together."

The eight brothers greeted the two with a smile; it was obvious that they too, had seen the battle their brothers had fought the women. The gate of the wall creaked open a bit. Reuben and Levi went to open the gate, finding hundreds of men and women in front of them. The ten brothers started running toward those waiting for them. Battle roars, erupting from their mouths, shook those trying to defend their city.

Some of the men fled in terror, while some stood fiercely against the brothers. A long and tedious battle ensued; at the end the ten brothers stood their ground, feet planted in the blood of their enemies.

The brothers began scanning the city, with arrows and spears thrown from spires and towers scattered throughout the city. A prayer arose from the brethren, knowing that danger hovered over their heads, as they walked through the city. Many hours passed as the brothers raided the city, destroying their enemies, men and women alike.

The kingdom of Gaash and the kingdom of Horon also came to war with the sons of Jacob.

The fierce battles lasted for six days, at the end of which the seven kingdoms fell to the Israelites. The great captivity and the mighty spoils taken, were led by the children of Israel and their servants toward the city of Shechem, to the plot of land which Jacob had bought many days before.

"We will not enter the city," Israel said to his sons, "lest more of the Canaanite kings come to fight with us and besiege the city."

The camp was spread out like the sand of the sea, beyond counting children and women; sheep and cattle; camels, horses, and donkeys; as well as all manner of vestures, vessels, and valuables.

Israel and his sons remained outside the city for ten days, awaiting more battles. After this period, they entered the city of Shechem, confident that there was no imminent combat.

"Father, it seems to me that the battles are not over yet," Simeon said to his father, who was diligently returning to his studies. Israel looked up from the scroll in which he was writing: "What's going on?" he asked, disappointed that he would have to deal with war again.

"A group of people on horseback are approaching the city. They look like men of war, but the strange thing is that they are a very small group, maybe two hundred people." Simeon felt foolish for bothering his father for a handful of warriors advancing toward the city, but he was comforted by the fact that his father had ordered him to do so if anything happened. "They may be the vanguard, followed by thousands more soldiers. We really do not know."

Israel slowly rolled up the scroll, then took his sword and bow leaning against the wall: "Come," he said to his son with a smile, responding to Simeon's unease at disturbing him. "We will go and welcome them. Are your brothers ready?"

"Yes Father, everyone is at the gate with the servants." The father and son walked to the city gate.

Naphtali approached his father, bowing with a smile: "I went for a light morning run beyond the vanguard, to see if there was another army behind them. But there is nothing up to a distance of two to three days of walking; there is no trace of fighters behind them or in any other direction," he told his father.

Israel smiled at his sons: "Then we will go out of the city to welcome our guests." Israel, his sons, and his servants went out of the city gate, waiting for those who were approaching. Four people split from the group, which stopped about a mile from the city gates. The four continued to ride toward Israel and his sons.

A short minute passed. "King Japhia of Hebron is in the lead," Israel told his sons, "I wonder what he wants."

Japhia and his three escorts stopped a few yards from Israel and his sons and dismounted, prostrating themselves on the ground, Israel and his sons were shocked.

"King Japhia of Hebron, what brings you here?" Jacob demanded angrily.

"Please, my lord. We do not seek war, but to make peace with my lord," said Japhia. "We and all the Canaanite kings came to ask my lord for peace between us."

"Peace?!" Issachar snorted with contempt, "Since when do you want to make peace?!"

Japhia looked at Israel with embarrassment: "The delegation behind me consists of twenty more Canaanite kings. Each of them comes with his three senior ministers, and each of the ministers has three servants. We did not come with an army or soldiers, but only kings, ministers, and their servants. We do not want war, but peace."

Israel beheld the king of Hebron. The honorable man looked humbled and downcast: "If it as you say, send one of your men and call only to the kings; let them come and stand before me," he said with suspicion.

Japhia gestured to one of his ministers, and that one hurried out toward the group of people standing in the distance. Twenty men approached Israel and his sons, bowing their heads to the ground in submission. "We have heard what you did to the seven kings of the Amorites with your powerful sword and your great arm," said one of the kings to Israel. "No one could defy you, and we fear for our lives and the lives of our people; so, we have come to beseech your honor to make a peace treaty with us."

Israel looked at his sons. On the face of it, everyone seemed to believe the kings who bowed before them. "We will make a covenant with you: as long as you do not attack us, we will not go to war with you. However, if you attack, your fate will be far worse and more bitter than the fate of the seven kings who fell before us. You must know that if you act foolishly, then we will kill not only the men, but your wives, your sons, your daughters, and everything which is yours."

The kings nodded humbly before Israel. "We brought an offering to my lord," said Japhia. "May we call our ministers and our servants to bring our offering to my lord?" he asked.

Israel nodded, a little alert lest the kings attempt a ruse. The ministers and the slaves came to Israel, bowing before him, placing many and sundry royal treasures at his feet.

"Can I ask a thing of my lord?" asked Japhia pleadingly. "The captives my lord has taken from the seven kingdoms are our people. We know that your way is completely different from ours, and our wives and sons who are in your hands are unaccustomed to your ways."

Israel looked at Japhia with a contemplative look, as if pondering whether to accede to his request; but what he thought was: Thank God he asked for it. The burden of all these women and children is enormous, and moreover the loose women may lead my sons, astray, God forbid. I wish he would also ask for the loads of sheep, cattle, and all the booty? All this is just a burden that weighs on us. "

"Let it be, according to your word," said Israel, as if he had reluctantly relented at the request of Japhia.

Japhia looked at Israel, not believing what he heard. His gaze turned to the kings with him, seeing the joy fill their faces, even as they hoped Japhia would continue with the next request they had planned.

He bowed down to Israel: "If my lord will allow me to ask anything more of him, in his kindness and compassion upon us," he bowed hopefully. "My lord knows that these captives must support themselves. Would my lord in his grace deign to give us the flocks...?"

Israel restrained Japhia with a hand and turned to his sons: "Bring them all the captives and all the booty we have taken from them."

Japhia looked at Israel in astonishment, shocked by the man who so easily gave up the legendary wealth he had taken for granted. "We promise that every year we will pay taxes to our merciful lord," Japhia told Israel.

Israel smiled. "If you will forgive me, I have many things to do," he told the kings who bowed down before him. As he returned to his study, he reflected: Blessed are we to be rid of all this...

Chapter Fifty-Two

The Dreamer

The sky was gloomy, the sound of thunder shook the broken heart. A light drizzle fell, mingling with the tears of mourners.

Only seven years after her younger sister Rachel had passed away, Leah breathed her last. Her father-in-law, her husband, her six sons and one daughter, and her six nephews accompanied her coffin to Machpelah Cave, where she joined Abraham, Sarah, and Rebecca in their eternal repose.

Kings and princes from all over came to Hebron to pay their last respects to the wife of Israel. The outpouring of grief for the lost matriarch was vast, throughout the city.

Israel and all his sons mourned the death of Leah. Fifteen-year-old Joseph and his seven-year-old brother Benjamin embraced their father, trying to comfort him, grieving the loss of the aunt who had been a mother to them for the past seven years.

The year of mourning for Leah passed, then another. The bond between Joseph and Jacob only became stronger, as they studied the Word of God together.

One day, Israel was in his chamber, deep in thought, when Joseph unburdened himself about his older brothers. "Father, I cannot make heads or tails of their behavior. Did you not teach me that it is forbidden to eat the limb of a living animal? You said, as long as the animal is convulsing, its meat may not be consumed. How is it then, that my brothers slaughter an animal and eat of its meat immediately, while the beast is still convulsing? I told them that it is forbidden to eat like this, but they laughed at me and told me that I do not understand anything.

"And what about the way they associate with the local girls? My brothers tell me that they only buy from them and sell to them, but…" Joseph looked at his father, who seemed to be ignoring him.

He pressed on: "But they dismiss me, claiming I'm a child who understands nothing. I'm not a child; I'm already seventeen years old, and they still disrespect me."

Joseph sounded upset at the thought of his brothers' behavior toward him. His hands played with his curls absentmindedly.

Israel looked at his beloved son in pain. He thought: The poor boy was orphaned at eight. Benjamin was orphaned at birth; he never got to feel the warmth and love of a real mother. All his life he grew up with Bilhah; who really tried to give him the warmth and love of a mother, but it's not the same. Benjamin has never felt it, so he doesn't know what he's missing. Benjamin never went through the process of losing his mother because he never knew her. Meanwhile, Joseph has spent more than half his life missing that maternal love and embrace, something which he can never enjoy again…

"That's not the whole of it," Joseph continued, his voice piercing the mists of Jacob's swirling thoughts. "They don't even treat each other fairly. Leah's sons disrespect the sons of Bilhah and Zilpah, as if Leah's sons are the masters and Dan, Naphtali, Gad, and Asher are their slaves!"

"I understand…" Jacob replied, but he still seemed sunk deep in his thoughts, pondering how he could repair the tears in the fabric of his family. "For now, let us pick things up where we left them off yesterday." Israel changed the subject, turning from the distressing issue of fraternal relationships.

"Yesterday we talked about the purpose of faith, the way we can connect with the Creator whether times are good or otherwise. The simplest and easiest way is to actually think of the Blessed Creator as if He is your best friend, sitting in front of you, perfect, ready and waiting to hear all that hurts and bothers you. Think of Him as a kind of friend who can solve all the problems you have, no matter how great or small; a friend who is always there for you. It may sound simplistic or facile, but it requires great effort to internalize. It took me fourteen years to learn this in Eber's seminary. It took me fourteen years to realize that there is only one place that you can really always turn to. Know that He is always there with you and for you."

Joseph listened to his father, thirstily drinking in his words, happy that his father chose him from all his sons to be his attendant, feeling that his father invested more in Joseph's studies than he did with all the brothers. "I see..." Joseph hoped to return to the previous conversation, knowing that this was difficult for his father.

"I know you understand, Joseph," said Israel, trying to convey the message to his son in the best way possible, "but when it comes to this, you need to do more than understand, you need to feel it. Saying things is no big deal, but to feel... to experience... to internalize... to live... That demands a lot more of you. Not always what you think you see, you really see; not always what you think you know, you really know; not always what you think you understand, you really understand. There are things that take a while to internalize, to live with. As long as you are not in a place where you can see the whole thing from all angles, it is always better to keep an open mind. In order to rebuke someone, you must put yourself in his place, exactly within his reality, within his consciousness, his mind, his past, his thoughts, his character, his desires, et cetera. As long as you cannot do this perfectly, it is preferable to keep from saying anything. I know this is difficult, but believe me, my son: this is the best course."

Joseph looked down, picking up on his father's subtle rebuke, knowing that Jacob was right.

Israel caressed the hand of his son lying on the table: "Do me a favor, go to Bilhah; tell her that I want her to give you what I made for you." He put a hand to Joseph's head, stroking the brown curls: "I think you'll like it."

"Ugh! The spoiled brat is here again!" Simeon looked scornfully at Joseph, who was advancing toward his brothers.

"Look at him dressing up in his new colorful coat. He's parading around with it like he's some girl," Levi said angrily.

"I think Father told my mother to make it for him," Dan smirked with hate. "When I saw her working on it, I thought it was a gift for a bride."

Reuben pursed his lips contemptuously: "Look how he waves hello, as if any of us want to see his homely hairless face."

"The amazing thing about this kid is that he thinks anyone of us is capable of loving him. He acts like we're a bunch of fools who don't understand that everything he sees us do, he runs to tell Father and interprets it pejoratively," Reuben sneered.

"Hello, my dear brothers," Joseph said with a shining smile. The ten brothers pretended to be engaged in their work, ignoring their brother who came to visit them in the pasture.

Joseph disregarded his brother's hostility, feeling that he should straighten things out with them. "I have to tell you something!" Joseph said to his busy brothers.

"Then tell us and get out of here," Gad responded dismissively.

"Yesterday I had a funny dream. In the dream, I saw us binding sheaves in the field, and suddenly my sheaf stood upright, and the big finale was," Joseph smiled, barely stopping himself from laughing, "that all your sheaves turned and bowed to my sheaf."

The ten brothers straightened up from their work and turned to their cheeky brother:

"These are your dreams?! Do you want to lord and rule over us?! Do you think about that all day?! How to subjugate us?!" The brothers advanced toward Joseph angrily.

"Listen to me carefully, boy!" Reuben said, "Fly away from here, and never come back, or we'll show you who bows to whom!"

Joseph looked at his angry brothers: "No, you don't get it..."

Dan approached Joseph with clenched fists: "What we get or don't get is none of your business! You need to get gone, got it?"

Joseph walked away from his brothers, wiping the tears from his eyes: "Don't they see this dream is nonsense? Why would I dream of sheaves? I should have dreamt of sheep; we're no farmers. The dream is ridiculous. They don't understand me at all…"

All the children of Israel were sitting with their grandfather and father around the great table, the smells of the steaming stews filling the large room. The brothers talked to each other with loving smiles, recounting their experiences and their plans for the future. The atmosphere among the ten boys was relaxed and delightful. It was heartwarming for the whole family to be together.

Next to Israel sat Joseph and Benjamin, whispering to each other.

Israel watched his sons with pleasure, rejoicing in his good fortune: "Does anyone have anything interesting to tell us?" he asked his sons with a smile, looking at each of them in turn.

"Yes, Father!" Joseph was the first to jump up. "I have something very funny and interesting to tell."

Israel clapped his son on the shoulder with a grin: "If so, please tell us all."

"Yesterday, I dreamed that the sun, moon, and eleven stars bowed down to me!" he said with a smile to his father. The brothers' eyes glared at Joseph, as if trying to rip the flesh off him. The same thought went through everyone's minds: he is not satisfied with the brothers; he wants Father and Mother to bow to him too!

"Are not you ashamed?!" Israel rebuked him, "Do you want me and Rachel your mother — who is already dead — and your eleven brothers to come and bow down to you?!"

Israel looked at ten of his sons glaring at Joseph. He thought: He draws too much fire upon himself.

Meanwhile, Isaac thought to himself: It will be interesting to see when and how things unfold.

Israel thought to himself: The boys are in Shechem; they went to graze the flocks in the good pasturelands there. Three years have passed since I made an alliance with the people of the country. The Canaanites have grown stronger and stronger during these years. There is a fear that they will hate us and try to start a war against my sons again. I have the feeling that something bad is approaching.

Israel's concerns allowed him no peace of mind. His ten sons herding sheep and goats in Shechem could be in danger. The people of the land could not be trusted, he feared. He had to take action, urgently.

"Joseph, please, go visit your brothers who are shepherding in Shechem, and see how they are," he said to his beloved son, who was standing in front of him.

He thought: Unfortunately, Joseph is not particularly popular with his brothers, but I hope this mission I send him on will straighten things out a bit. They may not like him, but they certainly will not hurt him. He can take some delicacies and wine with him, and this will allow some thawing in their relationship.

"Benjamin will remain here as my attendant," Israel told Joseph. He thought: Joseph will be following my commandment, and no harm ought to befall those who fulfill a divine directive like honoring one's parent!

Joseph smiled happily at his father. Many weeks had passed since the painful confrontation at their family dinner. He thought: I have to explain myself to them, I hope they are not too angry with me.

"Father, I am at your disposal," he replied.

CHAPTER FIFTY-THREE

Sale

The road, dotted with spring flowers, delighted Joseph's heart. Leaving Hebron for open spaces was not an everyday thing for him. The flapping butterflies looked to him to be showing captivating smiles, the verdure singing a merry tune. His striped coat of many colors was the perfect garb for the bracing freshness of the vernal setting, with the hues of the flora matching his wardrobe. His legs carried him effortlessly as the meadows and hills spread before him. The journey was a pleasant one, feeling freedom and merging with the beauties of creation. He hummed a cheerful melody as he skipped lightly from rock to rock.

"I will finally get to see the place where my father and brothers fought the seven kings," he thought with a smile. "What heroes they are! I don't know what I would have done in their place. I hope I wouldn't have run away like a rabbit."

Years ago, before their relationship had soured, Joseph's older brothers had told him about their battles with the Amorite kings, and his youthful heart is still thrilled at the war stories. The tale of Simeon and Levi's retaliatory operation in Shechem inspired him to see the city that his two brothers had conquered, when they weren't yet teenagers.

Then his thoughts became troubled: Why don't they tell me anything like that anymore? It must be my fault because I don't think enough before I speak. Anything can be interpreted positively or negatively, and I always look at their actions in a negative way. Why do I do that?

A small tear ran down his cheek, soon evaporating in the sun. His conclusion was clear: I owe them a real apology!

The city wall of Shechem was visible from far off. Joseph recognized the place unequivocally from his memories of his brothers' descriptions. When he saw none of them, he thought: Perhaps they are on the other side of town; after all, our flocks are too numerous to vanish without a trace!

Joseph made a circuit around the city, looking for his missing brothers.

"What are you looking for?"

The clear voice from behind Joseph's shoulder made him jump. Joseph quickly turned on his heels, preparing himself for battle against the man who'd materialized as if out of the ether. The elegant face surprised Joseph; the perfect beauty and grace left him speechless; compassion and mercy filled the visage of splendor and grandeur.

"I am looking for my brothers," he told the stranger. "Please tell me where they are grazing."

"They traveled from here," the figure smiled compassionately. "I heard them say they were going to Dothan," the figure said and disappeared as if dissipating into the air.

Joseph looked at where the figure had stood a few seconds earlier: "That must have been an angel of God appearing before me," he thought as he tried to subdue the vibration that passed through his body. "I have to keep going towards Dothan."

Joseph recovered after a few moments. "I have a task to fulfill!"

Levi jumped up, feeling something poke him in the ribs. He had been lying on the soft lawn but was disturbed by Simeon's angry sneer.

"Get up and see who has comes to visit us!" Simeon whispered venomously to his listless brother. "Unfortunately, you won't be happy to see his shining face."

Levi's face expressed disgust: "Why is this tattler coming here? Finding more juicy gossip to tell Father? Showing off his new dress?"

"Maybe he just wants to see if his slaves work well. Perhaps he'll deign to grant us the great privilege of bowing before him," Simeon laid his hand on the sheath of his sword. "I ought to behead this creature and be done with him."

"Why, brother? Maybe he came to tell us another beautiful dream," Levi looked with disgust at his younger brother advancing toward them. "Maybe this time he dreamed we all kissed his feet, begging him to give us the right to serve him."

Joseph's waved hello to them, indicating he had seen them.

Simeon declared, eyes burning with fire, "You know, there's a word for what he is, and it's not gossipmonger or dreamer, it's pursuer. He plots to destroy our lives! He is trying, in every way, to prove to Father that we are wicked, that Father should banish us. He is essentially saying we are like Ishmael and Esau, bad seed, the chaff to be discarded from Abraham and Isaac, who must be distanced by holiness and dwelling with the Divine Presence."

Simeon looked at Levi and saw that he agreed, declaring: "We will do what must be done."

Meanwhile, Joseph saw that his brothers were not responding to his wave. He thought regretfully: They must be mad at me; they're not responding. Simeon and Levi, what courage these two brothers have! Not that the rest are cowards, but these two ...

Joseph hurried his pace, pondering how he could apologize to his brothers for his actions.

"Hello, my dear brothers," he said with a smile as he arrived, but he was met with an icy stare. He extended his hand to Simeon in friendship, but his older brother grabbed him, crushing his hand in his viselike grip.

"Simeon, you're hurting me!" he said in alarm, trying to wrest his wrist free, but to no avail.

Simeon twisted Joseph's arm, then put his other arm to Joseph's throat: "Every dog has his day, and for you, pup, it's your day of reckoning!"

"Enough! Enough! I'm sorry!" Joseph tried to free himself from his brother's grip, knowing he could not remove the arm over his throat.

"I have not yet decided what his sentence should be," he mused to Levi, dismissing with a smile Joseph's attempts to free himself. "There are many ways to execute such a cur. What would be most fitting? Now, I am partial to beheading, but there are other options... Stoning, burning, perhaps strangulation?" He tightened his stranglehold. "They're all good. The simplest way is to choke him and throw him into one of the pits and get rid of this Josephine trouble!"

"What do you think you're doing?!" Reuben's shout boomed at them, interrupting the execution summary. "Let him go!"

Simeon glared at his older brother over the gasping Joseph, whom he still held in a headlock. "Our family garden needs some weeding!"

"Who gave you permission to do that?!" Reuben's eyes gleamed at his brother.

"Permission?!" Levi laughed. "Who needs permission when he commits sedition? It's your position he's trying to usurp, big brother!"

Reuben snorted at this, staring at his brothers. "What makes you say such a thing."

"He is a pursuer!" Simeon protested, raising his voice. "He is trying to get us banished!"

"So, you kill a pursuer?!" Reuben asked innocently.

"Sure! Whoever comes to kill you, arise and kill him first!" Levi shouted.

Reuben rubbed his forehead as if considering his brother's words: "As far as I can remember, Father taught us that the pursuer is to be stopped by deadly force only if necessary. If a less drastic action suffices, that is all the law allows."

"Is all well?!" Judah asked. He and the six other brothers came running from the pastures, alerted by the shouting. "What's going on here?" he asked, puzzled, staring at Joseph in Simeon's grip.

"Simeon and Levi say that Joseph is a pursuer; they may have a point," Reuben summarized. "But as I recall, the pursuer must not be killed, if the pursued can be saved by less drastic action. In this case, the pursued — who we are — cannot take his life if he can be neutralized by merely wounding him."

"Reuben is right," Judah told Simeon and Levi. "You must not kill him!"

"So, what do we do with him? Send him home to tell Father everything that happened here? What do you think will happen to us then?"

The ten brothers stared at each other, trying to find a practical solution to their predicament.

"I have an idea!" Reuben said with a smile, "Here is an empty cistern. We'll throw him in. There are probably snakes and scorpions in the pit. If he deserves death, they will kill him; if not, he will be saved. In the meantime, we can think of a proper solution with clear heads."

Reuben looked at his brothers, who agreed, some readily, some reluctantly. Meanwhile he thought: This will buy me some time until their fury dies down; then I can get him out of the pit. If I can bring him back to Father, perhaps that will atone for my indiscretion in lying on my father's bed.

The brothers stripped Joseph of his striped coat, while he begged for his life. They quickly carried their brother, throwing him into the deep pit.

"Let's eat something; then we'll be able to think," Dan said with a smile to his brothers.

Naphtali nodded: "But let's put some distance between us and the bawling brat."

The expression on the faces of the nine brothers seemed extremely serious.

Reuben eschewed the midday meal, as he fasted through the daylight hours as a measure of penitence for disrespecting his father. He left his brothers to their repast as he went to pray.

The sound of crying and pleading reached their ears faintly.

"If he hasn't been stung by the pests in the pit, he probably does not deserve death," Judah cut the thunderous silence while eating. "It is inconceivable to leave him there to die of starvation!"

"Why not?" Simeon said angrily, "He did not feel sorry for us! He tried to drive a wedge between us and Father."

"You're right, but…" Judah and his brothers looked off into the distance as they heard a new sound coming from the north. A caravan of Ishmaelites came into view, transporting merchandise on camels. "He tried to distance us from Father so, we shall distance him!" Judah said as he found the perfect solution, "We will sell him to these Ishmaelites, who seem to be making their way from Egypt, and we will not lay hands on him, for he is our brother, our flesh!" Judah looked at his smiling brothers with satisfaction: "Let us go and talk to them," he told his brothers happily.

"I tell you, he's a hard worker. He's just too uppity, so we're tired of him. Here, he keeps trying to escape to his family in the north of the land of Canaan. If you take him to Egypt, he will realize escape is hopeless," Simeon said with a smile to the Ishmaelites.

"How much do you want for him?" demanded the Ishmaelite merchant.

Simeon thought for a second, "Forty pieces of silver," he replied.

The Ishmaelite snorted contemptuously: "I swear you will not take more than ten from me for a slave!"

Simeon looked thoughtful, "Ten silver pieces?! What shall we do with ten silver pieces?" To the Ishmaelite he said: "It's a deal!"

He thought: I would give him away for free, just to be rid of him.

However, when the brothers ran towards the pit, they found seven Midianites standing on the edge of the pit, holding the half-naked Joseph, examining the find they had come across.

"What are you doing? Leave him alone, he is our slave!" Naphtali shouted at the Midianites.

Each of the Midianites placed a hand on the hilt of his sword. "Your slave? By the look of it, maybe you are his slaves and you rebelled against him; or you are just trying to rob us of the slave we found!"

Simeon advanced toward the seven Midianites with a sword in his hand: "I tell you that this is our slave, and if you try to take him, you will have to deal with me!"

"So?!" spat one of the Midianites contemptuously.

"Then you will share the fate of the Shechemites. Don't you know what we did when they abducted our sister? Or what happened to the seven Amorite kings who tried to avenge them?" Simeon approached the seven Midianites defiantly, "Do you want the wild animals to feast on your bones too?"

The seven Midianites moved away from Joseph, leaving him to his masters, realizing who stood before them.

"A wise choice, friend, one which will redound to your benefit," Simeon said with a smile as he led the merchants to the merchandise. "Buy him, and you won't regret it." He patted the merchant on the shoulder.

"If you are willing to sell, I'll give you twenty pieces of silver for him, and we need not fight over him," the Midianite told Simeon. "That way everyone will be happy!"

Simeon looked at the Midianite "For the sake of peace, I agree!"

The Midianite inspected Joseph with a smile, examining the white teeth, touching the sturdy body. He tried to summon a tough look on his face. He relished the profit he would make when he sold the slave in Egypt. "Here's the amount we agreed upon!" he said as he poured twenty pieces of silver into Simeon's hands. Joseph was loaded on a donkey, while weeping over his bitter fate.

The lead merchant burst out laughing as they walked away from the sellers: "Twenty? I'll get two thousand silver pieces at least for him!"

"Or we'll lose our heads — and our families will perish too!" his companion said.

"What?!"

"Do you think this boy is really a slave?! Look at him, he's clearly a Hebrew! He is probably one of the family of Israel. When Israel hears that you bought and sold his son, that will be the end of us — and all our cities! You think you're a great trader? You'll bring destruction on all of us!" The friend looked frightened, to the depths of his soul.

The leader thought for a moment, "What do you propose we do?" He thought, and in his heart, he saw horrors from the stories he had heard about the war of Israel against the Amorites.

"I suggest we chase down the Ishmaelites and sell him to them at the price you bought him for. Maybe that's how we'll be saved from your nonsense."

The Midianites caught up to the Ishmaelites, selling Joseph for the same price.

Knowing that he was doomed to go down to Egypt, the weeping Joseph was loaded onto one of the camels, where he stopped crying as the smell of gum, balm, and aromatic resin rose in his nostrils. "At least they're not carrying naphtha," he thought with eyes red from crying.

"Where is he?!" Reuben screamed at his brothers.

The surprised brothers looked at the agitated Reuben in astonishment. "Why are you screaming?! Are you trying to deafen me?" Simeon said to his older brother defiantly. "What's your problem? Do you miss the twerp?"

"Simeon, do not upset me! I asked you, where is he?" Reuben advanced to his brother, his anger growing.

"Who knows? He's gone now, the scheming brat. He is over and done with and will never return! So much for his dreams of grandeur!" Simeon sneered.

Reuben went to his brother, grabbed him by the throat: "Did you kill him?!" he asked in horror.

Simeon angrily moved his brother's hand away from his throat: "I did not kill him. I do not know why, but Judah convinced us not to kill him, but to sell him. So, when a group of Midianite merchants passed through here, we sold him to them."

"You sold him?!" he screamed in disbelief.

"Yes, don't worry. The money is right there. Not much, but enough to buy some nice shoes." Simeon took out a moneybag. "Here, I'll give you your share for selling that snake." Simeon stood with his hand outstretched to his older brother, who refused to take the money.

"Don't get any bright ideas, big brother. We have taken a dread oath, promising to never tell what happened here today. The nine of us convened a court and decreed excommunication — in this world and the next — upon anyone who breathes a word of what transpired here. We even made Joseph swear never to reveal this to Father, although I don't think he'll ever have the chance. So, smile, take your blood money, and forever hold your peace, lest our curses befall you and your seed."

Reuben reluctantly took the money: "How could you have done this? What will we tell Father about his beloved son?"

"We have no choice; we have to tell Father something," Judah said sadly. "We'll have to lie to him."

"It seems to me that the best thing to do is to take the striped coat we stripped off of him, tear it, and pour goat's blood on it and bring it to Father," Levi said seriously. "Obviously, Father will draw his own conclusions, and we will not have to lie to his face."

The brothers looked at each other, thinking of the advice: "And who will bring him the coat?" Naphtali asked.

"We will draw lots, and whoever draws the lot will have to do it."

The coat was torn, the goat was slaughtered, the blood was smeared on the coat, and Judah drew the lot.

Judah's hands shook, a lump in his throat as he stood on the threshold of his father's study, paralyzed. The knowledge of Israel's impending sorrow and sadness almost made him flee, pick up and run away as far as possible. "I must do it, let things fall as they may!" he said to himself, forcing his feet to cross the threshold of the study.

"Father," he said in a whisper, as if wishing to disappear from the world, "we have found this." He mumbled apprehensively to his father, who looked up from the scroll at his son with a smile, "Do you recognize it? Is it your son's coat?"

Israel's eyes widened in terror. He got up quickly, picking up the coat in his hands. A shrill voice burst from his mouth as he collapsed on the ground, hugging the blood-soaked coat, wetting it with a burst of tears. "Oh Joseph! Joseph, my dear son! It is my son's coat! An evil beast devoured him!" He cried bitterly: "Joseph has been torn apart!" Jacob grabbed the collar of his garment and rent it. He wallowed in the dirt, raising ashes on his head. "My son, my dear son, my dear soul has been torn apart and is no more."

His bitter cry brought all the inhabitants of the camp to his door. The news burst out like fire in a field of thorns, breaking hearts, clouding souls. "Joseph was preyed upon by an evil beast as he went on his father's mission to his brothers in Shechem!" Word of mouth spread it almost instantaneously.

Benjamin sat down next to his father, weeping bitterly with him. In fact, he was upset. He found himself unable to cry from the bottom of his heart for his devoured brother: He wondered if he still harbored resentment that Joseph had dreamed of him as one of eleven stars bowing down to him. Heartbroken, the nine-year-old suffered a different kind of torment.

The brothers returned to their father's house, trying to comfort him after his loss. A week passed, a month, but Israel remained disconsolate. "I will go to my grave mourning my son," he cried incessantly. "I was promised through prophecy that if all my sons lived, I would be saved from Hell, but now it appears the netherworld is my fate! My seed from Rachel will not succeed in ridding the world of evil, because Joseph is gone."

"You and your suggestions!" Simeon berated Judah in front of the other brothers, "Look what you have brought upon us! Look what you have done to Father!"

"What I did?!" Judah wondered. "You wanted to murder him! Why am I to blame for Father's misery?"

"You could have persuaded us not to do anything to him! Do you think we really would have killed our little brother?! Because of you, Father is suffering! You constantly act like you're in charge. Whenever an issue arises, you tell us what to do; but now you're trying to shirk responsibility! We won't listen to your advice anymore."

"What are you talking about?!" The cry surprised the brothers. Benjamin had come to look for his brothers; he'd heard them arguing and came to find out why. The brothers hadn't noticed their little brother.

Simeon ran to Benjamin, gripping his hand tightly: "Listen to me carefully!" he admonished his little brother. "If you breathe a word of this, you will be excommunicated from this world and the next world!" Simeon told his kid brother the truth about Joseph. The shocked Benjamin looked at his older brother in disgust. "I guess I have to do what you say," he said after a moment, "but it makes me sick to be in your presence!" Benjamin wiped the tears from his eyes and left the room quickly.

"We ought to take wives," Levi told Reuben.

Reuben smiled in agreement: "You're probably right, brother; it's time to expand the family."

Reuben married Elioram daughter of Hivai the Canaanite. Levi took Adina, great-granddaughter of Eber, as a wife. Judah married Ilith, daughter of Hirah the merchant, Shua of Adullam.

All the other brothers married as well, welcoming their mates into the Covenant of Abraham.

However, Israel's mood was not improved by the arrival of grand-children. His mourning and sadness remained as on the day he heard the bitter news about Joseph.

CHAPTER FIFTY-FOUR

Exile

As the caravan arrived at the noisy marketplace, Joseph woke up. His eyes were now dried out; he had no tears left to shed. Day and night had passed repeatedly as he bounced along amid the ships of the desert.

The travails of travel had been bad enough, but then the Ishmaelites had started beating him to stop his tears. Their blows had come to an abrupt halt miraculously, their raised arms frozen in the air; their paralysis passed only once they had sought the forgiveness of the slave they had bought. After that wondrous occurrence, the Ishmaelites had looked at him askance, afraid to do anything to arouse the ire of the boy they'd acquired.

The marketplace overwhelmed Joseph's ragged senses: the pungent aromas, the shouting sellers, the swirling colors. He firmly shut his eyes as some immodestly dressed women passed in front of him.

The convoy of Ishmaelites made their way to the heart of the bustling market. Joseph could hear the traders shouting: "Slaves for sale! Today only, save when you buy a slave!"

Joseph opened his eyes a little, squinting at what was happening. A dark-skinned man was placed on the stage, wearing nothing but a tiny scrap of cloth that barely covered his loins. The man's body was pawed at, his mouth opened to examine his teeth, every inch of him inspected as if he were an animal.

"Strong and young! Healthy teeth! Sir, if you are interested, I'll sell him to you for sixty silver pieces!" said the slaver with a smile to the interested customer.

"Sixty?! He's not worth even forty! You know the market is flooded. You can't trick me; I know the prices. I'm willing to give you thirty-five, but not a penny more!" The prospective buyer looked at the seller.

"It's a deal! Forty-five, let's shake on it!"

"I said thirty-five! How did you get to forty-five?!"

"You're right, forty is a great price!" said the slaver, pleased with himself.

The prospective buyer grabbed the slaver by the neck: "Stop playing the fool! Do you want thirty-five or not?"

The slaver sighed with a rueful grin: "Well, my friend, I agree, but only because we are friends."

The slave's hands were bound, and he followed his new master in submission.

The Ishmaelite merchant approaches the slaver, whispering a secret to him. The slaver's eyes opened wide with financial greed, and he quickly went with the Ishmaelite to the camel Joseph was on.

"Take him off!" he said with shining eyes. "Wow, where did you get this slave?! How much do you want for him? A hundred?"

The Ishmaelite burst out laughing: "My dear friend, do you think me a simpleton? Don't confuse me for one of the fools you usually deal with. I know how to appreciate goods as well as you!"

"So how much do you want?" The merchant circled around Joseph apprehensively, eager to touch his body, gazing at him mesmerized.

"Look at him! He is no fieldhand; he should serve in Pharaoh's household, or at least in the household of one of his ministers." Ponderously, the Ishmaelite offered: "How does a ten-percent commission sound? But you must find us a high-class buyer, not someone from the sleazy crowd you associate with."

The slaver's eyes twinkled, as if struck by a brilliant idea: "Wait for me here! I'll be back in a few moments. I have a great customer!"

A large crowd gathered around Joseph and the Ishmaelites, trying to offer massive sums of money to purchase the fair-skinned slave. The Ishmaelite ignored the suggestions as if they were ludicrous.

The crowd suddenly parted in awe, as the slaver returned, along with guards escorting one of Pharaoh's most important ministers.

The slaver launched into his blandishments. "You know, my lord, that I would not have bothered an important and honorable person like yourself had it not been for the wonderful commodity I have to offer today. My lord knows my wares are always the finest, but this item is so exceptional, I have never seen his like in all my life. This slave would make an excellent servant for my lord; you will not find anyone better and more attractive than him. My lord, I tell you that you will never regret this purchase. If I could afford him, I would buy this slave myself, but I am not worthy. Such a fine specimen should only be acquired by someone as honorable and noble as my lord."

The slaver fell, prostrating before the minister, who approached with dignity, his face like cast copper, unblinking at the display of fealty

The minister stopped before Joseph, his half-closed eyes flying open in shock, his mouth agape in astonishment. "Where did you kidnap him from?!" he asked the slaver after a few moments of hesitation. "This boy is no slave! You must have kidnapped him from one of the royal houses, and now you want to sell him at a profit. Do you not realize this will end in war?!"

The Egyptian slaver glared at the Ishmaelite trader: "Tell Lord

Potiphar, captain of the guard, where you got this boy from. Tell my lord that you did not abduct him, that you paid full price for him."

The Ishmaelite merchant advanced towards the minister, prostrating himself fully in humility: "My lord, we did not snatch this slave out of nowhere, but bought him from Midianite merchants…" The merchant told the minister what had transpired since they had purchased the slave, omitting some details about beating him on their way to Egypt and the contention he'd had with the initial sellers.

"I will buy him," the minister finally said after hearing the long story. Potiphar turned to his aide, who was walking beside him: "Pay him whatever price he asks," he ordered, without knowing how much they would charge him. "Bring him with us," he told two of his guards, "and be very careful with him! This is not a cheap commodity!"

The slaver whispered to Potiphar's aide: "He will cost you a sum of four thousand silver pieces. Believe me, he cost me more. But for our esteemed Lord Potiphar, I offer a discount."

Potiphar's aide smirked at the merchant's fraud: "Take your money, you wretched schemer. 'He cost me more,' really? We've heard about you. You've never seen such a sum, let alone held it in your hands."

Lord Potiphar had Joseph put in a nice room in his house and ordered that food be brought to the slave. Joseph bathed and dressed in the fine clothes that were brought to his room, his spirit restored thanks to the meal. He took some small comfort in the fact that all the dishes brought before him were vegetarian, since the Egyptians worshipped sheep. He then went in to rest on his comfortable bed.

Lying there, Joseph thought: I have two options. Either I can bitterly lament my fate and the injustice done to me, wallowing in grief and angst; or I can try to find the good in my experience, to seek happiness even though I am far from my father and family.

However, the thoughts of the last few days gave him no rest.

He ordered himself: You must avoid these thoughts absolutely. You can ponder it all later! You must figure out what the Lord wants you to do, what duty demands of you!

Amid a sea of thoughts, reflections, and deliberations, Joseph sank into a deep slumber, indulging in the silence given to him.

As day broke, Joseph opened his eyes and looked around, hoping to see that everything he had been through was actually one of his strange dreams, like the ones about sheaves and stars. However, the Egyptian accoutrements made it clear to him that his new location was very real.

He said to himself: There is work to be done!

He ignored the pains along and across his body, leaping to his feet. Joseph put on the clothes that lay by the bed, apparently placed there as he slept. It was time to do his job, whatever that turned out to be.

Leaving his room, he walked the corridors of the spacious estate, looking for his new master. He asked a dark-skinned man in the hall, who seemed to work there: "Potiphar?" Joseph picked up the name of his new master in the man's reply. The servant, surprised by the elegant young man standing in front of him, then bowed and gestured for Joseph to follow him.

The servant opened the doors wide, and Joseph found himself standing in front of a huge room, with a spacious bed in it, on which Potiphar lay sleeping.

Joseph nodded to the servant and entered the room discreetly. He arranged his master's clothes, waiting for the moment when he would wake up. When Potiphar stirred, Joseph handed his master fresh attire.

Potiphar's eyes opened wide in surprise. The new slave served him as if he already knew all his master's habits and desires. A captivating smile lit up his eyes, as if his sole wish were to serve his master.

Joseph accompanied his master on his daily rounds, managing to learn a few words in the unfamiliar language, maneuvering between the known and the unknown.

In what seemed to be no time at all, Joseph learned enough of the Hamitic tongue to communicate nicely with his master. Understanding the language, he began to offer ideas on how Potiphar might improve his various enterprises.

It wasn't long before Potiphar prospered, thanks to the wise young man he had bought.

Potiphar hugged the shoulders of his slave lovingly: "Joseph, I'm very glad you're with me. Since your arrival, I have finally achieved peace of mind. Business is booming, Pharaoh appreciates me much more, and everything is getting better — all thanks to you!" he gushed.

"My lord," Joseph replied with his captivating smile, "it is all thanks to the Lord. He is the source of everything good!"

"Joseph, can you come please?"

There was the voice that troubled his soul. Lady Zulaikha, Potiphar's wife, had been trying to seduce him since his first day in her home. Now she was calling him again. "Darling, can you bring me the shoes please?"

Joseph entered the room, his eyes lowered to the ground, refusing to look at his master's wife: "If it please you, my lady," he said, handing Zulaikha her shoes without meeting her gaze.

"Please sit down, darling, rest a bit," she said to Joseph, trying to imbue her voice with a husky, seductive tone.

"I beg your pardon, my lady, but I have many affairs of my master, your husband, to attend to," Joseph said, trying to vanish from the room.

"But all I'm asking you is to sit with me for a bit. Please, look me in the face. Why do you refuse to do so? Am I so ugly in your eyes?"

"My lady, forgive me, I cannot speak to your appearance; but I am confident you are not ugly, and I would never think such a thing." Joseph stepped back, attempting to escape.

"Slave, I have not dismissed you yet!" declared Zulaikha in an aggressive but shaky voice.

Joseph felt the stare aimed at him, not allowing him to leave. "Lady Zulaikha, I am sorry if I have offended you in any way."

"Are you sorry? You know, I was considered one of the loveliest women in the whole land of Egypt. All Pharaoh's courtiers courted me before I agreed to marry Potiphar. I could have married any man I desired! Even now, years later, I am still among the great beauties of Pharaoh's court."

Joseph moved restlessly: "Of course, my lady."

"And you... you are as handsome and striking a man as I have ever laid eyes on."

"By the grace of God, Who forms all of us. It was not my doing," he replied in a whisper.

"Your eyes ..." she said longingly, "they have no equal."

"There will be nothing special about them when they are closed in my grave, my lady, a fate which awaits us all," he retorted.

Zulaikha felt the rage rising inside her. The situation was intolerable: a slave who refused her advances? It made her tremble with fury. No man had ever turned her down, but the soft-spoken Hebrew refused to even look at her.

"Do you know who you're dealing with?!" she hissed venomously. "You presumably do not know me well enough yet. I can make you spend the rest of your days in agony. One word of mine, and you will find yourself tortured in a royal dungeon. You would beg me to get you out of there. I will bring you to your knees, until you understand that you cannot refuse me."

Joseph remained silent, but he thought furiously: I know very well who I am dealing with! You are the wife of Satan, the wife of the ancient serpent who tries to seduce me and make me sin like you did Adam, during the one hundred and thirty years he was separated from his wife. You are the same one who makes people sin all the time, who has done so since time immemorial. You are the same one that discards one form and takes on another, in order to distance a man from holiness and his Creator.

Zulaikha looked at Joseph's downcast face, hoping that her words would make an impression: "I will let you go for now, but ponder what I told you. You can live a beautiful and happy life if you listen to me; but if not..." A smile rose to her lips. "Well, I think a boy as smart as you would not be so stupid as to tell me no again."

Joseph turned on his heel and hurried out of the room.

"My dear friend, I do not know how to tell you this, you are a magician!" Potiphar hugged Joseph tightly. "How do you do that? You buy goods that have no chance of being sold, and suddenly their price skyrockets, as if the whole world were waiting for such a product to come to market."

The wide smile on Potiphar's face proved that business was excellent. "I'm telling you, since I bought you, my wealth has doubled at least three times, and all in less than one year." Potiphar chuckled. "To think someone would buy these ridiculous clothes... My friend, you are truly a wizard, like the thaumaturges of Pharaoh's court!"

Joseph smiled at his master: "I am happy if my lord is happy, but I am neither thaumaturge nor wizard nor magician. It is Divine Providence that makes things happen this way."

Potiphar laughed uproariously. "Of course, of course, you tell me that, but I know that it's magic! If only..." He stopped laughing abruptly. His face was overcome with grief, as if suddenly recalling something sad. Potiphar sighed from the depths of his heart, looking at Joseph, debating whether to spill his secrets to him.

"If only..." Joseph repeated. "Did something happen, my lord? Is something wrong with the business?" he asked his master anxiously.

"No, it's not business, it's personal. Between me and my wife." Potiphar muttered, as if unsure how much to share, then shrugged. "The truth is I don't know what's going on between us. We sent our only child away from the capital for her schooling, and I thought we would grow closer; but for almost a year now the situation has been deteriorating, and lately it has become unbearable. Zulaikha has always been… my wife, but suddenly it seems to me that she does not want me. She avoids me, she says she is not feeling well, she uses all sorts of excuses to distance herself from me. And even if she wanted to be with me, I no longer feel physically capable of satisfying her!"

Joseph lowered his eyes. He knew the source of his master's pain, but he could not tell him the true cause of his trouble.

Potiphar put a fake smile on his face: "At least the business is running well…"

CHAPTER FIFTY-FIVE

Zulaikha

eminine laughter filled the room. The five friends sat together, sharing their daily experiences.

They were the elite of Egyptian society, the ladies of the court, the wives of Pharoah's most trusted advisers. Dressed in their finery, they sat in Zulaikha's salon. They lived an elegant and indulgent life of bright colors, intoxicating aromas, and luxurious sensations. They were the famed beauties of the land, married to the most powerful men in the kingdom, and their time was spent seeking out pleasures, acquiring and enjoying them.

However, their hostess seemed to be distracted, as one of her companions could not help but note. "Zulaikha, I don't understand what's happening to you! Excuse me, my dear, but you cannot neglect yourself like that. I have not seen even one smile grace your face since we arrived. You look like you are unwell but do nothing to take care of yourself."

Zulaikha sighed in pain, looking at her friends laughing. She felt miserable, entirely remove from their joy: "There's nothing to do!"

Her friend rose and came to sit next to Zulaikha, embracing her shoulders in sympathy, trying to soothe her mysterious pain.

"Zulaikha, you must tell us what you are going through. You don't eat, you don't drink, you constantly look like your world has been destroyed. Why have friends if you won't tell them what ails you?! You know we love you and want the best for you. Maybe we can help you with something," she said gently.

"You cannot understand," replied Zulaikha, tears welling up in her eyes. "You do not have the tools to understand the humiliation and frustration I feel every day." The tears became sobs: "He doesn't even look at me! Not even a glance..."

Her friends looked at each other in amazement, until the one sitting next to her asked: "Who? Potiphar?!"

Zulaikha gestured dismissively. "Are you serious? Potiphar? You cannot understand... It's Joseph!" she gasped, heartbroken.

"Joseph? Who is Joseph?!" they demanded, almost in unison.

Zulaikha spoke longingly: "Joseph is... Joseph is... he is a slave, whom my husband bought almost a year ago."

"A slave?!" Her friends were shocked. The one with her arms around Zulaikha got up and stepped away in disgust. "You're in this state... because of a slave?!"

In frustration, the mistress snorted: "Yes, I'm going to die because I long for a slave! That sounds crazy, right?!"

"Zulaikha, I don't understand what your problem is! Take him and do with him what you will! You are the mistress, so you are... the mistress! Look, I know what slaves are. I have enough of them at home, and none of them have ever refrained from doing whatever I command them. I have a hard time believing that you do not know how to make chattel do what you want!"

The friends smiled at each other, a secret they all shared. "Now if you have a problem with one of your slaves, we will send you one of our best." They laughed: "And you know we have many!"

Zulaikha waved her hand in dismissal: "I know what you have! I have the same, more than I know what to do with! But Joseph... he doesn't even look at me. "

"Enough, I'm tired of hearing that strange name, Joseph! Like he's got something extra, more than any other slave! I do not know what you are going through, but it seems to me that you should call a doctor," declared her friend, with barely contained rage.

"Or some other slave..." said another of her friends with a leer.

Zulaikha raised her teary eyes, wiping her face. "You know what? I know you're mocking me! I can see that! I would mock you too! But let's do an experiment. You're all talented women, mistresses of your households! You all wear very expensive jewelry! You're all so attractive and experienced!" She smiled to herself: "Please, get up from the couch. Do not be afraid, I will not do you any harm. I will only illustrate to you, what I go through every day, all day!"

Zulaikha took four apples and four knives from the serving table. "Please, peel the apples when I tell you to start. All I ask is that you try to make him just look up and gaze at you. The first to succeed will be given my entire jewelry box! Just get him to glance at you! Whoever succeeds will win all the jewelry! But if none of you do, then I will take yours. Ready?"

"Zulaikha, be serious!" Her friends laughed at the very thought. "What is this nonsense? Why do we need to peel an apple?"

Zulaikha looked at her friends devilishly: "I'm very serious, every last item of jewelry. As for peeling the apple, you'll soon see. Ready?"

She strode towards the doorway, her friends exchanging glances behind her back, wondering if the mistress of the house had gone mad.

"Joseph!" Zulaikha's voice echoed through the mansion: "Joseph, come to my salon!"

Zulaikha stood by the doorway, waiting. A light footstep approached. "Start peeling!" Zulaikha commanded her friends.

"Joseph, please come into the room, I need you to bring me the new dress I bought from over there," Zulaikha said in a foggy voice. Joseph quickly entered, his eyes fixed on his shoes, making his way through the salon towards the wardrobe. As he walked, he thought: That snake brought reinforcements to fight me! A diamond-encrusted ring was thrown at his feet. Joseph continued on his way, trying to escape the suite as quickly as possible. More jewelry was thrown at him, as Zulaikha's friends tried to distract him from his duty. He quickly took out the dress, turned on his heel, marched back to Zulaikha, and handed her the garment. "As it please you, my lady," he said, leaving the room without lifting his gaze once.

The friends remained wide-eyed, their eyes fixed on the doorway through which Joseph had disappeared so quickly, memorizing the young man's figure, and sealing it in their memories. The friends tried to recover, to return to reality, their eyes fixed on Zulaikha with compassion. "Wow...!" they whispered longingly.

"Do you understand? And you thought me a fool or a madwoman?" she spat venomously. "Now, look at your hands and see what has slashed my heart, day after day, month after month!"

The women looked at their hands and began screaming. Their palms were filled with blood, as they had sliced their flesh absentmindedly while Joseph had distracted them. While the slave had been in the room, they had felt nothing.

"Serves you right for making fun of me!" Zulaikha derided them viciously. "Now that you've seen your hands, maybe you'll feel the stabbing in your hearts too... And don't forget to leave the rest of your jewelry!"

"Ugh, her actions cross every boundary of decency!"

Joseph was sitting in his room, trying to find a way deal with Zulaikha. "I thought she would stop it, but the pressure is only getting worse, day by day. Master of the Universe, help me to be free of her. I cannot go on like this! All day long she's just enticing me, attempting to seduce me. I cannot bear this! I have no peace of mind anymore, and I'm starting to lose my sanity!"

The commotion in the mansion distracted him: "At least tomorrow I will have a break. They have an idolatrous holiday, and everyone is going to celebrate, the masters and the slaves together. I alone, as a worshipper of the One God, will remain to do my work. At least tomorrow she will not be able to drive me crazy."

The unusual silence brought a smile to Joseph's face. A sensation of peace and tranquility filled his soul, sure that he was the lone occupant of the great estate for the next few hours. The usually bustling mansion was silent, only the sound of his footsteps echoing through the house.

"Joseph!" The call froze Joseph in his place. "Joseph, come to my room, please," Zulaikha said calling from the entrance to her suite.

Joseph approached, his heart pounding; he had thought there was no one else in the house, but here she was. His mind was confused. "What will I do? How can I avoid her now? It is not going to stop! How can I be saved from this evil beast?!" His hear was about to explode: "How am I supposed to withstand such an attempt?! Everything is twisted here: no family, no friends, far from Father!"

"Please come in," Zulaikha whispered, trying to hide the excited tremor in her voice, "I need you to help me with something."

Joseph entered the room, knowing that it made no difference whether the door was closed or not. They were alone in the house. "Yes, my lady," he said, feeling the horror of death upon him, as if he were being carried to the gallows with no hope of escape.

"I didn't feel well this morning, so I didn't go with the rest of the household to celebrate," she smiled. "I do have a new pair of shoes in honor of the occasion, and I need your help getting them on."

Joseph's eyes were focused on the footwear. "Of course, my lady," he replied. A shiver passed through his body as he picked up the shoe.

Zulaikha sat down on the divan, raising her dress to expose her feet. Joseph approached in fear, trying to put her shoe on her with eyes closed.

But when he stood up and turned to leave, he felt her hands resting on his shoulders, grasping his tunic from behind. "Joseph, I beg you..."

Thoughts ran through his mind, quick like lightning: "I must run away! How much longer must I suffer, Lord?! Perhaps I can convince her that I am lacking in male potency? Will she leave me alone then? No, she is utterly besotted. Yet it is forbidden! How long, Lord?!"

"At least look at me!" cried Zulaikha fatally, her desperate cry interrupting his reverie.

His eyes still shut, and his arms stretched out in front of him, Joseph turned his head. He opened his eyes a bit when his arm hit a mirror. He was struck by the face peering back at him, so much like that of his father, from whom he had been abducted. The thought struck him: Can a son of Israel really do such a thing?

Joseph moved his arms as he leaned back, wriggled out of the tunic his master had brought him as a gift, fleeing from the room as if his soul depended on it. He felt pain in his fingertips, as if a liquid had flowed from them.

"You do not care about me! All that matters to you is your fortune and honor!" Zulaikha's screams echoed throughout the mansion.

Potiphar, who had returned with all his slaves and servants from the feast, stood stunned before his shrieking wife. Some of the manservants and maidservants who came before him stood beside Zulaikha, their faces stunned by what their mistress had told them a few moments earlier: "*See, he has brought in a Hebrew to mock us; he came in to lie with me, and I cried with a loud voice. And it came to pass, when he heard that I lifted up my voice and cried, that he left his garment by me, and fled, and got him out.*"

Now she repeated her accusation to Potiphar: "*The Hebrew servant, whom you have brought to us, came in to mock me. And it came to pass, as I lifted up my voice and cried, that he left his garment by me, and fled out.*"

The captain of the guard looked at his wife with a despairing look on his face. To himself, he wondered who had in fact done what to whom; but he knew that he could not admit that aloud.

Zulaikha continued to rage: "You must punish him! Show him no mercy! Do you know what he did to me?! He came in when I was asleep and had his way with me! You must behead him forthwith!"

Potiphar looked at his wife with pity mixed with anger, certain that his wife was hiding the truth from him.

"Do you think I am lying?! Check the divan, see I'm not lying! What do you think that vile stain is?" The manservants and maidservants gazed at Potiphar in amazement.

"Heaven forbid, my love, I don't suspect you of lying, not for a moment," he replied in a weak voice.

Gathering his strength, he ordered a servant: "Summon the guard!"

"My lord," the lieutenant reported privately a short time later to Potiphar, "we apprehended the Hebrew slave. He was sitting in his room, as if waiting for us to come. He did not object to the arrest. His attitude was very bizarre, almost as if he were relieved to be chained and taken away to the royal dungeon."

Potiphar sighed heavily, "And what about the test I asked you for? What did the thaumaturges say after you gave them the sample?"

The officer paused a bit, thinking of how to tell his superior about the discovery: "The thaumaturges say that, most likely... it's egg whites," he whispered.

Potiphar sighed again, bemoaning his predicament.

"Now what, my lord? Shall we execute him?" asked the lieutenant, assuming there was nothing wrong with killing a slave to cover up the lies of his superior's wife.

Potiphar thought for a moment, "No! Do not execute him! Tell the warden that the slave is mine, and that I am asking him to protect and preserve him. I need to think about how to proceed. Tell him that the slave I entrust to his keeping has a rare talent, and he should feel free to avail himself of his prisoner's services until I take him back. " Potiphar placed his hand on the lieutenant's shoulder: "I ask you to keep what you know and what I told you a secret, my friend. I promise you it will pay off for you."

The officer nodded understandingly to Potiphar, smoothly pocketing the precious stone the captain of the guard had slipped him. "Certainly, my lord. The matter will be shielded behind a wall of silence."

"Joseph, my dear friend, what have you brought me today?" The warden sat in his room, full of pleasure, smile smeared across his face.

"Boned fish with steamed vegetables, my lord," the prisoner said to his jailer. "And another little thing, my lord, the land on the edge of town we were talking about — buy it as soon as possible; it will be worth three times as much in two weeks. "

The warden looked at Joseph with a smile. "Tell me, how do you know all this? You are sitting here in the royal dungeon, but you know what to buy and what to sell all over the country."

Joseph placed the laden tray in front of the warden: "You know, my lord, that I have my sources. As far as I know, you have never lost following the tips I give you, my lord. I hope that things will continue in the same manner," he said with a smile.

"You're not wrong, my friend; you probably do not even know how right you are." The warden smiled at Joseph with great affection. "Ah... something else," he said with a full mouth, "we have two new prisoners today, and the truth is that they are both my colleagues: the chief butler and the chief baker. His Majesty had an awful luncheon today: first he found a fly in his wine, then a hair in his bread. You should have seen Pharaoh's face — I pray I never witness such anger turned on me! Anyway, they are to be brought here until His Majesty decides what to do with them. Take good care of them; as I said, both are my friends."

One morning not long afterward, Joseph happily went to the cell where the chief butler and the chief baker were imprisoned. He held two trays heavily laden with hearty breakfasts.

Joseph opened the door with a wide smile, but the two officials responded with anxious frowns. "Good morning, my lords," he grinned, hoping to improve their moods. However, the officials only scowled in response, frustrated.

"Friends, what troubles you so? I hope I didn't wake you up. I was sure you'd arisen long ago. Have I done something wrong?" Joseph asked, trying to smile at the displeased officials.

"No, it's not you, Joseph," said the chief butler with a downcast face.

"I hope there's been no quarrel between you," Joseph said, examining his grim face.

"We haven't been fighting," the baker said heavily.

"If it's because you've heard a rumor about your cases, rest assured that's not true. I know nothing has developed yet, and we're still waiting for Pharaoh's decisions."

The chief butler shook his head: "No, it's not that, my friend." The official waited a bit, debating whether to tell Joseph or not. Finally, he confessed: "We've just had disturbing dreams, shaking us to our core! We cannot interpret them."

Joseph looked at the depressed officials. "My friends, interpretations belong to God!" he said with a smile. "Please tell me!"

The chief butler looked at Joseph, thinking: He is a young man, admittedly, but very talented and smart.

"In my dream, behold, a vine was before me; and in the vine were three branches; and as it was budding, its blossoms shot forth, and the clusters thereof brought forth ripe grapes, and Pharaoh's cup was in my hand; and I took the grapes, and pressed them into Pharaoh's cup, and I gave the cup into Pharaoh's hand." The chief butler looked at Joseph in the hope that he would be able to interpret the obscure dream.

"This is the interpretation of it: the three branches are three days; within yet three days shall Pharaoh lift up your head and restore you to your office; and you shall give Pharaoh's cup into his hand, after the former manner when you were his butler."

The chief butler smiled lovingly at Joseph, feeling color returning to his cheeks as his misery fled. The young man looked at the official with a smile and blurted out, almost reluctantly. *"But when it shall be well with you, show kindness, please, to me: recollect me and recall me to Pharaoh, and bring me out of this house. For indeed I was stolen away out of the land of the Hebrews; and here also have I done nothing that they should put me into the dungeon."* Joseph regretted the words as soon as he had said them, but it was too late.

In the meantime, the chief baker smiled at Joseph hopefully, realizing that Joseph was right. In his dream, he had seen the chief butler restored as well, so he knew that the interpretation was correct. However, his own dream remained symbolic and enigmatic to him.

He told Joseph: *"I also saw in my dream, and behold, three baskets of white bread were on my head; and in the uppermost basket there was of all manner of baked food for Pharaoh; and the birds did eat them out of the basket upon my head."*

The baker's face fell when he saw the gloomy look on Joseph's face.

"This is the interpretation thereof: the three baskets are three days; within yet three days shall Pharaoh lift up your head from off

you and shall hang you on a tree; and the birds shall eat your flesh from off you," Joseph said with certainty.

The baker began to cry, while the chief butler's gaze was downcast, as he too had seen within his own dream this bitter fate for his colleague.

Three days passed, and the king issued his decree, while celebrating his birthday. The chief baker was hanged, while the chief butler was returned to his original post. He poured the king his wine while the memory of Joseph came to mind again and again. The chief butler pushed to the corner of his mind the request of the Hebrew slave, reluctant to mention it before the king.

CHAPTER FIFTY-SIX

Dreams

"Can you stop driving me crazy with your nonsense?" Pharaoh's face flushed with anger. "If the interpretation is beyond you, just admit you don't know! Stop making up all sorts of ludicrous ideas to attempt to justify your position at court! What is the connection between the drivel you are trying to sell me and my dream?" Pharaoh shrieked with cynical mockery: "'Seven daughters you shall bear, seven daughters you shall bury.' 'Seven lands you shall conquer, seven lands you shall concede.' How do these predictions explain my dreams? Here's one for you: 'Seven thaumaturges sang, seven thaumaturges hang!' That one at least has a nice ring to it!"

The thaumaturges looked at each other apprehensively, aware that their inability to interpret Pharoah's dreams to his satisfaction could cost them their lives. The great obstacle was that Pharaoh had told them that his dreams had included both allegory and explanation; he had forgotten the latter part but would know it when he heard it. Unfortunately, every interpretation they'd proposed so far had rung false.

The chief butler approached his monarch gingerly. As he

presented a goblet of fine wine, he thought: With Pharaoh in such a foul mood, it is hardly the time to remind him of my past mistakes. However, if I can help soothe his spirit today, he will remember it with favor for the rest of his life!

"Your Majesty, may I speak freely?" he asked submissively.

The king snorted contemptuously. Now even the sommelier is trying to play soothsayer. "Speak then!" What did he have to lose?

The chief butler squirmed a bit. "I beg your Majesty's pardon, but... I must recall my sins today. Pharaoh was wroth with his servants, and put me in jail, in the house of the captain of the guard, me and the chief baker."

"Yes?!"

"One day the baker and I had dreams: each of us had a vision of our own. We also were told what the meaning of the other's vision was."

"Get on with it!" Pharaoh urged, impatient due to sleeplessness.

"In the prison with us there was a Hebrew boy, some slave of the captain of the guard — certainly unfit for a prominent position, possibly mentally incompetent. I don't know why we told him the dreams, but we had no other options. The amazing thing was that he interpreted them precisely, like an idiot savant! The chief baker was hanged, while Your Majesty graciously restored me to my position."

Pharaoh rose to his feet: "Who is this slave? Where is he now?"

"Joseph, Your Majesty, his name is Joseph," the minister said apprehensively. "As far as I know, he is still in the royal dungeon."

"Bring him to me immediately!"

The loud knocks on the heavy iron door alerted the warden, who had been enjoying his extravagant meal. The official struggled to make himself presentable, running to the door anxiously: "If anyone is rapping on the dungeon door, it must be by Pharaoh's own direct and urgent command!" He tried to comport himself properly.

Joseph caught up with him at the door, wiping the warden's hands as he marched toward the heavy door. "Just a moment, please," he said, pulling out the large ring of keys to open the door.

"By the king's order, we have come to retrieve Joseph from the royal dungeon," the lieutenant told the warden, looking — as it were — through the slave who had opened the door for him.

"Joseph?" the warden repeated morosely, knowing that the long period of prosperity he had enjoyed was now at an end.

"I am Joseph," was all that the young man said to the lieutenant, but his thoughts were a maelstrom.

The previous night, he had been considering the mysterious ways of God. He had realized that exactly two years had passed since the chief butler and chief baker had experienced their fateful dreams; two years since he had erred by begging the former: *"Recollect me and recall me to Pharaoh;"* two years of suffering for putting his confidence in flesh and blood.

Then a presence had filled the room. Joseph's eyes had widened, seeing the figure he had encountered while searching for his brothers in Shechem. The figure told him: "I have to teach you a few things for the next part of your journey," and began to teach him many and sundry languages. Joseph tried to remember, to understand, to absorb, but the words would not settle in his memory. The figure pondered for a moment, then declared: "Jehoseph will be your name!" With the power of this new facet of his identity, God's name intertwined with his own, the young man felt the multiple tongues miraculously become etched in his mind...

Joseph's reverie ended abruptly when the lieutenant snapped: "Come with me!"

"My lord, the cauldron is on the fire. You will have to see to it that your soup does not burn," Joseph said as he left his prison, smiling at the shocked warden.

As they left the dungeon and came into the light, the lieutenant looked at Joseph's tattered prison garb. "Sorry, but you cannot appear before the king like this. You need to be shaved, bathed, and dressed to be presentable in court."

Joseph was escorted by a squad of royal guards to the bath, barber, and haberdasher. He could not help but wonder what God had in mind for him next. The bright lights dazzled the eyes accustomed to the darkness of the dungeon.

His years of imprisonment had taught him how to instill peace and patience in his soul. The absolute knowledge that he was being led by the Creator of the Universe gave him the confidence to cast aside his emotions and accept everything he went through with equanimity.

Freshly cleaned, coiffed, and clothed, Joseph was brought into Pharaoh's throne room, which was spectacularly spacious, high-ceilinged, and broad. Joseph followed his escorts with assuredness, glad to have left the dank and dark behind him.

"Are you Joseph?!" a voice boomed down from on high.

Joseph looked up, seeing the king of Egypt for the first time, on his lofty throne, atop seventy steps of gold. He nodded affirmatively.

Without preamble, the king announced: "*I have dreamed a dream, and there is none that can interpret it; and I have heard say of you, that when you hear a dream, you can interpret it.*" His voice conveyed doubt that a slave, newly freed from prison, could accomplish what the famed thaumaturges of his court had failed to do; but he retained a faint hope that his chief butler's idea might bear fruit.

"I beg Your Majesty's pardon, but I have never said that I know how to interpret dreams. *It is not in me; God will give Pharaoh an answer of peace.* If the Lord wishes to explain the vision, I am his conduit to inform Your Majesty; but if not, then I am helpless. God willing, may the former be the case."

Pharaoh waved his hand in disapproval, trying to dismiss Joseph's strange words. "Now you listen to me! *In my dream, behold, I stood upon the brink of the river. And behold, there came up out of the river seven cows, fat-fleshed and well-favored; and they fed in the reed-grass. And behold, seven other cows came up after them, poor and very ill-favored and lean-fleshed, such as I never saw in all the land of Egypt for badness. And the lean and ill-favored cows did eat up the first seven fat cows. And when they had eaten them up, it could not be known that they had eaten them; but they were still ill-favored as at the beginning. So, I awoke."*

Pharaoh shivered at the frightening memory.

"And I saw in my dream, and behold, seven ears came up upon one stalk, full and good. And behold, seven ears, withered, thin, and blasted with the east wind, sprung up after them. And the thin ears swallowed up the seven good ears."

Pharaoh paused; his story told. Sweat beaded his brow as he remembered the terrifying visions. Joseph was his last lifeline, a thin strand keeping him from drowning in a sea of desertion. Pharaoh waved his hand dismissively at his court magicians. "These are my thaumaturges, whom I consulted; not one of them could give me a satisfying answer as to what these dreams mean."

Joseph looked at the king with a smile, seeing the mental distress experienced by the mighty king, feeling that the solution ought to be clear and simple to all. "Your Majesty! First, the two dreams are actually one, communicated to the king using two analogies. Now, I believe that the king has changed a few details in his description of the dreams. First, did not the king see himself standing in the Nile itself, not on its bank? Second, did not the king see that before the thin cows ate the fat cows, they stood alongside the fat cows?"

Joseph saw Pharaoh's eyes open in astonishment; he nodded in agreement, impressed by the slave's knowledge. Despite the chief butler's derogatory remarks, there was no doubt that Joseph was in fact intelligent and eloquent.

"Now, as I said earlier: both dreams have the same message, which God is sharing with Pharaoh. It is clear that the dreams revealed to you are of great significance to the whole land of Egypt, not some private or marginal matter," Joseph reprimanded the thaumaturges.

"The seven good cows and the seven good ears of grain herald seven years of abundance and fullness; the seven thin cows and the seven thin ears of grain predict seven years of famine."

Joseph looked at the king, seeing in his eyes confirmation of his interpretation. *"That is the thing which I spoke to Pharaoh: what God is about to do He has shown to Pharaoh. Behold, there come seven years of great plenty throughout all the land of Egypt. And there shall arise after them seven years of famine; and all the plenty shall be forgotten in the land of Egypt; and the famine shall consume the land; and the plenty shall not be known in the land by reason of that famine which will follow; for it shall be very grievous."*

The thaumaturges gasped in shock and horror at this ominous forecast.

"And for that the dream was doubled to Pharaoh twice, it is because the thing is established by God, and God will shortly bring it to pass," Joseph said with equanimity and without inflection.

Pharaoh's eyes darted towards his frightened thaumaturges. Their expressions revealed that they had no idea what to do next. Joseph's calm affect raised hope in Pharaoh's heart for a solution. "And now..." the king prompted, hoping for a remedy.

Joseph glanced at the thaumaturges amusedly: *"Now therefore let Pharaoh see to a man discreet and wise, and set him over the land of Egypt. Let Pharaoh do this, and let him appoint overseers over the land, and take up the fifth part of the land of Egypt in the seven years of plenty. And let them gather all the food of these good years that come and lay up grain under the hand of Pharaoh for food in the cities and let them keep it. And the food shall be for a store to the land*

against the seven years of famine, which shall be in the land of Egypt;
that the land perish, not through the famine."

Pharaoh and the thaumaturges looked at Joseph, amazed at his
wisdom. *"Can we find such a one as this, a man in whom the spirit*
of God is?" Pharaoh asked his embarrassed courtiers.

"Climb one step towards my throne," said Pharaoh, knowing that
Joseph understood the language of the land of Egypt. Joseph did as
he was ordered.

"Do you understand what I am saying to you?" Pharaoh asked in
the language of Midian.

"Certainly, Your Majesty," Joseph replied in Midianite. Pharaoh
gestured for him to climb to the next step.

"Rise further up!" said Pharoah in Assyrian.

Joseph ascended further: "As you say, Your Majesty," he answered
in Assyrian.

In seventy languages Pharaoh spoke to Joseph, and in seventy
languages Joseph answered the king. For every language that the
young man answered in, he climbed another step, to the astonishment of Pharaoh and his thaumaturges. Egyptian law said that the
most educated man in the kingdom, who knew more languages than
other people, would become the king of Egypt. Joseph reached the
last step, standing face to face with the king.

"Peace be upon you, Your Majesty," Joseph whispered to Pharaoh
in the Holy Tongue.

Pharaoh looked at Joseph in shock, feeling as if the earth trembled beneath him: "What did you say?" he asked in Egyptian.

Joseph repeated the phrase.

"What are you saying?! What language are you speaking?!" the
king whispered to Joseph.

In Egyptian, Joseph responded: "I said: 'Peace be upon you, Your
Majesty.' My native language is the Holy Tongue, the one with which
the Lord created the world."

Pharaoh felt terror take over him: "You must teach me this language," said the king, trying to calm himself.

"Happily, Your Majesty," Joseph said with a smile, knowing that the endeavor was futile. As they stood on the seventieth step for a long time, Joseph patiently taught the king of Egypt several phrases, but Pharaoh could not manage to get his mouth around the words.

"You must not reveal to anyone that you know one language more than I do," Pharaoh said to Joseph casually, knowing that his status as king depended on the slave facing him.

Joseph smiled at Pharaoh: "Surely, Your Majesty."

Pharaoh looked at Joseph unbelievingly: "Will you swear to me that you will not tell?"

"I swear," Joseph told the king.

Pharaoh smiled with relief and raised his voice again: "*Forasmuch as God has shown you all this, there is none so discreet and wise as you.*" The thought passed through his head: You know a language even I do not know.

"*You shall be over my house, and according to your word shall all my people be ruled.*" Looking at Joseph, Pharaoh wondered if the young man understood the significance of this decree. Joseph neither batted an eye nor changed his expression.

"*Only in the throne will I be greater than you!*" said Pharaoh, trying to impress the young man who had been a prisoner only hours earlier.

"*See, I have set you over all the land of Egypt.*"

There was no response. Pharoah thought: Does he think all this is only for appearances' sake?

He knew Joseph was the only man who could save Egypt. He pulled the signet ring from his finger and put it on Joseph's. "Come with me," Pharaoh summoned Joseph, and they made their way down from the height of the throne.

"Run and bring royal robes for this man! Summon all the royal ministers immediately!" the king commanded his servants.

They ran and returned quickly, dressing Joseph in luxurious clothes.

The royal ministers looked in amazement at the slave who was wearing royal robes. Pharaoh took a precious gold chain in his hand and placed it on Joseph's neck. "Bring the viceregal chariot, and bear him throughout the city, announcing: This is Abrech! He is like a father (*ab*) to the king, even though he is tender (*rach*) in years, because he is so great in his wisdom. I appoint him viceroy over all of Egypt!" he ordered his ministers.

"But he is a slave!" the minister of justice objected. "And it is written in the laws of Egypt that a slave cannot occupy a high office!"

Pharaoh looked with a piercing smile: "I know the laws well! Now, look at his bearing, which is so aristocratic — is it conceivable that he is truly a slave? If you say so, then it is time to amend the law... or replace the justice minister!"

The king shifted his gaze from the minister to Joseph, hoping to see his heart skip a beat. "Do you understand what I mean? *I am Pharaoh, and without you no man shall lift up his hand or his foot in all the land of Egypt.* "

"I understand," Joseph said mildly.

Pharaoh felt frustrated at the discipline of the man facing him. The realization that this young man controlled himself unconditionally amazed him. "What did you say your name was?" he asked after a few moments of hesitation.

"Joseph," he replied.

Pharaoh thought for a moment, trying to roll the name on his tongue. "No, that won't do. From now on, we will call you Zaphenath-paneah, my dear friend. This is a worthy name, for you possess the ability to decipher (*paneah*) that which is hidden (*zaphun*) in a man's heart."

To his servants, he ordered: "Go and announce in the streets to all the people that Pharoah commands all citizens to leave their houses and see the man whom the king has selected to be viceroy of Egypt."

Pharaoh turned his gaze to his ministers: "Come on! Take Zaphenath-paneah and place him in the viceregal chariot. Pass before him and say what I told you, immediately!"

The chariot began its journey around the capital. Tens of thousands of people left their homes, standing in the crowded streets, watching the man who had risen to greatness. Joseph sat in the chariot, his eyes fixed on his feet, hearing the shouts of the people who had come to see him, sensing, and seeing the jewelry thrown into the chariot by young women hoping to catch his eye.

A strange item hit his arm, and he was drawn to it almost against his will. It was a golden pendant which popped open, revealing a message inscribed in the Holy Tongue! His eyes read excitedly the familiar script from his father's house: "This girl is Asenath, daughter of Dinah, daughter of Israel, son of Isaac, son of Abraham." He read the words over and over again.

"Halt!" he abruptly told the charioteer, who immediately complied. "Minister of the Interior, come to me!" Joseph called out to the cohort of ministers accompanying his chariot.

The minister approached Joseph, his face sour at the indignity of being forced to obey a slave.

"Please find out who the woman who threw this ornament at me is," Joseph ordered in a slightly excited voice, "We will wait here until you locate her and bring her to me."

The minister approached his duty with a heavy sigh, hoping that the day would be over as soon as possible.

A few minutes passed, and the minister parted the crowd, approaching the chariot with a smile, leading a young woman, about twenty years old. "Here is the woman! This is the daughter of

Potiphar, your erstwhile master," the minister told Joseph.

"I thank you very much, my dear friend. You have helped me greatly, I will not forget you," Joseph thanked the minister of the interior.

He looked up a little. It was as if his half-sister Dinah stared back at him. "Please, ride with me in the chariot, my lady."

"Do you know who you are?" he asked the young woman.

"What? I'm Asenath, the daughter of Lord Potiphar and Lady Zulaikha," she replied with downcast eyes. "I came back to the capital to find a husband."

Joseph gazed at her, seeing on her face that she was not disclosing the full truth: "Do you know whose daughter you really are?"

Uncomfortably, she thought: this is Zaphenath-paneah, decipherer of hidden things. Pharaoh says he can read the secret of any heart! She revealed, with mixed emotions: "It took me years to learn the truth, but my birth mother was actually Dinah, daughter of Israel."

"And I am Joseph, son of Israel! Dinah and I have the same father, but different mothers," Joseph said, to Asenath's surprise. "So have you found a husband?" he asked.

"Not yet," Asenath said, smiling captivatingly.

Joseph felt a blush rise over his cheek: "Will you marry me?"

Asenath felt as if the whole bustling world around them fell silent: "Yes," she said as her heart skipped a few beats.

She recalled Zulaikha's cries and complaints against herself and her dreams: "Every night, I see visions in my sleep that I will have children from Joseph. But now Joseph is in prison! What will become of my dreams?!" She would sob incessantly in the darkness of the night, when she thought no one could hear; but her adopted daughter, in her suite surreptitiously, overheard her words and wept with her.

She thought, not without some sympathy for Zulaikha: Her dreams must have been about me; since she raised me as her daughter, my children would be like her own offspring. "Happily!" she agreed, eyes sparkling with joy.

Thirty-year-old Joseph married the twenty-two-year-old daughter of his half-sister. Two sons were born to them, Manasseh and Ephraim. Meanwhile, Joseph led the whole nation for seven years with a firm hand, scrimping as if the famine were nigh, even though the harvests were bountiful and grain abundant. Seven years passed, seven years of imposed privation amidst profusion, parsimony amidst plenty.

CHAPTER FIFTY-SEVEN

Tamar

"**S**o, what should we do, Father?"

The voice of his young son pulled Judah out of his reverie. Judah put his head in his hands, painfully contemplating the complex issue, thinking of how he'd gotten here, over the course of a decade...

For a few years after Judah married Ilith, daughter of Hirah the merchant, Shua of Adullam, his life had seemed charmed. A beautiful wife, three sons — but now Ilith had tragically passed away, leaving Judah a widower.

Judah had sought a wife for his firstborn Er, and Tamar had seemed perfect, a young woman so modest that her face was never seen. All those who knew her praised her, because the girl was as attractive as she was modest. She had lost her own father, and so she had been married off by her mother.

Then, a few months after Er and Tamar's marriage, Er had suddenly died. Judah had asked Onan his son to marry his brother's wife, to bring a baby into the world to bear his older brother's name. However, a few months after that marriage, Onan died as well.

Judah had asked Tamar to return to her childhood home so his little boy, Shelah, could have a chance to grow up; then Shelah and Tamar could marry.

The years had passed, but Judah could not make peace with the idea of marrying off his youngest and last surviving son to the woman who had already buried his two older brothers.

Now, he replied to Shelah: "In truth, my son, I don't know," wallowing in the frustration that accompanied him constantly.

Had everything taken a turn for the worse from the day of Joseph's sale? All his brothers remained angry with him, saying that if he had wanted to, he could have discouraged them from doing anything to Joseph. The thought that their father, Israel, was in constant sorrow because of his inaction allowed him no rest. Judah did not really believe his brothers saying that just as they'd accepted his proposal to sell Joseph, they would've agreed to return him to his father. Still, the bothersome thought that they might have agreed brought to his heart a feeling of profound melancholy — a feeling that had intensified now that he was a widower and doubly bereaved father.

"But Father, I just don't understand how Tamar could be to blame," Shelah objected, trying to find a solution to the complicated problem. "Tamar remains chained in her mother's home, unable to move forward with her life. The levirate duty devolves to me, and I am willing and ready. If there is some reason that our marriage is undesirable, then she can be released through the unshoeing ceremony and marry any man she wants. If, on the other hand, there is no objection, why should I not fulfill my levirate duty?" Shelah dreaded raising such a touchy subject with his father, but the situation did not sit well with his well-developed sense of justice. "With all due respect, Father, I cannot understand your position, which is neither here nor there."

"Look, my son, the situation is not that simple. There is a type of a woman who may never marry, because any husband of hers will die, due to her temperament or her fate," Judah tried to justify his actions. "Now, it's true that once is happenstance, twice is coincidence, the third time is fate; but this is a matter of life and death. I cannot wait for you to be the third victim who proves the pattern. Two deaths are enough in this instance; I cannot lose my last surviving son!"

Shelah looked his father in the face, trying to find the words to express himself without defaming his dead brothers. "If that were the case, I would understand and accept your refusal to let me marry her. However, you know as well as I that it was not Tamar's temperament or fate that caused Er and Onan's death, but their temperament and fate. You know as well as I do that Er did not want Tamar to become pregnant, because he thought that would make her unattractive; so, he took measures so she would not conceive. Onan did the same, though his motivation was that he didn't want to father a child who would be considered Er's heir. It was their desires which caused their lives to be cut short! The Lord killed them because of their lustful drives." Shelah teared up. "I don't want to upset you, Father, but it is difficult for me to hear an injustice and not try to stop it. In my humble opinion, Tamar suffers for a crime she didn't commit."

Judah sighed from the bottom of his heart: "You are right, my son. On the other hand, I fear greatly for your life. You are the last thing I have left on earth after the death of your mother and two brothers. For many years, all of you filled my world, but now all I have left is you."

Judah sighed again, rising his feet: "I must get going now. Your grandfather Hirah is waiting for me. We have to go to Timnah to shear the flock. I very much hope that there I will have some leisure, away from town, to think through the matter and arrive at a conclusion. I very much hope that I will return from there with a practical plan for the future."

Judah and Hirah made their way together to Timnah. Two of Judah's servants accompanied them, walking a little before their master at his command, to give him privacy during his conversation with his beloved father-in-law. The close relationship between Judah and Hirah gave the feeling that their bond was not merely that of family, but of true friendship.

"You know, what? Being with you depresses me," Hirah told Judah, much to his surprise. "Not that I'm sad to see you, but I'm sad to see you act as if you have nothing left to live for. You're still in the prime of your life, but you act like a doddering old man. Your great-grandfather Abraham was a century older than you when his wife died, but he went and remarried. Now, you've been a widower for almost a decade, but you act as if you might die any day. True, my cherished daughter Ilith was a wonderful woman, but there is no need for you to remain alone forever. A year or two of mourning, that's understandable; but it's been nearly ten years!"

The long road to Timnah seems even longer as Judah pondered his predicament. He thought: The truth is that Hirah is right. *It is not good for man to be alone.* The situation I create is ultimately for the worse. Perhaps I am immiserating Tamar just to keep Shelah from leaving the house — lest I feel abandoned and empty, again experiencing the loneliness I did when Ilith passed away. Moreover, what good is my refusal? If Shelah is not meant to marry Tamar, then he should release her; and if I mean to encourage him to fulfill his levirate duty, it ought to be done as soon as possible.

Hirah walked beside Judah silently; a torrent of words would only do harm, distracting his mind. He thought: The dam around Judah's heart every time I bring up remarriage seems to have cracked a bit. If I continue to talk to him about the issue, he will raise more barriers against my proposal. Instead, I ought to let the weight of the waters break through on their own.

Indeed, Judah had begun to think the same thing: Despite the pain and sorrow of Ilith's death, I must overcome and marry a new woman. Hirah is correct. I must not bury my life just because I buried my wife. What happened has happened and it cannot be undone. The Creator of the World leads man in all his ways, but a man must make decisions about the rest of his life. He must behave in the way the Creator guides the world, accepting with love what is destined for him, whether what he experiences seems positive or not.

His face, toughened and impassive for almost a decade, broke into a smile. A feeling of lightness filled Judah's heart, uplifting him. The grin widened due to a genuine feeling of accepting reality and faith. From the mouth which had not produced a laugh in years came a light chuckle as Judah paused to say: "Did I ever tell you I love you?" Then he laughed richly, while Hirah stood there, shocked by his companion.

"Not in recent years," Hirah replied, grinning from ear to ear in response. "But I always knew that!" he remarked, laughing with joy and affection.

Judah gave Hirah a firm embrace: "Thank you, brother. I am very glad you are my friend, and I love you very much."

"So, what's the good news?" Hirah asked with a smile.

Judah laughed aloud again: "My friend, it seems to me that you have outdone yourself! You will very soon have to spend a fortune on a wedding gift."

The two friends hugged each other and kept going. The boys accompanying them watched their master happily, shepherding the animals in front of them. The journey continued with gaiety and laughter. Judah and Hirah began to recall happy memories of their shared past, things that once seemed annoying and oppressive, but become the subject of mirth with the passage of time.

"In a few more minutes, we will come to Enaim Gate, where there are two springs. From there, it's not far to Timnah," Hirah said. "It seems to me that we ought to go in for a drink at the inn there, and then we can continue to our destination."

Judah, Hirah, and the two boys entered the inn to quench their thirst. As they walked in, a young woman sitting at the far end of the room stared at Judah. Hirah poked Judah in the ribs playfully. "It seems to me that the woman in the corner has her eyes on you," he observed, smiling. "Maybe buy her a drink? She looks right for you, my friend."

Judah looked at Hirah: "Will you stop teasing me? So what if I told you I was going to get married? That doesn't mean it should take place today, and certainly not with a woman sitting around staring at men."

Hirah looked at Judah, then at the woman sitting alone: "I'm not teasing; she really looks to be someone special, my friend. I know you do not look at women, but recommend you check her out. This woman is not something ordinary and simple. Her gaze is fixed on you like she wants you to talk to her." He looked at Judah reprovingly. "Didn't you say you love me? So do me a favor and talk to her."

Judah glanced at the woman in question, quickly looking away: "Are you kidding?! She must be some prostitute looking for a customer. This is not the kind of woman I'm looking to marry!"

Hirah glared at Judah angrily: "How did you come to such far-reaching conclusions at a glance? I'm sorry, but that's not the Judah I know. Look closely at her, you'll see that you're being ungenerous."

As they watched, a young man entered the inn and tried to sit down next to the woman, but she rebuffed him. "You see?" said Hirah to Judah. "She rejected that fellow immediately. A woman of the kind you suggested would never do that." Hirah quickly thought, "I'm going to ask her if you can order her a drink," he said, getting up before Judah could stop him.

Hirah returned to the table with a wide smile a moment later: "She agrees," Judah said, "I ordered you two drinks. I told you before that I thought she was for you, but now, I'm sure. You should have seen how she blushed with shame when I told her you'd buy her a drink "Get up, do not embarrass the woman. Even if she's not right, at least you'll have tried!" Hirah urged Judah, who arose hesitantly. Years had passed since he'd talked to any woman, and now chatting someone up at an inn... He thought resignedly: I took it upon myself to walk the path God chooses for me happily. If she's right, good; if not... then no!

Judah approached the table where the woman sat alone. His heart raced like that of a warhorse in battle, sweat dripping down his forehead, his whole body vibrating. "Hello..." he said to the woman. The voice came out of his mouth shaky and weak.

"Hello," the woman replied with downcast eyes and a flushed face.

Judah stood his ground, debating whether to stay or flee for his life; but the woman's blushing face gave him the feeling that she could be his future wife. "May I sit here?" he asked shyly.

"Yes..." the woman replied weakly.

"My friend said you are willing to talk to me..." Judah tried to find an opening to start a conversation with the strange woman. "I'm sorry if I'm a little awkward... I'm not used to talking to women... Since my wife passed away, a decade ago, I have not had a conversation with a woman..." he apologized.

The woman shifted in her chair uncomfortably. "Well, I'm not used to this either," she said, with a bashful grin spreading across her face.

Judah sat down, resolving in his heart to quickly find out what needed to be found out and do what he had to do. "As I mentioned, it's been more than a decade since I was widowed. Until recently I didn't think I would try my hand again, but my friend, who spoke to you, who is actually my former father-in-law... He convinced me that I should. So, excuse me, but may I ask a few, how shall I put it... direct questions?"

The woman nodded: "Ask away."

"First, I want to know if you are married or single," Judah asked, focusing on his target.

"The latter," the woman said.

"What do you believe in?" he asked.

"I believe in the God of heaven and earth, the sole Creator who created all the worlds," she said resolutely. "I am from the seed of Shem son of Noah," she said, explaining the source of her faith.

Judah looked at the woman, sensing the truth of what she told him, realizing that she could be his wife: "Do you know who I am?" he asked, hoping this had been the reason for her staring at him.

The woman nodded: "Yes, you are Judah, son of Israel, son of Isaac, son of Abraham the Hebrew."

"Would you be willing to marry me? Are you pure?" The words came out of Judah's mouth as if of their own accord. Judah felt an inexplicable urge, impelling him to do things in a hurry, as if an unknown hand were pushing him to do so.

"Yes, and yes," the woman said. She answered the questions as readily as if she had known them ahead of time.

Judah looked toward Hirah, sitting with the two lads. His eyes met Hirah's, looking at him. "My friend and one of the boys can witness our betrothal," Judah told the woman.

She nodded affirmatively, a blush of excitement covering her face.

Judah quickly got up, walking over to Hirah, who was smiling at him. "Come witness my betrothal," he told the surprised Hirah.

"My friend, you are swift," Hirah said to Judah. "Are you sure?"

"One hundred percent!" Judah said, pushing his friend towards the woman's table. "But I must give her something in order for the betrothal to be valid," said Judah, rummaging in his pockets. "I have nothing on me!" he realized, frustrated. "I'll send goats from my flock when we get there, in exchange for the betrothal money?" he suggested, unsure.

Hirah clicked his tongue: "No good... you need something tangible now."

"If you give me a pledge until you send the goat..." the woman whispered, embarrassed.

"Pledge... Pledge... What pledge shall I give you?" Judah felt agitated, impatient to settle the matter.

"Perhaps the signet ring, and the cloak on your shoulders, and the staff in your hands," the woman suggested shyly.

"Now we may proceed," Judah smiled, relieved. "You are hereby betrothed to me by this pledge, until I send you a goat, by the faith of Abraham, Isaac, and Jacob." Judah took off his cloak and gave it to the woman, along with his signet ring and staff.

"As for the consummation, you need not bring her beneath your roof back home," Hirah said, "as we'll be staying at this inn tonight. Congratulations, my dear friend." He hugged Judah lovingly and hurried to arrange their accommodations with the innkeeper.

The next morning, Judah and Hirah left early to oversee the shearing of his flock at Timnah — and to pick out the kid goat for his new bride. They returned to Enaim Gate as soon as they could, and Hirah offered to deliver the bride-price while Judah waited by the bank. The soothing sound of the rippling water filled his being as he thought about what he'd done.

His thoughts came in quick succession: I hope Hirah finds her. I know it was not lust that pushed me to marry in such a hurry, but I do not know what it was. Perhaps it was a mistake? I believed everything she said. Maybe she was not telling the truth?

"Judah!" Hirah's cry roused Judah to his feet.

"He's back..." Judah's heart skipped a beat in anticipation. "What do you have to say, my friend?" he asked, his eyes fixed on the kid goat walking after his friend. Where was his bride?

"My brother, I'm sorry, but I couldn't find her. I searched and asked everywhere if they'd seen the woman I described to them, but no one knew anything. I tried to find some piece of information about her location, but the people told me there was no such woman around." He looked depressed: "I apologize; I feel that everything has gone wrong because of me..."

Judah wrestled with his next move: "Look, I sent the goat in exchange for the pledge, I did what I could do... if she has disappeared what can I do? Let her keep what she has! We cannot make a mockery of ourselves." He was mortified and pained by the bitter development

In the room, lit by warm light streaming from the wide-open windows, a light breeze blew, shaking the trees in the orchard outside. The three judges sat discussing various matters. Isaac, Israel, and Judah sensed the strange whispers among the people awaiting their verdict.

"Can anyone explain to me the meaning of these murmurs?!" Isaac said, raising his face above the scroll before him: "What are all these mutterings today?!"

One of the litigants got to his feet, smirking: "Apologies, Your Honor! We are very sorry, but a very unfortunate rumor is circulating, and it is creating quite a stir..."

"Rumor?!" Isaac said with an angry face, "What rumor can justify this commotion?!"

"Excuse me, Your Honor. There really is nothing that can justify our behavior, but the gossipmongers say that Tamar, the Honorable Judah's daughter-in-law, has become pregnant. We all know that she is sitting in her mother's house, waiting to be married off to the

Honorable Judah's son Shelah; yet the woman is pregnant from some stranger, apparently!" The man looked at the three judges, who were surprised by the terrible news. "I am sorry to be the bearer of bad news, Your Honors."

Isaac and Israel looked Judah. Judah hid his face in his hands. Surely, he was to blame for dallying and keeping Shelah from marrying Tamar, resulting in this disgrace; nevertheless, what she had done was akin to adultery, an act which could not be countenanced. He had to apply the full severity of the law.

He thought: This generation must appreciate the weight of this offense; we must act in a way which will be seen and heard, far and wide.

Judah raised his face, brow furrowed but determined: "Take her out, and she shall be burnt!" he ruled. "Justice overtakes mercy! She has done a forbidden deed, and she must bear her punishment!"

The people sitting in the room were silent in fear, their eyes watching Isaac and Israel on the bench, nodding in agreement with the words of Judah.

The noise outside the walls of the house woke Tamar from her sleep. She opened her eyes, lovingly stroking her belly which had begun to grow. "Who's making such a ruckus outside?" she asked herself, struggling to sit up. Then she heard her mother sobbing at the door to their home. She got to her feet and made her way downstairs as quickly and carefully as she could.

The sound of crying came from the door of the house. Tamar hurried her steps toward the horrified cries. "Mother, what's going on?!" she asked in a panic, seeing her mother barring the door as a crowd of angry men approached the house.

Tamar's mother turned toward her daughter, terrified: "They say they come by order of Judah your father-in-law to execute you by fire!" The mad look of fear penetrated Tamar's belly: "They say you committed an unspeakable act, so your sentence is immolation!"

Tamar felt like a bird trapped in the hunter's trap: "I must do something! I must save the boys who are inside me!"

The troop of men seemed to rejoice at Tamar's plight, sadism and schadenfreude on their faces.

"I must tell Judah that he is the father of my sons, that he unwittingly fulfilled the levirate duty!" She had not thought much about anything else since learning she was pregnant. The joy of having Judah's offspring growing within her overshadowed any concerns of how her situation might appear to others. "I have to let him know, but how? I cannot humiliate him in public!"

The pressure on the door increased, the crowd beginning to push Tamar's mother out of the way, so they could seize her daughter and carry out her grisly sentence.

"The pledge!" Tamar recalled. "I will send him the pledge he gave me! If he admits that I am pregnant by him, well and good; if not... I will have to sacrifice my life..."

"I beg of you," Tamar pleaded, as the men forced open the door and apprehended her, "just give me a few minutes, and I will come with you willingly."

The men laughed out loud: "Do not try to escape; the house is surrounded."

"I will not try to run away, I just want a few moments to get ready, and I will surrender myself to you," she said, hoping for understanding.

One of the men chortled to his friends: "She must want to throw something decent on to come before the court. Such playacting! Commit such vile deeds, and now act like a righteous woman? Have it your way, we'll wait right here. Now hurry up!"

Tamar entered her room and began frantically searching for the pledges that Judah had given her. "They must be here!" She thought in frustration as she quickly opened the closets. "I put them here!"

Despair began to take root in the woman's heart; it was a veritable act of Satan that the pledges had vanished — at the moment when her own life and the life of her offspring were at stake!

Tamar looked up, hearing the men threatening to enter and grab her with their hands. She raised her eyes heavenward and said: "Master of the Universe, Who answers those who turn to Him in time of distress, enlighten my eyes so I may find my three pledges; by them, three souls will be saved who will be the ancestors of three souls who will sanctify Your name in public. I know that my actions may be seen as indefensible, but I know that I had to do it in order to bring the souls that are within me into the world, so that the people of Israel may merit a Redeemer who will deliver them at the end of days. "

Tamar lowered her gaze in tears, and to her astonishment the three pledges were miraculously revealed before her eyes. "Thank you, Master of the Universe," she said as she grabbed the cloak, the ring, and the staff.

Tamar wiped away her tears and went out, back straight, to those who wanted to burn her.

"Honored sirs, I have one last request before you take me to my execution!" A wan smile was on her face.

The confused men looked at each other. "Last request? What is it?"

Tamar handed the ring, the cloak, and the staff to the man who seemed to be the leader of the group. "Please, take these to Judah, and tell him that I said that the owner of these items is the father. Ask him to recognize whose cloak, signet ring, and staff these are."

The man took the objects. "Take her to the pyre, but wait for me," he told the group of surprised men. "I hope this is not some feeble attempt at delaying the inevitable!" he upbraided Tamar.

Tamar smiled in shame: "I hope so too..."

The door to the courtroom opened, and Judah looked up. "Is it done?" he asked with a heavy heart, seeing his servant return.

"Ah... no, my lord... not yet..." he replied in confusion, trying to explain the meaning of the delay.

"What happened? She absconded?" Judah asked, trying to root out the feeling that he would be happy if that were the reality.

"Ah... no, my lord, she did not run away... she made one last request before we carried out her sentence..."

Judah grinned. "One last request?! What did she ask for?"

The man approached Judah, handing him the objects Tamar had given him: "She asked that I give you these items, which allegedly belong to the man who impregnated her. She said that you may know who the man is." The man placed the objects in front of Judah without looking at him. "I believe that this is a ruse by which she hopes to put off her sentence for a few more moments. I will carry it out immediately, my lord, rest assured." The man turned, about to leave.

Isaac and Israel looked at Judah's surprised face, his mouth open in astonishment, unable to utter a word.

"Halt!" Isaac commanded the man who was about to leave. His ancient voice stopped the servant as if he'd been nailed to the floor.

"Do you recognize these objects?" Isaac asked Judah.

Judah tried to recover his composure, a maelstrom of emotions spinning in him. He realized that he had been with his daughter-in-law, unwittingly performing levirate marriage. He marveled at the initiative of his pious daughter-in-law, who had been abandoned in her mother's house without being remarried or set free; he was impressed by the courage she had shown in order to get out from under the decree imposed on her. He was also happy to know that his bride from the inn was pregnant. A light peal of laughter burst from Judah, astonishing all the onlookers. "Yes, I know to whom they belong, they belong to me! *She is more righteous than I; for I gave her not to Shelah my son.*"

Isaac and Israel looked at Judah seriously: "Are you sure?!"

"Definitely!" Judah answered.

Judah looked at the confused servant: "Run quickly to the pyre before they do something stupid. Get Tamar and bring her to my house. Tell them that Tamar is my wife, and they must not mistreat her!"

The man lingered a little, taking in the surprising development.

"Why are you waiting?! Run!!!"

The man quickly ran to his gang. A scream rose from his mouth, alarming the men who had begun lighting the pyre they had prepared for Tamar. The fire was extinguished, and Tamar was led to the house of Judah, only the hem of her dress scorched by the fire.

Four months later, after being safely ensconced in Judah's home, Tamar went into labor with twin boys.

One put out a hand; and the midwife took and bound upon his hand a scarlet thread, saying: "This came out first." And it came to pass, as he drew back his hand, that, behold his brother came out; and she said: "Why have you made a breach (perez) for yourself?" Therefore, his name was called Perez. And afterward came out his brother, that had the scarlet thread upon his hand; and his name was called Zerah.

CHAPTER FIFTY-EIGHT

The Descent to Egypt

"**A**re you a gang of fools?!" Pharaoh hurled the golden bowl of soup before him at the minister of police's face: "What do you expect me to do?! Do you want me to force him to do something against his will?! If he said that, then so be it! "

The minister of police was afraid to evade the bowl thrown at him, so he allowed the soup to land on him. As it dripped from his hair, onto his face, he struggled to find the right words: "But Your Majesty... The people are not willing to accept his words... they are not amenable to his orders..."

Pharaoh mimicked his minister mockingly: "Your Majesty... the people are not willing to accept his words... they are not amenable to his orders..." Then he threw his goblet at the minister, and the wine ran down his clothes. "Then tell them to die! Do you understand?! Tell them they have two options: either die or do what he says!"

The minister began to cry: "But why, Your Majesty? Zaphenath-paneah is viceroy, but he is not king of Egypt. You are!"

Pharaoh put his head in his hands and spoke as if to himself: "What can I do when I am surrounded by idiots!"

Pharaoh stared at his official: "Tell me, you hapless nincompoop, how long has the famine been going on?"

"Two months, Your Majesty," the minister replied quickly.

"Very good..." Pharaoh said with a pained smile, "and how long was there satiety?"

"Seven years, Your Majesty," replied the minister.

"Well done!" Pharaoh grinned, "And for how long did we know the famine would come?"

"Seven years, sir."

"And why did you not store surplus grain during those seven years?" he probed, though he knew the answer.

"We did, Your Majesty, but it all rotted," the minister reported.

"Zaphenath-paneah also stored grain, right?"

The minister nodded.

"Has the grain he has accumulated gone bad?"

"No, Your Majesty," admitted the minister.

"You still do not understand, dolt?! Zaphenath-paneah decreed that your grain would rot, while his would not. He can alter the decree so his grain will rot as well, and then..." Pharaoh seemed at a loss. Knowing that he was in the hands of Zaphenath-paneah deflated him.

"Then what shall we do, Your Majesty?" The minister of police felt as if he were about to burst into tears at the humiliation he was about to experience and convey to those who came to him.

"What shall you do? You shall do whatever he tells you! If he says that those who are uncircumcised are not to be given food, do not give them food. You've seen it with your own eyes: he gathered grain in quantities beyond number, and it has all remained perfectly preserved. Meanwhile, you barely managed to collect enough to fill a few sacks, and even that meager amount has now rotted away."

Pharaoh smirked, accepting his bitter fate. "So those are your options: circumcise yourselves and live or refuse and die. Now get out of here! You have ruined my appetite!"

Israel sat in his darkened study. The sound of children at play could no longer be heard. The feeling of hunger had begun to seep into the camp. He knew that the food depots in his possession would not suffice for very long; and even if the food could last, the children of Esau and Ishmael would probably go to war against him if they saw that he and his family had enough to eat.

The remaining eleven sons of Israel stood before their father, whose pained face showed the traces of two decades of misery. *"Behold, I have heard that there is provender in Egypt. Get you down there and provide for us from there; that we may live, and not die,"* Israel told his sons heavily.

The brothers looked at each other, the thought of going down to Egypt did not appeal to them to say the least, but they might be able to find their brother there and bring peace to their mourning father's heart. "Father, who should go down?" Reuben asked.

Israel sighed: "It seems to me that you will all have to go down. I understand that a great sorcerer named Zaphenath-paneah is in power there. He sells grain only to a father according to the number of children he has. Whoever tries to deceive him will not be able to obtain provender from Egypt again. He also requires that everyone who comes to buy food from Egypt write his name, his father's name, and his grandfather's name, as well as the number of children he has, and according to that he sells the grain. Moreover, he won't sell again to anyone unless enough time passes for the buyers to use up the food, by his calculations." Israel looked thoughtful. "This sorcerer seems very strange, according to what they say about him."

The brothers looked at their father: "Then we will all go," Reuben said with a smile, trying to impart optimism to his voice. "In a few days we will return with grain for everyone, and everything will be fine."

Israel looked at his sons: "All of you except Benjamin. I need someone to help me, and he is the youngest of you, so he will stay with me. Whatever you bring with you, share also with him. Still, when you enter Egypt, do it separately. Try not to draw too much attention."

Meanwhile he thought: Benjamin cannot undertake such a journey; both his mother and his brother perished while traveling.

The ten brothers set out on their journey, riding donkeys. The road was arid and dry, the parched soil looking as if no water had touched it in years. The sun beat down on the riders' heads, drying out their skin.

Finally, they approached the border of the land of Egypt. The brothers held a consultation before entering the land of the nonbelievers.

"I count ten gates," said Naphtali, who returned from inspecting the area. "I suggest each of us enter through a different gate so as not to attract too much attention, as Father said."

"The first thing we do inside is look for Joseph," said Judah. "We have no choice but to look for him among the dens of iniquity. An attractive lad sold as a slave in Egypt? I shudder to think what he may have been forced to do, God forbid."

"If we find him, we will try to buy him back;" said Simeon, "and if they refuse, we will have to take him by force!"

"See you at the central market," Judah told his brothers. The brothers set off, each to a different gate.

The minister of police addressed Zaphenath-paneah respectfully: "My lord asked us to inform him when the men giving these names arrived. Each of them entered through a different gate." He handed the list to his superior, happy that he could fulfill the request of the man who saved the country. While once the minister had resented the viceroy, he had changed his mind once the circumcision decree had been carried out. The pain was gone and forgotten, dissipating into the feeling of widespread economic wellbeing created by Zaphenath-paneah's stewardship of the state. All the people of the neighboring countries came to Egypt, leaving behind them the best of their silver and gold in exchange for the grain that Zaphenath-paneah had collected. As for Egypt itself, every parcel of land and all property had been acquired by the viceroy — on Pharaoh's behalf. Taxes amounting to twenty percent of the total economy of the country were brought to Pharaoh. The only ones exempted were the priests, whose land remained in their hands and who did not have to pay for their grain.

"Thank you, my friend," said Zaphenath-paneah to the minister, "when did they enter?"

"Yesterday, sir. Probably in the afternoon," the minister replied.

"Do you know where they are now?" asked Zaphenath-paneah.

"Certainly, sir," the minister replied with self-importance, "from the moment my lord told me to be on the lookout for these individuals, I ordered two policemen be assigned to follow each of them."

"Excellent, my dear friend," the viceroy smiled at the minister, who relished the reassurance he inspired: "And where are they now?"

The minister smiled lewdly: "They seem to be making their way around the central market, which my lord knows… Well, the district is famous for…" He laughed. "Its reputation is worldwide, one might say!"

"What are they doing there?!" demanded Zaphenath-paneah firmly, stopping the minister from describing the bordellos any further.

The minister regained his composure: "They... they seem to be looking for someone there. Someone by the name of Joseph. The truth is, they don't seem to be partaking in any pleasures of the flesh, but are focused on locating this individual."

"I see." Zaphenath-paneah smiled. "Fine, let them have the rest of the day to search; but tomorrow, make sure they are brought to me.

Do it gently; I don't want to see anyone of them injured."

A hand was placed on Asher's shoulder. He turned quickly to see who was touching him, finding a group of policemen led by a senior officer. "Sir," said the officer to Asher, "Zaphenath-paneah, viceroy of Egypt, requests that we escort you to his palace, the Grand Granary." Asher looked around to see if his brothers were around.

"Your nine brothers are already making their way to the Lord Viceroy," the officer said. "He just wants to check how much grain you need to take to your homes. The law in Egypt does not allow people from foreign countries to stay here for more than a week."

Asher accompanied the policemen, knowing that if he wanted to, he could have objected to their request; but three days had passed with neither hide nor hair of Joseph. Perhaps it was time to return to the land of Canaan, to their families.

The ten brothers were ushered into the Grand Granary, where huge sacks were piled up along one side of the great hall, while along the other were stacks and heaps of silver and gold. In the middle of the great hall stood a man in the finest attire of Egypt, his clothing immediately establishing his lofty status. His face was framed by a dark brown beard and a golden, bejeweled headpiece. The ten brothers bowed respectfully to the viceroy of Egypt, who looked elegant and aristocratic. Next to him stood a page, who seemed eager and intelligent, despite his young age.

The lord considered the brothers with a scolding look: "Where did you come from, and why did you come to the land of Egypt?" he asked in a language the brothers did not understand.

The page adroitly translated the words of his master into the language of the land of Canaan.

Reuben replied, "We came from the land of Canaan to buy grain for our household."

The page translated Reuben's words.

Zaphenath-paneah spoke harshly. "My lord says that you are spies, and you have come to uncover the secrets of Egypt.

The brothers looked at each other in amazement. Reuben objected: "No, my lord, your servants came to buy provender. We are all sons of the same man we; we are honest men, not spies!"

Zaphenath-paneah laughed aloud: "If you are brothers, why did you enter by ten different gates and not one?! Why did it take you three days to get to me? If I had not brought you to me, who knows how long it might have been before you came here! "

Reuben felt he had to counter the man's suspicions: "My lord, we are twelve brothers, from the land of Canaan. One was lost, while the youngest remains with our father. We have been looking for our lost brother since we arrived, because he was sold as a slave to Egypt."

"'He was sold'?!" the viceroy demanded. "Who sold him?" He raised a silver goblet and looked into its reflective surface. "Do you not know that I am a diviner? In my goblet I can see that two of you destroyed the city of Shechem when you were young, and that all of you destroyed several kingdoms in the land of Canaan. Now you have come to do the same to the land of Egypt!"

"Forgive us, my lord, and I will explain what happened," said Reuben, trying to find a way out of the entanglement that surrounded them. "Our brother was a rebel, and he committed unspeakable acts. He wanted to subjugate us, so we sold him as a slave. As for the Shechemites, they abducted our sister, so we fought to save her from them. The other kingdoms came to wage war upon us; they attacked us, and we had no choice but to fight them in self-defense."

Zaphenath-paneah laughed at the excuses: "And what would you do if you found your lost brother?"

"We would buy him back at any cost," Reuben replied firmly.

"What if his owner refused?" Zaphenath-paneah looked into the silver goblet in his hand to see if Reuben would speak the truth.

"We would fight him," Reuben said, knowing that the man would know if he lied

"Ahhh... I told you so! You are spies! You are here to destroy the land of Egypt!" yelled Zaphenath-paneah triumphantlyy.

"My lord, that is not the case!" the brothers objected, perplexed by their predicament, begging for benevolence.

Zaphenath-paneah was not moved. Brooking no argument, he declared: "*Hereby you shall be proved, as Pharaoh lives, you shall not go forth here, except your youngest brother come here. Send one of you, and let him fetch your brother, and you shall be bound, that your words may be proved, whether there be truth in you; or else, as Pharaoh lives, surely you are spies.*"

He fixed his gaze on them. "Which of you shall go and retrieve this younger brother you claim? What, no volunteers? Until you decide, you shall all be imprisoned."

Zaphenath-paneah clapped his hands three times, and a large detachment of soldiers entered the Grand Granary.

Judah saw that his brothers were readying themselves to fight, but he dissuaded them. "We will keep that option in reserve; for now, we must accept imprisonment, while we ponder our next move."

The brothers relaxed, following their captors to the dungeon.

For three days, the brothers sat in the dungeon, debating how they could convince Zaphenath-paneah that they were not spies. Surely if only one of the brothers returned, with nine of them missing, their father would never be persuaded to send Benjamin to Egypt as well!

The creaking sound of the heavy bolt pulled the brothers to their feet, but little light came in through the small window which showed a slice of starry sky. Then the heavy door opened, and in front of the brothers stood Zaphenath-paneah, his page beside him. The light of the torches behind the viceroy blinded the eyes of the brothers.

"I have decided to give you a second chance to prove that you are not spies," Zaphenath-paneah told the brothers, through his page. *"This do, and live; for I fear God: if you be upright men, let one of your brethren be bound in your prison-house; but go you, carry grain for the hunger of your houses; and bring your youngest brother to me; so, shall your words be verified, and you shall not die."*

The brothers looked at the viceroy in amazement. Thoughts began to run through their minds: We were sure that he imprisoned us solely due to his wickedness, but for some reason he is willing to release nine of us, so our families will not starve. Moreover, he says he fears God, meaning he doesn't want to abuse us capriciously.

Simeon whispered to Levi: *"We are verily guilty concerning our brother, in that we saw the distress of his soul, when he besought us, and we would not hear; therefore, is this distress come upon us.* Look, this nonbeliever shows us compassion, though he is no brother to us; we did not even appeal to him, but he senses our distress and exhibits compassion toward us."

Levi nodded sadly, deeply sorry for his unworthy deeds.

Reuben hissed at his brothers: *"Did I not say to you, 'Do not sin against the child,' but you have not heard, and his blood is required here!"*

The page was silent, while the brothers spoke to each other in the Holy Tongue. Zaphenath-paneah turned on his heels and left the cell.

Joseph moved away from his brothers to a far corner, wiping from his eyes the tears washing over his face with excitement. A few minutes passed and the viceroy returned to the cell. The ten brothers waited outside the cell for the viceroy to return and speak. He raised his hand in the direction of Simeon: "You will return to the cell!" he ordered.

"I?!" Simeon wondered, thinking: Why should I be arrested? After all, I was opposed to the sale; I wanted to execute him. Isn't selling a man into slavery worse than killing him?

"Surely you won't abandon me in this wretched dungeon, will you?" he asked his brothers in the Holy Tongue.

"What do you want us to do: let all our families die of starvation?! We must bring them food; then we can come back for you."

Simeon grinned grimly: "Well, let's see who can get me back in that cell! What, because I went in willingly at first, I'll return with no resistance? Away with you then, brothers! I'll do it myself!"

Zaphenath-paneah gestured with his hand toward seventy soldiers who stood some distance from the brothers. The soldiers approached Simeon, determined to drag him back to his cell. Simeon looked at the warriors approaching him with a slight smile on his face. A scream came out of Simeon's mouth, filling the prison and shocking the soldiers. A peal of laughter erupted from Simeon.

Zaphenath-paneah whispered something to his page. The page slowly approached Simeon, who glanced at him. The young boy launched a surprising and mighty punch towards Simeon's belly, folding him in two in pain. Shocked, Simeon felt a huge steel hand grip him, casually toss him into the cell, and lock it behind him. Groaning in pain, Simeon mused: This punch comes from Father's house!

The nine brothers made their way toward the land of Canaan, leading their own heavily laden donkeys and Simeon's animal as well.

Jacob rose. The sound of the children's cheering distracted him. About two weeks had passed since his ten sons left for Egypt, and now according to the shouts of joy, his sons had apparently returned.

Jacob came out of his gloomy study to welcome his returning sons. His eyes stared in horror at Levi leading two donkeys. A brief review revealed that Simeon was missing. Jacob hastened his steps toward his returning sons: "Where is Simeon?!" he asked his sons, who were bowing before him submissively.

Reuben looked at his father. How could he soften the blow? "Simeon is in Egypt, Father," he said, trying to sort things out.

"What is he doing there?! Why didn't he come back with you?!"

"When we got to Egypt, we did as you told us, and we each entered the country from a different gate. Apparently, the fact that we each entered the country alone caught the attention of the police. As you know, they checked our names and probably realized we were all brothers. So, we were called to come before Zaphenath-paneah, the viceroy. He performed divination with his silver goblet, discovering that we had once fought with Shechem and the other kings, so he came to the conclusion that we were spies who had come to expose the land of Egypt," Reuben looked at his disheartened father. "At first, he spoke to us very harshly, and put us all in the dungeon. Then he took us out and put Simeon back. He said that as soon as we brought our little brother before him, he'd believe that we aren't spies and release Simeon."

"How did he know you had another brother?!" demanded Israel angrily.

"Ah... he started asking about our family, and we told him we were twelve brothers, that one was dead, and the other was at home."

The rest of the brothers busied themselves with their donkeys, trying avoid the difficult conversation taking place between their father and eldest brother.

Levi opened his pack, voicing his astonishment at seeing the bundle of money he had given to the man who sold him the grain, deep inside his saddlebag. At the hotel where they'd lodged along the way, he'd discovered Simeon's bundle of money in the grain he had brought, and now his own. The other brothers also searched inside their saddlebags, discovering their own bundles of money inside their sacks of grain. Awe and fear overtook them.

Tears welled up in Jacob's eyes: "*Me have you bereaved of my children: Joseph is not, and Simeon is not, and you will take Benjamin away; upon me are all these things come.*"

Reuben's heart was broken by his father's weeping: "Father I promise you, give me Benjamin, and I will go and retrieve Simeon. *You shall slay my two sons, if I bring him not to you; deliver him into my hand, and I will bring him back to you.*"

Jacob looked at his son as if he were a madman: "Slay your two sons? They are my sons too! *My son shall not go down with you; for his brother is dead, and he only is left; if harm befall him by the way in which you go, then will you bring down my gray hairs with sorrow to the grave*". Sobbing, Jacob turned on his heel and went back to his study.

While the provisions brought from Egypt dealt with the immediate crisis, the cries of the young returned over the next few weeks, leaving Jacob unable to concentrate on his studies. The sorrow haunting him for the last twenty-two years had intensified due to Simeon's plight. Fatigue and despair had filled his days since the loss of Joseph, compounded by the grief of being orphaned when Isaac passed away years later. Jacob felt cut off, a father without his son and a son without his father. As he scrutinized his scrolls, he felt that his mind was as hamstrung as his spirit. Isaac had been a lifeline, keeping Jacob from drifting out into a sea of grief, tethering him to the Word of God. Now, there was nothing to prevent the exponential growth of his sadness.

The study door opened. Serah, Asher's daughter, went to her grandfather to serve him lunch. He reflected: At least little Serah tries to lift my spirits, always smiling. She brightens my mood, even if only for a few moments. However, today even Serah seems morose!

"What is wrong, Serah? Why the long face?" Israel asked in pain.

A tear fell from the girl's face: "What can I tell you, Grandfather? Everyone is hungry, the little children keep crying, and the young mothers are starving. Those who are nursing have no milk to breast-feed their infants, and no food can be found anywhere. The grain Father and my uncles brought from Egypt is almost gone. We eat portions that are not enough for babies. We have no strength to go on like this anymore. I wear the same face as everyone else, God help us!" sighed Serah from the bottom of her heart.

Israel looked at his granddaughter in agony, realizing he must do something: "Please call my sons to come to me."

The children of Israel stood in their father's study. They showed the signs of hunger more than anyone else, as they would regularly give up their own portions to their desperate wives and children.

"Return, get us some provender from Egypt," Israel told his sons.

The brothers sighed deeply: "Father, the lord in Egypt warned us that we could not go back to ask for food without our little brother with us. If you send Benjamin, very well; but if not, there is no reason to go down there, it will just make things worse. Without Benjamin, he will probably imprison us as spies, or perhaps decapitate us — and Simeon too."

Israel felt helpless, caught between the rock of endangering Benjamin and the hard place of hunger. "Why did you do me wrong by telling the man you had another brother?!" he asked in frustration.

"The man asked us about our family, our homeland, our father, and brother, were we supposed to know that he would ask us to bring our brother down to him?" Judah argued in pain. "Father, please, allow me to take Benjamin with us, and we will go bring food for the whole family. Then we will not perish — neither we, nor you, nor our children. You have my pledge, you may seek him from me, if I have not brought him before you and presented him before you alive, then I will have sinned against you for all time. I will be excommunicated from this world and the next," Judah swore before his father. "Had we not hesitated, we could have gone back and forth twice; Simeon would be back here, and everyone would have food!"

Israel sighed, seeing no choice: "*If it be so now, do this: take of the choice fruits of the land in your vessels, and carry down the man a present, a little balm, and a little honey, spicery and ladanum, nuts, and almonds; and take double money in your hand; and the money that was returned in the mouth of your sacks carry back in your hand; perhaps it was an oversight; take also your brother, and arise, go again to the man; and God Almighty give you mercy before the man, that he may release to you your other brother and Benjamin. And as for me, if I be bereaved of my children, I am bereaved."*

Tears welled up in Israel's eyes as he embraced his sons before parting. The brothers hurried to load their donkeys and return to Zaphenath-paneah.

CHAPTER FIFTY-NINE

Theft

The Grand Granary was full cheek by jowl. People from all the neighboring countries had come to buy grain from Egypt. The viceroy rationed the grain equally, with everyone paying the same price. Manasseh, Joseph's son, entered the chamber, whispering something secret to his father.

"Bring them in, but right now, I am only interested in seeing if they brought Benjamin with them," Joseph told his son.

The brothers were brought to the edge of the grand granary, and Joseph observed his brothers standing at a distance. *"Bring the men into the house, and butcher an animal, and prepare; for the men will dine with me at noon,"* Joseph told him.

"Come with me, please," the page told the brothers.

The brothers followed the page, and they were overwhelmed by the glorious estate he led them to. Gardens and orchards were in full flower, peacocks and songbirds among the colorful flora. Glory and majesty sparkled from every corner of the magnificent ivory building standing before them. The brothers looked at each other anxiously.

"Because of the money that was returned in our sacks at the first time are we brought in; that he may seek occasion against us, and

fall upon us, and take us for slaves, along with our donkeys!" Dan worried, alarm on his face, as he shared his concern with Gad.

Asher, looking at his older brothers as if urging them to do something, opined: "We need to explain to the lad that they made a mistake last time and never took our money."

Reuben approached the page: *"Oh my lord, we came indeed down at the first time to buy food. And it came to pass, when we came to the lodging-place, that we opened our sacks, and behold, every man's money was in the mouth of his sack, our money in full weight; and we have brought it back in our hand. And other money have we brought down in our hand to buy food. We know not who put our money in our sacks."*

The page replied with a smile: *"Peace be to you, fear not; your God, and the God of your father, has given you treasure in your sacks; I had your money."* The boy laughed happily at Reuben's startled face. "Come to the salon, gentlemen; I will soon bring your brother Simeon out to you."

Reuben thought: That laugh reminds me of someone....

"Oh, my dear brothers, how I missed you!" the amused voice of Simeon boomed behind the heavy door. The door opened and Simeon went out to his surprised brothers. The thought that Simeon was being tortured in a pit in Egypt had weighed heavily on their hearts since they left him behind, but now Simeon was revealed to be luxuriating, dressed in lush robes. The brothers hugged him with a surprised look.

Simeon kept talking, it seemed that the only thing he'd been missing was his brothers' company: "I hope the journey was not too difficult. It's true that it took you a little longer than I thought, but accommodations here are fit for a king. You look a little skinny, my dear brothers. Come in, wash your feet, take a load off. I'll tell the servants. They'll bring you something to eat and drink in the meantime. "

Simeon chuckled and called out: "Salim, bring my brothers something to eat and drink, and also bring bowls of water to wash their feet, they have come a long way!" Simeon looked at his astonished brothers: "As soon as you left, they brought me here. I almost feel at home here. If I could, I would bring the whole family!"

Judah asked: "Isn't this Zaphenath-paneah's home?"

Simeon shrugged. "I guess so?" he said, bewildered. "The truth is I have not seen him here, but my intuition tells me that the interpreter boy who accompanied you is his son. He is a very friendly boy. His name is Manasseh, he does not talk much, but is very respectful. His little brother, Ephraim, too, a charming child. They live here. I got to see their mother once. She does not look so Egyptian to me. Maybe Zaphenath-paneah brought her from another country?" Simeon chortled. "With his position and wealth, he can afford anything."

The servants entered, bearing trays laden with delicacies and fruit, holding large jugs of water and bowls to bathe the feet of the guests.

"Sit comfortably, my dear brothers, they will take off your shoes and wash your feet. You should not feel uncomfortable; that is their job," Simeon giggled at the surprised faces.

Manasseh entered the salon: "Zaphenath-paneah will come here at noon. He wants to have lunch with you, if you agree," he told the brothers, who opened their eyes wide, amazed at what was happening.

"Ah... of course... it would be our honor, sir," said Judah, feeling confused.

"Thank you," said the boy humbly, "then rest in the meantime. My master will arrive in a few hours... I will bring you a little lamb soon, and you may prepare it according to your customs, if it pleases you."

The brothers watched the boy in amazement, sharing a thought: The Egyptian boy intends to bring us a lamb so that we can slaughter it! Don't the Egyptians worship sheep?

The morning hours quickly passed, after preparing the lamb brought by the boy in the yard, the brothers rested in the spacious salon. The divans were so inviting, they could not help but nap a bit.

The door of the palace opened: "Sorry...", Manasseh said, "my master wishes to meet you now." The brothers jumped up in front of the boy standing at the entrance to the room, readying themselves to face the viceroy again.

"Please, come with me to the dining room," the boy asked.

The brothers quickly picked up the gift they had brought with them for the ruler of the land, arranging their garments for the strange meeting. The brothers followed the boy to a large room, where the table was full of appetizers of various kinds. Gold cups and plates sparkled on the table, at the head of which stood Zaphenath-paneah. The brothers presented the gift and bowed.

"Peace be upon you," said Zaphenath-paneah with a bright face as his page translated his words, "Is your father well, the old man of whom you spoke? Is he yet alive?"

"Your servant, our father is well, he is yet alive," they replied, bowing and prostrating.

Zaphenath-paneah surveyed the faces of the brothers, who stood in front of him with downcast eyes: "Is this the youngest brother of whom you spoke?" he asked the brothers. The brothers nodded in silence, fearing what the strange man might think. "God be gracious to you, my son." He said, gently, "Come, sit next to me." Benjamin approached Zaphenath-paneah with apprehension.

Joseph looked at Benjamin, whose gaze was downcast: "Son, do you have another brother?" he asked.

"I had a brother, but he is gone," Benjamin replied painfully.

"Do you have a wife? Children?" Joseph lightly probed.

"Yes, I have a wife and ten sons," Benjamin replied, fearing that Zaphenath-paneah would ask him to bring them to Egypt.

"And what are their names?"

"Bela and Becher and Ashbel, Gera and Naaman, Ehi and Rosh, Muppim and Huppim and Ard."

Joseph smiled: "Those names are a little weird."

"They all memorialize my brother," he told Zaphenath-paneah and began to explain the names of his sons.

Joseph felt a tremor pass through his body, he felt a raising wave threatening to break upon him and destroy his plans. He steeled himself, thinking: The time is not yet ripe! He turned on his heel. "I will return soon," he said, feeling the tremor in his voice. He ran out of the room, leaving the brothers astonished.

"He always seemed like a madman to me," Simeon whispered to Levi, seeing the ruler of the land of Egypt running out of the room for no apparent reason.

Joseph ran into his bedroom and slammed the door behind him, bursting into sobs. All he wanted was to hug his brothers, to reveal himself to them. He told himself: Not yet! They need to look into their own hearts and demonstrate that they truly repent for their actions.

"Sorry," Zaphenath-paneah said as he returned to the dining room, "I remembered something important I had to do." The brothers nodded to the strange leader, ignoring his odd behavior.

"Let's sit down to eat," he told them, gesturing toward the table. "My wife and sons will also sit down to eat with us, but at a separate table, if that does not bother you," Zaphenath-paneah told the brothers, who quickly looked away from the lady of the house, remarkable in her modesty, sitting together with her two children at a table set for three.

"Now, how shall we sit?" mused Zaphenath-paneah as he rubbed his forehead. He picked up his magnificent silver goblet inlaid with gems. He tapped his finger on the goblet, a slight sound rising from it. "Strange..." he said as if spoking to himself, "I thought Judah was the eldest; he's always speaking first. But the goblet tells me that

Reuben is the eldest." He looked at him. "Reuben, son of Leah, sit down here," he said, pointing to a chair. "Simeon, Levi, Judah, Issachar, and Zebulun join him because you all share the same mother. That's what my goblet says." Zaphenath-paneah pointed out the brothers in order, showing them their places. "Gad and Asher, sons of Zilpah, sit in these places. Dan and Naphtali, sons of Bilhah, sit in these places. You, Benjamin, sit next to me because I too, have no brothers. I also had a brother whom I lost, so we shall sit together."

The brothers looked at each other in fear of the man who seemed to know all their secrets. Zaphenath-paneah snapped his fingers, and servants entered bearing full trays, placing before their master's foreign guests plates laden with lamb, even as they glared at the desecration. The master received a plate laden with vegetarian food: "Put it next to him," he told the servant, pointing to Benjamin. The three plates placed before the wife and sons were also brought before Benjamin. "He probably feels bad about scaring Benjamin by ordering him to come here," Levi whispered to Simeon.

Fine wine was poured out before the brothers. They had not indulged for twenty-two years, from the day they sold Joseph, but they partook in honor of their brother Simeon. The table was filled with peals of laughter as the men drank their fill; for the brothers, long out of practice, did not take long to become wholly intoxicated.

Manasseh's voice boomed the next morning: "Honored guests!" The brothers, roused from their slumber on the luxurious divans, shocked to hear him say: "Morning has come, and my master has commanded that you all depart at once!"

The brothers blinked, trying to get a grip on reality, not sure if it was all a dream. No, Zaphenath-paneah's palace was still there and very real.

"Gentlemen, your donkeys are ready, loaded with grain and waiting for you at the gate of the estate," the boy hurried them along. "Sirs, I urge you to leave as soon as possible. I believe you do not want to stay and live in the country of Egypt." The boy spoke in a flurry, while the brothers rushed to get ready to travel. "You better hurry before my master changes his mind…" The brothers quickly followed the page, who led them to their laden donkeys. They swiftly took the donkeys from the guards, leading them out of the city to return to their father and their families.

"Father, in a few minutes they'll be beyond the city limits," Manasseh told Joseph.

"Very well, now chase after them. As soon as they leave the city, stop them and say to them. 'Why have you repaid good with evil? That goblet is the tool of my master's divination! You've acted egregiously." Manasseh smiled at his father, trying to understand why his father was behaving so strangely towards the men he knew to be his uncles.

The donkey caravan was abruptly halted by the galloping troop of cavalry. The brothers looked back to see Manasseh leading the charge, rushing toward them.

He reined in his steed, dismounting to challenge them furiously, much to their surprise: "How could you do this? How could you steal my master's goblet? It is his tool of divination! Why have you treated him like this, after he paid you such uncommon honor?"

Judah approached the boy in submission, choosing his words carefully: "*Why does my lord speak such words as these? Far be it from your servants that they should do such a thing. Behold, the money, which we found in our sacks' mouths, we brought back to you out of the land of Canaan; how then should we steal out of your lord's house silver or gold?*"

The bizarre accusation left them shocked; they knew that none of them would ever steal. "*With whomsoever of your servants it be found, let him die, and we also will be my lord's slaves!*" they said confidently.

Manasseh replied: "That is what the law says, if one of you is a thief, then you are all his accomplices! However, my lord does not want that. He says that whoever has the goblet in his possession will become my master's slave, but everyone else can go free. Now, nine of you have shown yourselves to be honest men, bringing back the money returned to you all the way from Canaan, so I will not begin with you. Instead, we shall search the other two." Manasseh pointed to Simeon and Benjamin: "Unload your donkeys, please," he commanded.

Simeon and Benjamin did as asked, confident that nothing would be found. Manasseh went to Simeon's saddlebag and inspected it, declaring: "It's not here. Now it's your turn!" he said and went to rummage through Benjamin's pack. An angry smirk appeared on his face as his hand closed around something hard. "Well, well, what have we here?" he demanded furiously, pulling out the purloined goblet.

The brothers tore their clothes, their faces fell in shame. Simeon approached Benjamin, punching him between the shoulders: "Pilferer, son of a pilferer! I see you take after your mother!"

"I swear to you I did not steal the goblet," cried Benjamin sadly.

"Stop dawdling and come back to the city with me! There, we'll see what my lord deigns to do with you lot!" spat Manasseh angrily, leading the embarrassed brothers after him to his father's house.

"Well?! What do you have to say in your defense? Ingrates!" Zaphenath-paneah sat on his throne, arms crossed, facing the brothers falling on their faces in front of him. He was furious at the thieves. "What did you think?! That a man such as I wouldn't know who stole his goblet?!"

Judah raised his body slowly above the ground, knowing that he was finished and would never be able to return to his father again: "*What shall we say to my lord? What shall we speak? How shall we clear ourselves? God has found out the iniquity of your servants;*

behold, we are my lord's slaves, both we, and he also in whose hand the goblet is found. This is not about theft; it appears that God wants to punish us for our youthful indiscretions. You are merely the instrument for His Will." Judah's eyes filled with tears, his body trembling with sorrow, realizing God was punishing them for selling their brother long ago.

Zaphenath-paneah waved his hand in contempt: "Whoever has sinned against me, he alone will be punished by me! The man who has the goblet in his hand, he will be my slave for the rest of his life; now the rest of you can return to your father in peace."

The brothers got to their feet and watched Manasseh approach Benjamin chaining him before them. "Get out of my sight! I do not want to see you again!" said Zaphenath-paneah angrily to the brothers.

The brothers looked at each other helplessly, confident that they were in the right but could not prove it to Zaphenath-paneah. "There is nothing to do," Reuben said sadly, knowing that their father was finished, and that there was no escape.

Nevertheless, Judah met Zaphenath-paneah's gaze, feeling fury building within him. "*Oh, my lord, let your servant, please, speak a word in my lord's ears, and let not your anger burn against your servant; for you are even as Pharaoh.*"

Zaphenath-paneah looked at Judah dismissively. "You have something to say? Out with it!"

"Very well, my lord, I do not understand what has transpired here! From the moment of our arrival, you interrogated us in the most bizarre manner: 'Do you have a father?' 'Do you have a brother?' Tell me, what is it you wanted? To marry our sister?! Or did you think we wanted to marry your sister?! Still, we innocently answered you, telling you about our elderly father and the son of his old age, whose mother and brother had perished. Then, you decided you wanted to have a look at him. Now, you want us to leave him to be enslaved?!

Is this how you 'have a look,' as you said?! This is how the Egyptian government works?! Now that you accuse him of being a thief, he should stay with you?! I tell you I will stay in his place, but you are not ready to accept it. Why would you want a thief to be your slave?! Now, it would be reasonable enough if he had stolen the goblet out of desperation, if he were so indigent that he had no choice but to steal something he could sell for food; but that is not the case! Benjamin lacks nothing! Since he stole, let him pay it back and go home. What interest do you have in a madman, who compulsively steals even though he has everything he needs? If you want a slave, I am more qualified than he. I can serve you better than he in a domestic capacity; and if you want someone to serve you in a military capacity, then all the more so I am the superior choice!"

Zaphenath-paneah looked at Judah, amused: "So longwinded! Still, you are not the firstborn, but the fourth-born. Why are you talking and not Reuben, Simeon, or Levi?!"

"I gave my father a pledge for the boy," Judah said in pain. "No one gave a pledge but me."

"What's the pledge? Silver? Gold? Gems?" Zaphenath-paneah asked with a smile. "I will give it to you, and you may give it to your father!"

"Neither silver, nor gold, nor precious stones," Judah replied, "but this is what I said to my father: 'If I do not bring the boy before you, I will be banished from you in this world and the next world!'" Judah began to cry: "How can I face my father if the boy is not with me?! "

Zaphenath-paneah glanced at Judah, then looked at the silver goblet in his hand. "Interesting... My goblet tells me that you bereaved your father by selling one of your brothers, and you did it all for ten pairs of shoes. You sold your brother for shoes... Am I right?!! You didn't care about the grief your father would experience; you did not offer a pledge for the brother you sold." He stared at Judah. "The boy you sold did not sin, while this one is a thief! And just as you told your father that your other brother was devoured, you will say the same about this one. It appears this boy has an evil nature; that is why he stole and was caught." The viceroy grinned contemptuously: "This poor motherless boy... your father could not raise him right alone!"

Judah felt rage rising within him, taking long and deep breaths. "Now listen to me carefully!" he told the viceroy as he approached him, "Two of my brothers destroyed Shechem, when they were adolescents; the seven kingdoms of Canaan fought against us, and we destroyed them all. The sound of my voice will bring pestilence to Egypt, and if I draw my sword, both you and Pharoah will lose your heads!"

With peace of mind, the viceroy looked at agitated Judah, gesturing to his son Manasseh, standing next to him. The lad kicked the ground hard. The pillars of the palace shook, dust filling the throne room.

Judah was astounded. He thought: This kick comes from Father's house! He screamed furiously, shaking the earth like a thunderbolt going from one end of the world to the other. A slight moment passed, and beside Judah came Hushim the son of Dan, whom the quake had alerted. He had rushed from the land of Canaan to aid his uncle. Judah and Hushim screamed together, the ground quaking and heaving. Zaphenath-paneah's throne of stone split, and he fell to the ground before them. Judah approached the lord, blood dripping from both his eyes, two hairs on his chest sticking out, tearing his clothes. Joseph thought: He's really angry! He knew the signs of his brother's fury.

Zaphenath-paneah looked straight into Judah's eyes; he angrily kicked his broken throne, reducing the marble slabs to so much gravel. Judah, heart afire, thought: How does this nonbeliever have such power?!

Judah stretched out his hand to his sword, intending to unsheathe and behead his opponent. The sword got stuck, refusing to come out of the sheath: Judah thought, in frustration: A nonbeliever? No, this man may be a foreigner, but he must be God-fearing!

Legions of fighters began to rush into the room to fight the brothers. Judah looked at them with contempt; a scream of anger came out of his mouth, terrifying them all.

Judah glanced at his brothers. The brothers nodded in agreement: "There are twelve great cities in Egypt," Naphtali said.

"Everyone take a city!" said Judah, intending to destroy the land. A hand was placed on Judah's shoulder, soothing rather than attacking. Judah looked behind in amazement: "Calm down, Judah, we will give you your brother Benjamin," said Manasseh with a reassuring smile. "There is no need to destroy the country."

Judah looked at the boy and saw the truth in his words. He calmed his stormy spirit, glancing at his brothers as he announced: "The war is over."

Zaphenath-paneah looked around: "Take everyone out from before me," he commanded Manasseh, with his throat slightly hoarse. The brothers watched as all the soldiers and servants left, amazed at being left alone with the viceroy.

There was silence in the throne room, a scene of postapocalyptic devastation. Dust drifted through the palace. The brothers and Zaphenath-paneah looked at each other in silence. "You said you entered Egypt through ten gates to find your lost brother, right?!" he broke the silence. The brothers nodded, without saying a word.

"Did you find him?"

The brothers shook their heads.

"Do you think he's still alive?" he asked.

"Probably not," Judah said sadly.

Zaphenath-paneah smiled at the brothers. "I bought him for twenty pieces of silver. Do you want me to call him, so you can see him?" he asked, but didn't wait for their answer: "Joseph son of

Jacob!" he cried, in a voice which echoed through the ruined palace. "Joseph son of Jacob! Come and talk with your brothers."

The brothers turned around, searching the room, trying to figure out which direction Joseph might come from, waiting for one of the palace doors to open. The minutes ticked by, but nothing happened. The brothers, annoyed, turned on Zaphenath-paneah angrily, thinking he was mocking them.

"Why would you look in the corner?" he asked. "I'm Joseph!"

The brothers looked at the viceroy, considering his face, trying to imagine what he looked like without the beard and headpiece. Their hearts started beating so fast, they thought they would pass out.

"I am Joseph; does my father yet live?" Joseph said, sobbing.

The brothers were shocked. Could it be... or was it just another trick?

Crying from the bottom of his heart, he begged: "Come here, please." They complied, and he tearfully told them: "*I am Joseph your brother, whom you sold into Egypt. And now be not grieved, nor angry with yourselves, that you sold me here; for God did send me before you to preserve life. For these two years has the famine been in the land; and there are yet five years, in which there shall be neither plowing nor harvest; and God sent me before you to give you a remnant on the earth, and to save you alive for a great deliverance. So now it was not you that sent me here, but God; and He has made me a father to Pharaoh, and lord of all his house, and ruler over all the land of Egypt.*"

Close-up, they could see how much Joseph resembled their father; now they were shocked they hadn't seen it before. Dumbstruck, the brothers still managed to convey ruefulness, remorse, and regret.

"*Hasten and go up to my father and say to him: 'Thus says your son Joseph: "God has made me lord of all Egypt; come down to me, tarry not. And you shall dwell in the land of Goshen, and you shall be near*

to me, you, and your children, and your children's children, and your
flocks, and your herds, and all that you have; and there will I sustain
you; for there are yet five years of famine; lest you come to poverty, you,
and your household, and all that you have." And behold, your eyes see,
and the eyes of my brother Benjamin, that it is my mouth that speaks
to you." Indeed, his monologue was in the Holy Tongue, undeniable
evidence of his identity. *"And you shall tell my father of all my glory*
in Egypt, and of all that you have seen; and you shall hasten and bring
down my father here." Joseph fell on Benjamin's neck with a cry of
longing and release, embracing and kissing his brothers with sincere
love and reconciliation.

A royal decree was issued by Pharaoh to give Joseph's brothers
whatever they might need to bring their father and their families
from the land of Canaan to the land of Goshen. The fear that Joseph
would leave the land of Egypt made Pharaoh swear that he would not
harm Israel and his sons. The convoy of loaded wagons was waiting at
the entrance of the city, Joseph and his entourage accompanying the
brothers as they left to bring their father and their families to Egypt:
"Please, do not rehash the past while you travel. If Father does not
believe you, just point to the wagons. They prove that I am still alive,
because they will remind him of the subject we studied the day I left."

The brothers neared Hebron, wondering how they'd tell their father
the good news without the shock and surprise overwhelming him.

"Father, you're back!" cried Serah happily, running out to jump
into Asher's arms in love; he affectionately hugged his little daughter, with a smile on his face. "She will know how to inform Father
about Joseph," he told his troubled brothers, "She always plays and
sings to him."

The mission was duly given to Serah. The little girl eagerly ran
to her grandfather's study, waiting for him to rise for prayer. Serah's
sweet refrain merged with Israel's solemn prayer, his concern for his

sons' welfare only intensifying his sadness.

Joseph is alive and well
In Egypt-land, so they tell.
He has a wife and sons, two
Come down now, he waits for you!

The tunes merged, the lyrics intertwined, a melody of longing bearing tidings of joy began to penetrate into his supplication, uplifting him with a feeling of bliss he had not felt for many years. His heart, wallowing in the dirt of lamentation as if chained to the earth, began to rise. His communication with the Creator, soaring with Serah's song, snapped the shackles of misery and mourning. The dejection and desolation which had haunted him for more than two decades melted away, his soul thawing. The realization that his beloved son had been found alive in Egypt dawned within him, as Serah inspired him. Israel concluded his prayer, finding it hard to tear himself away from his act of devotion to the Rock of Ages, but he needed to confirm the message.

"Yes, dear grandfather," said Sarah with a loving smile to Israel, "Joseph is still alive, he rules in Egypt, and he has two sons: Manasseh and Ephraim."

Israel looked up at his returning sons, his heart longing to believe, but still finding it hard to accept. "The wagons, Father," the boys said with a smile, "Joseph said that they would remind you of the last subject you studied with him, the day he disappeared."

The eyes of Israel were filled with tears of happiness: "*It is enough; Joseph my son is yet alive; I will go and see him before I die.*"

The journey to the land of Egypt began, Jacob and his offspring making their way to the land of Egypt. Passing through Beersheba, they brought thanksgiving-offerings for the miracles they'd experienced. After twenty-two years of not receiving prophecy, Jacob received the Word of God: "*I am God, the God of your father; fear not to go down into Egypt; for I will there make of you a great nation. I will go down with you into Egypt; and I will also surely bring you up again; and Joseph shall put his hand upon your eyes."*

Israel hurried, knowing it meant the commencement of the exile decreed on the seed of Abraham in the Covenant Between the Parts. It was all worth it, he felt, as long as he could see his beloved son.

Sixty-six descendants of Israel went down with him to Egypt. Adina, the wife of Levi, gave birth to Jochebed at the time of their entry into Egypt. Joseph and his two sons, in Egypt, completed the count of seventy souls. Judah was sent from Israel to the land of Goshen to build a study hall for his father that would be ready when he got there.

Joseph ran to his chariot, quickly harnessing his horse, his servants watching their master in amazement. Urging the horses into a gallop, he sped towards his beloved father. He thought: Twenty-two years of distance, twenty-two years I could not inform my father that I was still alive. Twenty-two years of anticipation are about to end. The chariot advanced towards the slowly rolling wagons. Joseph stopped his chariot, jumping out to run towards his father's wagon.

Israel looked at his beloved son, his heart beating as if it might burst from his chest, out of joy, associating his bliss with his Creator. *"Hear, O' Israel, the Lord our God, the Lord is one,"* he said with devotion before turning to embrace his beloved son.

A few days passed, and Joseph presented five of his brothers to Pharaoh. Before the meeting, he warned his brothers to tell Pharaoh that all their lives they had been shepherds and knew no other craft. Even Israel was presented before Pharaoh, and he blessed him as sages do when meeting people of high rank.

Israel's arrival in Egypt meant that the famine ceased. The children of Israel dwelt peacefully in the land of Goshen, enjoying the abundance that was given to them by Joseph. As the family of Egypt's viceroy, they were released from all duties and labor.

During the seventeen years that Israel lived in the land of Egypt, Joseph refrained from being alone with his father, lest he ask him about the circumstances of his disappearance and or his justification for not making contact during the twenty-two years he lived in Egypt. The fear that dissuaded Joseph was that in anger, his father might curse his brothers for their actions, and they would be utterly destroyed.

Chapter Sixty

Parting

A light breeze blew through the throne room. The petition-ers gave him not rest; worry over affairs of state constant-ly occupied his mind. Dealing with the needs of the many did not leave enough time to deal with spiritual matters. The hours ticked by, another issue arising as soon as one issue was settled. Ministers entered to receive advice, courses of action, and then leave, making way for the generals and army commanders who came after them.

"At least I do charity all the time," Joseph comforted himself, "If I am doomed to stay away from the study hall, at least I am practicing that."

Joseph sighed heavily, longing for the time when he could sit with his sons and teach them. He was comforted that at least they could study with his father, since he was unable to due to his role and the fear of questions that might arise if he were to be alone with his father.

His last conversation with Jacob had been a troubling one.

"I called you, because I want to ask you something, my dear son," Israel had looked at his son with a pleading expression. "If it please you, put your hand upon me, and assure me you will act in kindness and truth: do not bury me in Egypt. Machpelah Cave in Hebron is where I must be interred, alongside my forebears."

Joseph had looked at his father, wanting to argue that Jacob was not going anywhere; but his father's imploring and irrefutable look proved to him that it was not proper for him to say so. "I will do as you say," he had said, tears welling up in his eyes.

"Swear to me," Israel had begged.

"I swear to you," Joseph had said in tears.

Israel had bowed down to the Creator of the world in gratitude for the fact that Joseph had promised to bury him in the ancestral tombs.

Joseph smiled as his son, now a sturdy and handsome young man like Joseph had been at the age he was sold. How wonderful it was that Jacob, whose time with Joseph had been cut short, could enjoy his experience with the next generation. In particular, Jacob rejoiced to hold the baby on his knees during the circumcision ceremony, as he welcomed yet another grandchild into the covenant of Grandfather Abraham.

However, the young man's usually smiling face looked very preoccupied; he bowed to his father and kissed his hands lovingly.

"What troubles you, darling?" Joseph asked anxiously.

Words didn't come easily. "I don't know what's happening to Grandfather; something odd, I've never seen anyone in such a state."

Joseph jumped up from his throne: "What happened to him?!" he asked, his voice startled.

"I don't know, he is lying on the bed, barely able to lift himself to a sitting position. He looks pale and very weak, as if a heavy weight bears down on him." The young man thought for a moment: "He said he asked God to become sick before he departed the world, so that he could command his sons and family before he died."

"Quick, run, call your brother and go to Grandfather's house. I will meet you there," Joseph said and hurried out to head for his father's.

Ephraim's dire message about Jacob's worsening condition was no exaggeration. Still, Jacob did his best when he was told by one of the servants that his son the viceroy was coming, gathering his strength to sit up in his bed.

Joseph and his two sons stood at the entrance to the room. A sad draught was felt when the door opened, a feeling of haze and oppressive darkness. Joseph hurried to his father sitting on the bed; the sight of Israel's weakness shocked his devoted son.

"What ails you, my father?" he asked painfully.

Israel smiled through the torment, striving to look good, to the best of his ability: "Apparently, I've received a gift from God to be sick before I leave the world," he said; an outburst of coughing stopped him.

Joseph hugged his father, waiting for the coughing fit to pass.

"It is terrible for a person to die suddenly, with no warning. It is a great gift that I can prepare to leave this world and prepare myself for the journey that awaits me," Israel said with a smile. He looked at his son, trying to hide the pain. "You see, my son, the end of my life has come... Do not try to deny it," he insisted, seeing Joseph's dismay to at hearing such things. "It is my privilege to tell you the following!" Joseph kissed his father's hands in gratitude for the privilege given to his seed. "*God Almighty appeared to me at Luz in the land of Canaan, and blessed me, and said to me: 'Behold, I will make you fruitful, and multiply you, and I will make of you a company of peoples; and will give this land to your seed after you for an everlasting possession.' And now your two sons, who were born to you in the land of Egypt before I came to you into Egypt, are mine; Ephraim and Manasseh, even as Reuben and Simeon, shall be mine. And your issue, that you beget after them, shall be yours; they shall be called after the name of their brethren in their inheritance.*"

Joseph kissed his father upon hearing the news that his two sons would receive portions in the land just like their uncles.

"You know that I made you swear to bury me in Machpelah Cave, even though I did not bury your mother there, but on the road to Bethlehem. However, you must realize that this was by the Hand of God; there is good reason that your mother is buried there specifically. I hope you understand my actions were justified and well-intentioned."

Joseph nodded, trying to overcome the feeling of disappointment that his mother would not have her husband buried beside her.

Israel looked at Joseph's sons; he sought to bless them, but he could not shake the feeling that among their descendants would be wicked men undeserving of any blessing. A gloomy spirit of sadness rested on Israel: "Who are they?" he wondered, seeing the behavior of their descendants.

"These are my sons, whom God has given me here," said Joseph, presenting to his father the documentation of his marriage to Asenath. "Master of the Universe, please, give the inspiration to my father to bless my children," Joseph prayed from the bottom of his heart.

"Please bring them to me," said Israel, smiling, feeling his spirit return to him. "I did not dare to hope to see your face again," he said to his son with love, "but now God has shown me your seed as well."

Joseph brought his sons closer to his father, directing the older Manasseh toward his father's right hand, and the younger Ephraim toward his father's left hand. Israel smiled, understanding the actions of his son. He interlaced his arms, placing his right hand on the head of Ephraim and his left hand on the head of Manasseh. Israel raised his old eyes, looking at Joseph. Israel said in prayer: "*The God before whom my fathers Abraham and Isaac did walk, the God who has been my shepherd all my life long to this day, the angel who has redeemed me from all evil, bless the lads; and let my name be called in them, and the name of my fathers Abraham and Isaac; and let them grow into a multitude in the midst of the earth."*

Joseph noticed that his father had rearranged his hands, the opposite of his intention. Without thinking, he reached out to his father to replace them. He exclaimed: "Not so, my father, for this is the firstborn; put your right hand on his head."

Israel smiled, thinking: Young people always think they are smarter than adults. *"I know it, my son, I know it; he also shall become a people, and he also shall be great; however, his younger brother shall be greater than he, and his seed shall become a multitude of nations,"* he said, looking at his two grandchildren. They looked calm, unmoved by what was going on above their heads, though they knew the importance of the matter. "There is no envy in these children, and they exhibit complete self-nullification," Israel thought happily. *"By you shall Israel bless, saying: God make you as Ephraim and as Manasseh."*

Joseph's sons came out from beneath their grandfather's hands, accepting with love and peace the blessing bestowed upon them.

He went on: *"Behold, I die; but God will be with you and bring you back to the land of your fathers. Moreover, I have given to you one portion above your brethren, which I took from the hand of the Amorite with my sword and with my bow,"* with my prayer and my supplication."

Joseph felt pain and sorrow over the impending separation, mourning the many years he had been sentenced to be distant from his father.

"Now please gather your brothers, and bring them to me, and I will tell you what will befall you at the end of days," he told Joseph.

The twelve brothers came to their father's sickbed. There was considerable sorrow in their eyes, seeing their father at the end of his days. Thoughts about the past and the future came up, flooding their heads with memories of days gone by, trying to suppress the thoughts about the future without Father.

"Hear me, my dear sons. There is a sick evil in the world and its name is divisiveness. A land that has divisiveness will be destroyed; a city that has divisiveness will be destroyed; a house that has divisiveness will be destroyed. Your power is in your unity! If you remain united, no nation or people will be able to hurt you; and if not, then you will be ravaged!"

Israel concluded his will. He thought: I must reveal to my sons the end of days! A strange feeling entered his heart. The words he chose to say to his sons went away as if he had no permission to say them.

"Perhaps, God forbid, one of you has doubts about the Holy One, Blessed be He?" he asked, looking at his sons.

"*Hear, O' Israel, the Lord our God, the Lord is one*," they replied. "As your heart is whole with God, so are our hearts whole with God."

"Blessed be the glory of His kingdom forever and ever," replied Israel, feeling the truth in their words.

Israel felt that the authority to reveal to his sons what he wanted had been revoked him. His eyes shut with holy meditation, he thought: At least I can rebuke them before I pass away.

"*Reuben, you are my firstborn*," he told Reuben, "you deserved to have three more parts over your brother: birthright, priesthood, and kingship. However, you lost it all when you disrespected your father." Reuben hung his head, accepting his sentence, hoping for forgiveness.

"*Simeon and Levi are brethren*. The anger that you felt for Dinah without consulting me was disastrous. *Cursed be their anger, for it was fierce, and their wrath, for it was cruel; I will divide them in Jacob, and scatter them in Israel.*"

Judah began to retreat, fearing his father would upbraid him over Tamar. Instead, he was told:

Judah, you shall your brethren praise; your hand shall be on the neck of your enemies; your father's sons shall bow down before you. Judah is a lion's whelp; from the prey, my son, you have gone up. He stooped down, he crouched as a lion, and as a lioness; who shall rouse him up? The scepter shall not depart from Judah, nor the ruler's staff from between his feet, as long as men come to Shiloh; and to him shall the obedience of the peoples be...

Israel blessed Judah with kingship, then went on to bless the rest:

"Zebulun shall dwell at the shore of the sea...

"Issachar is a large-boned donkey...

"Dan shall judge his people...

"Gad, a troop shall troop upon him; but he shall troop upon their heel.

"As for Asher, his bread shall be fat, and he shall yield royal dainties.

"Naphtali is a hind let loose: he giveth goodly words.

"Joseph is a fruitful vine, a fruitful vine by a fountain; its branches run over the wall...

"Benjamin is a ravenous wolf; in the morning, he devours the prey, and at evening, he divides the spoil."

Israel looked upon his sons with love, seeing on their faces the acceptance of rebuke with humility and joy over the blessings. "May all these blessings be with you all," he told his sons.

"I am to be gathered to my people; bury me with my fathers in the cave that is in the field of Ephron the Hittite, in the cave that is in the field of Machpelah, which is before Mamre, in the land of Canaan, which Abraham bought with the field from Ephron the Hittite for a possession of a burying-place. There they buried Abraham and Sarah his wife; there they buried Isaac and Rebecca his wife; and there I buried Leah. The field and the cave that is therein were purchased from the Hittites."

He slowly lifted his legs onto the bed, shifting from sitting to lying there. He closed his eyes and smiled as he breathed his last. The sound of crying signs burst from the brothers' mouths, realizing that their father had gone on his last journey. Joseph fell on his father's body crying, with a kiss to say goodbye upon his warm hand.

Heavy mourning fell on the Egyptians at the death of the man who had brough the famine to an end; the father of the man who had saved them from death has passed away, leaving the country exposed to imminent natural disasters.

Seventy days had passed since the death of Israel, forty days of embalming, and thirty days during which all of Egypt mourned.

"Your Majesty," Joseph sent messengers to Pharaoh, "my father made me swear to bury him in the land of Canaan in Machpelah Cave, where his forebears and wife are buried. Now the time has come for me to fulfill my oath, to bury my father in his tomb; then I shall return to Egypt."

Pharaoh looked with displeasure at the messengers, turning down the request. "My viceroy will make an appeal in person!" he demanded.

"What is wrong with being buried in the land of Egypt?!" the king demanded when Joseph appeared.

A sour look appeared on Joseph's face, but he immediately insisted: "There is nothing wrong, but my father made me swear that I would bury him in the land of Canaan, in the ancestral plot!"

"I think it is just nonsense. Do you think Egypt lacks the resources to produce a funeral with all the pomp and circumstance you could want? The honor he will receive here at interment will be much greater than in the land of Canaan," Pharaoh promised. "Moreover, you and your family live here; why bury your patriarch so far away?"

Joseph looked at Pharaoh angrily: "My father made me swear! That was his last request from me, and I do not intend to break my oath! The reasons he asked to be buried there are his and his alone!"

He thought: Although I do know some of the reasons. If he is buried here, he may be turned into an object of idolatry, since his arrival ended the famine. Second, there is the fact that when the dead are resuscitated in the far future, anyone buried abroad will have to roll through underground tunnels to reach the Promised Land. Last, there are the plagues Egypt is destined to experience, like lice, which target the dirt of the earth...

Pharaoh broke out in a huge smile as he countered his viceroy's objection. "Ah, an oath! Yes, I know how your laws work. You can consult sages of your faith, and they have the power to release you from the vow." Pharaoh looked delighted at this stroke of genius.

"I have never made such a request in my life, and I have never broken an oath. Would you like me to start now?" Joseph smiled mischievously. "Then I should also consult the sages about the oath I made to you a quarter-century ago. Remember when I swore I would not reveal that I know one more language than you, the Holy Tongue? Once released from my vow, I can inform all of Egypt — and then, by right, claim my throne!" Joseph whirled around to do just that.

"Just a minute!" cried Pharaoh, "I was just jesting with you! I certainly agree you should go to Canaan! You know how much I appreciated your father; I would not want to make him sad!"

Joseph turned to look at the frightened Pharaoh: "I am glad Your Majesty agrees," he said with a smile. "We will make a state funeral. All the adults among his offspring will go escort him on his last journey."

Pharaoh nodded, knowing that he must do as Joseph said. "The elders and the nobles of Egypt will go with you as well, and the chariots and cavalry will accompany your father's coffin."

Joseph left the room without adding anything, knowing that the military forces sent by Pharaoh were there guarantee his return. He thought: At least if Uncle Esau stirs up trouble, we'll have backup.

The funeral procession began. The children of Israel lifted up the coffin, three on each side. Manasseh and Ephraim took the place of Joseph and Levi to carry the coffin. A massive procession accompanied the great man.

At the threshing-floor of Atad, across the Jordan from the land of Canaan, all the people sat and wept for the father of the nation. The kings of Canaan emerged to wage war against the prospective invaders, but upon seeing Joseph's crown lying on his father's coffin, they immediately placed their crowns there too, knowing that thanks to Joseph their people, too, had survived the years of famine.

The mourning at Atad lasted seven days; then the people continued their journey toward Machpelah Cave in Hebron. Just short of their destination, they were surprised to encounter hostile forces — Esau's horsemen and soldiers.

"Where do you think you're going?!" he asked the pallbearers.

"To bury your brother, Jacob, our father," Joseph told his uncle.

"What dump are you going to toss his body into?" Esau smirked, revealing his toothless mouth.

"In Machpelah Cave, alongside Leah," Joseph replied with a sigh.

"You better look for another place. This one's reserved for me!" Esau retorted angrily. "See, our father left us two places in Machpelah Cave, one for each of us." Esau pointed to Jacob's coffin: "He buried Leah there in his place, but that's his problem. The other belongs to me!"

Levi approached Esau: "Our father bought the place from you. We all watched him give you piles of gold and precious stones for that place in particular and for the promise to inherit the land of Canaan. You even signed a bill of sale!" He said angrily.

"What bill?! Show me the bill in question!" Esau reached out his hand awaiting to take the putative parchment from Levi.

"We don't have it, it's in Egypt," Levi said in disappointment, hitting himself for not having the foresight to bring the document with them.

Esau laughed: "So, either you go and get the bill, or you look for another place." Jacob's twin sat down on a large stone: "I'm waiting!

I have nothing but time." Esau smirked. "I just hope he doesn't start to stink too much. The truth is, I couldn't even stand his scent when he was alive!" Esau's men roared at the helplessness of the mourners.

Joseph realized that their hand was being forced. He called Naphtali over: "Brother, you are the fastest. Run to Egypt and retrieve the bill."

Naphtali nodded. "It will probably take me a few hours; I'll do my best," he said and set off.

The mourners stood, sun beating down on their heads, illuminating the cave in which the soul of Israel had longed to be buried.

"What are we waiting for?" Hushim son of Dan asked his father. Dan looked at his son, who was hard of hearing, realizing that he had missed the back and forth. "Esau, Grandfather Israel's brother, is delaying the burial," he explained to his son. "Naphtali has gone back to Egypt to retrieve the bill of sale. Esau knows we have the document, but he wants to antagonize us before letting us bury Grandfather."

Hushim looked around, staring at the coffin, contemplating his grandfather's disgrace. His gaze shifted to Esau sitting with a toothless smirk on a rock, laughing contemptuously at his deceased brother. He thought: This scoundrel, this miscreant dares to defile this solemn occasion?! He took his cane in his hand and approached Esau from behind. One mighty whack fractured the old man's skull, knocking his eyeballs out of their sockets and up to Israel's coffin.

Judah saw Esau flailing between life and death. He drew his sword from its sheath and cut off Esau's head. "Now I understand the prophecy of Grandmother Rebecca. *'Why should I be bereaved of both of you on one day?'* This is the day she spoke of, the burial of both!"

Esau's forces grabbed his body — bedecked in gold and jewels — and fled as quickly as they could. His head was thus buried at the entrance to Machpelah Cave, his body on Mount Seir, where he lived. "Let's continue the funeral procession," Judah said with a smile, "he will no longer interfere."

Israel was buried next to his wife Leah, and the mourners spent another day mourning him at Machpelah Cave. The following day, they set out to return to Egypt.

Along the way, they came across the pit Joseph had been tossed into almost forty years earlier. Joseph stopped to acknowledge God's salvation: "Blessed is he who has done a miracle for me in this place."

CHAPTER SIXTY-ONE

Joseph

"I hope now he will not take the opportunity to have his revenge," Judah told his ten brothers starkly. They were clustered around the family table, with the chairs of Jacob and Joseph empty.

Simeon rubbed his neck: "Did you hear the blessing he made by the pit?! As if it all happened yesterday!"

Levi looked at the empty chairs: "Since we returned from the funeral, he has not come to sit with us."

"It seems to me that we should talk to him," said Reuben. "What if he were to be told that Father requested that he forgive us?"

The brothers nodded at each other in agreement.

"But who will we send to him?" Simeon asked, "Certainly not me!"

All eyes were fixed on Dan and Naphtali; the sons of Bilhah squirmed in their chairs uncomfortably.

"He loved you more than the rest of us. We cannot send Benjamin since he was not part of the sale. You two must carry out the mission."

Dan and Naphtali looked at each other, sighing at the heavy task on their shoulders.

"We will accompany you," said Judah, "but we will wait outside

316

until you reconcile with him, and then, we too, will come in and ask his forgiveness." His expression was quite sober. "The truth is that one must be a very great person in order to be able to forgive such an act completely."

Joseph stood up with a loving smile towards his brothers, overjoyed at the visit. Dan and Naphtali looked very stressed from the meeting. "Hello, dear brothers. I'm so happy to see you," Joseph said as he rose from his seat to embrace his brothers.

Several weeks have passed since their father's burial, weeks in which Joseph had not seen his brothers. He had mused: When Father was alive, we would sit down to eat together, and Father ordered me to sit at the head of the table. For Father's honor I had to do so. Now that Father's dead, how can I sit at the head of the table, with my older brothers sitting at the sides of the table, as they will surely insist that we act as we did when Father was alive?

Unsure what to do, he had simply avoided joining them for meals.

"What brings you to me today, my dear brothers?" Joseph asked with a beaming smile, "I'm sorry I haven't seen you much since the funeral, but there is so much work I need to catch up on, you see!"

Dan and Naphtali looked at Joseph, trying to find the right words to say to their royal brother. Finally, Naphtali blurted out painfully: "Your father commanded before he died, saying: 'So shall you say to Joseph, forgive, please now, the transgression of your brethren, and their sin, for that they did to you evil.' And now, please, forgive the transgression of the servants of the God of your father."

Naphtali's words struck Joseph like a blow from a gauntleted arm. He was mortified, in agony. Joseph fell to his knees in bitter weeping.

He thought: He knew! For years I did not sit with my father privately for fear that he would ask me something, and now it's clear to me that he knew everything. All I wanted was to study with him, but I avoided it because I was worried what he might ask me about how I got to Egypt.

And he knew everything!

Joseph's weeping grew louder, as the memories of the days when he moved away from his father on different pretexts buffeted him. Sobbing bitterly, he thought: He knew and did not say a word all these years! The door opened. Joseph's brothers entered, and they saw him kneeling in bitter tears. Tears flooded the brothers' eyes, seeing the grief inflicted on their brother. Joseph's brothers fell on their knees before him, crying: "We are your slaves!" They accepted fully their culpability, ready to give their lives to the brother who nullified himself in order to forgive the terrible crime they had committed.

Joseph said with tears suffocating his throat, "Fear not; for am I in the place of God? Could I do something to you if it were against the Will of God? True, you meant evil against me; but God meant it for good, to bring to pass, as it is this day, to save the lives of many people."

The brothers embraced their righteous sibling, beating their breasts in grief.

"No, you must not worry anymore." He tried to raise a conciliatory grin on his face. "Before you arrived, they thought I was a slave; but when you arrived, they realized that I come from an illustrious family. Would I harm you? If I do that, they will all say that I was playacting, that I was a slave all along, who falsely claimed membership in a family not his."

Joseph rose from the ground, inviting his brothers to join him at the table: "I will sustain you and your families; you will take hold in the land of your settlement," he told his brothers with a loving smile. "It would not be good for your sons and daughters to wander within the land of Egypt. It is best that you take care to keep far away from the idolatrous Egyptians."

The brothers nodded, agreeing with their sibling, acknowledging that he was right.

Fifty-four years had passed since the death of Israel. Those who came down to Egypt lived in great prosperity and enjoyed their closeness to Joseph, who ruled Egypt securely. The nascent nation of Israel prospered in the land, free from taxes and levies, free to worship God in a state of economic abundance.

The eleven brothers were called to the bed of their royal brother, who smiled at his sadfaced brothers. "Do not despair, my brothers," Joseph asked, *"I go the way of all the earth.* I thank God that I have such close kinsmen as you, and that God made me the conduit to shower blessing upon you, your children, and your families. But every person comes to an end. I know that I will not have the privilege of being buried in Machpelah Cave; this is reserved for the patriarchs and matriarchs. Moreover, I also know that Pharaoh will not give you permission to raise my bones out of the land of Egypt. Still, I have one last request before I depart: *I die; but God will surely remember you and bring you up out of this land to the land which He swore to Abraham, to Isaac, and to Jacob. God will surely remember you, and you shall carry up my bones from here."* Joseph begged his brothers.

The brothers watched their dying sibling with tears streaming down their faces: "We swear to you that we will raise your bones, our dear brother."

Joseph smiled at his brothers, closed his eyes, and returned his soul to his Heavenly Father, a broad smile on his face.

The brothers fell to their knees, tearing their garments in bitter tears over Joseph, first among Jacob's sons to pass away and go on to his heavenly reward.

Joseph's body was embalmed, and his coffin was placed in the Nile — until the time came for him to be raised, by the Word of God.

Made in the USA
Las Vegas, NV
13 November 2024

11777993R00177